AMERICAN BLONDE

LOUIS KAPELEF

JENNIFER NIVEN's three previous novels are *Becoming Clementine*, *Velva Jean Learns to Fly*, and *Velva Jean Learns to Drive*, which was chosen as an Indie Reader's Group Top Ten Pick. Niven has also written three nonfiction books. *The Ice Master* was named one of the top ten nonfiction books of the year by *Entertainment Weekly*, has been translated into eight languages, has been the subject of several documentaries, and received Italy's Gambrinus "Giuseppe Mazzotti" Literary Prize. *Ada Blackjack* was a Book Sense Top Ten Pick and has been optioned for the movies and translated into Chinese, French, and Estonian. *The Aqua-Net Diaries*, a memoir about Niven's high school experiences, was optioned by Warner Bros. as a television series. She lives in Los Angeles. For more information, visit jenniferniven.com or follow her on Facebook.

Praise for *Becoming Clementine*

"Unforgettable and heartfelt."

—Pam Jenoff, bestselling author of
The Kommandant's Girl and *The Diplomat's Wife*

"I devoured *Velva Jean Learns to Fly* and immediately began spreading the word: This one is not to be missed!"

—Cassandra King, bestselling author of *Moonrise*, *Queen of Broken Hearts*, and *The Same Sweet Girls*

"Velva Jean Hart is a heroine with grit, grace, determination, and enough humanity to hook readers with ferocious tenderness, making them want to find and befriend her. Niven's writing shines."

—*Booklist* (starred review)

"A sweeping adventure that takes the reader from the streets of Nashville to the belly of a WWII bomber."

—Benjamin Percy, award-winning author of *Red Moon* and *The Wilding*

"In this fun, fast-paced, heartwarming sequel to *Velva Jean Learns to Drive*, we follow the beloved young heroine from her mountain home to Nashville. But soon after Pearl Harbor is attacked, Velva Jean begins singing a new song—one full of patriotism, courage, and feisty independence. The perfect read for any girl of any age who yearns to soar beyond her dreams."

—Susan Gregg Gilmore, author of *The Funeral Dress* and *Looking for Salvation at the Dairy Queen*

Praise for *Velva Jean Learns to Drive*

"A touching read, funny and wise, like a crazy blend of Loretta Lynn, Dolly Parton, a less morose Flannery O'Connor, and maybe a shot of Hank Williams. . . . Niven makes some memorable moon-spun magic in her rich fiction debut."   —*Publishers Weekly* (starred review)

"In this story Jennifer Niven creates a world long gone, a mountain past where people suffer failure, loss, and betrayal, as well as the strength and joy of connection and deep love. *Velva Jean Learns to Drive* takes us far into this soaring, emotional country, the place where our best music comes from."

—Robert Morgan, bestselling author of *The Road from Gap Creek* and *Gap Creek*

"A fluid storyteller."   —*Wall Street Journal*

"Velva Jean learns to . . . not only drive, but to soar. This beautifully written coming-of-age story captivated me, and I recommend it to anyone who has ever longed to 'live out there.'"

—Ann B. Ross, author of the bestselling *Miss Julia* novels

"Spirited."   —*Parade*

JENNIFER NIVEN

American Blonde

A PLUME BOOK

PLUME

Published by the Penguin Group
Penguin Group (USA) LLC
375 Hudson Street
New York, New York 10014

USA I Canada I UK I Ireland I Australia I New Zealand I India I South Africa I China
penguin.com
A Penguin Random House Company

First published by Plume, a member of Penguin Group (USA) LLC, 2014

LIBRARY OF CONGRESS CATALOGING-IN-PUBLICATION DATA
Niven, Jennifer.
    American blonde : a novel / Jennifer Niven.
      pages cm
    ISBN 978-0-452-29821-7 (pbk.)
    1. Young women—Fiction. 2. Appalachian Region, Southern—History—20th
century—Fiction. I. Title.
    PS3614.I94A83 2014
    813'.6--dc23
                                    2013039066

Printed in the United States of America
10 9 8 7 6 5 4 3 2 1

Set in Granjon
Designed by Eve. L. Kirch

Once upon a time, there was a town that didn't exist.

—Penelope Niven

Contents

Miss Red, White, and Blue

1945 ~ 1946

ONE

Six days after setting sail from Scotland, my brother Johnny Clay and I stood pressed against the railing of the *Gray Ghost*. It was June 21, 1945. We were only two of fifteen thousand passengers. Soldiers filled the upper decks, so crushed together that I was afraid I might have to jump overboard to breathe. The fog settled thick around our shoulders as we waited for the first sight of land.

Ever since I was a little girl, growing up in my brother's shadow, it was important that I see things first. But this time I'd decided to let him win. He needed to win because the war had changed him. Every day I looked at his face, searching for some trace of the boy I knew—my brother, my best friend, champion gold panner, rider of the rails, paratrooper—and sometimes he was there and sometimes he wasn't. Today he was somewhere in between, here one moment and then gone again, like the sun on a cloudy day.

Thanks to a German bullet, Johnny Clay would always limp, but he didn't mind this because all the best cowboys limped. The thing that troubled him more was the middle finger of his left hand and the fact that—also thanks to a German bullet—it was missing from the knuckle up. My brother was vain, and limping was one thing, but missing a finger was another. He was a gold panner and a guitar player. These were the things he could do best, once upon a time when he was whole, even though he'd done other things—roped cattle, flown and jumped out of planes. Now, if you asked him what he was going to do with himself, he'd tell you he guessed he might do anything he set his mind to. But he'd say it in a far-off way, as if he didn't really mean it or care much at all.

The fog was so heavy that I could barely see the water, but as the ship went churning through, the spray hit my face. Before the war, the *Gray Ghost* had been the *Queen Mary*, the grandest ship on the ocean, but since 1942 she'd been used to transport troops across the world. Soldiers crowded to my left, to the back of me, to the right of Johnny Clay. I stood, my arm against my brother's, staring out into nothing and thinking over everything I'd seen and done since the last time I'd been home to North Carolina, early in 1943. If you asked me what I planned to do now that I was going home again, I would tell you that for the first time in my life I didn't know.

"What do you think New York City looks like, Johnny Clay?" I wondered if it was grander than Paris, where I'd worked as a spy, where my name had been Clementine Roux, where I'd cut and dyed my hair and pretended to be French, and where I had been captured by the Germans. I stared out at the fog and saw all the places I'd been: Scotland, England, Germany, and the villages and cities of France. I thought of the pieces of me I'd left behind, a piece here, a piece there, scattered like bread crumbs. How much of me was left?

My brother leaned over the rail, so far that I felt myself reaching for him, ready to pull him back. He said, "See for yourself."

All at once, the haze lifted, and in the distance I could see the black outline of land. Something appeared through the clouds—at first a dusky mass, like a haint, but then a form. A crown, a torch held high. The Statue of Liberty. The torch had been dark since the war began but now it burned bright through the mist.

The soldiers started to cheer. Two dirigibles flew low in the sky. A helicopter passed over the ship, then another. From somewhere, a song was playing, as if the city was singing. Smaller boats steamed past, blowing three long whistles. The *Gray Ghost* responded with a rumbling, knee-shaking blast—like thunder. Flags flew from the tops of buildings and from the windows, which were open and filled with people leaning out. A brass band played on the pier: "God Bless America."

I laid a hand on my brother's arm, lightly, hoping he wouldn't move it away. I said, "Oh, Johnny Clay. It's beautiful."

• • • • •

We pushed down the gangplank, carried by the crowd. Fifteen thousand soldiers fighting to be first on shore. I held tight to Johnny Clay's hand, my feet barely touching the wood of the dock. With my other hand, I held tight to my hatbox, my Mexican guitar, my mandolin, until Johnny Clay took them from me. I didn't need to walk because the men around me were pushing me forward. Thousands of people lined the pier and the harbor, waving, crying, shouting out names. Banners held high, flying in the breeze that skimmed off the water: "Welcome home, boys! Well done!" Handkerchiefs to mouths. Sobbing. Laughing. The first of the soldiers off, straining to find loved ones in the ocean of faces and waving hands. Men in uniform kneeling down to kiss American ground. Newsreel crews gathered, interviewing the returning heroes. Confetti falling like rain. I wanted to cover my ears from the noise, but I didn't dare let go of my brother's hand. It was his bad hand. I tried not to feel the knuckle, the smooth knot of it where the skin had grown over.

Just like that, we were on land. Back to America. *Home.* From somewhere, I heard my name and turned. I could see a man running, holding on to his hat. "Velva Jean Hart?"

"Yes, sir?"

"You're the little girl pilot, the WAVE . . ."

"WASP." I wasn't a WASP anymore—Women Airforce Service Pilots, responsible for ferrying planes and bombers to military bases. The WASP had been disbanded in December. I wasn't anything anymore, just a girl wanting to get back to her family and her mountains.

"Right, sure, WASP. You were in the British papers."

Was I? I didn't remember. I'd been too busy worrying over Johnny Clay, sitting at his bedside in the base hospital, praying for him to wake up, to get better, for months, and then waiting to go home, to be told he was strong enough, to find a ship with enough room to take us.

"Martin Seever, *New York Post*. Mind if I ask a few questions?"

"Okay."

"How old are you, honey?"

"Twenty-two."

"Where're you from?"

"North Carolina."

"Charlotte?"

"Alluvial. It's in the mountains."

"You the brother?" The man with the hat looked at Johnny Clay.

"Yessir." Johnny Clay narrowed his eyes.

The brass band played "Battle Hymn of the Republic" as men kissed their wives, parents, children.

"How did it feel to be rescued by your sister? Is it true she picked you up herself and carried you into the plane?"

I thought Johnny Clay was going to punch the man. I said, "There was another man, an agent." I didn't want to say too much. *A Frenchman. I don't know his real name but I still have the gold ring he gave me.*

"Now before this, you let yourself be captured by the Germans and placed in a French prison, is that true?" The reporter was looking at me again.

"It was supposed to happen that way, but I was taken early."

Martin Seever, *New York Post*, was writing down everything I said. He wanted to know how I got out of prison, was I tortured, what did the Nazis do to me, how did I find the agent, how did I free myself from the train that was sending me and all the others to Ravensbrück concentration camp. I told him Johnny Clay helped free me, he and the other agents. We fought off the Germans together as we escaped through the Palatinate Forest to France.

"Is that where you found the plane?" This was from another man, with a notebook and a cameraman.

"Just outside the forest on a German airfield, yes."

A third reporter appeared: "Had you ever flown a German plane before?"

"No."

"You were shot at by Germans and Americans on your way to England?"

"Yes."

We were surrounded. They asked us to pose for pictures, the Statue of Liberty in the background, holding up two fingers in the V for Victory sign. One of the men had a moving picture camera. He said he was Ed Dale with *News of the Day*.

Johnny Clay said, "The newsreels?"

"That's the one."

Ed Dale pointed the camera at us. "Look right into the lens. Smile and wave. Put your arm around her, son, lean on her just a little. Wave that hand, the one missing the finger. Now, honey, you look up at your brother and then back at the camera, right in there. Thatta girl. Remember—you're happy to be home. You're a brave soldier but you're grateful just the same. You're a daring aviatrix, second girl in history to fly a bomber across the ocean. You're a war hero—the girl who saved her brother after he was shot by the Germans, the girl who stole a German plane and not only saved the life of her brother but of a secret agent, important to the Allies. But you're also just a little girl who loves her country and now you're back in that country and the war is all but over."

I tried to do everything he was telling me. I ran a hand over my hair, which was wild and too curly from the salt air. The color had grown out where I'd dyed it almost black, and it was back to its regular color, not quite honey, not quite gold, not quite brown. I touched my bottom lip where there was still scar tissue, courtesy of a German interrogator. My face was wet from crying. I reached a hand up to wipe the tears away and Ed Dale said, "No, no. Leave them there. That's perfect. Now blow a kiss to America."

The sun broke through the fog and I tilted my face to the sky, closing my eyes for a second to soak it in. And then I looked into the camera and blew a kiss.

TWO

No one was waiting to meet us because they didn't know we were coming. A few old men sat outside Deal's General Store drinking Coca-Colas and chewing tobacco, but I didn't recognize their faces. They narrowed their eyes in our direction, like we were strangers and not to be trusted.

We walked past them, past Deal's, up the hill toward Sleepy Gap, which sat high up in a holler on the side of Fair Mountain. As we walked up the hill, Johnny Clay and I didn't speak a word. His leg was giving him trouble, but the closer we got to Sleepy Gap, the faster he started walking. I walked faster too, until we were practically running. Then we were racing, just like we used to when I was ten and he was twelve and we were trying to get home for supper.

We came up over a rise in the hill and I could see the big red barn, the chicken house, the smokehouse, the root cellar, and Daddy Hoyt's fiddle studio, where he made his violins. The first of the houses was a narrow weatherboarded two-story. It had a tin roof and a porch on the front. I could picture the newspapers, yellowed and curling, that lined the walls inside and filled in the cracks. They were the ones I'd learned to read from.

Johnny Clay threw our bags down in the grass and we were past Mama's house and around to the back, where another house sat. This one was made up of two log cabins connected by a dogtrot, or breezeway, and a shared red roof. Five blue stars hung in the front window—for my brothers Linc and Beachard; Johnny Clay; Sweet Fern's husband, Coyle Deal; and me.

The front door stood open and just as Johnny Clay was getting ready to holler, an old woman walked out onto the porch, shading her eyes with one hand. *Granny*. She was thin and tough as a strip of tanned leather. Her white hair was pulled back in a bun. You could see the Cherokee in her—in the cheekbones, in the eyes—as she took her hand away. She blinked against the sun and let out a shout. Then her arms were around us, and she was small but strong and she was crying. I breathed her in—the smell of lavender and lye soap that she made every year.

A man came out of the house. *Daddy Hoyt*. He was tall and sturdy, even with the rheumatism that made his back ache and caused him to stoop. He wore his herb-gathering pants, overalls with what seemed like a hundred pockets, which meant he was planning to spend the day in the woods, collecting the healing plants he needed. Granny was talking and crying and calling out to Aunt Zona, to Ruby Poole, to everyone on the mountain to come see, come now, the children are home.

They were all around us, and suddenly a man was hugging me. At first I didn't recognize him and almost pushed him away. His black hair was cropped close and there was a long scar at the hairline. *Linc*. My oldest brother. His wife, Ruby Poole, was crying and Aunt Zona's girls were crying, and I heard myself say, "Where's Aunt Bird?" at the same time Johnny Clay said, "Where's Hunter Firth?" and started to whistle for that old brown dog.

Someone said they'd died last winter, both of them old, both of them weary from living such full, long lives. Then a voice rose up behind us, coming up over the hill, traveling toward us like a bullet.

"Is it true? Are they back? They said at Deal's—the train just came—and two people, a boy and a girl . . . Where are they?"

A woman appeared. Her brown hair had gone almost gray and was pinned up off her neck. Her face was round and plain except for a smudge of pink lipstick. An old blue apron was tied around her waist and she was followed by one, two, three, four children of various ages.

Sweet Fern. She must be thirty-two now, almost thirty-three. She'd been twenty when Mama died, when she was left to raise Johnny Clay and me.

My granddaddy was looking at me. He had seen Johnny Clay's hand and leg, had noticed the missing finger and the limp. Nothing ever got past him. Daddy Hoyt was a healer and a medicine man, trained by the Cherokees, the wisest person I knew. He was looking us both over, making sure.

· · · · ·

That night, I sat at Granny's table and held hands with Ruby Poole to the left of me and Linc to my right as Daddy Hoyt said grace. "Well, sir, here we are. We've had quite a time of it lately, but it seems the worst is over. I want to thank you for getting these young people home to us. It's not Thanksgiving, but we're giving thanks just the same."

Linc and Coyle had both come home early, Coyle in January and Linc in May, discharged because of injuries. Coyle, shot through the arm, which now hung at his side, still working, still movable, but crooked. Linc, sent home with a head injury, minor enough to survive, major enough to end his war career. He looked up now and caught my eye. He squeezed my palm, and I glanced around the table, bowed head by bowed head, taking everyone in. I had my own scars but I wasn't wearing them on the outside.

Daddy Hoyt said, "If you would continue to look after Beachard who's still fighting in the Pacific, we certainly would appreciate it. And look after the rest of the brave men and women who aren't lucky enough to be home yet with the folks that love them."

Our hands broke apart and the food was passed—the very same food I used to dream about at Fresnes prison in Paris, where we were given coffee made of sawdust and bread rotten with maggots.

The children were practically grown. The youngest, Russell, was nearly eight. He sat next to his mama. Ruby Poole—dark hair curled over her shoulder, lips painted red, pretty as any Hollywood starlet in the movie magazines she loved to read—rested one hand on his head, the other on her stomach. She was pregnant, barely a month along.

Johnny Clay said to Linc, "You sure didn't waste a minute once you got home."

Sweet Fern said, "Johnny Clay."

For a long while I couldn't eat and I couldn't talk, which was fine because Johnny Clay was doing enough talking for everyone. At some point, he pulled out the gold bookmark that he swore had belonged to Hitler and passed it around. He said, "Careful now. Don't you drop it or lay a scratch on it." Johnny Clay took the bookmark from Dan Presley, Sweet Fern's oldest, and held it up to the light so that we could all see the inscription there. The words were in German but the initials were clear: *A.H. herzliche Grüße von E.B.* Then he carried the bookmark over to Granny, as if he were bringing her something holy. He said, "I brought this back for you. I thought you could put it on your mantel along with these." He fished two bullets out of his pocket. They were clean, nearly as bright gold as the bookmark, but there was a time they'd been covered with my brother's blood.

Just as everyone finished eating, I picked up the fork with my left hand, which was the way I'd learned to do in France so that no one would suspect I was American. Across the table, Sweet Fern and Coyle watched my hand and then looked at each other. No one had asked me yet what had happened to me, what I'd been through, and I was grateful.

· · · · ·

The story of my brave escape made it from the *New York Post* all the way to the *Hamlet's Mill Gazette*, and when the newsreel clip played at the theater in Waynesville, everyone on the mountain found a way to go and see it. I signed autographs for folks I'd known all my life who brought me casseroles or homemade pies or samplers they had stitched. The papers called me Miss Star-Spangled Banner, Miss Stars and Stripes. Margaret Truman, daughter of the President, wrote to me from Washington, D.C., to tell me I was "an inspiration," not only to her but to America. General Henry Arnold sent me a telegram. Jacqueline Cochran, head of the WASP, wrote to congratulate me on my bravery and my "fine example to women everywhere."

The newsreel called me Miss Red, White, and Blue: *She's the little girl who rescued an important operative! Government secrets were in her hands! This All-American sweetheart was one of the vital keys to the Allied effort in this war! She saved herself from the hands of the Germans and stole an enemy plane to rescue her dying brother and return him to Allied land. This little girl deserves more than just her brother's gratitude— she deserves the gratitude of a grateful nation.*

Johnny Clay was getting mail too—mostly from girls who saw him in the newsreel and sent him pictures of themselves. They wanted to take care of him and help him get better. My brother threw these letters in the trash, all except one—a package from Helen Stillbert, my friend from the WASP, which contained a note for me and some books for him, which was funny because I'd never known Johnny Clay to be one for reading.

He began taking off in the mornings with his gold pan or one of Daddy's old guns. He'd come back hours later and I would hear him whistling up the hill. Sometimes I smelled liquor on him, which made me think of Daddy, and other times he smelled like the woods and the earth, as if he was a part of them. One night, he got into a fight outside the Hamlet's Mill Theatre, and the next morning Sheriff Story walked him up the mountain so he could have a word with Daddy Hoyt. He said if that boy wasn't careful, he'd get himself locked up for good, or worse.

• • • • •

We'd been home a little over a month when, on August 15, Dan Presley came hollering up the hill followed by the rest of Sweet Fern's children and Sweet Fern herself. Her face was wet, her eyes red. Before Dan Presley could holler again, she said, "Japan surrendered, Velva Jean. The war is over."

That night, everyone came down from the mountains—Blood and Bone and Witch and Fair and Devil's Courthouse. We gathered in Alluvial, slapping each other on the back and shaking hands and congratulating one another on winning the war, as if each of us had single-handedly been responsible. There was food and music and home-made wine, and the children drew their names in the air with sparklers.

"What are you going to do now that the war is over, Velva Jean?" someone called out.

"I don't know," I said. A voice inside me was telling me to be on my way, stop wasting time, go, go, go.

The world after a war is a good world, I told myself. A happy world. A secure world. In this world, I might do anything.

• • • • •

One month later, just past noon on Friday, September 28, a stranger came walking up our hill. He found me on Granny's front porch, where I was helping Daddy Hoyt separate the plants we'd collected that morning.

The man said, "I'm looking for Velva Jean Hart." He stood in the yard fanning himself with his hat, his face shining and red, either from the heat or from climbing the hill. He had a thin blond mustache that gave him a slick look, and blond hair with plenty of pomade, which was starting to melt in the afternoon sun.

I came down the steps to meet him. "I'm Velva Jean Hart."

"Lowell Grann." He held out his hand and I shook it. "I'm with Metro-Goldwyn-Mayer in New York. We've seen your newsreel with the footage of you and your brother. You're quite the hero."

"Thank you." By this time, Granny and Ruby Poole had appeared.

The man said, "We've been trying to get ahold of you. We've sent telegrams, tried to phone you. We don't usually do this kind of thing in person, but you aren't easy to reach." He looked around at the woods as if now he could see why. "Lucille Ryman is head of talent at MGM. She'd like to offer you a test."

"What kind of test?"

"A motion picture test."

"To do what?"

"To be an actress."

Ruby Poole said, "The movies? Oh, Velva Jean!"

"She can sing," Granny said. "Prettiest voice you ever heard. Better than any singer you got out there in Hollywood."

The man wiped his forehead. "I'm sure that's true." He said it as if he didn't believe it for a minute, as if this was something people said to him all the time. "Ms. Ryman wants you in Los Angeles. I'm to arrange for your ticket. On the next train, if possible. You're quite the national hero, Miss Hart, and we want to keep you in the public eye while you're already in it. I won't be able to accompany you, but someone will be there to meet you in California."

I finally found my voice. "I have a friend at MGM. Barbara Fanning. We trained at Avenger Field together. We were WASP together. She was at MGM when the war started, and after we graduated she went back." Until the studio renamed her, she'd been Eloise Mudge, and the last time I'd seen her was spring of 1944 at the funeral of our friend Sally Hallatassee, a pilot like us.

"Barbara Fanning's one of our most popular stars."

Ruby Poole said, "She's playing Mallory in *Home of the Brave*, Velva Jean. The movie based on the book. Nigel Gray is Daniel, and I read that Ophelia Lloyd came out of retirement to play Martha Washington. It's going to be the biggest picture ever made."

"What would I do at MGM, Mr. Grann? You wouldn't put me in movies right away."

"You would train, take classes, prepare."

"Music classes?" Ruby Poole had once told me that the stars were given music lessons. Even Joan Crawford and Bette Davis had to study when they first began.

"We have the finest music teachers in the world." He could tell he had my interest. "We teach types of music you've never heard of. Every instrument. Every vocal technique. Song styling, phrasing, interpretation of lyrics. Do you think Judy Garland could sing when she came to us? Yes, of course, but not like she can now."

Before I could ask anything else, Johnny Clay said from the porch, "You should go, Velva Jean."

I turned to look at him. I hadn't even known he was there. "You could come with me."

He glanced at the man, at Daddy Hoyt and the rest of our family. "Velva Jean, I need to find my own way, ride my own coattails for a while." The shadows and the sharp angles of his face and collarbone had started to fill in thanks to the sunshine, the fresh air, and Granny's home cooking. " 'If now is only two days, then two days is your life.' "

I glanced at the book wedged in his back pocket. I was going to write to Helen and tell her to stop sending packages to my brother. I said, "What's that supposed to mean?" Even as I asked it, I thought: You know what he's talking about. You feel that way too.

"It means if you only got two days, you need to treat those two days like a lifetime. You need to find your place and figure out what it is you're supposed to do there, and I need to find mine."

Lowell Grann cleared his throat and replaced his hat. "Miss Hart. I will be on the four o'clock train. If you're interested in our offer, you can find me down at the general store. If not, I wish you luck. But I want you to realize that this is an opportunity that doesn't come around often. There are thousands of young women and men across this country who would give everything they have for an opportunity like this. We may see a thousand people a month, all wanting a chance. Of those, we might test five and sign only one. Wouldn't you like to be that one?"

He touched the brim of his hat and started down the hill.

Hollywood. All my life, I'd only dreamed of one place—Nashville—but Judge Hay, of the Grand Ole Opry, and Darlon C. Reynolds, record producer, weren't the ones who had traveled all this way to ask me to come with them. In Hollywood, I could train with the finest music teachers in the world and get all the experience I ever needed so that I could go back to Tennessee and show them I was ready. *We teach types of music you've never heard of.*

Everyone stared at me as Lowell Grann disappeared out of sight. I thought, I want to be that one. And then I started to run.

THREE

On October 2, four days after I'd left North Carolina, the Santa Fe Super Chief pulled into Los Angeles, California. I walked through the depot, carrying Mama's old suitcase and my hatbox, which, after all these years, still held my treasures. My Mexican guitar was strapped to my back.

I felt a fluttering in my heart as I left the station, stepping out into sunshine. It was a warm, cloudless morning. The palm trees swayed overhead. The air smelled like roses and wildflowers. The streets shone white. Layers of hills rose in the distance. Heavy red roses and other bright flowers bloomed everywhere. Fat oranges and lemons hung from trees. I didn't know any place could be filled with so much color anymore. *California.* It was a different world, a different planet. *A new world, a new life.*

I set my bag down and waited on the curb. Cars rolled past, pausing long enough to pick people up or drop them off. Here I am, I thought. Yessir, here I am.

After twenty minutes, I fished in my purse for the number Lowell Grann had given me. *Someone will be there to meet you,* he'd said, but here I was, alone. I took one last look around and then picked up my bag and headed back into the station. I found the Traveler's Aid desk and asked where I could find a telephone.

The man at the counter said, "If it's a local call, you can use this one."

At that very moment, I heard my name. "Hartsie!" For a minute, I thought I'd imagined it, but then I heard it again: "Velva Jean!"

A woman flounced toward me—dark glasses, hair tucked under a scarf, mink coat with the collar turned up. I didn't recognize her at first, even after she hugged me, her perfume turning the air sweeter. She held me out at arm's length, her lips and nails a feverish red, and said, "Don't look so terrified, Hartsie; it's me."

"Mudge?"

"That old nickname. No one's called me that since I left the WASP." She took the suitcase from me, linked her arm with mine, and said, "Where are your bags?" Her voice sounded throatier, huskier than I remembered.

"These are my bags."

From behind her glasses she raised one eyebrow, then she hugged my arm tight against her and we walked out into the sunshine. She steered me toward a long red car, bright as a ripe apple, one wheel sitting on the curb, the front bumper jutting out over the sidewalk so that people had to steer around it.

She tossed everything into the back except for a thick stack of bound rainbow-colored paper and the fattest book I'd ever seen. "Hold these for me."

I slid in beside her, holding them on my lap. *Home of the Brave*, it said on the cover of the bound paper stack. *Home of the Brave*, it said on the cover of the book. The car looked new, but a pile of lipsticks filled a compartment in the dash, and the ashtray was filled to the rim with red-smudged cigarette butts.

Mudge took off her sunglasses, and started the car. "I'm to bring you to the studio with me, orders of Lucille Ryman." She looked at me square, her eyes on my face, my dress, my shoes, then my face again. "Now what else have you got to wear?"

· · · · ·

We drove directly to Bullock's department store, where Mudge picked out a capped-sleeve cotton dress that was the pure, sweet green of spring grass. It cost 150 dollars, and Mudge told them to bill it to her account. "It's the least I can do, after you've traveled all this way," she said. "Besides, you needed it."

We headed down Sunset Boulevard, the mountains to the north, the ocean to the west, past Schwab's Pharmacy, the Garden of Allah, Ciro's, the Cafe Trocadero, and the Melody Room.

"Hold the wheel." I reached for it as she shrugged off her mink, flinging it in the back as if it was nothing more than an old napkin, and untied the scarf so that her black hair came spilling out. She ran her fingers through it, fluffing the ends, checking it in the rearview mirror. She lit a cigarette before taking the wheel back. "Don't ever start smoking because once you do you'll never want to give it up. Cigarettes are worse than men."

Something flashed silver on her dress.

"You're wearing your wings." The wings we'd earned as WASP.

She held up her collar, turning it toward me. "Sisters forever, Hartsie." She smiled into the distance, her hand resting on the pin as she smoothed the collar flat again. "No matter what."

· · · · ·

Culver City was a mix of farmland and dime stores, bars and diners, small houses and ugly apartment buildings. Depending on the breeze, one minute the air smelled like cow manure and the next like fresh baked bread, which Mudge said came from nearby Helms Bakery. Metro-Goldwyn-Mayer sat grandly in the middle of this, a sprawling, white-columned fortress.

The red car turned down a narrow street and rolled past a handsome white building shaped like the bottom half of an *H*. Four stories, tall windows, rounded corners, a covered walkway leading to double glass doors. Mudge paused in front, rolling down her window. "Louis B. Mayer himself works there, along with all the producers, directors, publicists." She turned to me. "I want you to watch out for the executives. Every one of them has a button on his desk that locks the door behind you, along with a private interview room, which is used for 'casting,' if you know what I mean. They promise you the moon, but it doesn't mean they plan to get it for you."

We paused at the East Gate, which wasn't a gate at all but just a paved drive with a stop sign separating the two lanes, along with a guard station no bigger than an outhouse. She flashed a bright red smile at the uniformed guard.

"Morning, Miss Fanning. Where's your driver?"

"I gave him the day off. Jimmy, I want you to meet the newest MGM contract player and future movie star, Velva Jean Hart. We were pilots together in the war."

The guard ducked his head so he could see me. "It's a pleasure, Miss Hart. I look forward to your pictures."

Mudge gave me the tour: There were the casting offices— see the people all lined up, waiting? There was the writers building, and, just past, music departments A and B. Over there was the portrait studio, where I would pose for pictures, one of the most important parts of the job when you were just starting out. Over there, the research department, where they kept thousands of files on every MGM actor, past and present. Over there, the fire department—and if I thought that was something, well Metro had its own school, barbershop, dentist, funeral parlor, and railway station. It even had its own police department—a police force of fifty officers, four captains, two plainclothesmen, an inspector, and the chief, Whitey Hendry, who'd been there as long as any one could remember and who was also chief of police for Culver City.

Back down there was the commissary. And just past that, the art department. Wardrobe to the right. Scoring stages to the left. Makeup, where I would be reporting every day first thing, once a contract was signed. The rehearsal halls were air-conditioned, and how many other studios could claim that?

"One hundred seventy-six acres . . . four thousand employees . . . sixty stars, the most of any studio. More stars than there are in heaven . . . Clark Gable, Judy Garland, Lana Turner, Nigel Gray . . ." City streets, Western towns, a French railway station, European villages, a fifteen-acre jungle. It seemed like all the world was right here at Metro-Goldwyn-Mayer.

The general dressing room building looked like a two-story barracks left over from World War I. In front of this was what Mudge

called the "star suites"—two buildings, side by side. She paused just
long enough so I could read the names on the directory—Greer Garson, Judy Garland, Esther Williams, June Allyson, Lana Turner.
Then she unlocked one of the doors—"Barbara Fanning," it said in
gold—and showed me into her suite, which was as large as an apartment and done up in rich shades of blue. She said, "It used to be Garbo's," and I could hear the awe in her voice.

Near the dressing room building was Stage 5, and the office of
Lillian Burns, the dramatic coach. We walked inside and were greeted
by her secretary, who sat at a desk in the outer office, fielding telephone calls. She handed us a stack of bound white paper, which I now
knew was a script, and said I was to memorize pages seventy-five
through eighty and to be ready to test on Friday.

· · · · ·

For the rest of the day, I followed Mudge from the makeup and hair
departments to wardrobe to one of the interior sets of *Home of the
Brave*, on Stage 15, the largest in the world.

In addition to the legendary Ophelia Lloyd, the picture costarred
Nigel Gray, Hal MacGinnis, Phoebe Phillips, and the great Webster
Hayes, who, for the past three decades, had been known as America's
finest actor. The producer was Ophelia Lloyd's husband, William
"Billy" Taub, one of Mr. Mayer's top executives and the creative genius
behind *Immortal Wife*, *The Haunted Man*, and *Darrow*. Leslie Edgar,
who had won an Academy Award for *The Mill on the Floss*, was directing.

While the cameramen arranged and angled giant lights and cameras, Mr. Edgar, small as a cricket, talked to his actors in a soft, gentle
voice. Under the spotlights, I watched Mudge transform instantly into
Mallory Rourke, Revolutionary War–era lady, torn between the love
of two brothers, played by Hal MacGinnis and Nigel Gray. According
to the movie magazines Ruby Poole had loaned me for the train, Hal
and Mudge had fallen for each other their first day on the set. In person he was taller and broader than he looked in his pictures, while
Nigel Gray was even handsomer.

A man, about thirty, sank into the chair next to me. He closed his eyes and propped his cheek on one hand. He sighed, long and deep, and opened one eye. He studied me a good ten seconds before saying, "Never try to outdrink Webster Hayes."

I glanced over at the actor, easily twice his age. "I'll remember that."

"Don't let the grandfatherly demeanor fool you. He's got the constitution of an elephant. Or an Irishman. Which sounds funnier?"

"Elephant."

"Got an aspirin?"

"No. Sorry."

He frowned. "Bourbon, then?"

"I drank it all."

He held out his hand. "Sam." He had rich-boy good looks, but there was something rumpled about him.

"Velva Jean."

"Seriously?"

"What?"

"I've just never heard a name quite like it. *Velma Jean.*"

"*Velva* Jean."

"Velva Jean. Never heard a name like that one either. Let me guess. Secretary?"

"No."

He squinted his eyes at me. "Rodeo rider."

"No."

"Candlestick maker."

"Singer."

He shook his head. "Sorry, you'll have to pick something else. You're too pretty to be a singer."

"What do singers look like?"

He stared out into the distance. "Faces only a mother could love. That's why radio works so well for them." He nodded at the script in my lap. "So that's only for show? To throw inquisitive men off the scent?"

"I carry it with me everywhere."

"Smart girl. Have you read the book?" Now he nodded at the set. "They say every person in America has read it."

"Well, I haven't. I got back from England in June. They don't seem to be reading it over there."

This made him laugh. "I thought I'd seen your face before. It's a face you don't forget. You're the war hero."

Before I could reply, a man came striding toward us. He looked like a madman, shirt untucked, ink stains on his fingers, eyes wild behind glasses, early forties on a good day. His gaze lingered on me for a fraction of a second before he thumped his copy of the script with the cigar he was holding. "The pacing is wrong. Mallory has a monologue on seventy-nine, and by eighty-seven she has one again. We need to cut one of them, but make sure we keep the information about Joseph's whereabouts." His hair was brown except for a single white streak, which bobbed and shook across his forehead as he talked.

Sam sighed. "Until next time, *Velva* Jean." He stood, gave a little bow, and then, walking backward, watching me, he followed the madman, expertly dodging wires and ladders as if he had eyes in the back of his head.

The madman was now talking to the director. "Silence, everyone." Little by little, they fell quiet. "I'd like to introduce Sam Weldon, the writer of this fine book. Without him, none of us would be here." I glanced down at the book in my lap. There was his name below the title: *Samuel Weldon*.

Over the sound of halfhearted clapping, Sam said, "Now you know where to aim the gun."

The madman continued, "He's agreed to come on at this late stage and give us some help with the script. Actually, we've had him holed up here for a couple of months already, working away on a new draft for you."

"What made you decide to do it?" someone called out.

"Other than the money, you mean? The way I see it, everyone from Groucho Marx to William Faulkner to the President's dog has had a crack at this script. I figured it's my story, I might as well see what I can do. I certainly can't make it any worse."

· · · · ·

Mudge lived on a palm-tree-lined Beverly Hills street in an enormous white farmhouse with window boxes of pink roses, a rolling lawn, and a white picket fence. A policeman was parked out front. As we gathered our things from the backseat, she said, "He's only a precaution. Whitey Hendry assigned us guards for the run of the shoot." Inside, the rooms were spacious and cheery, lots of whitewashed beams and vases of pink and red flowers and overstuffed couches and throw pillows. The dining room was dark wood and mirrored walls, an enormous grandfather clock in one corner. There was an office, a game room, a sunroom, a breakfast room, five bathrooms, and five bedrooms, not including the maid's quarters.

We ate dinner on the broad brick patio that stretched off the back of the house, trellises of purple flowers climbing up toward the second story. Mudge's housekeeper, Flora Anderson, a wiry black woman with hair the color of a ripe tomato, served the food before leaving. Because of racial covenants, she wasn't allowed to live in the house, but traveled home at the end of each workday to Leimert Park, ten miles away.

When Flora was gone, Mudge said, "They wanted to put you up in a hotel, but I said oh no. I've got a great big house—bigger than I need, now that I've kicked out husband number three—and I just rattle around in it like an old spinster. I'm nearly thirty, if you can believe it, because I certainly can't, and that means I've got about four more years before they start making me play mothers and harridans. You can stay as long as you want, Hartsie."

"Tell me more about the guard out front."

She dropped her napkin onto the plate and lit a cigarette. She stared out toward the pool and the hedgerow beyond, the smoke curling up around her face. "There are a lot of crackpots out there, especially since I took the role of Mallory Rourke." She sighed. "Everyone's got an opinion about who should play her. And apparently they don't all agree I'm the best choice. 'We want Lana Turner,' 'We want Greer Garson.' Well that hurts my feelings, especially when they try to climb in my windows or leave threatening notes on my front step." She sighed again, flicked the ash onto the ground. "I'm starting to wish I could give them Greer Garson. I've had two days off in the past eight months—*two*. I'm tired, Hartsie. I wasn't this tired in the WASP. Sometimes I think I'm too old to do this."

"My sister-in-law says it's going to be bigger than *Gone with the Wind*."

"Mayer certainly hopes so. From what I've seen of the dailies, though, the film creeps along like a rich old uncle who refuses to die. It's either going to be the greatest movie ever made or the biggest bomb in box office history. But I wanted this part more than anything and I try not to forget it. Some days that's harder to remember than others, but with any luck I'll come out of this knowing I could do it, no matter what they said." She stubbed out the cigarette, took a drink. "I'm sick of talking about me. One thing you'll learn as an actress is that it's all anyone expects you to do. You'll get so you can't stand yourself. Tell me about you, Hartsie." She asked me about the past year—where I'd been, what I'd done—and then we started in on the other girl pilots we knew in common and where they were now.

When my eyes grew heavy, she finally said, "You go on up, honey. I could talk your ear off. It's just so good to have you here. I've missed you. I miss the WASP. I miss flying. It was a good thing, what we did."

"It was."

My room was at the top of the stairs, looking out over the swimming pool and garden. The wallpaper was a cheerful pink and green, and the bed, which faced two broad windows lined with matching window seats, looked large enough to sleep eight. A vanity table took up part of one wall, and the rest of it was given over to a door that opened into a small bathroom tiled in pink and black.

I unpacked my suitcase and hung my clothes in the wardrobe. Then I sat down and flipped open the script I'd been given to learn. *Under the Moon* was the story of a dull mouse of a girl who, for years, is overlooked by the man she loves, until the day of his wedding, when she finally tells him how she feels. I paced up and down and read her lines out loud, but no matter how I said them they sounded flat and forced.

After a few minutes, there was a knock on the door, and Mudge poked her head in. "How's the studying?"

"I don't have any idea what I'm doing."

She walked over and picked up the script. "Believe it or not, this is the same story I tested with, thirteen or fourteen years ago. The writing wasn't any fresher then."

"I'm trying to figure out why this Jane character would sit back and let the man she loved get away. All my life, I've been fighting for things I believed in. I don't know how to play a girl like this."

"Sure you do." Mudge sat down next to me. She'd washed off her makeup, and now I could see the dark shadows under her eyes. "She's just another role, like pilot or spy. And maybe she doesn't seem like us, Hartsie, and maybe you don't think you've got anything in common with her, but at the end of the day, all she wants to be is loved, and who can't relate to that?"

. . . . .

Hours after we finished running my lines and I'd gone to bed, I woke. The room was dark and still, and for a moment I didn't know where I was. Then I smelled the gardenias, the ginger, the warm salt air. I could hear voices coming from the backyard. Mudge was still up. But then there was a man's voice, deep and rumbling.

I opened the window and leaned out, but I couldn't see anything except the trees and the sky. All this life. All this color. It was hard to believe there was ever a place where the sun didn't shine every day, the houses weren't enormous, the lawns weren't manicured, the flowers weren't blooming, and the people weren't beautiful. I thought, That is a California sky filled with California stars and soon you're going to be one of them.

FOUR

I arrived at Stage 8 early. Casting director Lucille Ryman was around fifty, attractive, and dramatically blonde, while director Jack Conway was a good ten years older than that. He said, "Velva Jean Hart. The war hero. I've seen the newsreel." Then he barked, "She needs more makeup." A man rushed forward, carrying a small suitcase in his arms. He opened it as he stood there, and I could see brushes and pots of rouge and powders, and tube after tube of lipstick.

Ms. Ryman said, "Not too much. I want her to look like herself." She stood back, arms folded.

Mr. Conway said, "Fine, but we need to darken the lipstick."

The stage was made up like a Victorian home, the rooms laid out side by side. Through the doorway of one, a staircase led upward. Mr. Conway told me he wanted me to come down the stairs, and that I, as Jane, would find the man I loved waiting for me. That I only had a few precious moments to profess my love once and for all, before it was too late, but that I was frightened because this was the bravest thing I'd ever done. He went up the stairs himself and came down fast, nearly running, and then the rest of the way slowly, as if he was trying to be controlled and calm. He crossed into the living room, stopping in the doorway. He leaned against it, cleared his throat, and said my first line.

He moved again. "Then you cross to here. Then here and here, as if you're not sure where to land. You just flit about." He moved around the room, straightening the curtains, rummaging through a crystal candy bowl. "Then, finally, over to him. You don't have much time! He has to leave any minute for his wedding!"

I could hear footsteps clattering on the cold concrete as more people arrived. "Places!" Mr. Conway waved at me to get up the stairs.

I walked through the hall, feeling the bright heat of the lights. I went up the stairs, one at a time. Fourteen steps up, the staircase ended at a tiny little platform. I stood on the stair next to the top and waited. I waited and waited. Finally, he shouted: "Action!"

I tripped down the stairs, nearly somersaulting to the bottom, but caught myself just in time. I swore without thinking and then smoothed my hair and glided the rest of the way. A man sat on the couch, his gold head gleaming under the lights. He checked his watch, tapped his shoe. I leaned in the doorframe and cleared my throat and said, "Thank you for coming." I tried my best to flit. I flitted to the curtains, to the candy bowl, and then to the couch.

The man with the gold head didn't turn around because he was too busy pulling out a cigarette. "You said it was important and that it couldn't wait." His accent was British, and he sounded impatient.

I flitted a little more and then I sat down beside the man, this stupid man, this man I loved, and the minute I looked into his blue eyes—the deepest, truest blue I'd ever seen—I forgot to be mad. I also forgot every single line that came next.

My God. It was all there: the darkly golden hair, the twinkling eyes, the devastating smile.

Nigel Gray said, "There's only one thing to do in this situation." He glanced over his shoulder toward the doorway, as if he was making sure we were alone. Then he gazed into my eyes and took me in his arms and kissed me.

When we pulled apart, I said, "The moon." Something about the moon. The kiss should have been on the piano bench. We were supposed to sing a song.

He laughed and grabbed me by my arms, just above the elbows, and pulled me to my feet. He shook me once, twice. In that famed

British accent, his voice husky and low and just for me, he said, "Jane, don't you see? Don't you know?"

"Don't I know what?" My voice was a whisper. My lines were gone, but for some reason I could remember every word I'd read about him in the fan magazines. *Nigel Gray is an only child from London, son of the Duke of Sutherland. He is married to glamorous German actress Pia Palmer, who is currently in England making a picture.*

He laughed and kissed me again. This time it lasted longer. I tried to breathe with his lips against mine. I tried to breathe under the hot, hot lights. His grip tightened, as if to steady me, but it only made my head go lighter. At last he let me go and the room tilted, just a little, and I waited for it to right itself.

How many kisses were there? I'd only noticed one in the script. I said, "I love you."

He laughed again. Then I remembered this wasn't my line at all. I was supposed to let him know I loved him without telling him so. I covered Jane's poor face, which was actually my poor face. He said, "Darling, I love you too."

"But Maisie . . ." I was saying anything now. My lines were far, far gone. *Nigel Gray is impossible not to like. Give him a chance and it's easy to see that, beneath his beautiful exterior, he is a rock-solid fellow, the kind of gent you'd be lucky to have for a brother, a friend, or a fishing partner.*

"Hang Maisie. Don't you know it's always been you?"

His eyes searched my face, running over my forehead, my nose, my lips, back to my eyes. I thought he was going to kiss me again and then instead he crossed to the piano. He sat down and played a few notes. "Do you remember the song I sang to you, back when we first met?"

"I could never forget that." I walked over to the piano bench and sat beside him.

He began to sing and play. He had a rich voice, a decent voice, and he played well. Suddenly I remembered the words. I sang a verse with him and then another by myself, and then the chorus. My voice bounced off the rafters of the soundstage, echoing around us. I closed my eyes, blocking everyone out. I kept singing.

I don't know when Nigel Gray stopped playing, but suddenly I could only hear myself. I opened my eyes and he sat watching me. There was something behind his eyes, as if he were studying me and taking me in. The charming smile, the twinkle behind the blue dropped away, and I felt as if I could see the real him—not the actor him, but the man. I stopped singing and, without thinking, took his hand, as if he was lonely and needed comfort.

He said, "Don't you know it's always been you?" I couldn't remember if it was what he was supposed to say or if he was making it up now too. At that moment, it didn't matter because he leaned in and kissed me again.

When it was over, Mr. Conway said, "That was fine, Miss Hart, just fine."

Lucille Ryman shook my hand. "We'll be in touch."

Then Nigel Gray stood, eyes on me as he pulled a cigarette from a flashing silver case. "I'm going to keep my eye out for you, Jane." He tucked the case away, twirled the cigarette into his mouth, lit it with a flashing silver lighter, and, with a wave and a wink, swaggered off.

· · · · ·

Two days later, I still hadn't heard from the studio. I told myself: That's it. You forgot your lines and nearly fell down those stairs and made a fool of yourself in front of Nigel Gray and Lucille Ryman and everyone else. I tried to put it out of my mind, but every time the telephone rang I jumped.

On Sunday night, Mudge and I ate a late dinner by the pool— shrimp cocktail, chicken à la king, asparagus, baked potatoes, fruit, salad. She had come directly from the set and was still wearing Mallory Rourke's studio makeup and hair. I'd barely seen her all weekend because her days on the picture lasted fourteen, sixteen, eighteen hours, and sometimes the studio added promotional appearances on top of everything else.

I could tell there was something on her mind. When I asked her about it, she smiled a little sadly. "At the end of the day, they're all the same." I tried to pass her the plate of shrimp, but she said, "I'm allergic. I asked Flora to make them for you."

As I ate, I thought, I could get used to this. "Who's all the same?"

"Men." She pulled something out of her pocket. It glinted silver in the light. She unscrewed the cap and drank—the same flask she used to carry with her in the WASP, the one where she'd hidden her gin. She offered it to me, but I shook my head.

I said, "Hal MacGinnis is handsome." Hal had been a fighter pilot and captain. He'd earned the Medal of Honor, the Silver Star, the Bronze Star, and the Distinguished Flying Cross. He'd been a star before the war, but was an even bigger star now.

"He is." She sighed, pulling her legs up onto the chair, sitting cross-legged. "Do you ever wonder why we haven't been able to stay married to anyone, Hartsie? Maybe I shouldn't lump you in with me. At least you only tried it once."

"If I'd stayed home with Harley Bright, I never would have gone to Nashville or become a WASP. I never would have gone to war. I'd never have come to California. I'd be living in Devil's Kitchen cleaning up after Harley and his daddy and worrying about what to fix for dinner."

"Do you think you'll ever get married again?"

I stared out toward the pool and tried to picture myself married, and then I tried to picture a man who would make me want to want to be married. "I don't know."

"I will. I can't seem to help myself. But the thing I want to be remembered for is being a pilot. Being in the WASP. That's the best thing I've ever done. It was the closest I've ever come to being truly good." The words seemed to echo in the night air. "Until now. Until Mallory Rourke and this picture. Still, at the end of the day, I think I'd give it all away—the studio, the clothes, the cars, the house—for a good husband and a home full of children." She stubbed out her cigarette and smiled. "Of course, if you ever repeat that to anyone, I'll tell them you're a liar."

Just after eight o'clock, we were interrupted by the jangling of the telephone. Mudge jumped to answer it, asked who was calling, and waved the handset at me. "It's the studio."

On the other end of the line, Lucille Ryman said, "Congratulations, Velva Jean Hart. The newsreel didn't lie. I'll see you tomorrow morning. Eight o'clock at the Thalberg Building. Tell the receptionist you're there to see Billy Taub about your contract."

As I hung up, Mudge was watching my face, her eyebrows raised, the corners of her mouth curved upward. "Yes?"

"Yes."

She clapped her hands together, handed me her drink, and took the phone from me. She cradled the receiver between her ear and shoulder as she dialed a number. "Redd, it's me. . . . Don't flatter yourself. I'm about to ask a favor. A friend of mine has a contract she needs looking at and a career that needs tending. It's going to be a big one. . . . Because as much as I detest you, Mayer detests you more, and it's good to keep him on his toes, especially with something"—she looked at me—"that he's taken such an interest in. Besides, I trust you. And that's awful hard to find in this town."

She set the receiver down with a bang. "Redd Deeley is the best agent in town. Just as long as you don't marry him."

FIVE

The contract was for seven years. I would receive a guaranteed salary of seventy-five dollars a week for six months, paid whether I worked or not. At the end of that six months, Metro had the option to renew for another half year at twice that amount or they could drop me, just like that, and be done with it.

I was to accept all roles assigned to me and agree to all promotional appearances requested by the studio, as well as any travel arising out of my work; otherwise I would face suspension. I was not allowed to leave Los Angeles without permission, even when I wasn't filming. I was not allowed to do any television work or accept any other profitable employment, which included theater, radio, and recordings.

I was always to be on call to learn, study, and film the movies I was in. I was to be free to promote the movie or do anything MGM needed me to do, including being loaned out to another studio. I was never to refuse to sign an autograph. I was to give the studio approval over anyone I dated. And according to the "standard morals clause," I was to "project what the studio considers an appropriate image," which meant I must behave myself at all times.

Redd Deeley, square jawed and strapping, sat next to me across from Billy Taub, neat and tidy in a jacket and tie—the white streak of hair smoothed back—and looking less like a madman than when I'd first seen him on the set. His office was on the third floor of the

Thalberg Building, connected to the rest of the legal department by a network of intercoms and telephones. The door kept opening as men walked in and out, interrupting long enough for him to look over this or talk to them about that. He signed papers with a red pen, barely glancing at the page, and kept checking his watch. His desk was stacked with scripts, maps, drawings, lists, and three copies of the book *Home of the Brave*. An enormous framed picture of his movie star wife, Ophelia Lloyd, perched on one corner.

"You're unmarried, Miss Hart?" Mr. Taub stared up at me, a finger marking his place on the page.

"Yes, sir."

"Any plans to be married in the near future?"

"No, sir."

"We ask that you consult us when and if this changes."

"I will." I wasn't worried about getting married. I was worried about the fact that I wouldn't be allowed to do recordings. I said, "When you say I'm not allowed to record, do you mean any kind of music?"

"Is that a problem?" He glanced at Redd.

I said, "I'm afraid so. Seven years is a long time."

"Is it about the money?"

"No, sir. It's about having control over my music."

"Look, this is a standard contract. You can ask your agent there. Judy Garland, Kathryn Grayson—they've all signed it."

"I would agree to it if you could take out the thing about recordings. I'll give you a year at the most, but that's all I can do."

"You're quite the negotiator." He glanced again at Redd.

Redd sat back, crossed his arms, and smiled at him. "She's certainly making my job easier."

I said, "There are certain things I won't compromise on. The main reason I came here was because of music."

"You do realize we're not a music conservatory. Our purpose isn't to educate you and then send you out into the world for someone else to reap the benefits." From the picture frame, Ophelia Lloyd's eyes blazed at me.

"I realize that."

Mr. Taub and I went back and forth, back and forth like this, Redd interjecting now and then, until finally, when Mr. Taub could tell I wasn't going to change my mind, he stood and glowered at me. "Wait here." He snatched the papers and stalked off, rattling them as he went.

While Billy Taub was gone, I looked around, wondering where his private "casting" office was, and if he had a button on his desk that locked girls in. If he did, I felt pretty certain he'd never try to use it on me.

Redd said, "I'm glad to be working with you, Velva Jean. In this business, in this town, it's good to have a team of people looking out for you. You've got one of the best ones." For a second, I thought he was talking about himself. "Barbara isn't always an easy pill to swallow, but she's loyal. If she loves you, she'll fight to the death for you. If you cross her, you're on your own."

Fifteen minutes later, Mr. Taub was back, papers in hand. He said, "You've got a deal, Miss Hart. We've changed the recording clause from seven years to one year, and raised your salary from seventy-five dollars a week to one hundred fifty. I'm assuming that addresses your concerns?" He smiled.

"Yes, sir."

"Any others we should discuss at this time?" I decided it was actually a baiting kind of smile.

"I don't think so. No."

"I'm glad to hear it. The studio will open a checking account for you at the Culver City branch of the Security Pacific Bank. Do you need us to find you an apartment?"

"I'm staying with a friend right now."

Redd smiled at Mr. Taub once again. "I believe you know her. Barbara Fanning. The girls were pilots together."

Mr. Taub said vaguely, "Is that so?" as he plucked a pen from its holder and laid the contract out in front of me. There, in black and white, was "Velva Jean Hart" and a line above it. I held the pen over the page. For once, I wasn't going to think or question or wonder what if. In thick black ink, I signed my name.

・・・・・

Metro's head of publicity was Howard Strickling. He was as tall, dark, and handsome as the movie stars he handled, but he wore a navy blue suit that wasn't flashy or fancy and spoke matter-of-factly—with a sometimes stutter—as if he didn't have time to waste. He sat in a beaten-up leather chair behind a desk with a carved ivory lion looming at one end, a photo of Joan Crawford thumbing her nose on the other. He said he needed to hear my life story, every detail, and that I shouldn't leave anything out.

I told him about Mama dying when I was ten and Daddy going away, about being raised by Sweet Fern, and saving up my money to go to Nashville. I told him about marrying Harley when I was sixteen, and divorcing him when I was twenty. I talked about Nashville and Darlon C. Reynolds and my friend Gossie, who took me in, and learning to fly, and then applying to be a WASP. I mentioned half Creole, half-Choctaw Butch Dawkins; Ned Tyler, the boy I'd loved who died in Blythe, California, when his plane crashed into a mountain; the fact that I was almost killed myself at Camp Davis when my B 29 was sabotaged. Then England and France, the Resistance and Émile Gravois and his team and Gossie's aunt, who smuggled downed pilots out of Paris. Being captured by the Germans and tortured and shipped off to a concentration camp, which was when I escaped. Killing a man, maybe more, as we tried to get away, and then what he already knew from the papers about saving Johnny Clay and stealing a German plane to get us home.

Mr. Strickling said, "Miss Hart, it's come to our attention that your father has a police record. Perhaps you can explain."

I didn't ask how he knew. Mudge had already warned me that they would do their research and that it was better to get it all out in the open at the start.

"My father never meant anyone harm, but he did like to drink. He was happy when he drank, never mean. And he would never hurt anyone."

"'Drunk and disorderly,' 'drunken conduct in a public place.' He seems to have spent more than one occasion in jail."

"When I was growing up, the sheriff in Hamlet's Mill would sometimes bring Daddy in, more to keep him from wandering off or getting into mischief. My brothers liked to make him stay in jail a night or two because they felt it was good for him."

"When was the last time you saw your father?"

"I haven't seen him in years."

He sat back in his chair. "So for all you know he may actually be dead."

"I—well. I suppose he could be." Even after all Daddy had done and not done, even after all these years of not seeing him, it wasn't something I liked to imagine.

Mr. Strickling said, "Is that everything?"

"Yes, sir."

"If there's anything you're holding back, anything that might prove embarrassing if the media gets hold of it, now is the time to let me know. If you tell me now, I can make sure that anything like that stays out of the press. Or if we can't keep it out of the press, I can make sure it's revealed in the most positive light possible. I don't want any surprises when I open my morning paper."

"That's everything."

"Good. When were you born, Miss Hart?"

"November 5, 1922."

"We'll need to change the date. Shave two or three years off your age, maybe give you a more patriotic birthday. Not July fourth because that belongs to Mr. Mayer, but perhaps Lincoln's birthday." He pressed a button on a little box on his desk.

A woman's voice said, "Yes, sir?"

"Get me a list of patriotic days of the year, please, Doris, disregarding July four."

"Certainly, sir."

He handed me a stack of pages, longer than my contract. *What does*

your father do for a living? Where did you grow up? What are your hob-
bies? What is your favorite food? Where did you go to school? Who is your
ideal man/woman? What are you most afraid of? What is the bravest
thing you've ever done?

He said, "Once you fill out the questionnaire, we can create your
studio biography." He pressed the button on the box again. "Doris, get
me Bernie Hanser." To me, he said, "Bernie will be your personal
publicist. Good guy. Southern. From West Virginia, like myself." He
wrote something in my file and then closed it. "Talent is like a precious stone, Miss Hart. Like a diamond or a ruby. You take care of it.
You put it in a safe, you clean it, polish it, look after it. There's only one
of you, one of Nigel Gray, one of Barbara Fanning, and because of that
you have to be protected. It's what we do here."

· · · · ·

At wardrobe, they measured every inch of me. I learned that my hands
and feet were too big, my chest too small, and that I was, at five feet six
inches (and three-quarters), too tall, but "thankfully not as tall as In-
grid Bergman." The woman who weighed me said I could stand to
lose five pounds, "preferably on the hips and not the chest," because it
would make my cheekbones "more prominent." She asked me what
my regular diet was and when I said, "I eat anything I want to," she
scribbled something down on an index card and handed it to me. *Pre-*
scribed diet: eight glasses of water a day. Breakfast: plain toast. Lunch:
cottage cheese and fruit. Dinner: boiled vegetables and one small piece
plain fowl, fish, or beef. No desserts!

In the makeup department, I sat in a barber's chair under bright
lights while my teeth, smile, nose, eyes, eyebrows, ears, and cheekbones
were examined by a team of men in lab coats. They talked about me like
I wasn't even there, discussing what to do about my freckles (violet-ray
treatments) and my teeth (caps for the front two to make them more
even) and the little scar on my lip, which had been given to me by a Nazi
officer. My eyes and cheekbones were my best features, even if my eyes
were a darker green than they would have chosen, and my eyebrows
needed to be plucked and arched. One of the men drew on my face with

a fat black pencil, and when I asked him what on earth he thought he was doing, he said, "Trying out the possibilities."

In the hair department, the one and only Sydney Guilaroff—the man responsible for the most glamorous heads in Hollywood—stood back and studied me, his own head cocked, cigarette in one hand. He was a dapper, balding man, trim in a handsome gray suit with a lavender pocket handkerchief.

"A natural beauty. Good coloring." His assistant followed him, making notes. Mr. Guilaroff gestured as he talked, waving the cigarette like a baton. He came forward and touched my hair, holding the ends, examining the color and the feel of it. "It's too curly. We can give it a wave, which will take some of that out, control it more. The hairline is good. I don't think we'll have to lift it. The cut is terrible." For the first time, he spoke to me directly: "Who did this to you?"

I had done it to myself, in a bathroom in Paris, with a set of cutting shears loaned to me by a family from the French Resistance. "I did."

He frowned. "The color too, I see." He moved behind me and set his hands on my shoulders. He studied my reflection for about three minutes. "You're an American hero, are you not, Miss Hart?" Before I could answer, he snapped his fingers at his assistant, and said something to her about color number this, and number such-and-such and so-and-so. She wrote everything down, nodding so hard I thought her head would snap off. He beamed at me in the mirror. "What do you think . . . of *blonde?*"

Mudge arrived before I was done. She dropped her mink onto a chair and lit a cigarette. She said hello to Sydney, hello to Arlene Dahl, hello to Phoebe Phillips. She stood chatting with Sydney, watching him work.

Afterward, when he was finished, Mudge inspected my head from every angle. "Sydney, you're inspired. It's the hair she should have been born with. What do you call it?"

"Blonde."

"Not just any blonde, darling." She winked at me. *"American* blonde."

$\cdots\cdots$

Miss Burns taught drama, Miss Bates taught ballet and movement, and Miss Fogler taught voice—speaking, not singing. Her office was on the back of the lot in a little green bungalow.

I sat in a hardback chair and read aloud a poem that she'd handed me. Then I lay down on the floor and read it again, bouncing a book on what she called my diaphragm. Then I sat in the chair again and read a story from the book. She gave me a hand mirror and I recited sentences over and over in front of it: "I did not want to pet the dear, soft cat." And: "How. Now. Brown. Cow."

All the while she would say things like, "Sit on it, child! Make your voice come up from down there—down *there*. That's good, that's good."

Her own voice was full and lilting. She said, "My job is to place the voice because a resonant voice records better than a thin one. Now. There is a lot of work to be done here—goodness, a lot! But I promise you that when we're finished, that Southern accent will be exorcised."

I posed for publicity pictures at the portrait studio, swinging a tennis racket, balancing on ice skates, sitting atop a horse and then a bicycle, eating an ice-cream cone, petting a dog. In movement class, Miss Bates went over the proper MGM way to get up out of a chair while keeping the knees together, and how to tuck the bottom when walking. She demonstrated how to make exits and entrances. She said, "An actress has to have a look of authority when she enters a room. Body language is important. Posture is important."

She said it was a process, that it would take weeks and weeks of training until we learned how to hold our hands and our heads, and how to know the right angle for the camera. Once we learned, we must keep studying and practicing so that we never lost it. She said there were some actresses who had been at Metro for years who *still* hadn't learned, which was why they would never be movie stars.

The last class of my first week was with Sam Katz in the musical department, which was spread across five separate bungalows that Mudge called Tin Pan Alley. The windows to the bungalows were open, and I could hear someone on the piano, and someone else singing scales. Then another piano started up, but instead of fighting each other, the notes from the three different melodies merged together into a symphony of promise. *This is why you're here, Velva Jean.* I closed my eyes and listened for as long as I could.

Inside Sam Katz's office, the walls were covered in framed posters of the more famous MGM musicals. I strolled down these like an avenue, taking in every one.

Mr. Katz asked me to sing anything I wanted, and I chose one of my own songs, one written years before called "Yellow Truck Coming, Yellow Truck Going." While I sang, he perched on a desk and listened with no expression at all.

When I finished, he said, "Do you read music?"

"Yes."

"Do you play piano?"

"Guitar and mandolin, but I'd like to learn."

Mr. Katz pulled a stack of sheet music off the desk and handed it to me. "Pick one of these and sing it." I chose "Begin the Beguine," from *Broadway Melody of 1940.*

Afterward, he said, "You're a very promising diamond in the rough. You've got one heck of a voice, but we can help it be even better. Where did you study?"

"I didn't. But everyone in my family is musical. We kind of picked it up as we went along. I came here to train."

"You'll have to unlearn things as well as learn. I want to warn you that it's going to feel like starting from scratch. I've seen people come in here who think they know all there is to know about music, maybe they've had years of training, only to discover they don't know anything at all."

"In the end, all I care about is my voice, and what's good for it."

"All right then. We're going to assign you to Bobby Tucker to work on your phrasing. You'll work with Harriet Fields for pop singing, Earl Brent for jazz singing, and Arthur Rosenstein for vocal form. It will take a team, but that's what we're here for. With some hard work MGM might—just might—be able to turn you into a singer."

• • • • •

The office of Louis B. Mayer was on the ground floor of the Thalberg Building, and was the largest room I'd ever seen. Everything was white—walls, ceilings, lamps, chairs, sofa, grand piano, and an enormous leather crescent-shaped desk, which stood fifty or so feet from the door and was built on a platform. A man sat behind the desk wearing a dark three-piece suit and round wire-rim glasses.

At first I thought I was dreaming. Maybe I had died and gone straight to heaven and here was God himself to greet me, looking not like God at all but like the president of a bank or a stout little owl. The man's secretary, Ida Koverman—who had two assistants and a secretary of her own—looked like a kindly grandmother, but didn't act like one. She announced me, her tone clipped and disapproving, as if she was afraid I would track dirt onto the thick white carpet.

He said, "Thank you, Ida." She bristled out.

I began the long walk to the desk. I was wearing my new green dress and suddenly I felt gaudy and too bright. In the midst of all that white, the color of my own dress hurt my eyes.

The man stood and I could see that, even on the platform, he was short. He called out, "Miss Hart, lovely to see you. I'm sorry it's taken us so long to be introduced." He held out his hand. "Louis B. Mayer. Welcome to MGM."

He punched a button on his desk and from a great distance, there was the sound of a lock clicking into place, and I thought, Uh-oh. He waved to me to sit in one of the white chairs. After I'd taken my seat, on the edge of my chair, ready to outrun him or knock him down if he made a pass, Mr. Mayer sat, beaming. He was sixty, round, and balding, and didn't look at all like the most powerful man in Hollywood.

The windowsill behind him was covered in framed photographs—three women who, by the looks of it, were his wife and daughters, and J. Edgar Hoover. A pitcher of orange juice and a glass sat on one end of the desk, along with a white telephone, a day-by-day calendar, pens and pencils, and various papers.

He said, "You've got a fine singing voice. And of course you're quite the heroine." He leaned forward, hands clasped, eyes narrowing into bright little beads. "I can sense stardom. You have it. In my long career, it's rare to come across this kind of talent. I haven't done so nearly as many times as you would think. Greer Garson, Nigel Gray, Judy Garland." He delivered the lines easily, as if he'd rehearsed them. I thought: That isn't a platform at all. It's his stage.

He smiled, a kind uncle, a generous father. "Your name has to change; I'm sure you realize that. Double names aren't glamorous and they're too difficult to remember. We thought we'd let the fans choose your new name. After all, you're a national heroine. You belong to America, and because of that we think it's important they're in on this from the beginning."

"But people have read about me. They know me as Velva Jean Hart."

"They know you as the courageous girl pilot with the million-dollar smile."

I said, "Mr. Mayer, I thought you liked me in the newsreel. But now you want to change everything—my hair, my teeth, my birth date, my accent. My name."

"Don't think of it as changing you, Miss Hart. Think of it as enhancing what's already there and bringing out your very best."

"I'm sorry, but I can't let you change my teeth or zap off my freckles."

He stood so suddenly and with such authority that I stood too, without thinking. "You were a spy, Miss Hart. I'm assuming to be one you had to take on another identity, perhaps change your appearance, your name, your background. Think of acting as another form of spying. We figure out what role you need to play and then you play it, on and off the screen. You play it with everything you've got, as if your life depends on it. That's why we gave you a contract. Now, what's say I'll do my job and you do yours?"

He walked around from behind his desk, a neat and portly little man who would have come up to my ear if he'd been standing on the floor beside me and not on a platform. "If you ever have a serious problem of any sort, I hope you'll call on me and I will do everything I can to help you. You're part of the MGM family now. Welcome home."

· · · · ·

We celebrated at the Cocoanut Grove, with its live palm trees, Moroccan chandeliers, and ceiling of stars. Guy Lombardo and his orchestra played waltzes as Veronica Lake glided by with a man in a pin-striped suit. Lucille Ball and Desi Arnaz sat at one of the little round tables, smoking cigarettes and drinking cocktails.

Men and women crowded the dance floor, like a party on New Year's Eve. Frank Sinatra, Mickey Rooney, Ava Gardner, Carmen Miranda, Lana Turner, Artie Shaw, Jack Carson, Tyrone Power—more stars than in the MGM commissary.

Mudge said, "There's no such thing as dancing here. You come to sway." She wore a blue satin gown with a fur collar, and a clip of diamonds in her hair. Every time she turned her head the jewels caught the light.

We were joined by Hal MacGinnis and contract players Phoebe Phillips and Laura Burdine. Phillip Drake—mustached and dimpled, a younger Clark Gable—pulled up a chair and wedged it between Phoebe and Laura, and then Tom Vreeland appeared with a tray of drinks. "What are we celebrating?" he asked as he set them in front of us.

"The newest Hollywood star." Mudge raised her glass. "To Hartsie."

"To Hartsie," everyone echoed, and then we all clinked glasses as a photographer stopped to take a picture. Hal grabbed Mudge and kissed her. The flashbulb popped and shattered, and then another cameraman was there, and another. After they were done, I could barely see the table.

My head whirled with the dancers—movie stars, all of them. Even the people who might not be movie stars looked like they could be. Everyone so polished and beautiful, like brightly plumed birds.

"Do you want to dance, Velva Jean?" Hal stubbed out his cigarette and stood, as tall as one of the palm trees. I could still see a blur of red lipstick on his mouth.

"Yes." I took his hand and let him pull me to my feet, my head barely reaching the cleft in his chin. "I do."

To: Leslie Edgar; Sam Weldon
cc: Louis B. Mayer
From: Billy Taub
Re: *Home of the Brave*

October 10, 1945

Based on the strength of Velva Jean Hart's screen test, Mayer and I want to write in a part for her as Betsy Ross. Because of the overwhelming excitement regarding this girl, my mind is to add five or six scenes and perhaps a song or two for her to sing. *We cannot tell you how strongly we feel about this matter or how important we feel it to be.* We think it is the difference between a successful picture and an unsuccessful picture; the difference between a new star and a girl who will never make another picture here.... The curious charm that Hart had in the newsreel and in her test—the combination of exciting beauty and fresh purity—certainly ought to be within our abilities to capture.

One thought is that it would be powerful to have Betsy Ross present at the reading of the Declaration of Independence, and to welcome her own husband home at the end of the war.

To: Sam Weldon; Billy Taub
cc: L. B. Mayer
From: Leslie Edgar
Re: *Home of the Brave*/Ideas for scenes

October 10, 1945

Perhaps we can have Betsy present at a ceremony related to the June 14 Continental Congress flag adoption.

While her home is shared by the British and while the Continental Army is at Valley Forge, let's show her sneaking away to sew the bags as the enemy lodgers are sleeping in the other room, thus underscoring her bravery.

Re: her second husband, Captain Ashburn, we don't want to upset the ending with Nigel Gray's character returning home, but it may be possible to merge Betsy's loss at learning her husband's fate with Gray's triumphant homecoming, *both* singing a song as a kind of poignant duet.

To: Billy Taub
cc: Leslie Edgar; Sam Weldon
From: L. B. Mayer
Re: *Home of the Brave*

October 11, 1945

All possible scenes you mentioned sound good. Make sure they are interspersed throughout the film so that Betsy Ross doesn't disappear for very long. I like the idea of a duet at the end, as long as they are in separate locations, each thinking he/she is singing the song alone. This kind of ending could be even more powerful than the original, underlining her loss and his loss as well, but also his victorious return to the woman he loves.

Put in Phillip Drake or someone like him as Betsy Ross's second husband. And, if at all possible, create a scene for Miss Hart and Nigel Gray, however brief.

To: Billy Taub
cc: L. B. Mayer; Leslie Edgar
From: Sam Weldon
Re: *Home of the Ludicrous*

October 12, 1945

Schedule permitting, perhaps Lassie could tote Betsy Ross through the blizzard to Valley Forge so that she can deliver those home-sewn gunpowder bags herself. At this point, the dog seems to be the only MGM star *not* attached to the picture.

To: Sam Weldon
cc: Louis B. Mayer; Leslie Edgar
From: Billy Taub
Re: *Home of the Brave*/Ideas for scenes

October 13, 1945

Lassie is currently shooting *Courage of Lassie*, but write the scene with Betsy Ross struggling through snowstorm to Valley Forge alone and on foot, and have it to me with the others listed above.

SIX

Bright and early on the morning of October 22, I stood on the steps of the Thalberg Building sandwiched by Mudge, Louis B. Mayer, and Ophelia Lloyd while a throng of reporters elbowed each other, cameras flashing. Howard Strickling and my publicist, Bernie Hanser—suntanned and brawny, with a round, friendly face—stood, arms folded, off to one side.

Ophelia Lloyd, once the grandest movie star of all—until famously leaving the business at a too-young age—looked exactly the way she did on screen and in the photograph on her husband's desk: diamond necklace, diamond earrings, hair swept up and off her face, which was perfectly made up. Her lips were painted a deep bloodred, and her great, blazing eyes were large and dark. She wore the highest heels I'd ever seen—dancer's shoes with a strap around the ankle—but she was still a head shorter than I was. She might have been twenty-five or forty-five. It was impossible to tell.

Mr. Mayer beamed like a proud father as first Mudge and then Ophelia Lloyd said a few words in tribute to MGM's latest find—me. Miss Lloyd linked her arm through mine and told the reporters, "I know you will love this girl as much as I do, and that you will believe in her talent just as I do." Her voice soared and lilted, the only one like it in the world, in spite of what Mudge called her "assembly line studio British."

"I am excited to set foot once again on the Metro lot, where my career truly began, and share its newest star with the world. As you know, we held a little contest to find her a new name and, while we received thousands of entries, and while they certainly were clever and creative, none of them truly captured her particular brand of charm." She took a breath and drew her shoulders back so that she suddenly seemed taller than all of us. "Therefore, I have taken it upon myself to name her." She paused, her eyes sweeping the crowd, as if daring us to speak out in protest. "I am excited to introduce everyone, once and for all, to a girl who reminds me of myself only a few short years ago . . . Miss Kit Rogers."

The cameras flashed and popped. One of the reporters down front called out, "Wasn't that the name of your character in *Our Growing Daughters*, Miss Lloyd?" He was short and squinty, arms folded across a burly barrel chest, hands tucked into armpits, the only one in the crowd without a hat or a notebook.

"Yes it was, Zed. It was the role that gave me my start. And now I hope it will be as lucky for Miss Hart . . ." She laughed at this, waving her hand, *silly me*, "Miss *Rogers* . . . as it was for me."

Zed's eyes flickered to me. "What do you think of your new name, Miss Rogers? Or can we call you Kit?" Polite laughter all around. He was the only one who didn't join in.

What could I say? It sounded like something you would name a cat, but when the most famous movie actress in the world baptizes you after her favorite character, the one that made her a star, you've got to be polite about it.

I said, "It's an honor, Mr. . . . ."

"Zabel. Zed Zabel."

I knew his name from his newspaper column. "It's an honor, Mr. Zabel. I'll do my very best to live up to it."

Zed Zabel was looking at Mr. Mayer now, eyes aglint. "What can you tell us about *Home of the Brave*, L.B.? Have you mortgaged your house yet?" There were trickles of nervous laughter. *The period spectacle to end all spectacles*, MGM promised. *The budget to end all budgets*, reporters wrote.

Mr. Mayer said, "*Home of the Brave* is going to make *Gone with the Wind* look like a Poverty Row quickie. We've got Billy Taub producing, Colin Fedderson designing the costumes, and author Sam Weldon working on the last polish of the script. Not to mention these two beautiful ladies." Mudge and Ophelia Lloyd smiled royally. "It was a dark day at Metro-Goldwyn-Mayer when Ophelia retired from the screen, but we are lucky to have her back. The public demanded she return."

"Was that what persuaded you, Miss Lloyd?" This came from a red-haired man.

"Yes, it was, Dennis. I would not be standing here today, on the steps of this great studio, if not for the public. Everything I am, I owe to them, and I have never forgotten it."

Mr. Mayer boomed, "We're also lucky to have, in her very first movie . . . Kit Rogers." He glowed at me. "Usually, we at Metro like to take time to groom our new stars, but every now and then an actor or, in this case, actress comes along, and you just have to take a chance on them."

Zed called out, "The movie that much of a sinking ship, L.B.?" Some of the other reporters laughed. "And what do you say to the other Revolutionary rip-offs? I hear Warners has Flynn and Olivia de Havilland suiting up for *King's Mountain*, and got Zanuck's Tyrone Power as Benedict Arnold and Betty Grable as Abigail Adams. Sounds like they're giving you a run for your money. The question is if *Home of the Brave* and Metro are up for that kind of challenge."

Mr. Mayer narrowed his eyes in Zed's direction. "*Home of the Brave* is going to blow all other ships out of the water."

After the press conference was over, Miss Lloyd dropped her smile and air-kissed me on either cheek. "Best of luck to you, Kit, and do let me know if you need anything." She nodded at Mudge. "Barbara," she said, and her tone and look were cool.

"Ophelia," Mudge replied in the same exact voice. Miss Lloyd went tapping off, followed by a small army of assistants.

I shadowed Mr. Mayer as he shook hands all around and then walked off with Howard Strickling, who stuck close by him. As they opened the door to the Thalberg Building, I ran up the stairs after them, in time to hear Mr. Mayer say, "Never again. If I so much as see his fat, stupid—"

"Mr. Mayer?" He turned, blinking at me as if he were trying to place where he'd seen me before. "I want to thank you for your belief in me, but I'm not ready to be in a film. I'm afraid I'll only make a mess of things and make a fool of you, and I don't want to let anyone down, least of all myself. It would be like taking a plane up before I'd learned to fly."

"Nonsense. Your test was one of the best I've seen in years. I want to put you on screen while that face of yours is still fresh in the public's mind. Did you see those people out there? The cameramen and reporters? Well, now those people are out there"—he pointed toward the street, toward Los Angeles—"and it's burning a hole in them to tell your story. Let's don't ruin that for them."

He ducked inside, Mr. Strickling on his heels, the door swinging closed behind them. When I walked back down the steps, Zed Zabel was waiting. "Not getting cold feet, are we, Kit?"

Mudge blew cigarette smoke in his direction. "Go home, Zed. Don't you get tired of coming to parties you're not invited to?"

"Not on your life."

She steered me away from him, toward the soundstages. "You have to be careful with reporters, Hartsie. You'll need to watch out for Hedda Hopper and Louella Parsons. They'd sell their own children if it meant a good story, but if you're nice to them, they'll be nice to you. But don't trust men like Zed Zabel. He hangs around the nightclubs and the studios, trying to gain entry, just so he can unearth dirt to print in his filthy column."

I was barely listening. "Mudge, this movie is enormous and important. I'm not an actress. I'm not ready."

"Think of it as going up in a plane for the first time. At some point, you had to take the controls and fly it yourself. You can do this, and I'll be there." We paused in front of Stage 15. "Let's face it, girls like us don't get a lot of opportunities in this world. We *make* our opportunities. Never forget why you're here."

I felt like I had to keep moving, I'd written to my family the night before. *Until Lowell Grann came walking up our mountain, I'd never thought twice about being an actress or coming to California, but now that I am, I can see it was the right thing to do. I've never forgotten Darlon C. Reynolds telling me to get out there and experience every type of music, and I think he also meant every type of life.*

I hadn't heard a word from Johnny Clay since I left North Carolina, and I hoped that, wherever he was, he was okay, and that he was also finding his place.

· · · · ·

Later that morning, I was on my way to drama class when I ran into Sam Weldon outside the scenario building, where the writers worked. "So. Kit Rogers. Not sure how I feel about the new name." The script was tucked under his arm. With his other hand, he scratched his forehead, cigarette burning red. "Sounds too much like an Old West outlaw. You know, grizzled beard. No teeth. Makes it harder to know what to call you."

"How about my real name?"

"Too easy. I kind of like Pipes. Because you've got a hell of a pair. Seriously, if they had to butcher my story by adding songs to it, I'm glad you're the one singing them. Besides, there's not much more they can do to screw up this script."

"Has anyone ever told you that you're terrible at giving compliments?"

"Yes. I imagine you're good at it though. Southern belle and all."

"I take it you weren't happy having to write in Betsy Ross?"

"Let's put it this way. Historically, we don't even know for sure that she sewed the flag, but by the time L. B. Mayer and Billy Taub are done with her, moviegoers across the country are going to think she single-handedly won the Revolutionary War, not to mention that she was a hell of a singer."

A group of contract girls swished by in a cloud of perfume. They glanced at Sam—to see if he was someone, to see if he was watching—and he smiled like a rake in a novel. "Ladies." They went off giggling.

He watched them. I cleared my throat. He turned back to me. "Pipes. Sorry, what were you saying?"

"I wasn't."

"Right. Well then, what do you think of the story?"

"I haven't read it yet."

"If I didn't know better, I'd think you were trying to flatter me."

"I'm not."

He dropped the cigarette, stubbed it out with his shoe, shoved his hands in his pockets. "No, you're not. Much as I enjoy flattery, it's refreshing. This place is full of people who do nothing but flatter from sunup to sundown. They excel in flattery. They're paid a lot of money to flatter. Frankly, I'd rather be insulted. At least it's honest."

"Is that an invitation?"

I cocked my head and smiled. He cocked his head and smiled.

"Speaking of invitations, I'd like to extend a more overt one. Have dinner with me. If all goes well, have more than that."

"I'm afraid I'm busy tonight."

"Tomorrow night, then."

"I'm pretty sure I'm busy then too."

"Ah, the hard-to-get type. My favorite. Or maybe you're just old-fashioned. I'm not as crazy about that one."

"Good afternoon, Mr. Weldon."

"Good afternoon, Pipes." I could feel him watching me go and so I swished away like the contract girls, sending my hips from side to side like a metronome. He was still laughing as I passed Main Street.

I reported to Miss Burns and had a voice lesson with Miss Fogler. Then I met with Harriet Fields for pop music. She had the thinnest painted-on eyebrows I'd ever seen.

For ten minutes she told me about her work with the unparalleled Judy Garland, and then she said, "We're going to focus on scales."

I thought she meant for a few minutes, but she meant for the entire hour. I sang up and down, over and over. The only thing that changed was the vowel sound. "Sing ah," she'd say, smacking the piano with a baton. "Sing e." "Sing eh." "Sing oh." Then we started all over again with consonants. "Sing caw." "Sing muh." "Sing tee."

Afterward, I reported to Earl Brent for my jazz singing lesson. When he started me on scales, I said, "I just spent an hour doing this with Miss Fields. I'm as warmed up as I'll ever be."

"It's customary to spend the first several lessons vocalizing, Miss Rogers." But he stood and sorted through the sheet music stacked atop the piano. He pulled out three songs and said, "Let's see how you sight-read."

We started the lesson without accompaniment because Mr. Brent said this was the way of finding your key, the one you felt comfortable in. "The right key is almost always found in the last note." Once I found it, I set aside the lyrics and sang the vowels and then a single melodic line, the same one over and over, until my intonation was clear. I may have been singing nonsense words again, but at least I wasn't doing scales.

The thing I liked about jazz was that you could change up the rhythm, shortening and lengthening the notes in whatever way you wanted to. You could sing them one way once and a completely different way the next time around.

"Good work, Miss Rogers," Mr. Brent said at the end of our session. "I think you're coming along nicely."

As I walked out of his studio, the air seemed a little sweeter, the sun a little brighter. I thought, Maybe Kit Rogers can do this movie after all.

Back in my box of a dressing room, I vocalized as I checked my reflection, reached for a lipstick, ran powder over my freckles. Part of learning to sing all over again was practice. Practice, practice, practice. I swept my hair back with one hand and tried to decide if I liked myself as a blonde. Then I gathered my things, including my script, and on second thought went back for the *Home of the Brave* book.

I was halfway down the stairs when I saw Mudge, still in costume, walking out the door of her star suite. She glanced around, to her left, to her right. I opened my mouth to call to her, hand in the air, but then she looked behind her, nodding to someone, and Nigel Gray appeared. Without a word, she went one way and he went the other.

KIT ROGERS

1946 ~ 1947

The American Blonde

by Louella O. Parsons

Who is the young lady who stands to captivate a nation?

From the obscurity of an ordinary, simple home this patriotic Cinderella has quickly vaulted to the top in the motion picture world with a role—her very first—in the
biggest picture of all time . . . *Home of the Brave*. A picture
which is being rewritten just for her.

For starters, the girl can sing. But there is something in
her voice that transcends mere vocalizing. Kit Rogers is a
blonde-haired, green-eyed beauty, just nineteen years old.
Orphaned quite young, she is strictly the all-American
girl, with a charm and sparkle that stamps her a daughter
of Uncle Sam. As if that charm and sparkle weren't
enough, she was born on February 22, a birthday she
shares with President George Washington.

Miss Rogers made international headlines this past
summer as the brave and daring aviatrix who flew for the
WASP and her country, rescuing her brother from death
and thwarting the Germans' plans for victory. Miss Rogers was selected by Mr. Louis B. Mayer as being the ideal
young American girl of today. She has given up her smart
little uniform for pretty dresses and high-heeled shoes,
and traded in her pistol for a lipstick. Beauty professionals
predict her hair color, American Blonde, will become the
top requested hair color in the country, once *Home of the
Brave* debuts.

"When Miss Rogers came into my office," Mr. Mayer
tells me, "I knew she had that rare thing—personality.
She is beautiful, but more essential than beauty is that

quality known as screen magnetism, which she has in spades."

"I was so happy when they offered me a contract," declares Miss Rogers, "and I think Hollywood is the most beautiful place in the world. If only my poor dead parents could be here to see my dreams come true."

SEVEN

ome of the Brave was, at its core, the story of two brothers, Daniel (Nigel Gray) and Joseph (Hal MacGinnis), soldiers in the Revolutionary War who are fighting for their country and for the love of the same woman, Mallory Rourke (Mudge). While the brothers are at battle, Mallory and her sister, Anne (Phoebe Phillips)—secretly pining for Daniel—protect the family homestead, and Mallory smuggles secrets to the Patriots. Six years after the story begins, at war's end—after he has lost his brother and all of his friends and nearly lost his own life being run through by a sword—Daniel comes limping home to brave Mallory (as poor Anne watches on), carrying the battle-scarred flag, never imagining that the woman he loves has been at war herself.

It was to be an epic picture, shot in Technicolor and featuring a cavalcade of Metro stars in cameos. It would be MGM's tribute to our returning heroes and to our triumphant nation.

In the opening scene, George Washington (Webster Hayes), George Ross (Edward Arnold), and Robert Morris (Frank Morgan) call on young widow Betsy Ross (Kit Rogers), who, cut off from her family and struggling during wartime while still mourning the death of her husband, has no choice but to earn money mending uniforms and making tents and blankets for the Continental Army. When George Washington and his committee show her a sketch of the design for a national flag, she suggests the stars and stripes.

I was given seven scenes and three songs, one of them a kind of duet with Nigel Gray. The week before shooting my first scene, the two of us worked with Arthur Rosenstein in his studio. Rosie (as Nigel called him) was, with Sam Katz, in charge of the score. He was a large, white-haired bear of a man with glasses. After one time through the song, he pushed up his sleeves and announced, "Even though this isn't a conventional duet, it's still a duet, so we're going to rehearse together until we get it right."

We worked for two hours. Nigel was charming and polite. He wasn't a natural singer, but he knew something about how to breathe and drop his jaw and pronounce his vowels so they were clear and you understood every line. He knew how to interpret, how to pull back and give more where needed. We went over how to raise the soft palate and lower the back of the tongue to create a round space for a greater sound. We went over how to elongate our pronunciation and cap off the vowels.

Rosie was tougher than Earl Brent and Bobby Tucker. Time and again, he stopped playing, swiveled around to face me, and said, "Singing involves the entire body. Your gestures, your movements. The way you raise an arm or close your hand, the expression on your face. All of these are every bit as important as your tone and phrasing. Again." And he would swivel back to the piano keys and start playing.

All my life, whenever I'd felt like singing, I sang. No thought. No worries. But now it wasn't as simple as that. With each teacher—Rosie in particular—I was in the process of stripping away everything I thought I knew, and rebuilding as if I'd never sung before.

When Rosie became frustrated and I became frustrated, Nigel said, "I'd like to try something else. Let's see what happens if Kit and I move around a bit. See how we do when there's more than one thing going on. Maybe it'll help us to stop thinking it all to death." He was doing this for me, I knew. Nigel Gray didn't have to think things to death because he did everything easily. He took my hand and spun me as Rosie started to play. I spun out and then back into Nigel. Closer in, his eyes looked blue or maybe violet.

My verse came first, so I started to sing. He twirled me and spun me. His turn to sing, as we fox-trotted and waltzed across the room. Our voices joined on the chorus. I focused on my breath, on my diaphragm, on my phrasing, on the meaning of the words—so much to remember. It was the same as counting while you danced: one-two-three-step, one-two-three-step. But then I wasn't thinking it, I was feeling it, and all the one-two-three-steps went away, and I was Jane again, being swept under the moon into the arms of Nigel Gray.

·····

On January 22, I reported to the set, a jumble of wires and lights and people rushing this way and that. The most I'd had time to do was learn my lines and be fitted for my costume, a hand-me-down from Esther Williams, whose name was still stitched into the label. Mudge had promised to be there, but so far I hadn't seen her.

At nine thirty a.m., I rehearsed my first scene with Mr Hayes, Mr. Arnold, and Mr. Morgan, towering over all of them by a solid two inches. I only had six lines, not counting a few lines of a song. George Washington and his men would do most of the talking. Still, director Leslie Edgar, who I also towered over, took the time to explain to me each movement, each expression, in his soft, patient voice.

As I listened, as we ran through it, I did my best not to be too tall, while also telling myself what everybody else had been telling me: "Relax, don't be afraid, remember not to drop your G's, be sure to hit your marks, know when to speak, don't shout, don't whisper, don't look at the camera, don't fidget, remember your lines, don't stand there looking like a blank wall when the others are speaking, react, listen, *be* Betsy Ross!"

After we ran through it once, Mr. Hayes started bellowing for wardrobe. A girl scurried forward and bent down beside me. She tugged at my skirt, and set a pair of flats on the floor.

When the flats were firmly on my feet, Hayes barked, "She's still too tall."

"I'm sorry, sir," I said. "But this is as short as I get."

·····

Nearly three hours later, I sat alone, skirts carefully smoothed and arranged, in the window seat of Betsy Ross's parlor. Suddenly I was twelve years old again and at the Alluvial Fair, my first time singing alone in public. I stitched the flag and began to sing. I felt strange and stiff. I could feel my hands and my back tensing up until they ached, and then I gazed out the window. There, out of sight of the cameras, but sitting where I could see her, was Mudge. She was dressed in a smart navy suit—the Santiago Blues, our official WASP uniform. As she caught my eye, she touched the cap in a salute.

> *Sew thirteen stars in a field of blue—*
> *Sew loss and death and wars that cease—*
> *Sew thirteen stars in a field of blue—*
> *Sew hope, sew promise and peace.*

I stitched the flag and looked out the window at Mudge and that navy uniform and I thought of my brothers—Johnny Clay, Linc, Beachard—and all the men I knew and women too, including Mudge and myself, who had worn the stars and stripes.

We shot the scene three times, and when it was over and I'd gotten through it, my face was hot and my palms were hot and I thought: You did it, Velva Jean. You made it through your first day. Mudge and Leslie Edgar told me I was good, that I'd have a long career, and then Mudge was whisked off to wardrobe and Les was whisked back to the set. I stood by myself feeling lit up and limitless, and wanting the moment to go on and on.

"Very nice, Miss Rogers."

I turned to see Harriet Fields, who taught pop singing. "Miss Fields?"

"Mr. Katz asked me to be here for the first song."

"What did you think?"

She smiled in an apologetic way. "As I said, it was very nice. But I'm going to do you a favor. I'm going to tell you right now that no one expects you to be Judy Garland. Just feel comfortable with the songs you have to sing and do the best you can. "

As I watched her walk away, my face and palms were three times hotter. *No one expects me to be Judy Garland? Well, that's fine. Because I'm going to be better than Judy Garland. Just you wait and see.*

A voice behind me said, "She can go to hell." Sam Weldon stood, script under his arm, smiling at me with one corner of his mouth. "The question is how do you think you did?"

"I think I was pretty good, better than I expected to be." I tried to sound calm and cool, but my voice cracked. We came out of the soundstage and started toward the dressing rooms.

"You were better than I expected you to be too."

"Thanks."

"You might remember that flattery isn't my strong suit."

"I do." In the sunshine, I could feel the anger fading a little. "The thing that makes me maddest is she's never given me a chance. From day one, it's been 'Judy this' and 'Judy that.' I'd rather be judged on what I can do instead of who I'm not."

When we reached the stairs to my dressing room, I paused before going up. Sam draped an arm across the railing, "You know it's a shame."

"What's a shame?"

"That I don't date actresses. After that performance today, you proved you are one."

He still wore a cocky grin, but the expression in his eyes was sincere enough for me to say, "Thanks, Sam. Really."

"Don't mention it. Unless, of course . . ." He looked at me and I looked at him, and there was a kind of hum in the air as neither of us said anything. Suddenly, he leaned in and kissed me. He kissed me like there was no question that I would kiss him back, as if he had every right to kiss me outside my dressing room, in plain sight of everyone, his hands on either side of my face. I felt my arms reaching for him, wanting to wind around his neck, as if they had a mind of their own, and then I broke away and slapped him.

I don't know which of us was more surprised. He put his hand to his mouth, and said, "Jesus, Pipes."

"I'm sorry, but you can't go around kissing people like that."

"I don't go around kissing people. I thought I'd try kissing you. Let's face it, we've been wanting to since the first time we met."

"I haven't."

"You're not the only one. I've been thinking about it too." When I didn't say anything, he started to laugh. He said, "You should see your face." He laughed till he had to wipe the tears from his eyes. I could still hear him as I ran upstairs and went inside and shut the door.

January 26, 1946

Dear girl:

Thank you for your thoughtful Christmas gifts, and for the checks, which I wish you wouldn't send. We got along fine before, and I worry you don't keep enough for yourself. I'm putting most of the money away for the children, so that they can go to college if they want to. It's also there in case you need it someday.

Johnny Clay left here in November, and we haven't heard from him since. He said he was going to see a friend, and after that, he wasn't sure. I don't want you to worry that you haven't heard from him. That boy is just trying to find himself, Velva Jean, like everyone else after this war. You have to give him time.

Don't you worry about us either. In spite of a hard winter, we're all in good health, and everyone sends their love. Ruby Poole's baby came early—a little girl they're calling Mollie. Mama and baby are doing fine. We can't wait to see this picture of yours and to see your sweet face.

Granny says to tell you she's proud of you. You always were one to put your mind to the things you want and do them. You remind me of your mama in that way.

Love,
Daddy Hoyt

EIGHT

On March 1, Felix Roland replaced Les Edgar as director of *Home of the Brave*. Phoebe Phillips was forced to drop out of the picture due to pneumonia. And Nigel's wife, Pia Palmer, arrived from England.

Cast and crew gathered on Stage 15 for Felix Roland's first day on the set. He was a man with a reputation for hunting, gambling, womanizing, and hard drinking. Someone said he had begun his career as a stuntman, known for being the most fearless and reckless of them all. In other words, he was the exact opposite of Leslie Edgar.

On the sidelines, Billy Taub, looking rumpled but wired, chewed pills from a prescription bottle. Nigel sat in a chair, reading through the script and making notes on the pages, while Pia Palmer—cool and slender, dusky auburn hair swept up—lounged by his side. On the other side of him was a freckle-faced, doe-eyed girl of seventeen or eighteen, as slim as a Dresden figurine. This was Babe King, who would now be playing Mallory's sister, Anne.

"Have the fireworks started yet?" Sam Weldon appeared, lighting a cigarette. He was looking at Mudge standing across from us beside Hal, her face rigid.

"Fireworks? You mean because of Felix Roland?"

"Among other things."

Before I could ask him what he was talking about, Mr. Roland kicked over a chair to get our attention. The chair went clattering across the floor as he stood, arms crossed, his gaze moving over every single one of us like a searchlight. "Before we get started, I want to get this out of the way. Les Edgar is a great director. I respect him. No one can direct a dialogue scene like he can. It's bullshit that he's just a woman's director. He's not. He can direct anybody. But he's not here now. I've been working for three years straight on six different films. I don't want to be here any more than you want me here. You're tired, I'm tired, and we all want this to be over. I'm not here to hold your hand or be your pal. I don't give a goddamn if you're in the midst of a divorce or if you just lost your dog. I don't care if you go out every night and make love to a McCormick Reaper, as long as you're on time the next morning. We've got one month to wrap things up. If you've got questions on the script, ask the writer or the producer, but only on your own time."

The first scene was one Mudge had shot months before with Phoebe. It called for Babe King, as Anne, to sob as if her life depended on it. By now, Mudge could look at her lines once and know them. She had been in character for over a year, so Mallory was always somewhere nearby, within reach. Mudge could cry on a dime, but Babe was clearly having trouble, and the two of them had already been rehearsing for a week.

At first, the best Babe could do was cover her face with her hands and make sobbing noises. Mr. Taub called for glycerin tears, but Felix Roland said, "This is MGM. This is *Home of the fucking Brave*. They can use glycerin over at Fox or RKO. Or—where the hell are you from?"

"Columbia," Babe choked out.

"Or Columbia. Save the glycerin for Rita Hayworth."

They rehearsed the scene again and again, adjusting lighting and wardrobe when Mr. Roland thought they needed more contrast and color, but when it came to personal direction, he left it up to the actors. "Ham it up," he told them. "Just get in there and ham it up."

Finally, Mudge threw down the prop sword she was holding, and wheeled on Babe. "This is ridiculous. We've already shot this scene.

Phoebe could cry like that"—she snapped her fingers—"and now we're having to do it all over again and wait on you." She turned on Felix Roland. "Les Edgar knew these characters as well as the writer does. He was able to help us find their pulse and breathe life into them—"

"Which is exactly why he isn't here anymore," Mr. Roland barked at her. "We don't have time to locate pulses, Miss Fanning. We're over schedule and over budget as it is."

Babe interrupted him. "Stop it. Stop talking." She said to Mudge, "Don't blame him. You're right—I should be able to do the scene, no matter what. After all, that's what they pay me for." She sounded so upset, I was surprised she wasn't crying. "Slap me."

"What?"

"As hard as you can. I won't be responsible for holding things up." When Mudge continued to stare at her, Babe turned to Mr. Roland. "Or you do it. Or someone. Surely, one of you has dreamed of slapping an actress before. Now's your chance."

For a second, I thought the director was going to slap her, but then, without warning, Mudge hauled back and hit her. Babe's eyes went wide, her hand to her cheek, and then she started to cry.

They got the scene in one take, and afterward Babe dried her eyes like nothing had happened, and Mudge stalked off the set without a word.

My own scene was brief—a quick send-off for my husband, Captain Ashburn (played by romantic up-and-comer Phillip Drake), who was going off to war. Mr. Roland made certain I knew my marks, and then said: "You've lost one husband already. You can't stand it if you lose this one. On film, this scene will last ten seconds, so let's not turn it into *Birth of a Nation*."

He was awful, but we got it in one take. When I was finished I went outside to look for Mudge—at her star suite, in the makeup and hair departments. As I came out of the wardrobe building, Babe King was walking past. "Did you find her? Is she okay?"

"I'm sure she's all right. How's your cheek?" Out of costume, Babe looked all of twelve. Her nails were short and painted to match her lips, and a ring on one finger was her only jewelry. I could see her freckles.

She laid a hand to her face. "It's fine. Just embarrassed, like the rest of me. Are you headed to the dressing rooms?"

We walked there together, Babe telling me that she was under contract with Columbia, but Harry Cohn had set her free this once because, mean and nasty as he was, he knew a good picture when he saw one. This was her big opportunity, and she didn't want to muck it up.

They'd put her in the army barracks–style general dressing room building, two doors down from me. The door to her room opened and a woman appeared, bracelets clacking, her perfume crowding the air. It was hard to place her age, but everything about her was just a shade too bright—hair a little too blonde, face a little too made up. Babe frowned at her, as if she could see the woman through my eyes.

"What are we talking about, kiddies?"

"Mother, this is Kit Rogers."

The woman held out a hand glittering with rings, and I remembered something I'd read in the fan magazines. *Babe King moved to Hollywood when she was fifteen with her mother and her pet rabbit.* "Yilla King," she said. "I read about you in the papers. Babe's underage, you know, which is why I have to babysit her. Union rules." She winked at Babe, who looked away.

• • • • •

That evening, Mudge and I ate dinner silently, her mood hanging over us. At first, she made small talk, but her mind was clearly somewhere far, far away. I wanted to ask where she'd gone when she left the set, but instead I concentrated on my plain chicken and vegetables, wishing for real food.

We were just finishing our meal when Redd Deeley came muscling through the door, Flora at his heels. He snapped at Mudge, "I heard you walked off. That you threatened Billy Taub. Threatened?!"

"Redd Deeley, don't you barge in here without knocking." Mudge stood and threw her napkin onto her plate. "This isn't your house anymore."

Flora was apologizing over and over, and Mudge said, "It's not your fault, Flora. Don't you worry. If anything, he's my fault. I was the one who married him."

He shouted, "You listen to me. If you quit this film, you will be in court till your last day on earth. You will never work again on stage or screen. Taub and Mayer will see to that. And so will I. Do you understand me?"

She picked up a glass and threw it at his head. Flora started clearing the plates, taking away the ammunition. I stood up to help her as Mudge shouted back, "Get out. And leave your key."

"Not until you promise me you'll report for work tomorrow, and every other day until this picture is done."

"And what if I fire you?"

"Good luck finding anyone stupid enough or crazy enough to take you on."

"Redd, I can't go back. There's nothing left in me. I'm tired. I'm thirty, but I feel eighty."

"Is this about Roland or is this about Pia Palmer's arrival?"

She looked up at him, her face white.

"I thought so. You finish what you started. Don't treat this like one of your marriages." He sent something spinning across the table—a prescription bottle. "Treat this picture like what it is—the thing you love most in this world. You do what you can to see it through. And you know that when you walk away, after you've said your last line, you'll have done the best work of your career." When she only stood there, hand closed around the bottle, he said, "I'll take that as a 'Yes, Redd.'"

He marched out, slamming the front door as he left. Mudge sent the bottle of pills zinging into the wall. She said, "Of all the—" and then sank into her chair, put her head right down on the table, and sobbed.

I wrapped the glass in my napkin and dropped the pills one by one into the prescription bottle. When Flora came in to finish clearing the plates, I said, "That's okay, Flora. We'll take care of it." I looked at Mudge. She picked up her napkin, dabbed her eyes, and sniffed. "Are you all right?"

"I will be. I just need this picture to be over, Hartsie. And now this thing with Felix Roland and Les being fired and . . ." She shook her head. "Men like Les Edgar are the reason I became an actress in the first place. He doesn't deserve the treatment he's getting. None of us do."

"You're in the last stretch. You only have to do this a little bit longer. Remember the WASP and how we thought we'd never get through those last flight checks before graduation? Remember flying blind and what Puck told us?" Puck had been one of our instructors at Avenger Field.

In a small voice she said, " 'You know this.' "

"Yes. You know this. You can do this."

Flora crept back in, carrying dessert and a bottle of wine. She set down a new glass for Mudge, who reached for the wine. Mudge said to the both of us, "I'm sorry." Flora laid a hand on her shoulder before walking back into the kitchen. "Sorry, sorry, sorry. She's the only family I have, Flora—the only family —and you and the other girls from the WASP. My head is splitting." She reached for some water. "I'm just so tired. What's wrong with me?"

"You're overworked. You've been working too hard for too long."

She dropped her eyes, rubbed at a spot on the table, over and over. Gave a weak little smile. She held up the wine and I shook my head. From the prescription bottle, she popped out two little pills.

"How long has it been going on? With Nigel, I mean."

"How did you . . . ?"

"I saw him leaving your dressing room, and then Redd made that comment about Pia."

She sighed. "Since we started the picture."

"Is that why you left Redd?"

"Redd will tell you I left him and that Nigel was the reason, but actually he left me. Redd Deeley, like all men, wanted Barbara Fanning but what he got was Eloise Mudge. They're never as crazy about her."

"And Hal MacGinnis?"

"The studio put us together. It's good for business, good for the picture, good for Hal. He's queer, you know." I was beginning to feel like Alice in the rabbit hole, in a world where nothing was what it seemed.

She swallowed the pills, the smile fading. "Nigel's spent half his assets and his Metro trust fund to buy his way out of his marriage. Howard Strickling, Eddie Mannix, they're all trying to help, but Pia is impossible. And now she's here."

"He's her husband. Maybe she loves him."

"No she doesn't. Not anymore. She hates him and she hates me, and she's doing everything she can to keep us apart." She started to cry, silently, angrily, staring out into the room like a tragic widow. "I didn't want to fall in love with him, Hartsie. Don't you think I would have picked someone else if I could help it?" She took another drink.

· · · · ·

Mudge was back at work the next morning, sitting by herself between takes. She delivered her lines, did everything Felix Roland asked of her, behaved like a good, dutiful girl, was civil to others, and at the end of the day, drove off in her car and didn't come home until late. The next day, she followed the same exact pattern. And the next day, and the next. I wondered if she and Nigel had somehow found a way to see each other without Pia knowing.

Except for the biggest stars—Webster Hayes, Ophelia Lloyd, Nigel Gray, and Barbara Fanning—Felix Roland didn't bother to learn anyone's names. But he and Mudge managed to deal with each other politely. Two months after the director's arrival, Zed Zabel wrote in his column that Roland was the egomaniac to end all egomaniacs and that Mudge was becoming more and more like Mallory Rourke, this beautiful, terrible woman who could make enemies out of loved ones and loved ones out of enemies.

When she was home, she wandered around the house like a haint, keeping herself going with cigarettes and pills prescribed to her by the studio doctor—Seconal to help her sleep, and Benzedrine to wake her up. She seemed nervous, anxious, on edge. Sometimes she snapped at me or at Flora, and other times I would catch her crying. Sometimes she locked the door to her room and stayed away, and other times she

invited people over—the neighbors and the Helms Bakery delivery-
man and the studio guard who watched the house—and gave a party
with only an hour's notice. Flora said, "That girl's not acting like herself. I'm worried about her." We both were.

On the set, Sam Weldon said, "She's decided to behave herself at
work, I see, now that everyone's stopped speaking to her. What about
you, Pipes? Are you ready to misbehave?" Each day, he thought of a
new way to ask me out, and each day I said no.

I usually beat Mudge home even when I went out after work for
my studio-arranged dates—to Ciro's, with its walls and sofas of green
silk; Earl Carroll's supper club, which featured a revolving stage,
swings that could be lowered from the ceiling, and "the most beautiful
girls in the world"; the Palladium, where seven thousand dancers
swayed across the kidney-shaped floor as the lighting changed to suit
the music; and the Cocoanut Grove.

One night, I waited up for her and asked her where she'd been.
"Oh, I had a date with Hal," she said. I knew that wasn't true because
I had seen Hal earlier at the Trocadero.

Two days later, I asked her the same thing. This time, she said, "I
was just driving," as if she'd learned her lesson about making up stories.

NINE

Our first scene on June 5 called for Mallory Rourke to gallop through the Lot 3 lake on horseback. When Felix Roland shouted for the stuntwoman, Mudge said, "I can do my own stunts. I've done them before. I'm a pilot, for God's sake. Just because I'm thirty doesn't mean I can't ride a horse."

"No one's saying you can't ride a horse." Roland barely looked at her. He shouted again for the stuntwoman and went storming away.

Mudge picked up her skirts and followed him. "Let me do this, Felix. Please." He must have heard the same thing in her tone that I did—determination, the need to prove herself—or maybe it was that the stuntwoman wasn't anywhere to be found and he was, as always, in a hurry to move on. Or maybe it was that Pia Palmer was there watching everything and he felt sorry for Mudge. Everyone on the picture seemed to know about the affair, and Pia hadn't done much to make friends.

"All right," he said. "You've got one shot."

Fifteen minutes later, the cameras rolled as Mudge tore across the banks and into the water on the back of the horse. She was halfway across the lake when the animal reared up and sent her flying.

Felix Roland, Billy Taub, Nigel, Hal, Sam, me—everyone went into the lake after her, as the camera truck carrying six photographers and Technicolor equipment sat forgotten. The animal wrangler guided the horse back to shore, and then I heard the wail of an ambulance siren. The man-made lake was wide and long, but there was no current, no rocks, nothing but brown water, thick as sludge, that you couldn't see through. Parts of it were up to ten feet deep.

Suddenly, Billy Taub had Mudge in his arms—her head limp, black hair hanging like seaweed. He said, "I've got her," as if we couldn't see, and then he set her down on the ground.

"No one touch her," said the studio doctor, a man named Atwill, pushing his way through.

By this time, Mudge had opened her eyes and was looking up at all of us looking down at her. "I'm fine. Just embarrassed." She sat up coughing, and wiped the hair from her face. When she saw me, she said, "Some stuntwoman, Hartsie. I'm glad Jackie Cochran wasn't here to witness this."

Howard Strickling and Whitey Hendry arrived on the side of an MGM fire truck. Seconds later, the banks of the lake were swarming with men in uniform, men in suits. Mudge said, "Everyone does not need to be here. I'm okay. I'm fine. Nothing broken, nothing so serious that it will hold up filming. Just much, much more embarrassed now."

Dr. Atwill felt around her limbs and head and ribs. Finally, he said, "She's bruised her knee and I'm afraid she's cracked a few ribs, but she'll be fine."

Sam found me as Mr. Roland shouted once again for the stuntwoman. "You okay?"

"I'm fine. As long as she's okay."

"She's okay. She's stronger than you think."

Before I could ask how he would know, Babe's mother pushed Babe toward Felix Roland. "If you can't find anyone else, my daughter can do it. She's young, of course, but an excellent equestrian. She can wear a black wig and a black cloak and no one will ever know."

Roland looked over her head and all around, no doubt for the stuntwoman. When she didn't appear, he frowned at Mrs. King. "We've already wasted too much time on a scene that should have taken five damn minutes. Are you sure she's up for it?"

Babe's mother poked her so hard she jumped. "I'm sure," Babe said.

Ten minutes later, she was dressed in a black wig and black cloak, and ten minutes after that, the shot was done. As Mudge watched from the banks, Babe nailed it on the first take, body bent low over the horse, heels dug in, flying across land and water like hellhounds were on her tail.

· · · · ·

I met with Rosie afterward to go through my songs, which we would record once I'd wrapped my scenes. I stood at the piano and said, "Felix Roland is worried I don't know what I'm doing."

Sitting at the keys, Rosie frowned at me over the top of his glasses and pushed up his sleeves. "The only person Felix Roland believes in is Felix Roland. Now. These songs have to be as polished as the dialogue scenes. Each word carries meaning. You can't just throw them away. But we'll get there. You'll get there."

The one he wanted to work on was "The Star-Spangled Banner," a song that made me want to give up singing. It was the first song that ever made me think: You can't do this, Velva Jean. You aren't good enough. You don't have it in you. The thing of it was, it hadn't even been written till 1814, thirty-one years after the end of the Revolutionary War, but because one of the lines was in the title, Mr. Mayer said the audience would expect to hear it.

I told myself to focus on the meaning of the words instead of worrying about breath control and finding my soft palate and rounding my throat. Halfway through, Rosie banged on the piano and said, "You sound like Velva Jean Hart, mountain girl, not Kit Rogers, movie star. Yes, you are Betsy Ross, but you're also Kit Rogers. What is the thing that sets MGM apart from Warners or RKO or Paramount? The sound. You could walk blindfolded into a theater and know right away if it's an MGM movie up on that screen by the particular style and tone of the Metro voice. You need to put yourself aside and focus."

I thought, Maybe I want to sound like Velva Jean Hart. We started again, but this time instead of thinking about the words I was singing, I did my best to sound like everyone else.

· · · · ·

In my dressing room at the end of the day, I sat staring at the stack of sheet music, the words and notes a wild, spidery jumble on the page.

I jumped at the knock on the door. "Come in." When nothing happened, I stood and opened it.

Outside, a man leaned on the railing, as if he were made of time, chatting with someone down below. In the afternoon sun, his hair and skin burned gold. He turned around and flashed me a smile, the one that made women and men of all ages want to follow him anywhere. "Hey, little sister. I'm sorry I didn't get here sooner."

I threw my arms around him, and instead of picking me up or hugging me, he patted me, like I was a stranger. I said, "Dammit, Johnny Clay. I'm not letting go till you hug me proper."

His grip on me froze and then tightened, as if he wasn't sure what to do. And then he swung me off my feet, big arms around me, and squeezed the breath out of me. When he let me go, his face was wet, and I wasn't sure whether it was from my tears or his own.

He stood with his hands in his pockets, looking down at me. He wore a dark red shirt, the sleeves rolled up, underneath a gray vest and gray pants. His shoes shone like glass.

I said to him, "Are you a gangster?"

He laughed. "No, Velva Jean."

"What have you been doing? Why are you dressed like that? Why didn't you let me know you were here?"

He sighed and stretched his neck. His hair was longer, the wartime crew cut grown out, and combed back. He was as good-looking as ever, even more so, his skin and hair a deeper gold under the California sun.

"I can't believe you're a movie star. Look at you, Velva Jean. I mean, shit. You look like Ginger Rogers, and you sound like an English lady." He lit a cigarette. I watched his hands—the maimed finger, the scars on the knuckles. The lighter was sleek and silver, as shiny as his shoes. Initials were etched into the side, but I couldn't read them. He flicked the lighter closed and slid it back into his pocket. "I know all about me. I want to hear about you. You can tell me while you give me a tour."

I took Johnny Clay around the lot in the secondhand car I'd bought with one of my first paychecks, showing him Tin Pan Alley, the commissary, wardrobe, makeup, hair, the police department, the school, the soundstages. I wanted to introduce him to everyone. I wanted to say, *There he is, in person, my own brother standing right beside me, after all this time, he's here, he's here, he's here.*

Back in my dressing room, I said, "You promised to tell me how you got to California."

He sat in one of the matching club chairs, legs stretched out in front of him, drinking Coca-Cola from the bottle, taking his time getting settled, and finally he said, "Your friend Helen sent me some books after we first got home. Now, I ain't much of a reader, but I thought I'd give it a try since she went to so much trouble. So I took *For Whom the Bell Tolls* up to Devil's Courthouse, climbed up on the rock, and said, 'Okay, let's see what you got, book.' Three hours later, I finished it, the only book I ever read from start to finish. You ever read it?"

"No."

"This guy in the book, he knows he's going to die. 'There is only now,' he says. 'If now is only two days, then two days is your life and everything in it will be in proportion.' It took me a while to figure out what he meant, but once I did, I got to thinking about this two days business." He took a swig from his bottle. "Ever since I got shot the second time, I been nothing but angry at everyone, even myself. You probably already knew this, but I didn't." He fixed his eyes on me, as if daring me to say yes, I did know it all along.

"Daddy Hoyt guessed it."

He nodded. "Well, I wanted to wring the neck of every German and Jap on the planet. But this is what I figured out—all that anger goes back before the war. I'd like to kick the ass of every son of a bitch that ever hurt anyone or anything. I want to kill the sickness that took

Mama, and punch Daddy till he can't stand up for taking off on us. I been holding on to every bit of anger I ever had, since I was a boy—at Sweet Fern, at Danny for dying and leaving her alone, at Harley Bright, at Blackeye for what he did to Lucinda and making me nearly kill him. Even at you, Velva Jean. I mean let's face it, there's something humiliating about getting rescued by a girl, and not just any girl but your own sister."

He finished his drink, set the bottle down on the floor, and leaned forward. "The thing about carrying around all that anger is that it gets heavy after a while and your arms get tired. A couple of weeks after you left, I thought: What if I just give up that anger and decide to be happy while I can? What if this is my two days and I'm wasting it by being so mad?"

I stared at him like he was a stranger.

"So I started thinking about what I wanted to do with a year of unemployment, thanks to the Army. I thought about roping cattle or staying in the military. I went down to Hamlet's Mill for a week and followed Sheriff Story around to see if maybe I wanted to go into law enforcement, but I'm sick of wearing a uniform and taking orders. So that got me to thinking about music. You got another Coke?"

"What? Oh. Of course." I stood up, walked to the little refrigerator that sat in one corner. I pulled out a bottle, popped the top, and handed it to him. "So music . . ."

"Yeah. I mean I never been as natural at it as you, little sister, and I never been as focused, but I know I got a good voice and that I can play guitar better than a lot of 'em. Anyway, a buddy of mine was in Chicago trying to get up a band. He asked me to sit in. We been traveling the country ever since—Memphis, New Orleans, Austin. A guy down in Texas asked us to come to L.A., play at his club, with the chance to make a record." As if he suddenly remembered something, he checked his wristwatch: black band, square face. He stood, handing me the two empty Coca-Cola bottles. "I got to get back."

"But you just got here."

"Well, if you're free tonight you could come hear us. You got a piece of paper?" I handed him paper and a pen, and he scrawled down an address. "We go on at eight, which means nine. If you come, you make sure they know you're there so I can introduce you around. Bring some friends if you want. Make it a party."

I walked him back to the gate as slow as I could so that it wouldn't be over and he wouldn't be gone. I was afraid if I let him out of my sight that I might never see him again.

His eyes swept over the Thalberg Building, the gate, the sign that read "Metro-Goldwyn-Mayer."

"You done good, Velva Jean." He smiled, not flashy this time, but the sweet smile that he used to save for Mama. "I like to think I'm doing some good now too."

· · · · ·

At home, Mudge took up residence on the living room sofa, every part of her propped up with pillows, as if she were broken in a hundred places. The accident had made her unusually sweet and quiet, a sweet and quiet I hadn't seen from her in weeks. "Thank you, Flora," she said when Flora brought her a drink. "Thank you, Hartsie," she said when I brought her a new ice pack for her knee.

I sat down beside her. "My brother's here. In L.A. He wants me to come hear him tonight on Central Avenue."

"You'll like it there. The best music in town."

"I don't want to leave you like this."

"Flora's here, and I'm going to be sleeping anyway. I'm so tired and my head is splitting." As if to prove it, she yawned. "You go."

After I was dressed and ready, she said, "Did they find out what caused the horse to bolt like that?"

"Most likely a loud noise or a sudden movement."

"Is the police guard still out there?"

I checked. "Yes."

She nodded, set her glass down. "I think I'll close my eyes for a bit. I may even go to sleep. I may already be asleep right now. You have a good time, Hartsie. Tell that brother of yours hello for me."

"I will." I picked up the empty glass, and by the time I was at the doorway, looking back, she was sleeping.

TEN

abe King, Hal MacGinnis, and I headed south and east toward the high-rise buildings of downtown. I read each street sign to see if we were there yet. We sped past downtown, away from the lights, but we weren't going fast enough for me. I wanted to get there before Johnny Clay changed his mind and went home or took off somewhere else. *Hurry hurry hurry.* We turned down one dark road, little box houses on either side, close together. We turned down another dark road, and then onto a broad street, empty field on one side, a few clapboard shacks on the other.

Then, all at once, I could see the lights ahead. Hal swung the car toward them and into them, pulling over and parking so that we could get out and walk. He said it was the only way to see Central Avenue.

Pool halls, barbershops, barbecue joints, restaurants, five-and-dimes, doctors' offices, furniture stores, and jazz clubs lined the avenue on either side. There was an office for the colored newspaper, the *California Eagle.* The sidewalks weren't big enough to hold the crowds of hot dog hawkers, shoe shiners, street musicians, newsboys, fortune-tellers, bums, and men in brightly colored zoot suits. An armless boy shot marbles with his toes. Across the street from him, a little boy with a telescope was charging a nickel to look at the mountains of the moon. I could hear the music, blazing hot, coming from open doors.

The farther we walked, the more elegant and beautiful the

people—beautiful suits, beautiful gowns, beautiful faces. Hal said the heart of it all was the Dunbar Hotel, where everyone from Langston Hughes to Billie Holiday to Duke Ellington stayed, and the clubs that surrounded it—Club Alabam, the Downbeat, the Last Word.

The Downbeat's address was 4225 Central Avenue, which matched what Johnny Clay had written down. We ducked inside and off the street.

The club was built like a box, with a bar along one wall and the bandstand the other. The only seats we could find were at the bar, but there were mirrors behind it so you didn't have to turn around to see the stage. A tenor sax player named Gene Montgomery led the house band, which played a kind of wild and rowdy blues. Except for five or six others, we were the only white people there, and it reminded me of the juke joints I'd been to in Nashville and North Carolina, the music throbbing and pulsing until I thought my eardrums would bleed.

No one danced because there wasn't room, or maybe because they wanted to concentrate on the music. There were no live palms or stars on the ceiling, no green silk curtains and matching sofas, no revolving stage. The space itself was pretty plain. But I'd never heard music like this before.

"What in the world is it?"

"They call it bebop," said Hal.

The music was ugly and lovely and wild. It went off in every direction, like it couldn't be contained. Just when you thought it would go one way, it would switch on you and go another. It was a frustrating jumble of notes and phrases that didn't seem to be linked by anything. But you could hear the steam rising off the stage.

Just before ten o'clock, a new group of musicians wandered onto the stage. Three colored men—one with a hat—on piano, saxophone, and drums, and there came Johnny Clay, carrying a trumpet.

I said, "Since when does he play trumpet?"

Babe raised her eyebrows. "That's the best-looking boy I've ever seen."

Hal nudged my arm. "What's wrong, Velva Jean?"

I was staring at the fifth member of the band, who had just walked on, carrying a steel guitar, cigarette in his mouth, talking to someone in the crowd. He leaned down, grinned around the cigarette, and came back up laughing, sweeping the dark hair off his face. The hair was a little shorter than the last time I'd seen him, barely brushing his chin. He'd let his beard grow in a little. He still had the gap between his two front teeth. He wore a suit, but no tie, and at his open collar, I could see the Indian medicine beads and the dog tags. There was a new tattoo on one hand. There were the half-Choctaw, half-Creole cheekbones, the dark, hooded eyes. He fished in his pocket, came out with the broken bottle neck he used as a guitar slide, and said something to the band.

Babe said, "That one's good-looking too. They're all good-looking."

Johnny Clay had sat in my dressing room and talked about his friend, and I'd never once thought he might be talking about Butch Dawkins.

· · · · ·

They played for over two hours, and they were good. Even with part of one finger missing, my brother tore up that trumpet like he'd been playing all his life. He was better on the trumpet than he'd ever been on guitar. The drummer was a wild man, shouting out to the crowd, hollering lines of music every now and then. The piano player, the man with the hat, didn't look up from the keys once. The saxophonist jittered about the stage, like he couldn't keep still.

Butch Dawkins glanced up from his guitar every now and then, but most of the time, like the piano player, he bent his head over the instrument, lost in the music. He only introduced one of the songs, letting us know it was something they were still working out. In the same whiskey-and-cigarettes voice I remembered, he said, "I first heard this tune in Chicago. I thought, 'I've got to get a little bit of that song,' so I asked the fella if I could have the chorus." The music was different from any I'd heard Butch play before. Something in it smoldered, as if any moment he might let loose, but for now was holding himself back.

Around twelve thirty, the band walked off the stage, and someone else went on. A few minutes later, my brother made his way through the crowd, trumpet under his arm, stopping to shake hands with the people congratulating him on the show. He leaned against the bar, ordered a drink, and said, "Well, little sister? What'd you think?"

I said, "When did you learn to play trumpet?"

He laughed and laughed, delighted with himself. "Training camp. After I busted the lip of our bugler, they made me play reveille every morning for a month. I found out I was a natural." He looked down at his finger, the one that was half-missing, and then nodded at Babe and Hal. "Are these fine people your friends, Velva Jean?"

"Babe King, Hal MacGinnis, my brother Johnny Clay."

He shook hands. "Sure, sure, I recognize you. Y'all are movie stars." He winked at Babe.

I said, "You forgot to mention that Butch Dawkins was the friend you kept talking about."

"I was so happy to see you, little sister, it slipped my mind." My brother was nearly impossible to be mad at, something he knew.

At some point, he said, "The Downbeat closes around one thirty. What say we go over to Lovejoy's? They go till six or seven, and there's always a jam going on." Before I could say anything, he fixed a look on me. "Butch is going to meet us over there."

· · · · ·

Lovejoy's Breakfast Club, "Home of the Big-Legged Chicken," was located at Central Avenue and Vernon. Inside, we walked through a crowded, smoky hallway, up a crowded, smoky stairway, through another crowded, smoky hallway, and into a crowded, smoky room, where Johnny Clay's drummer was pounding away, and a man, as wrinkled as an old nut, sat at the piano.

Butch sat at a table by himself, bottle in front of him, guitar hooked over his chair, which was tilted back on two legs. His arms were crossed and he was watching the piano player. He didn't see us till we were standing there, and then he stood and nodded at everyone and said, "Velva Jean," like it hadn't been two years since we'd seen each other. He pulled out the chair next to his so I could sit down.

We ordered fried chicken baskets, and glasses for the liquor Butch had brought, and then a good-looking colored man walked up beside the piano and started to wail away on the alto sax. Johnny Clay said, "That's Charlie Parker, god of the future." While Hal sat across the table, drinking too much, Babe was next to my brother, laughing and talking. Next to me, Butch drank his liquor and smoked his cigarette and watched the musicians through heavy-lidded eyes. We sat close because there wasn't much room, and every now and then his arm brushed mine.

Finally, he reached for the bottle, poured himself another glass, and said, "I'm glad you're okay."

"I'm glad you're okay too."

He tilted the rim of his glass to mine so that it clinked like a piano key.

"I reckon it's a miracle any of us are here." He ran his fingers through his hair and leaned on the table, so our arms were touching. I studied the new tattoo, which looked like a bear claw. Under the table, his leg pressed against mine. Both of us sat, staring at the musicians, and I wondered if he felt the same thing I was feeling.

After all this time of carrying him around in my mind, wondering where and how he was, he's flesh and blood. Warm to the touch. Real.

As if he could read my thoughts, he propped his head on his hand, and gave me a long, sleepy look. He said, "Girl, you been on my mind."

· · · · ·

I was home by three, but I didn't sleep. I lay in bed flat on my back, resting on my side, facedown, stretched diagonally, curled into a ball. I closed my eyes, I opened them. I closed them. I opened them. It didn't matter what I did. I was wide awake, and Butch was everywhere.

ELEVEN

The last scene of *Home of the Brave* was scheduled to be shot on November 12—Betsy Ross's trek to Valley Forge. I was out of bed at two thirty every morning because I had to be made up and costumed and at Malibu Creek State Park by five thirty a.m. Framed by sloping mountains, on the edge of the Pacific Ocean, the Pennsylvania military camp of the American Continental Army sat in a valley of white, surrounded by oak and sycamore forests. The white spread endlessly—interrupted only by the log huts and tents of the encampment—created with artificial snow, a combination of confetti, foam, soap flakes, and liquid starch. Giant fans hooked up to generators, cords trailing for miles, blew the snow in gusts.

One thousand extras dressed as soldiers covered the ground like ants, some in ragged uniforms, some barefoot, some moaning from sickbeds, the victims of typhoid, cholera, or dysentery. On the first and second day, it rained, melting our fake snow. On the third day, the valley was covered in a thick, heavy fog.

On the fourth day, Felix Roland found me sitting alone in the dark, wrapped in a blanket, the air still cool and nightlike. At first I didn't recognize him because he looked older and thinner than the man he'd been when he first walked onto the set. There were rumors of a breakdown or nervous collapse, and no one had expected him back.

He said, "When you're out there today . . ." He squinted at the sky. At the curve of the horizon, there was a gathering of clouds, but no sign of fog or rain. "And it looks as if you will be out there—I want you to think about standing at the edge of a cliff and what it feels like in that moment to know you could jump or you could turn back." Something in his voice gave me chills. "For an instant, it's really a flip of the coin. You could live or you could die, and that choice is up to you." He stood and smiled, and it looked hollow, ghostly. "Or, if that doesn't work, just ham it up."

Thirty minutes later, as the giant fans created a swirling, roaring blizzard, I made my way through the snow, my poor face rouged pink for the freezing temperatures, my poor hands numb with the cold, clutching the hand-sewn gunpowder bags to my breast. At one point, I was supposed to collapse in the snow, too weak to go on. On the ground, looking up at the sky, I thought how easy it would be just to lie there.

Of course I wasn't Betsy Ross, and I wasn't lost in a blizzard. I was Velva Jean Hart under a California sky. But for those few minutes, I was on the edge of a cliff, looking down into darkness. One step, and I would be safe. One step, and I would be gone. I was amazed at the idea of it.

And then I thought of all the soldiers who were counting on my gunpowder bags, and before I knew it I was on my feet again and pushing through the storm.

We got it on the first take. And just like that, we were done.

Almost immediately, the wounded and dead walked off, smoking and talking. The set was pulled apart, tents collapsing, snow swept away, equipment shut down and unplugged and loaded onto trucks. As I stood watching, people marched by, nodding, shaking my hand, hugging me, already on their way to the next thing. *Good work, Kit. Good luck. Hope to do another picture together again.*

Ophelia Lloyd had already announced she was going back into retirement. Nigel would move on to his next film, *Latimer*, with Billy Taub attached to produce and Felix Roland to direct. Meanwhile, Mr. Mayer had purchased the rights to the comic strip *Flyin' Jenny*, in order to create a series of films for me to star in. Jenny was a pilot, spy, detective, daredevil, and, because I was playing her, a singer. Hal Mac-Ginnis was cast in the role of Jenny's patient, handsome boyfriend, Rick Davis, and Babe King would play her kid sister. We would start filming in a week, followed immediately by the second *Flyin' Jenny*. Metro planned to hold the release of both pictures till after *Home of the Brave* premiered.

A voice behind me said, "You know, I think I'll miss you most of all."

I turned to find Sam Weldon, eyes dancing, mouth curved into a smile.

"Are you going home?"

"I am. Will you miss me?"

"No."

He laughed. "At least you're honest. I'll miss you, Pipes. You're about the only thing I will miss."

"Well . . ." I wasn't sure what to say. "Good luck."

"I'd kiss you, but, let's face it, I'm too vain to risk injury. So I'll just shake hands." He held his hand out. When I didn't take it, he said, "Come on, Pipes. I don't want to leave knowing you think I'm a complete asshole."

"Only a partial one?"

"Yes."

I hesitated, then put my hand in his. He laced his fingers through mine. He turned my hand over, exploring the palm, the fingers. He looked down and I looked down, and we watched him do this like it was the most fascinating thing. I told myself to pull away, but there was something lovely about it. Something innocent. He said to our hands, "You make me feel as if I'm twenty. Or fourteen. I can't decide which." He looked up again. "Friends?" he said.

"Friends."

He said, "You're different, Velva Jean Hart." He dropped my hand like it was a hot potato. "I'd better get out of here before I forget that."

· · · · ·

With *Home of the Brave* behind her, Mudge became more and more her old self again. Mallory Rourke had gone away, taking all the stress and unhappiness with her. Now that the picture was finished, the studio guard in charge of watching the house had gone away too. The living room coffee table, the dining room table, and the desk in Mudge's office became covered with books about John Neville, Baron Latimer, his marriage to Catherine Parr, his rebellion and kidnapping, her struggle to survive in his absence, and his return to free her, after she was taken hostage by his enemies. Mudge was beginning her campaign to play the pious and patient Catherine. With Pia still in Los Angeles, *Latimer* would most likely be her only chance to be alone with Nigel.

I was already filming the second *Flyin' Jenny* movie when my work on *Home of the Brave* ended December 9 inside the scoring stage. The room was divided into three glassed-in booths and a large, open area with wood-paneled walls, padded doors, and a vaulted ceiling that reminded me of a church. Chairs, music stands, microphones, and a black grand piano faced an enormous white movie screen. The microphones looked like giraffes, necks extended, mounted on wheeled tripods. A square, boxed platform sat in the middle of the floor.

I knew from Harriet Fields that Judy Garland had once stood on this very platform and recorded "Over the Rainbow." I also knew that Miss Garland had recorded "The Trolley Song" from *Meet Me in St. Louis* in one take, and that even after she flubbed a line, Arthur Freed and the famous Freed Unit decided to keep it anyway because of the "pure, driving emotion of her delivery."

It was my turn to stand on the wooden platform. Rosie sat in the monitor booth with the technicians while a man named Howard adjusted the microphone to the right height and angle and then I said, "One, two, three," and, "This is Kit Rogers, recording 'The Star-Spangled Banner' for *Home of the Brave*," so they could find the right level for my voice.

Color flashed onto the white screen, and there was Betsy Ross, a widow for the second time, watching as the very flag she had sewn years earlier, after a fateful visit from George Washington, unfurls over the bloody battlefield. They played the scene through once, so I could get an idea of the timing, and then they started it over.

It was like stepping from one world into another. For months, I'd been Betsy Ross, and now, as they readied the score for *Home of the Brave*, shot retakes, created bridgeovers, montages, and other special film effects, I was pilot Flyin' Jenny. *Velva Jean Hart. Clementine Roux. Kit Rogers. Betsy Ross. Jenny Dare.*

I asked to watch the scene again. And then again. I was stalling, and they knew I was stalling. No matter how many times we'd been over and through "The Star-Spangled Banner," I still struggled with it.

"Ready," I said now.

Four lines into it, the strangest thing happened—I started to shake. I ignored it at first, but then I was crying. Just like a baby. I could barely get the words out, much less remember everything I was sup-posed to remember about controlling my breath and rounding my vowels. I shook and I cried, and I kept singing, the words spilling out in a mad, wet jumble, until suddenly Rosie was there, easing me down onto the platform. He snapped the microphone off so that the men in the monitor booth couldn't hear, and then he eased himself down be-side me. "Tell me."

"It's this song." I was being ridiculous, and I knew it, which only made me feel worse. "Not the song itself, but the music. All these high notes. And the way I'm expected to sing it, as if I'm Jeanette MacDon-ald or Kathryn Grayson."

Rosie said, "People make the common mistake of singing 'The Star-Spangled Banner' in the key it's written in, as if there's no other choice, but what they don't understand is that you can choose your own key. You just have to find it." He pushed his sleeves up over his elbows and said, "This is what we're going to do. We're going to con-centrate on breathing. Breath is the most important thing. It's your foundation. You need to be able to control your soft palate and tongue to create more space in your mouth." He stood and rested his hand on his stomach. He pointed at my stomach. "Take a deep breath. Now let it out. Don't lift your shoulders and suck in your stomach. I want you to breathe naturally, as if you're sleeping." He took off his glasses, set them on the music stand, and then lay right down on the floor. He stretched out flat, stomach rising like a pitcher's mound, eyes to the ceiling.

I lay down a foot or two away in the same position.

"I want you to focus on your breath, but don't get self-conscious about it. Breathe as deeply as you can and then let it out slowly with an 'S' sound." He demonstrated, breathing in and then out, hissing like a snake.

I closed my eyes and filled my lungs and then sent the air out, as slow as I could. Something hard flopped onto my stomach and I opened my eyes again—a book. Rosie said, "I want you to watch that book going up when you breathe in and down when you breathe out."

He sat on the platform, arms resting on knees, hands clasped, hunched forward, eyes on the book. Now and then he barked, "Relax," or "You're thinking too much," or "Feel, don't think."

Easy for you to say, I thought to myself. My breath was uneven and raggedy. The more I concentrated, the more strained it became.

"Close your eyes."

I closed my eyes. I let my mind drift where it wanted. I thought of the songs I had to sing, of all the songs I'd ever sung. I heard the words of my favorite hymn, Mama's favorite hymn, and let myself follow the notes like they were a road laid out before me. Finally, I stopped thinking and started feeling the air come in and go out, as the book moved up and down. It became a perfect rhythm. In, out, up, down. In, out, up, down.

The next time through, I didn't think. I breathed. Afterward, I had no idea whether I'd nailed it or not.

But I'm learning, I thought. I'm learning.

· · · · ·

Early Christmas morning, Mudge called me downstairs. Because she never got up before ten on the days she wasn't working, I came running, worried something was wrong. She waited near the front door, hair pulled back, face bare of makeup, still in her blue silk pajamas. She said, "I thought you were going to sleep all day."

"It's not even seven."

"Well your present was just delivered, and I couldn't wait any longer." She opened the door and went on out. Before I could follow her, she said, "It's chilly, Hartsie. Go up to my room and get us some sweaters while I guard the door. And don't try to peek out the window."

Upstairs, I sorted through rack after rack in Mudge's ocean of a closet before I found two button-up sweaters on one of her shelves. As I pulled them out, something fell onto the floor. I bent to pick up the thing that had fallen, which was actually a cloth box, no bigger than a biscuit tin. The lid had opened and the contents had spilled— various pins and medals and costume jewelry. Several of the pins had the same design, a half moon and stars, a lily, and a bird in flight, all intertwined. I scooped everything up and put the box back on the shelf.

Outside, even with the sweater, I shivered in the cool morning air. Mudge stood, hands on hips, beaming at the driveway and the dandelion-gold Oldsmobile that was parked there. "It has Hydra-Matic drive, powermatic shifting, and fashion-tone interior, and it's brand-new, even newer than mine. I remembered you telling me about that yellow truck of yours, so I had them paint it. I have to say I wasn't sure how it would turn out, but I think it looks pretty good like this." She walked up and down, patting the hood, opening the doors.

"I don't understand. . . ." The yellow was almost the same yellow as my truck, just brighter, shinier.

She held up the key. "Merry Christmas, Hartsie." She handed it to me. "Now let's take it for a spin." She ran around the car and climbed into the passenger's seat.

I slid behind the wheel, still dazed, still speechless. "Mudge, it's too much. You shouldn't have done this. The present I got for you is so small."

"If you don't start it up, I will."

I turned the key and the engine roared to life as if the car was ready to go, ready to take us wherever we wanted. The leather smelled brand-new. I suddenly had a pang for that old yellow truck that had taken me all over the mountains and to Nashville. It now sat parked behind Sweet Fern's house at home on Fair Mountain.

I backed carefully down the drive, and once we were on the street I said, "Where should we go?"

"Anywhere! And everywhere. Let's just drive."

We drove all over the city, windows rolled down, from Beverly Hills to Brentwood to the Pacific Palisades to the road that hugged the coastline. The morning started off cool and damp, but by nine thirty the clouds had burned off, leaving only sunshine. We drove as far as we could for as long as we could, both of us in our bare feet and pajamas, and then we pointed that beautiful yellow Oldsmobile back toward Beverly Hills.

· · · · ·

We had a party that night, and the last guest left at three in the morning. I was just turning off my light when I heard the sound of water coming from the bathroom down the hall. Underneath it, very faint, I thought I heard someone crying. I pulled on my robe and knocked on the door.

Inside the bathroom, Mudge sat on the tile, knees tucked under her chin. She'd either washed or cried the makeup off. The water in the sink was still running.

I sat down beside her. "Nigel?"

"Yes."

I held something out to her, wrapped in paper and a red ribbon.

"What's this?"

"Your Christmas present."

She sat up straighter, sniffling, tearing away the paper. She held up the gift—a little wooden carving of a girl, mouth open, hair long and wild, heart-shaped face, arms spread wide. "What is it? Is she . . . ?"

"She's flying. My friend back home made it for me from a very special tree, one that's been through a lot but is still standing, even after the most terrible storms. He's a wood-carver, but this is the only carving he's ever made from that tree. He wanted to make one that nothing could break."

She sat for a long time without saying anything, and then she started to laugh and cry all at once. "This is the nicest gift I've ever gotten." She leaned her head into mine and, holding on to the little figure, swept her back and forth through the air, making her fly.

SHOOTING SCRIPT/*Flyin' Jenny: Star-Spangled Blonde*/11-27-46

EXT. COUNTRYSIDE — DAY

A peaceful blue sky. A single-engine open cockpit goes into a dive, hurtling toward the ground like a bullet.

CLOSE-UP on the pilot, beautiful and blond, and now concentrating on bringing the plane level. 400 mph. 500 mph. She yanks back on the stick, ready to pull out, but at that moment the plane starts to shake, and suddenly the nose is engulfed in flames.

Jenny loses her helmet first, then her goggles. She's pressed against the hatch cover. Her flying suit is ripping to pieces. Her boots fly off. She jumps free, making herself count before pulling the rip cord. She drops through the clouds and lands in a clump of bushes.

Where she emerges in seconds, having improvised a dress out of the parachute silk, hair smoothed, skirt swirling around her knees. She is barefoot. She consults her compass.

> JENNY

East.

With determination, she starts off in the direction of the airport.

> JENNY

> That plane didn't catch

> fire on its own.

> Someone compromised the

> fuel. The question is — who?

To give herself courage, she begins
to sing "Facing the World Alone."

                              CUT TO:

INT. STARCRAFT AVIATION — ENGINE TESTING
CHAMBER — LATER

Engineer Swoop Lowe listens to Jenny
skeptically as she tells him of the crash.

                    JENNY

          The only thing I can figure

          is that someone added

          sugar to the fuel tank,

          but only a few of us had

          access.

                    (as it dawns on her)

          Actually, *you* had

          access . . .

Swoop Lowe attempts to shove Jenny into a whirling
plane propeller. Jenny's foot becomes caught
between the steel cable and cylinder of the test
stand, which keeps her anchored, and the saboteur
falls into the propeller instead . . .

WILLIAM TAUB AND OPHELIA LLOYD
CORDIALLY INVITE YOU
AND A GUEST
TO A CELEBRATION OF
"HOME OF THE BRAVE"
DECEMBER 28–DECEMBER 30
AT
BROAD WATER,
THEIR SANTA MONICA ESTATE
(PLAN TO ARRIVE AT TEN A.M. OR AFTER)
RSVP LYNN RIGNEY, SECRETARY TO MR. TAUB

TWELVE

On Friday, December 27, the studio sent two limousines to take us to Grauman's Chinese Theatre. Mudge and Hal rode in the first one with their publicists, and I rode in the other with Bernie Hanser, Johnny Clay, and Butch.

I wore an ivory gown with a white gardenia in my hair, a silk one because they weren't in season. My brother sat between Butch and me, pointing out all the sights. He leaned forward, taking it in, while Butch sat back, gazing out the window without saying a word. *Girl, you been on my mind.* We hadn't had a chance to talk, just the two of us, since the night at Lovejoy's. But he was here, in a tuxedo, hair brushed back off his face, lean and sexy. It was the first time I'd seen him dressed up like this and I couldn't stop looking at him.

As we turned onto Hollywood Boulevard, I could see the klieg spotlights from blocks away. The sky above the Chinese Theatre glowed like it was on fire.

The closer we got to the theater, the more shapes and shadows sharpened into view: the carved pagoda towers, the dragon across the front, silhouettes of smaller dragons on the copper roof, and two stone lions guarding the main entrance. The faces and waving hands of the crowd on the bleachers and on the sidewalks, roped off by a barricade. The flashing of cameras, like a lightning storm. I pinched my arm over and over with two gloved fingers. That same night, *Home of the*

Brave, the most talked-about film of the past decade, was opening in seven other theaters around the country.

Johnny Clay pulled something out of his pocket. Mudge's flask. He held it up. "She thought you could use it tonight."

He took a swig and passed it to Butch, who gave it straight to me with a look at my brother. "Man, it's like you were raised in a barn."

Johnny Clay said, "Don't let all that finery fool you. That's just Velva Jean under there."

I held the flask in my hand without drinking. "When did she give you this?"

"Before we left. You were busy getting ready."

The limousine rolled to a stop. I could hear the crowds now, not just see them. They were cheering at the sight of each beloved movie star, each glittering person who appeared under the lights. Webster Hayes stalked up the red carpet, followed by Babe King and her mother. Louis B. Mayer and his wife and daughters, accompanied by Howard Strickling and his wife. Nigel Gray and Pia Palmer, his hand on the small of her back as they stopped to pose for the cameras. Everyone in Hollywood seemed to be there—including Sam Weldon with a redhead I didn't recognize.

Bernie said, "As soon as you see Hal and Barbara, get ready. We let them get a good head start, then Kit and—which one of you guys is Kit's date?"

Butch said, "I am."

"You and Kit will go. I want you to pause, wave, and head up the red carpet. Slowly enough so they can snap pictures. You can sign a few autographs, Kit, but don't take too long getting to the entrance. There'll be radio. Say a couple words, pose for another picture or two, and then give one last wave before you go inside. And, whatever you do, don't forget to smile. Your brother will be right behind you, and I'll be behind him."

I slid the flask into my purse as a roar went up from the crowd. Hal and Mudge were on the red carpet.

When Bernie said go, Butch stepped out and offered me his hand. Together, we made our way up the carpet, my arm through his. Some of the stars lingered in the famous forecourt—I could see Billy Taub and Ophelia Lloyd, shimmering in silver. Hal and Mudge signed autographs and answered questions for the press, her silver wings gleaming on her gown. From the rope, Zed Zabel barked, "Does this mean the divorce is off? Are Nigel Gray and Pia Palmer reconciled? Is it true you're campaigning to play Lady Catherine opposite him in *Latimer*?"

Mudge's smile froze. Mr. Strickling said, "Now, Zed, why don't we talk about the picture? Or maybe you need to be reminded why we're here?"

Up ahead, I overheard Babe King answering questions about her mother, her pet rabbit, her love life, and her new nickname—Babe Fanning. "I don't think it's fair to either Barbara or me. I'm not trying to replace her. That was just an ugly rumor started by someone as a joke. . . ."

I stood, smiling dumbly, blinded by the bright, bright lights, gripping Butch's arm so tight I wondered if he had any feeling left in it.

I smiled. I waved. But the fans had no idea who I was. The camera flashes slowed, as if to say, *She doesn't matter. We don't care about her.* Members of the press seemed bored. They were already talking about who they'd seen, who they'd gotten on film.

Then the cameras started flashing again and I looked behind me to see who had arrived. Johnny Clay swaggered up the carpet. I watched as he signed autographs and shook hands, fans and reporters calling out to him. After he kissed her cheek, one girl swooned into a faint. I almost couldn't blame them. In his tuxedo, waving and winking and grinning like a fool, he looked just like a movie star.

A voice said in my ear, "No one will believe you're a singer in that dress." Sam Weldon stood at my elbow, cigarette in hand. In his tuxedo, he was as handsome as Nigel Gray. I didn't see the redhead.

"Did you misplace your date?"

"It's good to see you too." He glanced at Butch, at my hand on his arm, and the light in his eyes dimmed a little. "Sorry. Manners have always been a challenge. Sam Weldon."

Butch shook his hand. "Butch Dawkins. You wrote the book."

Butch nodded at the theater and the enormous *Home of the Brave* sign that hung over the entrance, blazing like a furnace. "I haven't read it yet, but I got real respect for what you do. People think writing's easy, but it's tougher than just about anything else."

"Thanks." He looked at me, back at Butch, back at me, and the expression on his face—like someone had let the air out of him—made me feel guilty for some reason. "And I wanted to hate him. Good luck tonight, Pipes."

"Good luck to you, too."

"I don't need luck. I need a complete mental examination." The cameras popped, one, two, three, four, five.

Zed Zabel called out, "What can you tell us about the picture, Weldon? Does it do justice to your book?"

"Not in the least."

"You started as a newsman. You claim to deal in accuracy, adhering to history, respecting the truth, yet Betsy Ross wasn't in the book, and now we hear she's all but taken over the picture."

"It's Hollywood. Haven't you heard? There's no place for accuracy or truth in this business."

"If you hate it so much, why are you here?"

Sam flashed a smile as bright as the klieg lights. "The most noble cause of all—money."

Above the laughter, Zed Zabel said, "Think you'll stick around?"

"They may not want me to after tonight."

"Is it true you've been hired to adapt another one of your books?"

"Sir, if I had a drink, I'd throw it in your face."

I pulled out Mudge's flask and handed it to him, causing everyone to laugh. Sam unscrewed the cap, studied Zed, studied the flask, and then drank down the contents to applause.

· · · · ·

The stage was the largest I'd ever seen, the screen covered by heavy red velvet curtains, and for tonight, the heavy red velvet curtains were covered by an enormous American flag. There must have been two thousand people walking down the red-carpeted aisles, settling themselves elegantly in the red seats. A chandelier hung from the ceiling, ringed by dragons. Chinese lanterns glowed on the walls.

We sat in the center section of the theater in one of the middle rows, Johnny Clay to my left, Butch to my right, Hal and Mudge sitting directly in front of us. Hal said, "Don't worry, everyone, I'll be slouching down once the picture starts so you'll be able to see the screen."

Nigel Gray and Pia Palmer glided down the aisle and sat at the end of Mudge's row. As Pia settled into her seat, she leaned into Nigel, perfectly at ease. In a moment, Mudge turned around and batted her eyes like Mallory Rourke. "So, Johnny Clay Hart. Are you going to Tauby's for the weekend?"

"I don't think we were invited, were we, Dawks?"

"No, sir."

Mudge said, "Oh well, you can be my plus one, and Butch can be Hartsie's. You have to see this place to believe it. Bigger than the royal palace, and right smack on the beach. There's nothing like waking up to the sound of waves outside your window." She looked at him through cat eyes. "Just bring your own hooch because there's no alcohol at Broad Water, ever since Ophelia famously went on the wagon. Speaking of, where's my flask?" I opened my purse and handed it to her.

Sam Weldon and the redhead came down the aisle and took a seat at the end of our row. When he saw me looking, he pointed at the redhead. "I found her." He sat back, draping his arm over her seat. Meanwhile, Mudge and my brother were laughing at something, which got Nigel's attention. He stared at both of them so long and so obviously that Pia Palmer craned her neck to see for herself.

Then the screen lit up. The lion roared. The music swelled. The credits appeared. *An MGM picture. A William Taub film. Directed by Felix Roland. Adapted for the screen by Sam Weldon, from his novel. Starring Webster Hayes, Ophelia Lloyd, Nigel Gray, Barbara Fanning, and Hal MacGinnis, with Babe King, Edward Morgan, Frank Mitchell, Phillip Drake,* on down the list. We were all clapping and cheering.

Johnny Clay whispered, "Where's your name, Velva Jean?"

I felt my heart sink. In front of me, I heard Hal say, "Where's Velva Jean?"

Suddenly, on a screen all its own, words flashed up in blazing red, white, and blue letters: *And MGM's Newest Discovery—Kit Rogers as "Betsy Ross." In William Taub's production of Samuel Weldon's* Home of the Brave.

A rousing overture followed— the musical score taking flight and carrying the audience with it—as the first lines of the book rolled across the screen. Then, just like that, Betsy Ross's face appeared. She was saying how honored she would be to sew the flag, how happy she was to be asked. Sketch by sketch, she looked at George Washington's design ideas and then she set these aside and told them her own vision for the stars and stripes. The men thanked her and left, and she started to sing.

I was singing up there, where everyone could hear it. People like Nigel Gray and Ophelia Lloyd. People like Harriet Fields, who'd made me think I couldn't do it. People like Jacqueline Cochran and General Hap Arnold and all the folks back home on Fair Mountain, who would see it at their local theaters. People like Darlon C. Reynolds and maybe Judge Hay of the Grand Ole Opry. People I didn't even know.

Too soon, it was intermission, and instead of getting up to find the ladies' room or stretch my legs, I sat right there—like almost everyone else—and waited for it to continue. Mudge didn't turn around this time, but sat looking at the screen, where the word *Intermission* blazed in red letters. Up there, she and Nigel were two young people in love. And now, after all they'd been through, on screen and off, they weren't even getting to celebrate together. I looked at Mudge, and it hit me, just like that, how alone she really was.

· · · · ·

Fifteen minutes later, the lights were dimmed once again. I was swept up in the story of these brave young soldiers and the brave women who waited for them at home, of the brave President who led them, and the brave widow who sewed the first flag. As Mudge and Nigel reunited on-screen, I started to cry. Across the rows of seats, I heard the sounds of sniffling and purses clicking open, of tissues being passed around. I touched Mudge's shoulder to let her know I was there. She took my hand and held it tight, and then there it came—"The Star-Spangled Banner." Not the orchestral version, but just my voice, by itself. In it, I didn't hear the frustration of the day I'd recorded it. Instead, there was the pain and loss and joy and triumph and hope of the war and the victory.

Following the last line of the song, the theater was silent as a tomb. Then, as one, everybody was on their feet, making so much noise I wondered if the roof of the theater might blow right off. I hugged Mudge, Hal, my brother, Butch. At the end of the row, Sam Weldon was slapped on the back by a dozen hands, and I saw the redhead plant a kiss on his mouth.

Velva Jean Hart, as Kit Rogers, as Betsy Ross, appeared in seven of the film's scenes, and she was good.

THIRTEEN

Afterward, we emerged from the dark of the theater into the white-bright klieg lights. I shaded my eyes with the hand that had been shaken, moments earlier, by some of the biggest names in Hollywood. For a second, I couldn't see because the camera flashes were blinding. I held on to Butch's arm and there, like the yellow brick road, was the red carpet stretching into the crowd that was gathered, into the night. Mudge wiped at something on my cheek, "Lipstick," she said.

Johnny Clay rubbed his eyes, pretending it was the lights, but he couldn't fool me. The movie had choked him up. He said, "Little sister, that was about the best thing I ever saw. You been working on your voice, Velva Jean. Yes, sir."

Mr. Mayer stood beaming, Mudge on one side, Babe King on the other. He leaned in to Babe and said something as Mudge, cradling an enormous bouquet of flowers, waved to the crowd and announced her gratitude to Leslie Edgar, without whom she couldn't have delivered such a fine performance. "Every night, after I left the set, I drove to his house and we prepared for the next day's work, even though he was no longer working the picture."

One of the reporters shouted, "Over here, Miss Rogers!"

"Kit!"

"Kit Rogers!"

Butch said, "Go on. I'll be here. I'm not going anywhere."

He nodded me forward so that I could shake the hands of the men and women who held theirs out to me, and so I could answer questions from the press: *Where did you come from? Is it true you're an orphan? That both your parents are dead? Is this your first picture? Is that your brother? Is he under contract to Metro too? Who's the gentleman you're with? Do we hear wedding bells? What do you call your new hair color? What's next for you, Miss Rogers?*

I told them *Yes, this is my first picture. Yes, that's my brother—he's a musician, not a movie star. That's my friend, he's a musician too. This color? It's called American Blonde. Yes, I am grateful—to Mr. Mayer and Lucille Ryman and Ophelia Lloyd and Arthur Rosenstein and my friend Barbara Fanning and all the nice folks who believed in me, most of all my family.*

Ophelia Lloyd swept in and air-kissed both of my cheeks. She said something about how proud she was, as my mentor, and what it meant to her to see the name she had chosen for me, the name of her favorite character, up on that screen. As she talked, I caught Sam's eye through the crowd. He held up his cigarette, like he was toasting me.

When can we next see you on the screen, Miss Rogers? Will you make a record?

I said I'd been working on a series of pictures based on the comic strip *Flyin' Jenny.* We'd already shot two of them, and the first one would be released sometime in January. In that moment Mr. Mayer appeared and said, "As you can imagine, we've got big plans for this little girl." Howard Strickling and Mr. Mayer's family fell in line behind him. "This is only the beginning, folks. You haven't even begun to see what she can do."

· · · · ·

Across the street at the Roosevelt Hotel, we danced in the ballroom and on the terrace and around the pool. Waiters in tuxedos and white gloves carried silver trays of scotch and champagne or caviar, raising them above their heads as they stepped, precise and delicate as ballet dancers, through the crowd.

We helped ourselves to the food, and people called out: *Kit Rogers, what a voice you have. You were wonderful as Betsy Ross. We loved you in the picture.* Someone bumped my elbow—Babe King, as breathless as if she'd been dancing all night. "Oh, Kit, can you believe it? Mayer's offered to steal me away from Columbia, not just for the next picture, but for good." Her mother was nowhere to be seen.

I said to Butch, "Do you want to get some air?"

Without answering, he led me through the ballroom and past the orchestra, through the lobby and the hotel bar and the Cinegrill restaurant, with its mural of moving pictures, champagne glass stools, and red Formica bar. We found ourselves outside on the terrace.

Nigel Gray and Pia Palmer, a good six inches separating them, sat by the pool watching the dancers. I heard someone say, "I'm surprised she would even come."

I followed Butch past everyone to the far end, which was emptier and quieter. We took a seat on one of the lounge chairs, side by side, facing the pool. He said, "This is your night. Are you sure you don't want to be mixing it up?"

"I'd rather sit here with you."

"In that case . . ." He took off his jacket and his tie, loosened his collar, and leaned back with the lazy grace of a panther. He nodded at my hair. "I like the flower."

I touched it, careful not to knock it loose. "It isn't real. Gardenias aren't in season. I wish they were because the smell reminds me of home." Summer nights on the porch, telling stories after supper, the air sweet and heavy.

"It's the flower of love. That's what someone once told me. Secret love." He smiled. I smiled. "So this acting thing—is this what you want to do now?"

"It's more about the singing than the acting for me." I let myself think of my voice, coming out over the screen so that everyone could hear it, of how my voice would carry itself to theaters around the country, maybe even around the world.

He pulled out some tobacco and a pack of white paper and began rolling a cigarette, right on his leg. "We're recording some songs for a little label down at Central. If you want to write anything or give me something you got, I'd love to hear it."

We talked about Central Avenue and music, and then our conversation shifted to what we'd been doing since we last saw each other at Camp Davis in North Carolina. He'd gone ashore on D-day with the 4th Infantry Division, 4th Signal Company. He'd fought at Saint-Lô, Hürtgen Forest, and the Battle of the Bulge. He'd lost more friends than he could count.

I told him about England and France and Germany, about Fresnes prison, and Romainville, and the cattle car to Ravensbrück.

Butch shook the hair out of his eyes. "My mama used to say, 'Where you been is gone, gone, gone. All you keep is the getting there.' The people I know who been at war, we all got the same story."

"It's what you do with it afterward."

"That's right."

We were quiet as the thought settled in. Butch said, "You know, at first I couldn't write about the past couple years, but lately it's all I write about. I don't play those tracks at the Downbeat though." He grinned. "I'm on my best behavior there." He took a drag on the cigarette, blew the smoke out ring by careful ring. "But it's not just about using where you been to help you write songs; it's about how you live the everyday."

We watched people jump into the pool in their evening gowns and tuxedos, the women coming up without their diamond necklaces and bracelets, and the men diving to retrieve them.

I said, "I like that so many people are here going after what they want. When I was growing up on Fair Mountain, the biggest thing anyone wished for was a new bait line down at Deal's."

"Never underestimate a new bait line." He cracked a smile at me, slightly crooked, gap between his teeth. Butch didn't smile a lot, but when he did, he was the best-looking man I'd ever seen. "You were good in the picture. You've always gone after what you want."

"So have you. It's a hard thing to do."

"It's harder not to. It's easy to forget what you want sometimes. Just don't let them change you or what you want to do." He nodded toward all the Hollywood people gathered in and out of the pool and then grinned at me again, dark hair falling down over one eye. "Now I sound like your brother, lecturing you. It's just that I'm invested." The look in his eyes was too direct, and suddenly I thought: Something's happening here. This isn't the Butch I knew before the war. He may not be speaking the words, but he's telling me something just the same.

Someone screamed from the pool, followed by wild laughter. The sound of it jarred me because I'd forgotten where we were. Judging by the look on his face, Butch must have forgotten too. He bumped my knee with his. "I should get on back. We're playing a gig tomorrow night and I'm still working on a couple of songs. You okay to get home?"

"The limo will take me. Do you want him to drive you downtown?"

"I'll take the streetcar or a bus or maybe I'll hitch a ride. Don't worry about me."

We made our way back through the Cinegrill, the hotel bar, and the lobby. On the street, we stood in the shadow of the lights, still blazing, from the Chinese Theatre.

I smiled up at him. He smiled down at me.

He said, "Congratulations on the picture. Thanks for letting me be a part of it."

"You're invited for the weekend." Even as I said it, I knew he wouldn't go, but I was spinning from the marquee lights and the champagne and him and the late, late hour.

His dark Indian eyes regarded me over his cigarette, and the way he looked at me made my neck go hot. "That so?"

I met his gaze, not blinking. "You said you've been thinking about me."

"You been on my mind."

"You've been on my mind too."

"Well then. I'm thinking we need to talk about all this thinking."

For one second, two seconds, three seconds, time stopped and everything was suspended. It was just Butch and me, alone on a street corner, no marquee lights, no cars racing past, no orchestra music, no people. I could hear my heartbeat in my ears like the drums on Central Avenue.

"But not here, girl. Not here."

Like that, the lights of Hollywood were burning around me again, and I heard the music, the car horns, the laughter and chatter of a thousand people. Time caught up, the moment had passed, and even though it was too late, I couldn't let it go. "Johnny Clay's coming for part of the day tomorrow, but he's not spending the night."

He stubbed out the cigarette. "All right then."

He reached out and for a moment I thought he was going to touch my face, but instead he unpinned the gardenia from behind my ear. My hair came loose, and I touched it where the flower had been as he tucked the gardenia into the buttonhole of his jacket, over his heart. "I guess I'll just have to go on thinking a few hours longer."

I watched him go, jacket hooked over his shoulder, making his way eastward down the street. Butch Dawkins had been on my mind for at least five years now, maybe more. I tried to remember what year it was I'd met him, when he and Johnny Clay first came riding up to Devil's Kitchen in Danny Deal's old yellow truck. I'd been a married woman then. It would have been 1940, or somewhere around in there. Butch had started out as Johnny Clay's friend, but then he became mine. We were friends who talked music and wrote songs together, and the last one he'd written, a song called "The Bluesman," had stayed with me like a ghost.

Tomorrow, I thought. He'd as good as said he would be there.

I crossed the street to the Chinese Theatre and stood on the broad forecourt, surrounded by the handprints and footprints and signatures of the stars, and found an empty square. I kneeled down and pressed my hands against the cement, until I could almost feel them making their mark. Then I pulled out my lipstick and wrote *Dear Sid Grauman, Live out there! Kit Rogers, 12/27/46.*

· · · · ·

At six a.m., Mudge and I packed our bags for the weekend and left the house. We weren't due at Broad Water till ten, but we wanted to watch the sunrise from the beach. We hadn't slept a wink.

I drove and Mudge sat beside me, one arm out the window, hair blowing in the breeze like a dark cloud. I glanced in the rearview mirror now and then to watch the sky lightening behind us, as if it were chasing us. I followed Mudge's directions, but before we reached the beach, she pointed me to the Santa Monica Airport.

"What are we doing here?"

"You'll see." As we passed through the gate, she said, "Pull up over there, Hartsie." She waved toward one of the hangars.

The airport had been the base of the Douglas Aircraft Company during the war, and the place still bore the look of wartime. A canopy of chicken wire stretched like a roof across the terminal, parking lots, and hangars. On top of this sat thin and flimsy wood-frame houses surrounded by fences, clotheslines, and trees made of wire with leaves made of feathers, spray-painted to look real. The runway was painted green like grass. The tallest hangar had been built to look like a hillside. From the air, the enemy would have thought this was just another neighborhood and never would have known there was an airfield here.

We were out of the car and walking across the pavement toward a sleek, thirty-foot-long dive bomber, painted black, a white star on the side and on the tip of each wing. Mudge threw her arm around me. "The Douglas SBD Dauntless. It's got a maximum speed of 255 miles per hour, a rate of climb of seventeen hundred feet per minute, a ceiling of 25,500 feet, a range of a little over one thousand miles, brakes so accurate that you can pull yourself out of a near-vertical dive . . ."

As she rattled off the facts and figures, a man strode toward us and shook our hands. "It's ready for you, Barbara."

"Thanks, Walter." She introduced us, and the man walked us through so we could go over the engine ourselves, like good, responsible pilots, the way they'd taught us to do in the WASP. Then we were inside the open cockpit, Mudge in the pilot's seat and me directly behind her. We tied our hair back, pulled on helmets and goggles, and went through the flight check.

Then we were off down the runway, and climbing into the early morning sky. And suddenly, there was the Pacific Ocean, stretching out across the horizon so that it looked as if the world ended with

California. As we flew, the sky turned golden, and when the gold-orange-pink of day finally reached us, we held up our arms and tried to touch it.

The blue of the water stretched out below us, behind us, in front of us. To the north I could see the road that hugged the coastline, weaving along, ocean on one side, and on the other, sloping green mountains and rugged cliffs. To the south, I could see the boardwalk, unfurling like a carpet. We dove low enough to see the paint-faded shacks advertising carnival prizes and fortunes, beer and barbecue, and went soaring over the Santa Monica Pier, with its roller coasters and Ferris wheel. The beaches were hard and tan, stretching out of the water and toward land for what seemed like miles. I loved the white dunes of North Carolina, but the ocean seemed broader here, as if there was nothing beyond it but more ocean and endless sky.

At first we sang at the top of our lungs, but then we shouted the things we didn't want anyone else to know, our voices drowned out by the roar of the engine and the wind and each other so that we only heard ourselves. Down we'd go, nose to the earth. *Butch Dawkins is on my mind!* Up we'd go again, into the sky. *Do I love him? I don't know!* We flew up the coast, where the cliffs grew higher and wilder, and islands of rock jutted out of the water. We swept low over those islands, low over the water, then back up into the sky.

We stayed up for an hour, maybe longer, and finally Mudge brought us in. Back on the ground, we climbed out of the Dauntless and onto the runway, and she laughed as she pulled off her goggles. Her face was flushed, her eyes bright, her hair windblown. She didn't look like a glamorous movie star. She looked like the girl I'd met at Avenger Field years earlier. "I wish there was a way to live up there, Hartsie. I haven't figured it out yet, but if I ever do I'll let you know."

The sky was bright blue by the time Hal and then Johnny Clay arrived, by himself. Even as my pulse continued to race from the flight, I felt a sinking in my bones. Butch had said he'd come, or I thought he had. I wondered if he'd ever meant to at all or if maybe I'd only heard what I wanted to hear. I told myself: Enjoy the moment. Don't let him take it away.

While Hal and Johnny Clay took their turn in the Dauntless, Mudge stood apart from me, eyes skyward. I could see how much she wanted to be back up there.

When the boys finally came in, she said, "Maybe we could go again, just for a few minutes," but Hal said, "Shit, people. It's past ten." We gathered our things and raced each other across the runway, Johnny Clay in first place, me in second, Mudge on my heels, Hal groaning in last place. I pushed myself like a racehorse in the final lap until I passed my brother, who cursed a blue streak.

As I ran, I felt strong and happy and grateful I was there, at this moment, with these people. I heard a tune beginning and I chased it. When Hal reached me, he scooped me up onto his shoulders, and the four of us sang "The Star-Spangled Banner" all the way to our cars.

FOURTEEN

road Water sat on Palisades Beach Road, a narrow ribbon of highway that wound along the seaboard. The house was a three-story, thirty-four-bedroom white Georgian mansion on twelve acres of Santa Monica beach. A parking attendant took the keys to our cars, and inside the main entrance, Ophelia Lloyd swept toward us, arms extended, and welcomed us to their home.

We were given the tour. One hundred eighteen rooms, fifty-five bathrooms, thirty-seven fireplaces, three guesthouses, two swimming pools, four tennis courts, an art gallery, a gold room decorated in gold leaf, a theater with a movie screen that rose out of the floor with the push of a button. We were directed through the living room and drawing room, walking under Tiffany chandeliers and over Oriental rugs, past life-size painting after life-size painting of Miss Lloyd in her more famous roles, to the double stairway that led to the ground floor and party room, painted white and gold and dripping with chandeliers, where two handsome men in uniforms stood behind a long wooden bar, which served only milk shakes.

Then it was back up a sweeping staircase, across marble floors, and suddenly we were outside. Eighteen broad columns stood at attention on the beach-facing side of the house, looking out over the sand, the ocean, and a long swimming pool with a Venetian marble bridge arching above the water. The air was surprisingly warm.

My bedroom was on the top floor, at the end of a long hallway lined with Oriental rugs and murals on either wall of English country scenes—horses and carriages, elegant estates, foxhunts. Mudge's room was next to mine, and Hal's was at the other end of the hall. Johnny Clay would leave after dinner for Central Avenue in order to be back in time for his show.

When Miss Lloyd said that several of the guests had already arrived, Mudge asked about Les Edgar. "He was such a part of the picture, it seems fitting he should be here too."

Miss Lloyd said, "No, Les won't be here. But isn't it fortunate that Pia Palmer could join us? I can't imagine what it must mean to Nigel." Mudge's face went blank as Miss Lloyd gave her a bright smile. To all of us, she said, "You're just in time for lunch, so please come down as soon as you're ready." Then she was gone, shoulders back, head high, gliding down the hall.

Johnny Clay wandered around my room while I unpacked. It was actually more of a suite, with its own living room and a terrace, which looked out on the ocean. It was thick with French antiques, and a giant flower arrangement sat on the coffee table, filling the room with spring.

My brother said, "There's a note." He pulled it out of the flowers. "'Welcome to Broad Water, Miss Rogers. Please enjoy your time away. You have earned it! I hope you will make yourself at home and let us know if there is anything we can do for you. Cordially yours, Ophelia Lloyd.'" He held it up so I could see the stationery—a thick, heavy cream—and her name, in flowing red letters, engraved across the top.

He said, "You know your friend Hal is queer." He opened the terrace doors, and the breeze blew in.

"Don't say anything about that to anyone, Johnny Clay."

"Mudge already promised to kill me if I did."

"Since when are you and Mudge such good friends?"

"Since she needs someone to talk to other than a girlfriend like you or Hal—a man who can listen to her heartbreak and make her feel she's still attractive." He picked up a piece of fruit and knocked on it. "Whoever heard of glass fruit? Just once I'd like to see a rich person who knows how to spend money."

"Did Butch say whether he was coming?"

"Coming where?"

"Coming here, Johnny Clay."

"Why would he come out here?"

"Because I invited him."

"Why?"

"What do you mean, 'why'?"

"I'm just going to say this once, little sister. You be careful. Next to you, he's about the best friend I got, and I'd hate to have to break his fingers. I mean it. He's not someone you mess with unless you know you want to mess with him. He ain't like me in that way."

"Has he said anything to you?"

"He knows better than that. If he said one word to me, I'd have to knock him flat. But I'm not blind or stupid. He don't lead girls on, and he don't flirt. Shit." He sighed. "He *doesn't* flirt. He wants a woman, he takes her, but there ain't—there *hasn't* been anyone who stuck. You're not the kind men mess with, Velva Jean. You're the kind that sticks. You go down that road with him, you got to be sure."

"Maybe he's not sure. Maybe I'm not the one he's looking for. Maybe he's not even looking. He might not be ready for someone who sticks."

"Maybe not. If he was, I'm the last person he'd tell."

There was a rap on the door, and Mudge and Hal came in. Hal said, "We all got flowers. Did yours have a note?" Johnny Clay handed it to him.

Mudge took a drink from her flask but didn't offer any to the rest of us. She frowned at the room. "You know this wallpaper cost nearly ten thousand dollars?"

My brother shook his head. "Rich people."

· · · · ·

Several of the guests sunned beside the swimming pool, including Pia Palmer in a black two-piece bathing suit. She looked at us and said, "How lovely to see you," in an accent as neat as a freshly made bed. Then she picked up a book and didn't look at us again.

We found a spot on the other side of the pool. Johnny Clay said, "That's one cool dame. A little too cool, if you ask me."

"Where did Mudge go?"

"Why are you looking at me, Velva Jean? I'm not her keeper."

Johnny Clay pulled off his shirt and dove into the pool. As I arranged myself on a lounge chair, I saw Pia watch him over the page of her open book. Hal yawned and stretched. "I'm going to say hi to the others."

He stood up at the same moment Mudge appeared, in a daring red swimsuit, hair loose under a bright red sun hat. She spread her things out on her chair—towel, sunglasses, magazines, flask. She looked exactly the same as she always did, but there was something brittle and controlled about her movements, as if a storm was brewing and she was trying hard to keep it away. I thought, Uh-oh.

She called out to Johnny Clay. "How's the water?"

"Why don't you come see?"

She laughed like this was the funniest thing, but it was the laugh she used on camera. Mudge said, "Watch my things, won't you, Hartsie?" and sat on the edge of the pool, kicking her legs and looking everywhere but at Pia Palmer. Johnny Clay swam up and tried to pull her in, and she splashed him, careful not to mess up her hat or her hair.

One by one, other guests appeared—Mr. Roland and his wife, Shelby Jordan, a stylish brunette, much younger than her husband, who was a publicist for Warner Bros.; Phillip Drake and his date; Bernie Hanser and his wife; and others I recognized from the cast and crew. Rosie and Sam Katz weren't there because they were already at work on another film score, and Webster Hayes had sent his regrets, which was no surprise to anyone since Broad Water was a dry county, so to speak.

Beach chairs were carried out onto the sand, and rackets were carried onto the tennis courts. We could soon hear the sounds of three or four games going on at once. Johnny Clay swam laps, cutting the water with long, mean strokes, as women around the pool watched, their husbands or boyfriends heading for the ocean waves with surf boards or standing around smoking cigars and discussing the pictures they were making.

At one o'clock, Babe King and her date, Redd Deeley, appeared from the house. Her mother wasn't anywhere to be seen. They made their way down the row of sunbathers, stopping at each chair to say hello. Babe's lips were brightly painted, but otherwise she didn't wear a stitch of makeup. In the sunlight, I could see her freckles. Under his arm, Redd carried a copy of a script—*Latimer*.

When they got to us, Mudge shaded her eyes from the lounge chair next to mine and looked up at them. "Redd Deeley, as I live and breathe. And look. How sweet. You've brought your child star, Babe Fanning. I'm sorry—Babe *King*. I hardly recognize you without your mommy." She took off her hat and fluffed the ends of her hair. "How are you enjoying my castoffs?"

Babe blinked her big doe eyes. "I wasn't aware they'd offered you *Latimer*." She took the script from Redd, smiled the sweetest smile, and clicked away as Mudge's mouth popped open. Redd followed, calling over his shoulder, "Sometimes I wonder if you know how you sound. There's only one child at this party."

Mudge shouted, "You'd be surprised what I know." She watched after them, and then turned to me. "What do you think she meant by that?" She lit a cigarette, sitting up straight and stiff, like she was on alert. "I can't lose *Latimer*. Not with Pia here. If I don't see him at work, I won't see him." Her voice cracked.

"You should talk to Redd."

"Maybe I will." She stubbed out the cigarette and went off after him.

I felt my eyes getting heavy, and soon I couldn't keep them open anymore, a combination of warm sun and the sound of the ocean. When I woke up, Pia was standing over me. She said, "I didn't want to wake you, but I wondered if you had some oil I could borrow."

From the chair next to mine, Babe said, "I've got some." She fished around and handed it to her. As Pia sat down, rubbing the oil onto her arms and legs, Babe raised her sunglasses and looked at me. "I'm so relaxed, I'm bored."

"Let's go for a walk or ride bikes."

"Bikes sound fun."

We tried to find our way through the house. I told Babe I'd meet her at her room, which was next to Hal's. As I walked to the other end of the hall, I could hear voices, loud and angry, coming from Mudge's room.

"Metro is my studio, not hers. She belongs with Harry Cohn and all his two bit thugs over at Columbia, not at Metro. Never at Metro." *Mudge.*

"She's better suited to the role. You'd hate playing such a plain, pathetic character. Let it go." *Nigel.*

"Let it go? Don't tell me you're sleeping with her too."

"Do you hear yourself? I don't know what's worse, the accusations or the paranoia."

"I'm sorry, it's just . . . this whole thing with Pia . . ."

"In case you're forgetting, we need her to sign the papers. That's why she's here."

"It's taking her an awfully long time to sign them."

"She's the one in control here. Not me, not you, not us. I love you. You know that. Don't pretend for one minute that you doubt it. I'm doing the best I can."

Glass shattered as something smashed against a wall.

Nigel: "I cannot talk to you when you're hysterical."

Mudge: "When will you realize she's not going to let you go?"

"Then screw the bloody divorce. I send her back to England and you move in with me."

"It's bad enough I'm your mistress, Nigel. I'm not going to live like one. We're going to live respectably or not at all. If you don't think I'm worth marrying, I'm sure there's someone out there who does."

I eased away from the door. As I did the floor creaked. I froze as the voices went silent. Mudge's door flung open. "Hartsie?" Her face was tearstained, and there was a red mark on one cheek, as if she'd been slapped.

"I'm going bike riding. I just came to change clothes. Are you okay?"

Mudge brushed the tears away, like she'd just remembered them. "Of course. I'm fine. I'll be down in a bit. Enjoy your ride."

Inside my bedroom, through the wall, I listened to the rise and fall of voices. They were quieter now. When there was no more shouting or breaking of glass, I changed into white shorts and a red blouse, and went to find Babe.

· · · · ·

When we went down fifteen minutes later, Nigel and Pia were on the tennis court with Felix Roland and Shelby Jordan, Bernie and his wife played cards in the shade, and Mudge and my brother were walking away, Mudge's arm through his. She steered him by the tennis courts, right under Nigel's nose, parading my brother like a prize horse. As she passed, Shelby said something that set Pia to laughing.

One of the servants helped Babe and me with the bicycles, and we wobbled off down Palisades Beach Road, singing songs and enjoying the breeze. I thought she seemed freer and happier without her mother around. We rode for an hour, all the way to the pier and back to Broad Water. Babe let go of the handlebars, holding her arms out like bird wings. "It's everything I thought it would be, Kit!" I couldn't tell if she meant the bike ride or the beach or the weekend or Hollywood or California, but whatever she meant, I agreed with her.

Johnny Clay and Mudge hadn't returned, and at four o'clock, Ophelia Lloyd appeared to announce sunset cocktails—nonalcoholic, of course—on the terrace. Guests wandered up to the house in tennis clothes and bathing trunks, and Babe said, "I'm going to take a shower."

"Me too." We were expected to dress for dinner, so I gathered our things, and then I picked up Mudge's as well because there was no telling when she'd be back.

· · · · ·

Sam Weldon swaggered onto the terrace just as the sun was setting. He kissed the cheek of our hostess and shook the hand of our host, who had finally appeared to greet his guests. Sam made the rounds like a politician, and when he reached Mudge, Johnny Clay, and me, he said, "I come bearing sustenance." From his jacket, he pulled a bottle, half-empty, and filled each of our glasses. Across the porch, Felix Roland raised his glass and said, "Thank God you're here, Weldon."

"Proposals of marriage will be accepted, Roland, but only from the women." Sam sank down beside me in an empty chair. "You first."

I took a drink of lemonade.

"You're looking lovely, Pipes." He glanced around. "Where's your date?"

"He's getting ready for a show."

"Is he a circus performer?"

"Musician. He and my brother have a band." I nodded at Johnny Clay, who sat with his feet propped on the railing, listening to Mudge. She was wearing her slinkiest evening gown, a light silvery blue.

"Brothers don't like me. Their sisters, on the other hand . . . well, you can imagine."

"Which is why brothers don't like you."

"You're a cold woman, Pipes. I take it you're not going to tell me about the date."

"I'm not going to tell you about the date. Speaking of dates, what happened to yours?"

"You'll have to be more specific." He slouched in his chair and got a concentrating look on his face.

"The redhead from last night."

He rubbed his jaw, narrowed his eyes at the distance, shook his head. "Again. The more detail you can give me, the better."

"You know what? It doesn't matter."

He poured some of the liquor into my glass, swirled it with a bartender's flair. "It's interesting. That we're both here. Dateless. I wonder why that is?"

"Don't read too much into it."

"I'm a writer, Pipes, which means I understand subtext. And fate." He sat back, swirling his own glass, and scanned the porch, his eyes moving from person to person. "The guest list reads like a who's who from the Hollywood gossip columns. Who knew our hosts had a sense of humor?"

Nigel called out, "There it goes."

We all watched as the sun dropped below the horizon. One by one, we fell silent as the sky darkened, and down the beach, the lights from the pier glowed like a carnival. The breeze blew in off the water, turning the air cool, and across the veranda, Pia pulled her chair closer to Nigel's. He put his arm around her, like it was habit. In a minute, Mudge got up and sat right down on Johnny Clay's lap.

Sam whispered, "I have a perfectly good lap myself, in case you're in need of one, Pipes." I turned to say something and he was still leaning in to my ear, which meant that now we were nose-to-nose. He set down his drink and mine, said, "Come with me," and then took my hand and led me into the house.

FIFTEEN

As he pulled me into the library, Sam said, "This room is worth every dime they spent on this monstrosity of a house." There must have been ten thousand books, leather bound and musty, some kept behind glass.

"It's beautiful," I said.

"You're beautiful. This is—I don't know what this is. The most provoking moments of a writer's life are when he can't find the words to describe something truly great."

I moved from shelf to shelf, running my fingers along the spines of the books. We'd had a library in Alluvial, in the house that belonged to my schoolteacher and her husband. They had let us come and read and take books home, and I'd hidden them from Sweet Fern because I'd known she wouldn't approve.

"I saw your brother in here earlier."

"Johnny Clay?"

"Unless you have another brother running around Broad Water this weekend, which, incidentally, is my worst nightmare. That and being eaten alive by fire ants. He had his nose so deep in a book, he didn't even see me."

I thought, What is the world coming to?

"Do they have your books here?"

"I hope so. They'd be lucky to be in such company."

I picked up a heavy leather volume, flipped through the pages, set it down. "Why did you sell the rights to *Home of the Brave?*"

"I got tired of having to say no. So finally I said yes, and I cashed their ridiculous check, even though I knew what they would do to the book. Two years to research it, four years to write it, and it only took them a month to tear it apart." He ran his hand along a panel in the woodwork, searching for something. "I wrote it after my father died because I wanted to say something about survival. I put it all into the novel, all of me, dividing everything I was feeling among all the many, many characters. And for some reason, it took. Maybe that's one reason I'm so protective of it."

"The story you wanted to tell still comes through."

He stopped searching for a moment to look at me, his hand resting on the panel. "Pipes. Does that mean you broke down and read it?"

"Yes."

"You know, it really is a shame I don't date actresses."

He pushed on the wood and a little door swung open, revealing a hidden cabinet. "Like the cabinets of Catherine de Medici. No jewels or money, unfortunately. However . . ." He opened another—this one contained bottles of something old (judging by the label) and dark. He scooped one of the bottles out and then opened more cabinets, each no bigger than a breadbox, all lined in wood. I set my hand inside one as if I expected it to disappear.

"Hoping for magic?" He closed the cupboards, the bottle now under his arm.

"Maybe."

His eyes danced over my face, settling on my mouth. "Tempting." He touched another panel, this one in the bookcase, and a large door, as high as my shoulder, sprang open. Beyond it was a curving flight of stairs, a white wall, and a window. Without another word, he ducked inside. I hesitated, then followed him in, creeping past him up the winding wooden staircase. "How did you know this was here?"

"I always check libraries for secret passageways. I even wrote one into a detective story." He popped the cork.

"Did you steal glasses too?"

"For you, Pipes, I'd steal the moon, but sadly, no." He offered me the bottle. I drank. He drank. He studied the label. "Not bad for 1787." He moved ahead of me. "Let's see where it goes."

We climbed the stairs like two detectives on a case. At the top, a narrow, low-ceilinged hallway ran half the length of the house— wood floors, Oriental carpets, fat painted lamps sitting on skinny tables. I said, "It's a house within a house."

At the end of the hall was a single room with two dormer windows and a view toward the Malibu mountains and the road that wound up the coast. Slanted roofline, a daybed, cozy chairs —it wasn't fine and formal like the rest of the house, which made me like it best.

Sam opened the window, and the night air drifted in along with the sound of the waves and the guests down below. We pulled up two chairs and drank the wine and watched the lights blink on across the mountains.

I said, "Who do you think uses this room?"

"I don't know. Probably her. Maybe both of them."

"But not at the same time."

"No."

"This house is too big for two people. I think it would be hard to find each other."

"Unless they don't want to find each other."

We sat for a few minutes without saying anything. I felt drowsy and happy, lulled by the sound of the ocean. I felt so happy, I started to sing. It was a song I'd written years ago about a girl who lived on a mountain near a little trickling creek, and how that creek fed into a stream that fed into a pond that fed into a lake that fed into a river that fed into the ocean. It was something I used to think about when I lived in Devil's Kitchen with Harley Bright, trying not to lose my mind. I'd walk in the creek that cut past his house and think, If only I could follow this, I'd reach the ocean.

And now here I was, and there it was.

When I finished the song, Sam was looking at me. Without a word, he reached for my hand.

"Tell me something. What's a girl like you doing in a town like this? You don't seem like someone who has to go to Hollywood because she can't do anything else. All these other people, I know why they're here. They'd never make it in the real world. All of them damaged in some way, dependent on the studios to guide them through life, telling them who to date and who to marry and what role to play."

"You're here."

"And I'm as fucked up as any of them. But you're different. I've been trying to figure it out."

I decided to quote his own words to me. "If I didn't know better, I'd think you were trying to flatter me."

He laughed. "I like holding hands with you, Pipes. I don't know when holding hands has ever excited me more. Or at all."

"I can't imagine you do a lot of hand holding."

He flashed me a wicked smile. "No, but I can imagine doing a lot of it with you. Of course, that isn't all I imagine. I want you. Epically."

"I imagine you want a lot of women."

"Not like this. Books should be written about it. Not just one book, but volumes." He was gazing out the window now, looking long and lazy and satisfied. "Not just volumes. A library. An adult library. But a library all the same. Do you think I have a chance?"

My mind stirred, my body stirred. Even as I listened to him, I wasn't sure if I should believe him or not. "Maybe."

"Come here."

"Why?"

"Because I want to kiss you."

When I didn't move, he pulled my chair around and in, so that it was facing his, and he sat up, leaned forward, suddenly awake and focused, eyes taking me in—really taking me in. "I want to kiss you," he said again, his eyes and voice serious. His fingers brushed my left cheek. "Kiss this cheek." His fingers brushed the other one. "And this one. I want to kiss your chin, your forehead, your nose . . . your lips." As he described it, I could feel him doing it, and my entire body went on alert, my heart running for him, my skin prickling like a storm was coming.

"I want to give you something to think about at night."

I whispered, "Why don't you do it, then?"

He whispered, "Because I'm afraid you'll slap me."

"What if I promise not to?"

"I might take the chance."

He touched my face.

"But I might want to build up to it, ease in."

He tucked my hair behind my ear.

"Just in case."

He kissed my left cheek.

He kissed my right.

He kissed my chin, my forehead, my nose.

Then his lips were on mine, soft and warm. And there was something behind it that let me know he at least meant some of what he'd said.

I heard a man's voice, coming through the wall. "Do you keep your room locked?" It was as clear as if he were in the room with us.

Sam froze. I froze.

A woman said, "In my own house?"

"I'll remember that later this evening."

"You're terrible." The sound of drawers sliding open, of someone rummaging, a muffled laugh, and then silence.

Sam said, very low, "Or maybe this is where they stash their lovers." We moved up and away from each other, and when I got to my feet he smoothed my hair and straightened my collar, the way Sweet Fern did with the children before she sent them to school. Then we set the chairs back carefully, making sure the room looked the same as when we'd found it. I was still breathing hard as, step by careful step, we crept away. We followed the stairs down, twisting and turning until we were outside the library.

I reached for the door, but Sam stepped in front of it. "By the way, I'm probably going to fall in love with you." His eyes were shining, the eyes of a wolf in moonlight.

• • • • •

After dinner, Mudge walked Johnny Clay to his car while Ophelia Lloyd excused herself with a headache, and Bernie and his wife announced they were going for a walk on the beach. Babe's mother had arrived at the end of the meal, and the two of them hadn't yet appeared, but the rest of us gathered in the game room around a roaring fire. A grandfather clock, stiff as a soldier, stood in one corner, and chimed the half hour. *Nine thirty.* Some of the men played cards, while others, Sam included, played a wild game of Ping-Pong. Hal, costume designer Colin Fedderson, and I sat in a corner and played Twenty Questions. Mudge walked in and joined Phillip Drake by the fire, flicking cigarette ashes into the flames. She talked and talked and waved her hands, ash flying everywhere, until finally he stalked away. She crossed to where we were and sat down beside me on the sofa.

Collie said in a biting way, "Making friends?"

"I told him he shouldn't let his mustache creep around his face like that. He ought to get it under control because otherwise he just goes around scaring people." Something about this struck her as funny, and she started laughing. Her face was flushed, either from the heat of the fire or all the gin she'd been drinking. The brown of her eyes had gone black. She chattered on about mustaches and snakes and how you couldn't trust them, not a one.

Hal frowned. "Why don't you give us your flask?"

"Because it's empty." She reached for Hal's ginger ale and took a swig. "The sun has dried me out." She gave him back his glass, then slipped off her shoes and massaged her feet. "Go on with your game. I promise to watch like a good girl. Not a mustache to be found here. No, no, I'm safe now." She narrowed her eyes at Pia. "As long as I stay right here and be very quiet and very good and very, very small, and then maybe I'll be invisible. Oh look, I already am." She laughed and laughed. "Sorry. I can't seem to stop it." Hal looked at me and shook his head.

Tauby had disappeared after dinner, but now he strode in, chomping on a cigar, and surveyed the room. "Let's choose a game we can all play together."

Collie was the one who suggested Murder in the Dark. One of the servants brought out a deck of cards, and Tauby himself removed three of the aces and three of the kings. He dealt the cards to each of us until the stack was gone. He gave the cigar three firm puffs and said, "The person who receives the ace is the Murderer. The person who receives the king is the Detective. Do not tell anyone whether you have these cards or not."

He stood, walked to the panel of light switches, and flicked them off. The fire cast shadows across the room. He pulled out his pill bottle, flipped it open, and chewed the pills as he talked. "We play in the dark, as the name implies. One of the servants will count to one hundred, and everybody must hide. No closets or cabinets, nothing closed in. You must be where the Murderer can find you."

Nigel said, "In this house, Tauby? We'll be playing for days."

Tauby stood with his back to the fire. "All right, we'll create boundaries." Half of his face was in shadow, the other half cast in an orange glow. "First floor only, no going upstairs or downstairs, and no going outside."

Shelby said, "The terrace?"

"Yes, but only on this level."

Hal raised his glass to Shelby. "Now we know where to find you."

Mudge called out, "And if you can't find her there, just look in Nigel's bed. Or Tauby's. Or maybe even Redd's, on occasion."

Shelby's smile disappeared as Felix Roland barked at Mudge, "Why don't you shut your mouth once and for all?"

Hal said, "Okay, that's it. We're cutting you off."

Maybe it was the fact that she was being locked up with Nigel and Pia for the weekend, but I couldn't shake the feeling that something strange was going on with Mudge. I laid my hand on her arm, and she was burning up.

Tauby raised his voice, as if he hadn't heard a word of it. "If you're the Murderer, you find the other players and kill them by tapping them on the shoulder. You can whisper, 'You're dead,' but otherwise be silent about it."

Collie added, "But the victims should feel free to perish with gusto. Make dying noises as you fall." He demonstrated with a scream, followed by choking sounds. He collapsed onto the rug and then whimpered and thumped and moaned before taking one last gasp and going silent. We all applauded. Beside me, Mudge jittered her leg up and down.

From the floor, Collie said, "Don't move until the game is over and the Murderer has been caught."

Tauby continued, "The servants will remove themselves after we begin, so that you don't confuse them for victims. If you run across someone who has been murdered, scream out, 'Murder in the Dark!' At that point, the person who locates the body will turn on the lights and whoever is still alive will gather here to determine the culprit, the Detective leading the investigation."

I said to Mudge, "Why don't you go up to bed? Sit this one out. It's been a long day."

She turned those black eyes on me, and I didn't like the look in them. "Sweet Hartsie. Dear Hartsie. Dear, *sweet* Hartsie. So dear. So sweet. I need an aspirin." She stood and practically ran toward the door.

I looked at Hal and Collie, propped up on one elbow, who were staring after her as if she'd caught on fire. "What in the world's gotten into her?"

Hal said, "You mean besides too much gin?"

Collie smirked. "And too little Nigel?"

We gathered in the middle of the room, and Sam found his way to me. In my ear, he breathed, "So many things we could do in the dark, Pipes. Remind me to find you once the lights go out."

We were told to scatter, as throughout the first floor the lights were snapped off. One of the maids came in and began to count, and I slipped out. I wasn't the Murderer or the Detective, so I needed to hide as soon—and as well—as I could.

My eyes adjusted to the dark, the only light coming from the fire-places that burned in various rooms and the glow of the moon, re-flected off the water, which crept in the windows. I heard a whisper as someone breezed past. I froze, and when I wasn't tapped on the shoul-der, I kept going.

The house was completely still. Then, ahead of me, I heard foot-steps. I turned and turned again until I was in the kitchen. I tried to remember the layout from earlier that evening, when Sam and I had passed through on our way to the library. I felt my way along the counter, which suddenly curved. As I ran my hand across it, I discovered an open space. I crouched down, trying to outline it with my hand, and found the pipe in the middle. The sink. I climbed underneath, into the open hollow, and waited.

It's funny how the other senses heighten when one sense is taken away. I could barely see, but I could hear every sound. It was a long time before I heard a scream, from somewhere far away. *The first victim.* After a while, another scream, closer this time. No one had yelled "Murder in the Dark," which meant the game was still on.

The minutes ticked by on the kitchen clock, and I started counting them. There was another scream and a series of moans, which told me Collie was the victim. Then silence again, then a kind of manic laughter, which sent a chill through me and caused the hairs on the back of my neck to stand up. A clock chimed the half hour. Moments later, a scream.

Then someone came into the room. He or she was trying to be quiet, but I heard each step as the person walked toward me. I held my breath until they went on past, and then, without thinking, I sighed. Suddenly, I felt a tap on my shoulder. "You're dead," the Murderer whispered. I let out a scream of my own and slumped onto my side, my cheek against the cool tile.

Sometime later I heard, "Murder in the Dark!" The lights flickered on. While I waited for the remaining players to solve the crime, I watched the clock on the wall. It was nearing eleven. It was cold on the floor, and I thought, If I had to die, why couldn't it have been in front of the drawing room fire?

It was almost eleven thirty when I heard footsteps. "Game's over, Kit." Redd helped me up.

"Who was the Murderer?"

"Nigel."

"Who was the Detective?"

"Roland. We're collecting the victims now."

"Where haven't you looked?"

"You could try the library and theater, over in that wing. I don't know that anyone's been there yet."

I found Shelby on the floor of the library, hand at her forehead, as if she'd been caught in a faint, and Phillip Drake in one of the reading chairs, head thrown back, eyes closed. The theater was empty, and so was the music room, but when I walked into one of the many bathrooms, as large as the kitchen, there was Mudge, lying on her side.

"Game's over. They caught the Murderer. It was Nigel." I turned to go, and when she didn't follow me, I turned back, hand on the doorframe. "Mudge?"

She lay still.

"Mudge?"

Her black hair fanned across her face and the tile, and it hit me for the first time how messy she looked. Mudge was too vain to be found like this, in a heap on the bathroom floor. She would have arranged herself to look as glamorous as possible. There was something else— the faucet was on and water was running in the sink.

I kneeled down beside her. She lay with one arm bent underneath her as if she had been trying to lift herself up. She was clutching something in her left hand—something white. Her purse was lying next to her, opened, the contents spilled across the floor—lipstick, powder, cigarettes, lighter, the flying girl I'd given her, and two bottles of pills. I pressed my fingers to her neck, and her skin was hot to the touch. I thought I felt a pulse, rapid and faint.

I turned her head gently and saw that her eyes were open, the pupils wide and staring, as if she had seen a ghost. "Mudge." I rolled her onto her back and pinched her nose and breathed into her mouth, trying to give her my own breath, to fill her lungs. I pressed on her chest, the way they'd taught us to do in the WASP, and then I breathed into her mouth again, counting. I thought, No, no, no. And then I shouted for help.

Mudge is only pretending. Or maybe she bumped her head in the dark. She might have knocked herself out without meaning to.

She didn't respond, and I kept at it, on and on, hollering for someone, anyone, praying silently, then out loud. *Please don't be dead. Don't let her be dead. Wake up, Mudge. Wake up, wake up.* I felt her wrist for a pulse, but the flesh felt empty, as if Mudge had gone away and left it there. I put my hand to my mouth, and tasted the gin from her lips on my own.

Felix Roland appeared, eyes startled, face red, as if he'd run fast and hard to find me. "What is it? What's happened? I could hear you hollering all the way from . . ." He looked down at Mudge, like he couldn't understand who or what she was.

"Call the hospital. Get help."

To Mudge I said, "Wake up." I lifted the hair off her neck. Underneath her makeup, I could see a faint bruise on one cheek, which could have been from earlier, from her argument with Nigel. There was a knot, barely visible, on the right side of her head, but that might have been from falling, maybe from hitting her head on the edge of the sink or on the hard floor. I didn't see anything nearby that could have been used to cause that bump—only a vase of flowers, undisturbed, and a dish of soaps. The white thing in her hand matched the mono-grammed towels—*T* for Taub—that hung on the racks. Everything else seemed to be in its rightful place.

Suddenly, her eyes fluttered. A slight intake of breath. She was saying something, or trying to. She was trying to grab my hand.

"Don't talk. Don't talk. We're getting help."

She was whispering.

"I can't hear you. Save your energy. Help is coming."

She said it again, and this time I heard it. "Rebecca," it sounded like, before her eyes closed and she seemed to drift off and away, and then her body started jerking like she was a puppet and someone unseen was making her dance. One seizure followed another seizure—wild, gruesome convulsions. The only thing I'd ever seen like it was Mrs. Garland Welch, who had gone mad with rabies when I was ten.

Just like that, Dr. Atwill, the studio physician, was pushing me out of the way, bending over her, on his knees. "Step back," he snapped, without looking at me.

I stood back. One by one, the other guests came. Babe King and her mother, hands over mouths, turning away. Redd, rushing forward, held back by Felix Roland. Bernie, followed by Shelby, then Collie. Bernie said lucky for us the doctor had been at Broad Water for an hour or more, tending to Miss Lloyd's headache. Felix rounded up everyone but me and sent them out of the room, directing them now as he had on *Home of the Brave*.

Someone tried to round me up too, but I shook them off. "Stop her," I shouted. "Don't let her do that!" As if everyone was to blame, as if she was doing it to herself.

Then Sam was beside me, so close I could hear him breathing. "Is it epilepsy?"

I didn't answer because if I moved or blinked or looked away she might die. And then Mudge went still, and the doctor sat back on his heels, pinched and defeated, and muttered, "There was nothing I could do. I'm sorry."

I heard my own voice. "It wasn't epilepsy."

I told myself she might have accidentally taken too much Benzedrine or Seconal. She might have eaten something with shrimp, which I knew she was allergic to.

Someone has killed her. Who would kill her?

And then I thought: Anyone. Anyone here might have done it.

SIXTEEN

Howard Strickling arrived just after midnight with Eddie Mannix, Metro's general manager, and Virgil Apger, the studio photographer. Minutes later, MGM police chief Whitey Hendry walked through the front door with three of his men.

All of us, hosts and guests, were seated in the living room, staring at the floor, at the walls, into space. Most of the women were crying. Babe's hands shook as she held her cigarette, the ash dangling and forgotten, her eyes huge and wet and staring. Shelby Jordan wiped one eye and then the other, until she gave up and let the tears run. Pia Palmer, cheeks damp, looked at me and then away.

Ophelia Lloyd sat in a chair, clutching a handkerchief, the color drained from her face so that the rouge on her cheeks was like two plastic checkers on a white board. Billy Taub stood by the fireplace mantel, furiously cleaning his glasses with a handkerchief, as if by cleaning them enough the image of Mudge's cold, dead body on his bathroom floor might disappear. Sam stood on the other side of the mantel, jabbing absently at the fire with an iron poker.

Nigel, drawn and hollow-eyed, said from his chair, "I didn't kill her."

Whitey Hendry was tough as a steel trap, even with gray hair and glasses. "We're not saying anyone killed her, Mr. Gray." He exchanged a look with Eddie Mannix and Howard Strickling that made it clear this was exactly what they thought. And then all three of them looked past Nigel at Pia.

"No, I mean I didn't kill her. In the game. I didn't walk up to her and tap her on the shoulder and say, 'You're dead.'" Pia stood behind him, one hand on the back of the chair, not touching him, staring down at the top of his head.

Howard Strickling said, "I need a copy of the dinner menu. She was allergic to shellfish, is that right?"

I answered, "Yes." I hadn't cried yet. I wasn't going to cry because in my mind, Mudge was still alive.

"Was there fish served at dinner? Shrimp?"

"Yes, but Mudge didn't eat any of it." I'd already been thinking this through. She hadn't eaten any at dinner, hadn't even touched the plate to pass it. There could have been a serving fork, used for the beef or the vegetables, that was mixed up with the shrimp, but the Taubs knew about her allergy. They would have warned the servants to be extra careful.

Eddie Mannix had a face like a bulldog. I had seen him before, in Mr. Mayer's office. He said, "Maybe she did. Cross-contamination. The cook uses a spoon to serve the shrimp, then uses the same spoon to stir the soup. She was deathly allergic, am I right?" He and Mr. Strickling exchanged another look.

"Yes, sir. But she didn't eat the shrimp. And she used her silverware to serve herself, not the serving spoons and forks. She always does that." *Did that*, I told myself.

Mr. Strickling said, "We need to see the body." *The body.* "Miss Rogers, you were the one who discovered it?"

"I was the one who discovered *her*."

Mr. Strickling said, "Show me."

· · · · ·

As Whitey Hendry and his men examined the scene, Mr. Strickling, Mr. Mannix, Dr. Atwill, and Tauby talked in a huddle. Nigel and I were the only other people there, standing forgotten outside the bathroom door. Whitey Hendry said, "Nasty bump on the head." He looked back and forth from Mr. Strickling to Mr. Mannix. "She could have tripped, knocked herself out, hit the countertop just so. . . ." He stood, demonstrating. "Accidents happen all the time. Especially in the dark, when you're not familiar with the place. Right, Doc?"

Dr. Atwill said, "Primula Niven." The men nodded. In May, the wife of David Niven had died after falling down a set of cellar stairs at the home of Tyrone Power. They'd been playing the game Sardines, and she had been looking for a place to hide.

"Same kind of thing," said Mr. Mannix, hands in pockets, rocking back and forth on his heels. He glanced past his colleagues to the bathroom mirror and smoothed the hair on his balding head.

The men moved out of the way so that Virgil Apger could have room to work. He took roll after roll of film, shooting Mudge from every angle. I heard him say to Tauby, "Shouldn't the police photographer be doing this?"

"Get them out of here." Mr. Mannix waved at Nigel and me. As one of Whitey Hendry's men ushered us into the hallway, Nigel said to me, "I was supposed to meet her during the game. But when I went to her room, she wasn't there. I drew the ace. It was perfect. The game would go on as long as I wanted it to. No one would know when I tapped the first victim. If I waited, there wouldn't be any bodies to find."

"So you would have had time to be together."

"But she wasn't there," he said again.

· · · · ·

We were instructed to tell the police that we'd found the body at twelve forty-five. This way, the police wouldn't know there had been a delay in calling them. I was to tell them I'd found the body in the bathroom, but that was all I was to say. Mr. Strickling and Mr. Mannix went over it again and again: an innocent game; a terrible accident; a call to the police as soon as we found her; just like Primmie Niven ("Mention Primmie Niven."). Yes, she had been drinking, even though it was a dry party. Most everyone had been drinking. The lights were off. No windows in the bathroom, so it was very dark. The servants could testify that the rug in the music room was always curling up. They'd tripped on it themselves many a time.

Dr. Atwill paraded around the room from person to person, passing out pills like he was the Good Humor man. When he got to me, he handed me a bottle of red pills. "We use Seconal to treat sleeplessness and tension. You need to remember that it's fast acting, even in small doses, but it will help you feel calm." He handed me the other bottle. "The white pills will give you energy."

"Benzedrine?"

"Yes."

I didn't trust pills. Except for the occasional aspirin, I'd been raised on mountain herbs and plants. Whenever I had a headache, Daddy Hoyt gave me a tea of pennyroyal leaves. If I caught a cold, I drank boneset tea.

I said, "No thank you." I gave the bottles back to him.

"Everyone uses them, Miss Rogers. When taken in the right combination, they're perfectly safe."

"I'd rather have aspirin." As Dr. Atwill doled these out and moved on to the next person, I turned to Sam. "Where are the police?"

"They'll be called before it's over, once Whitey and Strickling have the story straight."

It was almost one a.m. when Tauby placed the call. "There's been an accident," he said into the telephone. "Out of respect for my guests and my wife, no reporters, please."

The Santa Monica police arrived six minutes later. Instead of being separated, all of the guests and servants were interviewed together. Because I had found her, the detective in charge, Nick Agresta, asked me to come with them to the crime scene.

"Crime scene?" I repeated.

"The place you found her."

Through the short hallway to the bathroom, I could see one uniformed officer and one man in a brown suit, the man in the suit kneeling, the man in the uniform leaning over him from behind. But the body looked different. A corner of the rug was turned over, as if Mudge had tripped, and she was now lying on her stomach, head turned to the opposite side, the one with the knot on her forehead. Her eyes were closed. Her hair flowed across her shoulders, spilling onto the floor behind her so that you could see her face, which looked peaceful. There was something else—her purse, cigarettes, lighter, powder, pills, lipstick, and flying girl were gone.

No one was taking fingerprints. The police photographer was only shooting pictures of the detectives with the dead movie star, but otherwise he just stood around, chomping gum and talking to his colleagues about the size of the house.

Lieutenant Detective Nick Agresta was around thirty-five, with thick eyebrows and a hard chin. He barked at his men before turning to me. "Show us how you found the body, Miss Rogers."

"Not 'the body.' She still has a name." I tried to appear calm as I demonstrated how I had walked through the room to the bathroom, how I had checked for a pulse in her neck and her wrist and tried to bring her back, but otherwise touched nothing.

"What's going on in here?" Two more men strode in, one carrying a black bag, and the other wearing a gray suit.

Someone said, "What's he doing here?" as Whitey Hendry began briefing them on the details.

The man in the gray suit said, "No offense, Hendry, but I'd like to hear it from the detective in charge." As Howard Strickling, Eddie Mannix, and Whitey Hendry watched, clearly unhappy, the man with the black bag kneeled down beside Mudge, checking her eyes, the knot on her head. He had the soft, pleasant look of a country doctor— wire-rimmed glasses perched on the end of a long and rounded nose, two white patches of hair on his otherwise bald head. He began wrapping her hands and feet in plastic bags. While he did this, the gray-suited man called for the police photographer and told him to photograph her from specific angles.

Since the moment Mudge died, my head had been growing heavier, and it suddenly felt too much to carry around. I thought, If I could just sit or lie down, just for a moment. . . . Then Sam was there. He half-carried me, half-dragged me down the stairs until we were outside in the fresh sea air. My feet were moving but not working. My throat was dry. I couldn't swallow because it was like swallowing razors. "I need to go back in there," I croaked. "I need to hear what they're saying."

"What you need to do is breathe." He made me sit on the steps. He bent down beside me and held my face in his hand. "I need you to keep yourself together right now."

I breathed. Then, from a great distance, I heard my voice. "The air was too close in there, in the bathroom. I thought I was going to pass out. I don't see how anyone can breathe in there. They moved her, Sam. They're making it look like an accident."

"Maybe it was an accident."

"It wasn't an accident. She was having convulsions. My granddaddy's a healer. I've seen it before. That was something else. I know it was something else. Maybe she took too many pills without meaning to. I don't know. But if it was an accident, why are they going to so much trouble? They're not even taking fingerprints because they're so busy posing for pictures."

"I'm going to see what's going on, but I need you to be okay in case anyone comes around. Son of a . . ." Sam glanced over my head. "Like this guy." He sighed.

A policeman marched across the terrace. He said, "I'm going to want to talk to her."

"You can talk to her later."

Their voices overlapped like a fog. Sam said to me, "I'll be back. Are you okay? Pipes?" He took my chin in his hand again and tilted my face toward him. His dark eyes, usually so amused or unamused, were serious, and he looked both mad and worried. "I need you to trust me and I need you to be okay."

He followed the policeman into the house, and I sat rocking back and forth in the breeze. I stared out at the waves slapping onto the beach. There was something soothing about the sound. I stared at the waves until I could see a figure down at the shoreline. It was tall and broad and walked right into the water.

I waited for the figure to come back out, and when it didn't I told myself I'd imagined it. Maybe I'd imagined Mudge too. For a moment, I pretended everything was the same as it had been this morning and the day before and the day before that, and then I got up and ran down the stairs to the beach. I pulled off my shoes. The sand was hard and cold as I headed for the ocean. From the edge of the water-line, I could see the figure again, waist deep and still walking.

I started shouting. "Hey! Hey you! You there! Where are you going?" My voice was carried up and away by the breeze. I picked up my skirt and waded into the shallows, up to my shins, and the water was like ice.

The figure seemed to stop, to turn, and then it just stood there, the tide causing it to sway back and forth. The sea was choppy and rough, and as a large wave crashed in, the figure lost its balance. I was too scared to go after it—in this dark, in this cold, in this rough water—and so I stood frozen and useless, waiting for it to reappear.

The waves roared in, rolled out, roared in, rolled out, and suddenly there came the figure drifting with them. At first, I thought he was dead, but then he pulled himself up and brushed the hair off his face and waded toward me. It was Hal, and he was crying.

I put my arms around him and he carried me up onto the sand, away from the water, where we both sank onto the beach and he rested his head on his hands and just sobbed. I put my arm around him and rubbed his back, and finally just sat with my hand on his arm, grip-ping the skin where it was cold and wet, feeling the goose bumps under my fingers.

· · · · ·

Sometime later, Sam came to check on me in my room. When he knocked on the door, I said, "Come in," without thinking or caring who it might be. He found me sitting on the veranda, watching the waves.

He didn't say anything at first, just sat down heavily on the chair next to mine and looked out toward the horizon. Finally, he said, "The police are gone."

"And Mudge?"

"She's with the coroner."

The word sounded so final—*coroner*. Like *corpse* and *gravestone* and *funeral*. These were words without hope, words that meant endings. *The end.* My mind drifted. Sam was saying something else.

"What's that?"

"Do you want me to stay?"

"I'm okay."

He leaned down, a hand on each arm of my chair, his face inches from mine. "You let me know if you need anything. And, just in case, lock your door."

He made me get up and follow him out so that he could hear the lock click into place. I went back to the balcony, suddenly all alone, the most alone I'd ever felt in my life. I felt empty and washed away. The tide roared in, the tide rolled out. In, out. In, out. I finally fell asleep in my chair, and even after I did I could hear the roaring and the rolling, in and out, in and out.

ZED ZABEL'S HOLLYWOOD
"Barbara Fanning Falls to Death in Home of Movie Couple"
Await Autopsy to Determine if Inquest Needed in Death of Actress

HOLLYWOOD, December 30—AP—As the rest of the world celebrates the spectacle of Metro-Goldwyn-Mayer's *Home of the Brave*, Hollywood mourns Barbara Fanning, glamorous Metro star who most recently brought Mallory Rourke to life. Miss Fanning died Sunday from a head injury, suffered in a fall at the residence of *Home of the Brave* producer Billy Taub and his wife, actress Ophelia Lloyd (who plays Martha Washington in the picture).

The accident occurred during a weekend party attended by a small group of film notables, all friends of Mr. Taub and Miss Lloyd connected with *Brave*. Among them were director Felix Roland and his wife, publicist Shelby Jordan, screenwriter/author Sam Weldon, stars Nigel Gray, Hal MacGinnis, Phillip Drake, and Babe King, agent Redd Deeley, costume designer Colin Fedderson, and MGM's newest discovery, Kit Rogers, who, as many already know, is a longtime friend of Miss Fanning's.

A spokesman for Taub said that Miss Fanning apparently lost her way in the pitch-black house during a game of Murder in the Dark. The accident is eerily (and, some might say, conveniently) reminiscent of the one that befell Primula Niven in May, when, during a game of Sardines, she mistook the basement of Tyrone Powers's home for a closet and tumbled to her death down a flight of stairs.

Metro's biggest star, Nigel Gray, is reported prostrate over the loss. MGM said an inquest doubtless would be held, but no date has been set. Studio physician Dr. Edwin Atwill said the official cause of death was a "trauma sustained by accidental injury."

Coroner Benjamin H. Nigh asked police to investigate and said that results of the autopsy and investigation would determine whether an inquest will be held.

It is, of course, too early to know how this will affect the *Home of the Brave* box office, but the question right now seems to be: Can anything hurt it? In its first week of release, the picture has already broken records, leading both Warner Bros. and RKO to shelve their own Revolutionary War–era projects.

SEVENTEEN

Monday morning, I woke up in my bed thinking: I should get to the studio. I'll be late. And then the nagging feeling crept in—*something bad has happened. You're just too tired to remember. Something terrible.*

Like a flash, it came back to me. Mudge on the bathroom floor, the men from the studio, the coroner taking her away.

I wanted to go back to sleep so that I wouldn't have to think about it or remember, but instead I got up, pulled on a robe, and went downstairs. She was everywhere—her perfume, her photos, the throw pillows she loved to look at but hated to sit on, the piano she didn't know how to play, a pair of her high heels set neatly by the closet door because Flora had no doubt picked them up from the living room floor and put them there.

Even with all of this, the house felt empty, as if it had died too. Mudge's overnight bag was where I had left it in the entryway. I picked it up and carried it upstairs to her room, where I sorted through the clothes and shoes, her hand mirror, flask, magazines, hat, and her silver wings.

I set her powder and lipsticks and face cream on the vanity table along with her brush and comb. I didn't bother unpacking the other things, but I pulled out the jewelry. At the bottom of the bag, I spied a piece of cream-colored paper, Ophelia Lloyd's name at the top.

Dear Miss Fanning, Please enjoy your time at Broad Water. The only place off-limits to you is my husband's bedroom. Perhaps this time you will remember that. In other words, make yourself at home, but not too much at home. Cordially yours, Ophelia Lloyd.

• • • • •

Mudge's death covered the front page of every newspaper. The stories all said the same thing: During a celebratory weekend for *Home of the Brave*, beautiful and glamorous Barbara Fanning had died. The nation mourned Mallory Rourke.

At the studio, I drove past reporters looming and clamoring outside the gates and went directly to Howard Strickling's office, where Tauby, Miss Lloyd, and the rest of their weekend guests were gathered. Mr. Strickling and Mr. Mannix sat hunched over in their chairs.

Mr. Strickling said, "Because of the delicate situation involving Nigel and Barbara and the fact that he's a married man, our lawyers have advised us not to mention Miss Palmer's presence."

Tauby frowned. "But she was there when police arrived."

"She was in her room by the time they got there. Police detectives will be here at eleven to interview you. We ask that you remember the things we went over Saturday evening before the police and Coroner Nigh showed up." And then, in case we'd forgotten, he repeated them: An innocent game; a terrible accident; a call to the police as soon as we found her (at twelve forty-five a.m.); just like Primmie Niven ("Mention Primmie Niven.") . . . *That's all, thank you, the end.*

• • • • •

Three hours later, in Louis B. Mayer's office, two uniformed detectives and two plainclothes detectives thanked me for coming and offered me a seat beside Mr. Strickling, Mr. Mannix, Whitey Hendry, and two men I assumed were Metro lawyers.

Mr. Mayer sat behind his desk. He nodded at me. "No reason to be nervous, Kit. Just tell them what happened."

I recognized one of the suited detectives as Nick Agresta. Under thick black brows, he smiled at me, but it made him look slick instead of friendly. He said, "We won't keep you long, Miss Rogers. Since you were the one who found Miss Fanning . . ."

One of the lawyers said, "She's already given you her statement."

"Understood. Just a question or two. Procedure." He sighed. "Am I right that your brother was there? One Johnny Clay Hart?"

"He was there during the day. He left after dinner."

"What time would you say that was?"

"Around nine, maybe a little before."

"Why didn't he stay the night?"

"He's a musician. He and his band were playing Saturday at the Downbeat."

"Central Avenue?"

"Yes."

"Your brother was friends with Miss Fanning as well?"

"They'd only just met through me."

"I see. By the way, you were something else in *Home of the Brave*. Quite a splash for your first picture. Started your next one yet?"

"Yes, actually a while ago." I wondered what this had to do with Mudge and the investigation.

"Do we get to see more of Betsy Ross or is it another character?"

"Another character."

"One more thing." He fished a pen from his jacket pocket. "If one of you gentlemen has a piece of paper, I'd love to get her autograph for my niece."

"We can do better than that," said Mr. Strickling. "We'll get her publicist up here with a stack of photos."

Mr. Mayer buzzed Ida Koverman and told her to get Bernie on the line.

Mr. Strickling said to Lieutenant Detective Agresta, "How old is your niece?"

"Twelve, maybe thirteen."

"In that case we'll get him to bring up some official Kit Rogers merchandise—your niece is too old for coloring books, but how does a candy box, some badges, and a music box sound?"

"It sounds like I'm her favorite uncle."

I cleared my throat. "Did you want to ask me about the way I found her and what she went through before she died?"

The room fell silent, and I suddenly felt like the uninvited other woman, showing up unannounced. Nick Agresta made a show of flipping through pages in his notebook, where he hadn't written anything down. "I think I have all that here. I'll let you know if I come up with any other questions."

· · · · ·

Sam was waiting for me in the lobby of the Thalberg Building. When he saw me, he smiled, but it looked forced. "Pipes." He opened one of the glass front doors, and we stepped out into the day, bright and blue and sunny.

"I'm on my way to my music lesson, but I'm already late."

"I'll walk you." We went down the stairs and past the gate and the line of cars waiting to get in.

"The detective barely asked anything."

"That's because he's on the payroll."

"What do you mean?"

"The studio keeps men in every police department in the city, just in case Whitey Hendry can't get to the scene first. Strickling handles the press, Hendry handles the law."

"So why interview us at all?"

"Because it doesn't look good if they don't at least pretend to go through the motions."

"They can't get away with that."

"They can. And they have. And they will again as long as there's a studio system. It was worse in the thirties. Anyone could be bought back then."

In Tin Pan Alley, I could hear music coming from Rosie's studio. My Monday afternoon singing class. Just like any other Monday afternoon. Except that it wasn't.

"You said something this weekend about the guest list being straight out of the gossip columns. What did you mean by that?" We weren't walking now; we were standing.

"It's a small town, Pipes. Everyone's connected."

"But you were talking about the party."

"Babe King and Redd Deeley. Redd Deeley and Barbara Fanning. Barbara and Nigel Gray. Nigel and Pia Palmer. Pia and Felix Roland. Ophelia and Tauby, of course. Taub and almost every actress who's ever gone under contract to MGM. Taub and Shelby Jordan, who divorced him to marry Collie Fedderson, who divorced her so she could marry Roland. Which brings me to Collie and Hal—the jury's still debating that one, so mark it as conjecture at this point. Shall I go on?"

"Ophelia Lloyd and the mystery man from her bedroom." *Mudge and Tauby.*

"You get the picture."

"How do you know all this?"

"When I first got here I—let's call it *dated* a gossip columnist."

"Of course you did."

"It's good to see you smile."

"It's good to know I can." I could feel the smile going, even as I tried to hold on to it.

"Let me take you to dinner, Pipes." His tone had shifted. I could hear concern there, which was the last thing I wanted.

"I can't tonight." I might have gone to dinner with flirty, wise-cracking Sam, but instead it would be sweet, concerned Sam who was possibly in love with me, and he would only make me cry and lean on him, and I couldn't cry yet because I had to figure out what had happened to Mudge, and plan her funeral, and get through this somehow.

"Another time, then."

"Sure."

He smiled, easy, charming. "You just let me know."

Inside his studio, Rosie looked up from the piano. He pushed the bench back and lumbered toward me. "There you are," he said, and it was so simple and so kind and so like Daddy Hoyt. He patted me on the back and said it again. "There you are."

I wanted to run out the door, far away from him and all that sweetness and concern, but instead I let him lead me across the room and set me on the piano bench, where he said, "There you are, there you are," as I started to cry.

· · · · ·

On Tuesday, December 31, Nigel Gray met with reporters at his Mandeville Canyon home. He said he was glad to cooperate, glad to answer any questions regarding the death of Barbara Fanning and that he had nothing to hide. When asked about the nature of his relationship with Mudge, he said, "My wife and I have been apart for years. Due to our demanding schedules, we agreed long ago to end the marriage amicably, staying together in name only for the sake of our children. I didn't set out to fall in love with someone else. To be perfectly frank, as Pia will tell you, I'm married to my career. But then I began work on *Home of the Brave*, and—well—I met Miss Fanning."

At this point, Louella Parsons wrote, *He shrugged with all the innocence of a boy—a boy who has just lost the brightest light in his life.*

Where were the children now? Back in England with the nanny. And when did Pia plan to return to them? In a week or two. Would Nigel be going with her? He wasn't sure. It depended on his work schedule.

Throughout the interview, Pia sat beside him, looking "composed." When asked to comment, she said, "I am glad I could be here for Nigel during this time. I only wish I could have been there during the weekend, when he needed me. I will do my best to help him get past this. But don't forget that I also mourn the loss of my dear friend Barbara Fanning."

The headlines read: "Actor Nigel Gray Faces Questioning in Actress's Death." The newspapers speculated about Nigel's relationship with Mudge, as the gossip columnists, kept on a firm leash by the studio publicists, wrote about Nigel without using his name. Dorothy Manners reported, "They say the shocking death of Barbara Fanning was due to an accidental fall during a party game, but knowing the bright, laughing girl well, I believe she died of a broken heart and loneliness. She had been deeply in love with a married man who refused to leave his wife to marry her."

· · · · ·

I spent New Year's Eve night at home alone, my birthday present from Mudge on my lap. It was a 1930s National steel guitar, built out of brass and covered in nickel silver. The face was engraved with a lily of the valley design, the flowers and vines twining their way across the surface. The strings were raised high off the ebony fingerboard so they could be played with a metal slide, or an old broken bottle top, like the one Butch Dawkins always used.

I ran my hands over it, feeling the cool nickel, tracing the lilies. Then I tried out the metal slide, moving it across the strings, trying to sound out a melody on the guitar. The guitar was heavy and I wasn't used to the strings and the slide. I would have to learn to play it, just like I was learning everything else. In fits and starts, I played for an hour or two, maybe longer, and then I stretched out on the floor and closed my eyes.

I would need to talk to Mudge's lawyers about the will and deal with her papers and figure out what to do about Flora. Because Mudge didn't have any family, all the loose ends, everything there was to do, would fall to me.

Mudge will never know a single day of this year. As each week passes, she'll begin to disappear, until she'll be just a memory — that poor, dead actress who left us too soon. What was her name? She was in that movie, Home of the Brave. *You know the one. Fell down at Ophelia Lloyd's house and bumped her head.*

I must have drifted off, because I woke up to the sound of banging. A voice outside hollered, "Open up, Velva Jean. It's cold out here."

Johnny Clay stood on my front step. He hugged me hard and said, "We came to check on you and make sure you're okay."

Butch was walking up after him. He said, "I'm sorry about your friend."

We went on in and I sat on the sofa while Johnny Clay poured us drinks. He dropped down next to me and said, "What happened, little sister?"

I told them everything. When I was done, they had a hundred questions—about Nigel, about Pia, about Strickling and Mannix and Hendry.

"They said it was an accident."

My brother sat back. "You don't believe it."

"They're working awfully hard to cover things up and keep control over what we say and who we talk to."

"What happens next?"

"I don't know."

I thought of asking Butch why he hadn't come to Broad Water when he told me he would, but instead I said, "Tell me about the record."

Butch shook his head. "I was actually going to ask if you'd mind writing a song and singing it. But you got too much on that plate right now, girl."

An hour or so later, when my eyes grew heavy, Johnny Clay stood up and said, "I'll be back tomorrow to check on you. Unless you want me to stay."

"You go. I'm fine. I'll be fine."

I walked them out, and on the street in front of the house, a motorcycle shone black and heavy, with chrome that gleamed like a devil in the moonlight. I ran my fingers along the sleek, curved lines of it. "When did you get it?"

Butch said, "About a week ago. Want to try it out?" At first, I thought he was offering me a ride, but he waved at the seat. He showed me how to climb on, and I held on to my skirt as I swung my leg over, pulling it up just over my knees once I sat down. I wrapped my hands around the handlebars and closed my eyes. I could almost feel the wind on my face and in my hair. If I rode away right now, I could outdistance everything that had happened. I would be free.

"It's a 1940 Indian 440, bought off a guy I know down on Central Avenue. Four-cylinder engine that's been rebuilt to go faster, and rides as smooth as water."

"How fast can it go?"

"I don't know yet." A lazy smile crept across his face. "One hundred twenty, one hundred thirty miles per hour. You look good on there. I'll have to take you for a ride sometime." Johnny Clay was glancing back and forth between us, frowning.

I said, "I'd like that." Hang sometime, I thought. I wanted to ride right now, for days and days, until we ran out of land. I wanted to go faster than 130 mph, until I was only a blur to everyone else, to myself. I sat back, running my hands over the chrome.

"You sure you don't want me to stay?" Johnny Clay said.

"I'm sure."

I didn't want them to go and I didn't want to get down, but Butch held the bike steady, waiting. I climbed off, and stood watching as he swung onto it, and then Johnny Clay swung up behind, the air around us pulsing from the grumble of the engine.

I watched and waved as they rumbled away, like a B-17 taking flight. When the taillight faded, I went inside. The house felt too empty.

It was a brand-new year and Mudge was dead.

EIGHTEEN

The studio was closed New Year's Day, but I was back to work on Thursday, January 2. On Stage 4, I sat through rehearsal of the third *Flyin' Jenny*, which we were scheduled to begin shooting January 20. It felt strange to be back under the catwalks, in the great cavern of the soundstage. The cameras stood dark and still, like men turned to stone.

Les Edgar was directing. When we first saw each other, his eyes—red around the rims—looked so troubled and sympathetic that I wanted to run. Instead, I let myself be hugged, and when he asked how I was, I nodded and said, "I just miss her."

"I do too. She was one of my favorite people. She reminded me of why I got into this business in the first place—to direct genuine talent."

We were a small crew, just director, assistant director, wardrobe, cameraman, and a few others, including Hal, me, Babe, and Phillip Drake, guest-starring as Buck Rogers. Felix Roland's wife, Shelby Jordan, was on the set, but I couldn't imagine why since she worked for Warner Bros., not Metro. She sat by herself, one leg crossed over the other, twirling her sunglasses as she watched the actors.

Mudge hadn't even been dead a week, and there we were, business as usual. Report to the studio. Report to hair and makeup. Memorize lines. Learn songs. Take classes. Start filming the next picture.

"What's Shelby Jordan doing here?" I asked Babe.

"I don't know."

Everyone but Shelby stood in a tight circle as Les addressed us. "It isn't just the studio that has suffered a loss. Each of us has worked with Barbara, and so the loss is personal as well." Babe found my hand and squeezed it. "I want to know how you're doing and what you need, and together we'll get through this hard time."

· · · · ·

Johnny Clay came back that night by himself, driving my secondhand car, the one I'd given him. He left early Friday morning. Three hours later, I met Redd Deeley outside Stage 5 because he'd said he wanted to discuss something important. When I got there, he held up a key.

"What's this?"

"The key to your new dressing room." He began walking toward the barracks building, and I fell in step beside him.

"Why am I getting a new dressing room?"

"Not just any dressing room." He led me to the star suites, up the stairs and past the doors that read "Lana Turner," "Esther Williams," "Greer Garson," to one that read "Kit Rogers." He unlocked the door, pushed it open, and inside it looked exactly like a large, comfortable living room, decorated in cheery red and white. A red vanity table was built into the wall at one end, a door beside it leading to an enormous bathroom. Another door opened onto a walk-in closet. A full bar, stocked with various bottles and crystal glasses and a gold ice bucket already filled with ice, covered one wall. I could still smell the paint.

Redd handed me the key. "That's not all." From under his arm, he pulled out a sheaf of papers. "Your new contract."

"I'm not up for renegotiation yet."

"Apparently *Home of the Brave*'s box office is making Mayer feel generous. One thousand dollars a week. It's Christmas all over again."

"What's the catch?"

"No catch, other than pairing yourself romantically with Hal MacGinnis, which we could have predicted. Take a spin or two at Ciro's, eat a steak at Tom Breneman's, share a milk shake at Schwab's, let the public think you're an item. This is good news, kid. It's okay to be glad about it."

"I don't know what to say. Did everyone on the film get new contracts or just me?"

"You, Nigel, Hal, Babe, Ophelia. I don't know about the others because I don't represent them."

"Is this . . . normal after a movie does well?"

"Not at all. Not like this." Redd poured us each a drink.

I thanked him, took a sip. "Did Mudge ever mention a Rebecca to you? Maybe a girl at the studio or a part she played, or someone she knew while you were married?"

He narrowed his eyes into the distance. "No. At least I can't think of anyone. Maybe she was a friend outside of work? Or a fan?"

"Maybe she was family?"

He shook his head and gave a sad smile. "The only family Barbara had was me, her friends, Flora, and this studio." Then he tipped his glass back and drank.

· · · · ·

When I got home that night, I expected to see my brother, but instead Zed Zabel was parked in front of the house. As I pulled in the driveway, he stalked toward me like a man with a mission. "Busy day?"

"Go away, Zed."

"Be happy to after you answer a question for me."

"Just one?"

"For now. I want to know what went on at Broad Water last weekend."

"That's not a question." I brushed by him to the front door, digging for my keys.

"I'll rephrase it, then. What went on at Broad Water last weekend? Let me guess, Strickling and Mannix were first on the scene. Hendry too, I imagine. They gussied up the body, gussied up the guests, got everyone in line, and *then* called police."

"I can't talk to you."

"Can't or won't?"

"Both."

"All right, but you will. Once you get tired of being told to shut up."

"I don't know what you're talking about."

"You will. By the way? Congratulations on the new contract. I'm sure you'll do everything you can to earn it."

"Goodnight, Mr. Zabel." I turned the key and slipped inside, shutting the door before he could say another word.

· · · · ·

At ten thirty a.m. Monday, January 6, I reported to the Hall of Justice, a fourteen-story white granite building with an arched entranceway. Reporters were gathered outside its doors like vultures tracking the wounded. In an inquest, witnesses testify in front of jurors, but this was what they called an "informal" inquest, which meant we were to be interviewed privately in the coroner's office so that he could determine whether an inquest would be needed at all.

Bernie was in charge of getting me there on time, and as we walked toward the building, he said, "Don't be nervous. This is simply routine. They want to ask you a few questions, but nothing you haven't already answered for police."

We reached the front doors just as Mr. Mannix and Mr. Strickling were walking in with Nigel Gray. More reporters circled inside, humming and hovering until they caught sight of Nigel shadowed by Mr. Mayer's top two men. This shut them up instantly. The cameramen stood, cameras in their hands or at their sides, flashbulbs stilled. As we passed by, up the iron-and-brass stairs of the lobby, through marble columns, past marble archways, a copper-colored ceiling over our heads, someone said, "Well, there's the end of the whole goddamn case."

The Hall of Justice housed the sheriff's department, the public defender, the district attorney, and the municipal courts. The coroner's office was on the ground floor, in the windowless belly of the building. Unlike the one above, this hallway was cramped, the air smelling of formaldehyde.

Inside the chambers, the witnesses were assembled—Nigel, Billy

Taub, Ophelia Lloyd, Felix Roland, Bernie, Strickling, Mannix, Dr. Atwill, Whitey Hendry. The entire cast of Metro's loyalest supporters. Also Lieutenant Detective Nick Agresta, five of MGM's attorneys, and my brother.

I took a chair beside Johnny Clay. "What are you doing here?"

"Didn't you hear? The police invited me."

One after another, witnesses were called into the coroner's office. One walked out, another walked in. I glanced up, making sure no one was listening to us. I caught Nick Agresta's eye and looked away. "Why do they want to talk to you? You weren't even there."

"I don't know. They came to the Dunbar and told me to get my ass over here."

I heard my name. Johnny Clay nodded his head at me, winked, gave me that smile that said everything's okay, you'll see, we've been through worse, even though I knew a part of him must have been as nervous as I was. As I stood, Howard Strickling and two of the MGM lawyers stood also and followed me into the coroner's office.

As a mousy girl with a bored expression typed along, I stated my name and address and swore to tell the truth to Coroner Nigh, the man in the gray suit who'd shown up at Broad Water. The country doctor, Frederick Murdoch, who wasn't a country doctor at all but chief autopsy surgeon for the County of Los Angeles, made notes on a legal pad.

Coroner Nigh said, "Was the deceased someone you knew in life?"

"She was."

"What was her name?"

"Eloise Mudge."

"Her legal name was Barbara Fanning. Is this the person you mean?"

"Yes, but I wasn't aware she'd changed her name."

"She changed her name legally in 1935. On December twenty-ninth, you were the one who found the body?"

"I found her on December twenty-eighth."

"Why do you say December twenty-eighth?"

"Because I found her before midnight."

I heard one of the lawyers shift in his chair. He said, "Miss Rogers is confused about the time."

"I'm not. There are clocks all over Broad Water, which made it easy to keep track of what time it was."

The coroner made a note on a legal pad of his own before continuing. "She was dead when you discovered her?"

"No."

"She was still alive?"

"Yes."

Here, he frowned at Howard Strickling, who said, "I believe all of this has been covered and re-covered, Ben."

"I'm interested in covering it again." To me, the coroner said, "What time was this?"

"Approximately eleven forty-five p.m."

"The record indicates she was discovered at a later time."

"I found her at eleven forty-five p.m."

Mr. Strickling said, "You have to understand that it was a hell of a night. Miss Rogers was in shock—the discovery of her friend's body—"

"I didn't discover her body; I discovered her. She was still alive when I found her."

When one of the lawyers started to speak, Coroner Nigh spoke over him. "You are certain of the time you found her?"

I looked at Mr. Strickling. "Yes."

"What did you do when you found her?"

"I checked for a pulse and noticed a rapid heartbeat, very faint. I shouted for help and tried to resuscitate her."

"Did you discover any wounds on the person?"

"A bump on the forehead."

"What position was the body lying in?"

"She was lying across the bathroom floor on her right side."

"You didn't find her lying facedown, as noted?"

"No, sir. She was lying on her right side. I had to roll her onto her back to try to revive her." I could hear both Mr. Strickling and the lawyers muttering and shifting.

"And where did you learn this method of resuscitation?"

"During my time as a WASP."

"Dr. Edwin Atwill arrived shortly after and took over examination and treatment, is that right?"

"Yes."

"The person died not long after, is that right?"

"Yes."

"You were present at the moment of death?"

"Yes, sir."

"How would you describe the behavior of the person in that final moment?"

"She suffered violent convulsions before losing consciousness."

"She was suffering convulsions?"

"Yes, sir."

"The victim was not, to your knowledge, epileptic?"

"No, sir."

"Earlier that day, did the person act in any peculiar or unusual way prior to her death?"

"She couldn't stop laughing and she was talking nonsense, as if she'd had too much to drink. Her face was flushed and when I found her she was burning up, like she had a fever."

"The person had been drinking?"

"Yes."

"For how long?"

"I'm not sure what time she started, but I smelled alcohol on her after dinner. I think she had been drinking earlier in the day."

As Mr. Strickling emphasized that Barbara Fanning was by no means an alcoholic, that she was merely in a celebratory frame of mind following the premiere of *Home of the Brave*, Coroner Nigh consulted his notes and consulted Dr. Murdoch in hushed tones. Finally, he looked up again and said to me, "The statement is correct—that is your testimony in relation to the matter, under oath, is it?"

"Yes, sir."

By now, my heart was thudding in my chest, so loud I could hear it in my ears. I didn't look at Mr. Strickling or the lawyers, although I could feel their eyes on me. I folded my hands in my lap and stared straight ahead, until Coroner Nigh thanked me for my time and said I could go.

Back in the secretary's office, I sat down and caught my breath, as if I'd run for miles. Mr. Strickling and the lawyers followed me out and formed a huddle with Eddie Mannix and Whitey Hendry. When the next person was called—Nigel—Mr. Strickling and the lawyers followed him in. This happened with each witness. I wondered where Sam and Babe and Hal and the other guests were, and then everyone but Johnny Clay had been interviewed, and when it was his turn, Mr. Strickling and the lawyers thanked the coroner and Dr. Murdoch and put on their hats and went home. Johnny Clay went in alone.

Because I was the only one left, the secretary and I talked about movies and the weather until the telephone rang. She was still talking twenty minutes later when my brother walked out, shaking Coroner Nigh's hand, shaking the hand of Dr. Murdoch. The secretary stared at my brother, placing the phone in its cradle, and when he winked at her and kissed her hand, she almost passed out on the floor. "And what's your name?" he asked her.

"Lara," she breathed. "Lara Yacoubian. You should go out this way to avoid the reporters." She showed us the back door. After a short flight of stairs we were up and outside, on the Broadway side of the building. The sky was a bright blue. I breathed in the fresh air.

"What did they ask you?" I asked Johnny Clay at the same moment he asked me.

He lit up a cigarette, his hand shaking a little. "Shit, Velva Jean. Shit." He inhaled and let the smoke out. "They asked me how well did I know her, and what was going on between us. What did Nigel Gray think of the two of us being so chummy? Was he jealous? Did he say anything to me that day? Did he tell me to stay away from his girlfriend?" He inhaled again, let it out. "The worst kind of trouble is the kind you don't go looking for."

"I need to know something."

He fixed me with a look. "Was anything going on between me and Mudge?"

"Yes."

He didn't blink or flinch. He looked at me straight. "No. Not the way you mean."

"You looked friendly Saturday night."

"Yeah, but that's all it was, and that was mostly her anyway. She was sore at her boyfriend, and I knew it. I was only helping her out because the guy's a louse. Scout's honor." He held up his fingers and spat on the street, as if to prove it.

"The thing that bothers me the most, Johnny Clay, is that it's too much like the WASP. A girl died, but no one's doing anything about it. Instead of answering police questions—real questions—I'm signing autographs. They tell reporters she died from a fall, and they tell us what to say, and then they sit there in that inquest, ready to pounce if I tell what really happened. Meanwhile, I'm being handed new contracts and moving into a fancy new dressing room and starting new pictures. It's like my friend Sally Hallatassee all over again. Like the time I almost died because Bob Keene sabotaged my plane, and everyone just sat there and said, 'Accidents happen.'"

We rounded the corner and Zed Zabel stood leaning against the wall, as if the sheer weight of his ego was holding up the building. "Kit Rogers. I wondered when you'd appear."

Johnny Clay said to me, "Who's this?"

"No one." I kept walking, looking up and down the street in front of the Hall of Justice. I'd come with Bernie, but I didn't see his car.

Zed charged after us. "You ready to talk yet? Because I'm hearing some pretty nasty rumors about the cause of death. I wonder what you can tell me?"

I said to Johnny Clay, "Did you drive?"

"I took the streetcar."

"I can take you home, Kit. Give us a chance to have a nice, long chat."

Johnny Clay took my elbow, steering me away as fast as he could. "I don't like his face."

I heard a honking horn, and Bernie's car came swinging up along the curb.

Zed called, "Johnny Clay Hart?" We turned at the same time. Before I could ask how he knew my brother's name, there was a snap and a flash.

My brother threw down his cigarette and swaggered over to Zed Zabel. "Hey, nice camera. Can I see?" Before the reporter knew what hit him, Johnny Clay pulled the plate out of the camera and dropped it onto the ground, smashing it under his heel.

"Fuck you, Hart. I'll just charge MGM for a new one. We can put it on your sister's tab."

"You don't have to." Johnny Clay handed him a ten-dollar bill. As my brother and I moved away, Zed Zabel stood watching us go, too quiet for comfort. I took my brother's arm and held on to him firmly. He was here and alive and breathing. He said, "You're going to be fine, little sister. You need to trust me on that."

We were at the car too soon. I wanted to keep walking, keep my arm through his, but suddenly we broke apart.

"I can come back over tonight and stay if you want."

"I'm okay, Johnny Clay. You can't stop your life for me."

He screwed up his face and gazed up toward the sun. "I'm always going to be right here," he said to the sky. "I'll never leave you, Velva Jean. Don't you ever worry about that." It was what he'd said to me when Mama died.

"Promise?"

"Promise." He offered me his hand and we shook on it, just as we had when I was ten and he was twelve.

In the car, Bernie wanted to know about Zed Zabel—what he wanted, what he'd asked. As we headed northwest on Temple, crossing the streetcar tracks, I said, "Where were all the other guests? Hal? Babe? Sam Weldon?"

"There were so many of us that weekend. You know." He glanced at me, shrugged. "Mr. Mayer and the detectives in charge thought it best to offer only key witnesses; otherwise there would be so much repeat testimony. Longer for everyone involved, then no one gets anything done."

"Has this happened before with one of their stars? A sudden death like this?"

"I'm sure it has."

"Are they always so protective?"

"This is Metro, kiddo. We're a family. That means we look after our own. Someone's hurt or in trouble, we rally."

In front of the house, we said good night, and as I came up the walk I could see something on the front step. I tucked my purse under my arm and bent to pick it up—a bouquet of white gardenias, tied with twine. No note, just flowers. Gardenias in winter, even though they were out of season. Full and sweet and alive.

· · · · ·

The morning after the hearing, I was called to Mr. Mayer's office, where he leaned on his desk, hands folded, and explained the importance of loyalty and discretion while Mr. Strickling and Mr. Mannix looked on, as stoic as Mount Rushmore.

Mr. Mayer said, "Miss Rogers, talent is like a precious stone." I glanced at Mr. Strickling and resisted arching an eyebrow. *Really, Mr. Mayer? You don't say.* In my head, I recited it along with him. "Like a diamond or a ruby. You take care of it. You put it in a safe, you clean it, polish it, look after it. Miss Fanning was one of ours. In that way, she was our responsibility, one of our most important stones. Her death was tragic, but there's nothing we can do about the fact that she's gone." Mr. Mayer dabbed at his eyes, dry as they were. "What we can do is protect her and take care of what remains of her—her image and the way she's remembered—as best we can. You need to trust me to do my job, and I need to trust you to do yours."

"You mean lying?"

He flopped back in his chair as if I'd climbed over the desk and struck him. The corners of his mouth dipped so far down, they touched his chin. "I mean repeating the facts as we've discussed them, and remembering that we are, here at Metro, a family. Family looks after family." His voice was terse. "It's terrible enough that Barbara Fanning is dead. There's nothing to be gained by leaving the public with a last, gruesome image of her dying of convulsions on a bathroom floor."

CUPID STRIKES KIT ROGERS
"Love will help me through this sad time."
Modern Screen
January 8, 1947

Hal MacGinnis and Kit Rogers are costarring as Jenny Dare and Rick Davis in the *Flyin' Jenny* films, and now, it seems, they are costarring in life. Handsome Hal, who once dated the late Barbara Fanning, first met Kit on the set of *Home of the Brave*, her first picture.

It's a situation neither expected to be in, given the fact that they are in deep mourning for their mutual friend. Grief has brought them together because they understand what it means to lose someone so dear—and so suddenly. On the nights Hal works late, Kit waits for him as a dutiful sweetheart should. When he's finished, they tear away in his car (or hers) and take in a movie. If he's too tired, they just sit and talk.

Kit and her beau seldom join the café set because, as Kit says, "This isn't the time for parties. We just lost Barbara, and the last thing we feel like doing is dancing the night away at the Trocadero." They prefer private time, during which they share memories of Barbara Fanning, often share tears, and cheer each other onward. Their busy careers often make this difficult, but, as Hal says, "At least we know we can count on seeing each other on the set."

It's an upside-down situation, but love's a funny thing. No matter what they've been through and how they got together, we're still betting that their love will prevail.

NINETEEN

The funeral service was held Saturday, January 11, at Forest Lawn Memorial Park's Church of the Recessional, in Glendale. When we arrived by studio limousine, the streets outside were lined with cars, buses, and taxis. Thousands of people walked to the church from all directions, and thousands more gathered inside the cemetery grounds. I wore a gardenia in my hair.

It was unusually warm for January. The sun was blazing. There was no breeze. The limousine dropped Flora and Johnny Clay and me in front of the church, which sat on the side of a hill, surrounded by tall trees. It was a storybook chapel made of stone, and even though it only sat 150, some eight or nine thousand people surrounded it. Policemen barricaded a red carpet, which led from the cemetery road to the main entrance of the church. We walked down this as fans waved autograph books. "Kit!" they called. "Kit Rogers!" they shouted. I stared at the ground, at my own feet. When a girl threw her pencil in my direction, trying to get my attention, Johnny Clay picked it up and threw it right back at her. I heard the popping of flashbulbs and the shattering of glass as they dropped to the sidewalk.

Inside, the chapel was overfilled with flowers. My head went light from the smell. Through a doorway, I could see the pallbearers gathered. I caught a glimpse of the church itself, of people already seated, and, at the front of the room, the mahogany casket.

Someone ushered us into a back room, the one reserved for family. At twelve fifteen, Bishop Wade Lyman appeared and spoke in low tones. "It's time. If you'll follow me."

We were taken to the main entry, just outside the chapel itself. We stood outside the doors, waiting to go in, and when she saw the coffin, Flora's face crumpled. The church doors stood open, and I could hear the voices of the fans gathered outside.

A few minutes before twelve thirty, Redd Deeley arrived. A minute later, the voices of the crowd rose to a roar. I turned to see Billy Taub and Ophelia Lloyd walking up the red carpet, arm in arm. There was another roar as Nigel Gray, by himself, walked past the crowd, hands reaching for him.

Then Bishop Lyman was leading us up the middle aisle, and all the people already seated in the church turned to stare. There were famous faces and nonfamous faces. Down toward the front I passed Butch Dawkins and a young colored man, wearing their best suits.

A cross of pink roses sat in front of the coffin. An arrangement of yellow roses sat at the head, sent from my friend Gossie, who had never even met Mudge. A huge bouquet of white roses sat at its foot. A large attached card read: *Mr. and Mrs. Louis B. Mayer.*

Suddenly, I was looking down at Mudge, her eyes closed, her lips on the verge of a smile. Fresh roses were pinned to her shoulders, along with her silver wings, the only jewelry she wore. She held a nosegay of roses in her hands. She looked peaceful, as if she was sleeping, as if she was a fairy-tale princess waiting to be kissed awake. I said, "Mudge. It's me."

She lay still, her eyes closed, her lips on the verge of a smile. I was ten years old again and staring down at my mama, wanting her to get up, waiting for her to wake. I was twenty-four years old, saying goodbye to one of my best friends. After this moment, I would never see her face again.

I said, "I hope wherever you are, you're okay. I hope it's a better place, and I hope my mama's there to greet you. I hope you don't feel any pain ever again. I hope no one ever hurts you or breaks your heart. I hope you can be happy."

A little woman with white hair played "The Lord's Prayer" and "Ave Maria" on the organ. Then Bishop Lyman took his place at the altar. His voice rang through the church, bouncing from the rafters. I looked up at the altar, at the stained glass windows above the bishop's head. "Whenever there was a call," he was saying, "she always came; witness her war experiences flying for the WASP. Witness all the loved ones here today who loved her in return. She had a lot of friends. From the doors of hell, deliver her soul. May she rest in peace."

Bishop Lyman moved aside and a man took his place to sing "The Lord's Prayer." Then I walked to the front of the church, past the coffin. As I did, Billy Taub and Ophelia Lloyd stood and, side by side, left the church. People turned to watch them go.

I had chosen the songs—"Wild Blue Yonder," and "Beyond the Keep," which I'd written when I was in the WASP. As I sang, the people from each bench stood and, one by one, came forward to pay their respects.

The bishop signaled for the doors to open so that some of the people outside could come in at last to pay tribute. Over a thousand people filed in, walking past the casket. When I finished the song and they were still coming in, I started to sing an old marching tune from our days at training camp in Sweetwater, Texas.

> *In the land of crimson sunsets,*
> *skies are wide and blue,*
> *stands a school of many virtues,*
> *loved by old and new.*

As I was singing, another voice joined in. Loma Edwards stood, hands resting on the pew in front of her, chin up, shoulders back, eyes on mine. She had been bunkmates with Mudge and Sally Hallatassee and me at Avenger Field, but had washed out before graduation.

From somewhere on the other side of the church, another voice blended with ours. It belonged to a tall woman with wavy hair, standing with her arms at her sides. It took me a moment to recognize her because I hadn't seen her since the WASP. Our other bunkmate, Paula Hodges.

> *Gone before are many daughters,*
> *to carry on her name,*
> *may we live in faith and honor,*
> *yet to bring her fame.*

Another voice and another and another came chorusing in, as Janie Bowen and Ruth Needham and Shirley Bingham and my friend Helen Stillbert, all WASP, stood singing. And then a handful of other girls whose faces I recognized, but whose names I couldn't quite place.

And then one more voice joined in. A middle-aged blonde woman, perfectly made up, stood on the edge of one of the back rows next to a man in a wheelchair who I knew was Floyd Odlum, president of RKO. Even from across the room, I could see the silver wings gleaming on her dress. This was Jacqueline Cochran, the woman who had taught us to fly.

> *Long before our duty's ended,*
> *a mem'ry you shall be,*
> *in our hearts we pledge devotion,*
> *Avenger Field to thee!*

When we finished, the room went still. No one spoke. No one moved. No one breathed. And then Paula sang out, "If you have a daughter, teach her how to fly, If you have a son, put the bastard in the sky." Her voice, full and earthy, filled the church.

The rest of the WASP joined her till I thought we'd raise the roof. "Singing zoot suits and parachutes and wings of silver too, he'll ferry planes like his mama used to do." We repeated the lines twice, and on the last time through, the entire congregation was singing.

· · · · ·

At the cemetery, after the burial, Sam took me aside. He said, "I want to make sure you're okay, and I want to make sure you remember to eat a good meal. I guarantee she'd want you to take care of yourself and keep on living."

Someone walked up and coughed once just over my shoulder. Butch said to Sam, "Sorry to interrupt." He held out a white rose. "For you," he said.

I took it from him. *Thank you for the gardenias. Thank you for this.* I opened my mouth but nothing came out. I nodded at him because it was all I could do. My eyes were stinging and a lump was growing in my throat. He nodded at me and backed away, as if to say, *Go on, do what you need to do.* I handed Helen my purse and carried the flower over to the grave. I kneeled down and set it in the middle of the earth, a single white bloom. "Good-bye," I whispered. For that instant, the world seemed to go still.

From somewhere up above, I heard Helen say, "The car's here, Hartsie." And everyone was moving again, saying good-bye. I hugged and was hugged, one friend after another. I thanked them all for coming.

Sam put his hat on and kissed my cheek. His fingers brushed the other cheek like a warm breeze. "You know where I am, Pipes."

"I do," I heard myself say. "But I can't be any good to anyone right now, Sam. I'm sorry." I could see the surprise and maybe the hurt in his face. "I'm sorry," I repeated.

After a long pause, he nodded. "Okay then." He nodded once more. "Thanks for letting me know."

Johnny Clay was saying, "I'll see you back at the house, little sister."

Over his shoulder, I watched Sam walk away and told myself it was for the best.

Inside the car, Helen handed me my purse, and I sat back against the seat, feeling empty. The girls started talking over each other, catching up after all this time.

I stared out the window, the blue sky tinted dark through the glass. The crowd had gone, the cars had gone. The cemetery looked empty, except for a 1940 Indian motorcycle parked at the curb, a black Buick

Roadmaster, and three figures—my brother, Butch, and a young col-ored man—kneeling beside Mudge's grave, cleaning up the ground around it. I craned my neck so I could see through the back window as Butch stood, watching us go.

I promise you I'm doing everything I can to make sure we get to the bottom of this, Miss Cochran had said after Sally was killed. *We don't know that it's sabotage, but if it is, I plan to find out and something will be done about it.*

Only nothing was ever done about it. Not then, not now. Mudge's death was being swept under the carpet just as Sally's had been, and I owed it to her to find out what had happened.

ZED ZABEL'S HOLLYWOOD
"No Fanning Inquest"

HOLLYWOOD, January 13—AP—The DA's office said today no inquest will be held in the death of Barbara Fanning, screen star, who was fatally injured in an accident at the home of Billy Taub and Ophelia Lloyd on December 29.

The coroner's report said merely that the tragedy was accidental. Miss Fanning supposedly took a fatal fall during a parlor game after a dinner party.

District Attorney Carveth Rash said he's satisfied that Miss Fanning's death was accidental, caused by tripping over a rug in the dark and hitting her head. He announced that the investigation is formally closed.

With this news, Nigel Gray is on his way to England for a promotional tour for *Home of the Brave*, and Ophelia Lloyd has checked herself into Rockhaven Sanitarium for "a much needed rest." Her husband, Billy Taub, has begun preproduction work on the Nigel Gray/Babe King starrer *Latimer* with director Felix Roland, as Miss King moves into MGM, having officially left Columbia for what everyone knows are much greener pastures. Miss Fanning's onetime paramour Hal MacGinnis has signed a lucrative contract with *True Story* to write a series of articles about his friendship with the late star. And Kit Rogers is set to premiere her first starring picture for Metro, *Flyin' Jenny: Red, White, and Blonde*, January 15.

Some much needed uplift for the movie crowd in mourning. Seems like life goes on, and quite nicely, for those who keep their minds on the job.

TWENTY

On Monday, I shut myself in my new studio dressing room, and dialed Doan & Mills Funeral Home. While I waited for someone to answer, I looked at my list of things to do: *Write a check to Flora; answer sympathy notes; talk to attorney; go through Mudge's papers; respond to reporters.* Helen was staying for a few days, maybe longer, to help me sort things out, but even so, it was enough to make my head swim. I found a pen in a drawer and wrote: *Find out how Mudge died. Figure out who 'Rebecca' is.*

"Doan and Mills."

"Could I speak to Mr. McCrary, please?"

When the funeral director came on the line, I told him who I was and that I needed to arrange to collect Mudge's belongings.

He said, "I'm sorry. We never received them from the coroner's office. You'll need to get in touch with someone there." With a neat click, we were disconnected. I rummaged for the city directory. I flipped through the pages, and there it was—the number for the Los Angeles County coroner. I picked up the phone and dialed.

"Coroner."

"Coroner Nigh, please."

"I'm sorry, he's not in."

"Do you expect him back today?"

"Yes, but I'm not sure what time."

I thanked her and hung up. I picked up the phone again and dialed.

"Bernie Hanser."

"Bernie, it's Velva Jean. I've come down with the world's worst headache and I need to leave early."

"Sorry to hear that. Have you seen Dr. Atwill?"

"It's just a headache, Bernie. A bad one, but it'll go away after I get a little rest. I'll probably go on home and lie down for a while, maybe take a nap." I knew I only had a few more days, at most, before I would be expected to show up at the usual time without any excuses.

I picked up my purse and my script, and as I was letting myself out, I saw a man with a tool kit crouched outside Mudge's dressing room door, working on the lock. I said, "Excuse me?"

He glanced up, and then kept working.

"What are you doing?"

"Changing the locks."

"I can see that. Who told you to do that?"

He stopped what he was doing. "They need the room."

"We buried her *day before yesterday*. You can't do this. Leave the lock like it is. I'll take the blame. At least give me the chance to collect her things and get them out of there. I have to be somewhere right now, but I can do it tomorrow."

He sighed, dropped his tools, gathered them up, and stood. "Tomorrow."

· · · · ·

I took Wilshire Boulevard downtown to the Hall of Justice. In the coroner's office, I sat in the same hard wooden chair I had sat in my last time there. While the secretary talked on the telephone, my head went light from the formaldehyde. The room reminded me of a doctor's office—bland and badly lit, nothing to make you remember it after you walked out.

The secretary said to me, "Sorry about that, Miss Rogers. Can I help you?" Her tone was friendly and she seemed to remember me. The name plaque on her desk read "Lara Yacoubian, secretary to the Coroner."

I stood. "I'm here to pick up the personal effects of Barbara Fanning."

"And we have them?"

"Yes."

"You're sure?"

"That's what Mr. McCrary at Doan and Mills told me."

"I'll check." She pushed away from the desk.

"Also, I was wondering if I could speak to Coroner Nigh while I'm here."

She picked up the phone and punched a button. "Sir, Kit Rogers is here to see you. . . . Yes. . . ." She glanced at me. "No, sir." She hung up. "He's in a meeting right now."

"I can wait."

"Let me get Miss Fanning's things."

"Thank you."

I waited for ten minutes, wishing I'd brought something to read, thinking of my script in the car. When five more minutes passed, I stood up to stretch my legs, took a little stroll around the office, studied Miss Yacoubian's desk. Typical office accessories, blank piece of stationery in the typewriter: "Office of the Coroner." A neat stack of files, a framed picture of the secretary, arms around a dog, and fresh flowers in a bright green vase.

The telephone rang and I jumped. As I hurried back to my chair, I tripped over her purse, on the floor by her desk, and sent a stack of magazines sliding. I gathered them up and set them back where they'd been, but not before noticing they were movie magazines. There was my face on the cover. There was Mudge, and Mudge again. Pages were dog-eared, all having to do with *Home of the Brave*. I placed the purse on top of them and sat back down.

Not two minutes later, Lara Yacoubian walked in with a small bag labeled "Barbara Fanning." As she handed it to me, I glanced at the ring finger of her left hand, which was bare. I glanced back at her face. She worked in this place surrounded by windowless walls and formaldehyde, yet she had taken the time and care to paint her lips and style her hair and choose a pretty outfit.

She said, "This was all there was. Let us know if anything seems to be missing."

"Do things have a habit of going missing?"

"Sometimes. In high-profile cases. And Barbara Fanning is definitely high profile. Do you still want to wait for him?"

"If I could."

She shrugged to say she didn't care one way or another, and took her seat. She opened a file, began typing a letter. I waited, crossing my legs. In a moment, I switched to the other leg, feeling the weight of the bag on my lap.

I said, "I don't know if you remember my brother. He was with me the other day when we were here."

Her fingers froze on the keys. She glanced at the file she was copying and back at me. "Was he sitting next to you?"

"Yes."

"I remember."

"Well, he said to tell you hello."

Her face lit up like Christmas. "You can tell him hi back. Does he work nearby?"

"He's a musician. He and a friend of ours have a group they play with. Have you ever been to Central Avenue?" She nodded. "He plays there a lot. I think you'd like his music."

"Oh, I'm sure I would."

"He was friends with Barbara Fanning too." I smiled sadly and looked away.

She was leaning forward now, the ends of her hair dangling in the typewriter. "What was she like as a person?"

"Funny, smart. She loved children and animals. Especially dogs." Her eyes flickered down at the picture on her desk. "She was loyal. She was one of the loyalest people I know. *Knew.* Sorry. It's taking some getting used to."

"She was a great actress. She should win an Academy Award for *Home of the Brave*. I mean, you were good too, of course."

"Thanks, but she's the one who deserves it. She gave everything she had to that role." I looked down at my hands.

A few seconds later, I heard her say, "Oh hell," and then she marched over to the door to Coroner Nigh's office and knocked. She waited a moment before letting herself in, and closed the door behind her. In seconds, she was back, followed by Coroner Nigh himself.

He said, "Miss Rogers. I'm sorry to make you wait."

Once inside his office, he offered me a seat. He was barely in his chair before I told him why I was there. "I read about the DA's ruling in the paper. I know the investigation is closed. But why is it closed?"

"The DA felt that all evidence pointed to accidental death."

"Is that what you felt?"

"I can't answer that, Miss Rogers. The DA's decision stands. It doesn't matter what I think."

"So you don't think it was accidental."

"I didn't say that."

"I saw her die, and there was nothing natural about it. I saw the way Whitey Hendry and the others fixed up the scene before you got there." I told him about the studio photographer, the moving of the body.

"Pretty serious allegations, especially when I'm assuming you don't have those original photographs to prove any tampering was done."

"It's a serious matter. My friend is dead, and believe me, I want to move on. If there was a way to get my hands on those photos, I would, but you know as well as I do that if they still exist, they're locked up so tight in some secret location that they might as well *not* exist." I perched on the very edge of my chair. "Tell me there's no reason to second-guess anything that happened here. I want you to tell me that, if you believe it."

"It's out of my hands."

"I'm a war hero, sir. Did you know that? That's what they tell me anyway. I only did what I had to do to stay alive and survive. I did what needed to be done. That's what I'm trying to do here, nothing else. I don't want to get anyone into trouble, but I want to do what I can do for my friend because she's not here to fight for herself. She would have done the same for me."

He said, "I'm sorry about your friend. I wish I could give you the peace of mind you're looking for, but I can't."

• • • • •

I was almost to my car when I heard someone calling my name. Lara Yacoubian came racing toward me on high heels as tall as she was, her black hair turning reddish in the sun. She was carrying the bag of Mudge's personal effects. "You forgot this," she said when she reached me.

"Thank you." I had left it behind on purpose, hoping she would come after me.

As she handed me the bag, she said, "You met Dr. Murdoch, the chief autopsy surgeon?" I nodded. "Well, Dr. Murdoch said he needed more time. He sent the organs to the lab for analysis, but the DA closed the case before the results came back. Murdoch knew from the autopsy what didn't kill Barbara Fanning, but the investigation was closed before he could say what did."

"Is it possible to get a copy of the coroner's report?"

She shook her head. "The report was sealed."

Before I could thank her, she went hurrying away. I looked down at the bag, and on the top, under the label, was a card: *Frederick Murdoch, M.E. Telephone: CR6-6633*, and below the card a slip of paper with her name and number. *Please give this to your brother.*

• • • • •

At home, Helen was out, and Flora was already gone for the day. In Mudge's office, I sat on the corner of the desk and dialed Dr. Frederick Murdoch. The wall across from me was a floor-to-ceiling mural featuring a life-size Mudge in flying gear.

A woman's voice answered. She could have been the doctor's secretary or his wife—it was hard to know if I was calling him at the office or at home.

"Dr. Murdoch, please." I stared up at Mudge's smiling face.

"I'm sorry, he's not expected till later. Could I take a message and have him call you?"

"Thank you. No message. I'll phone him again." I clicked off.

In the living room, I sat down and opened the package of Mudge's belongings. Her perfume wafted out like a genie from a bottle. It was so strong that for one moment I expected her to appear. I sorted through the contents—a gold and diamond watch, a pair of gold earrings, and her purse. Inside the purse were her pressed powder compact, her lipstick, a lighter, the carving of the flying girl, and cigarettes. The two pill bottles were missing.

I opened the lipstick, winding the little stick of color out as far as it would go. It was half-used, the top of it rounded and flat. I turned it over to read the label: "Firecracker Red." I counted the cigarettes—four left in the package. I picked up the lighter, which was sleek and smooth, except for initials etched into one side: *JCH*.

I snapped the head of it once, twice, till a flame shot up. I waved it this way, then that, the fire flickering and fluttering and changing shape. That's why they're asking about Johnny Clay, I thought. Not only did everyone see them together the day she died; she was carrying his lighter.

. . . . .

It didn't take long to pack up three boxes of knickknacks and books in Mudge's star suite while one of the Thalberg Building secretaries paced around with a clipboard, checking things off her list: window treatments, living room sofa, living room chairs, living room coffee table, portable bar, lightbulbs. All of it was gone over in the nittiest, grittiest detail to make sure no studio property had been removed.

When she was done, the secretary handed me a copy of the list and said, "I am sorry about Miss Fanning. We're all going to miss her. I'll lock up behind you." Which meant she needed to make sure I didn't take anything I wasn't supposed to.

I bent down to pick up a box and when I stood, Babe was in the doorway. "Need a hand, Kit?"

"That would be great."

Between us, we managed the three boxes, carrying them past the guard gate and to the parking lot, setting them on the backseat of my Oldsmobile.

As I closed the car door, Babe said, "I read about the DA's decision. Why do you think they gave up so fast?"

"I don't know."

"You don't think—I mean, I'm hearing rumors around the lot about Nigel—that maybe it wasn't an accident?" I'd heard the same rumors: *Mudge and Nigel had fought and he had killed her without meaning to. Nigel had tired of her and purposely killed her to keep her quiet about the affair. Pia had killed her in a jealous rage.*

"I don't think anyone knows what happened."

"I'm sorry you had to be the one to find her. If it had to happen, I wish someone else had found her instead."

One of the publicists came walking toward us, waving and calling hello. We smiled and waved back and after he climbed into his car, Babe turned to me, serious once again. "Kit, I wanted to be the one to tell you—they're giving me her dressing room. I don't want it, but it's the only empty suite, and it's all a part of this new contract. I didn't want you to be surprised."

"Thanks, Babe."

"I'm not fooling myself into thinking she'd be glad about it." She smiled sadly. "It's strange, you know? I've worked so hard for so long and it feels as if I've arrived, finally, where I always knew I'd be, yet I can't really enjoy it. I shouldn't enjoy it. It would be wrong to right now."

Someone shouted her name, and we both looked. Yilla King stood across the street on the steps of the Thalberg Building, tapping her foot, tapping her watch. Babe sighed. "I wish I'd known her better. You're lucky you knew her so well."

With a quick hug, she walked away, heading for her mother, hair shining in the sun. I rearranged the boxes so they wouldn't shift too much, and drove home.

Flora was still there, dinner warming, house sparkling. She said, "I didn't know if you girls were planning to be in or out tonight, so I fixed something just in case."

"Thanks, Flora."

I said hello to Helen, and then went upstairs to my room and dialed Dr. Murdoch's office. This time, he was there. He came on the line, pleasant and distracted, and when I told him who I was and why I was calling, he got very, very quiet. For a second, I thought he'd hung up, but then he said, "I shouldn't be talking to you."

Not *I have nothing to say to you* or *I don't understand what I can do for you*, but *I shouldn't be talking to you.*

"If I could meet with you briefly, I promise not to take up too much of your time." I gave him my war hero speech, the same one I'd given the coroner, and then I said, "Please."

He rattled off an address, said to meet him at six the next morning, and hung up the phone.

TWENTY-ONE

I knew by the clock tower that it was quarter till six. The sky was still dark. My hair was pinned up, underneath a hat. I wore a light coat because the air was always cool this early in the morning. I was a spy again. I was in France, walking through the lobby of a Paris hotel, on the lookout for my contact, Dr. Frederick Murdoch, chief autopsy surgeon for the County of Los Angeles.

The Farmers Market was a maze of food stands and stalls, selling everything from homemade jam to fresh honeycomb to peanuts under canvas awnings. Farmers still made the daily drive into town to set up their displays of fruits and vegetables. But right now it was a ghost town. I found a bench, where I sat and waited. I was due at the recording stage by nine a.m., where I would lay down the songs from *Flyin' Jenny* for a soundtrack album produced by Metro's new record label. *Kit Rogers Sings Flyin' Jenny*. Songs like "Facing the World Alone," "Fly Away with You," and "Red, White, and Blonde." In my head, I went over the lyrics, and then I went over my questions for the doctor.

I told myself to be calm, but with each second that ticked by on the clock, my heart beat three times as fast.

As the clock struck six, I saw him—glasses, balding white head. Even dressed in a suit, he looked like a country doctor. "Dr. Murdoch?"

"Miss Rogers?" We shook hands. "I almost didn't recognize you. I'm afraid I don't have long."

As we took a seat on the bench, I thanked him for meeting me.

"You have questions about Miss Fanning's death?"

"Yes, sir. I was there when she died, and it didn't look natural to me."

"The district attorney closed the investigation."

"And sealed the coroner's report."

"Perhaps it's easiest if you tell me what you need to know, keeping in mind that I may not answer."

"Was Barbara Fanning murdered?"

Without so much as a blink, he said, "I can't tell you that. What I can tell you is that she did not die from a bump on the head suffered from a fall. That knot on her forehead was superficial at best."

"What did she die of?"

"Asphyxiation."

"She was—she was strangled?"

"Poisoned."

"Poisoned." I repeated it, as if that would help me make sense of it. *Poisoned.* "I don't understand." I felt dull and stupid and chilled completely through.

"Asphyxiation can cause petechial hemorrhages to form on the face and chest. This is most typically seen in strangulation, but can be present after any asphyxial death. They appear as small red or black dots, often around the eyes and cheeks, and as little red dots at the front of the eyes—subconjunctival petechiae."

"I didn't notice any—"

"They would have been difficult to see behind her makeup. On autopsy, I noted the dark blood and petechial bleeding in the lungs and heart, which also suggests poison."

"Do you know when? Or how—I mean, what kind of poison it might have been?" *And who—and why?*

"It may have been acute, possibly chronic." I shook my head to let him know I wasn't following. "She could have been poisoned that day or over a longer period of time."

"You mean a little here, a little there."

"Yes. Not enough for her to feel anything but under the weather. If acute, it could have happened anytime that Saturday. The process from ingestion to death might be several hours. As for what kind, I'm unable to say. Unfortunately, the toxicology laboratory is limited to a few test tubes. I sent the liver, kidney, samples of blood, and stomach contents to the Army Medical Museum to be analyzed, hoping to identify the type of poison, but the investigation was closed before I heard the results. Toxicology is in its infancy, so it's difficult to know if the tests would have detected anything. Far more significant in determining the type would be the mode of death observed by others. In other words, what were her symptoms before death, and what did the scene look like—the ceiling, walls, furniture."

"The running water in the sink."

"No longer running by the time Coroner Nigh and I arrived."

"You reported all of this, everything you've told me, to the coroner?"

"Yes."

"And he reported it to the district attorney?"

"Yes."

"But the DA closed the investigation." A voice inside me was saying: This can't be happening. It isn't real. Things like this don't happen.

"Miss Fanning was an extremely high-profile MGM star. Metro-Goldwyn-Mayer is an extremely lucrative studio." His eyes were kind, but his manner was matter-of-fact, as if to say, *This is just the way things are.* "I'm sorry."

"But there's got to be something we can do."

"I'm afraid the studio's power extends well beyond the movie screens. Especially if they think they're protecting one of their own."

The weight of his words made it hard for me to breathe. I sank back against the wall, as if I couldn't hold myself and all that weight upright any longer.

"Why did you agree to meet me?"

"Even though the investigation was closed, I was curious. For my own peace of mind, I contacted the laboratory regarding the report.

The organs and blood went untested and the stomach contents were reported missing."

"Missing?"

"I was told the contents disappeared along with the mouse they were tested on. The first time, in my forty years, that I've known this to happen."

We sat in silence, and then he said, "I've been a doctor for most of my life. The reason I went into medicine, trite as it sounds, was to help people. As far as I can see, a blocked investigation doesn't help anyone except the people blocking it. And those people don't interest me. I've made it clear to both the coroner and district attorney where I stand in the case of Barbara Fanning. There's little more I can do without risking my career. However, I believe we have an obligation to state the truth, no matter what."

"What if there were evidence?"

"I would do what I could to help."

Shop owners started trickling in, the sounds of chatter adding life to the place. He stood. "I wish you luck, Miss Rogers. I'd like to think this did you some good, but I'm afraid I've made a bad situation worse. Perhaps it's better you didn't know."

I stood. "Thank you, Dr. Murdoch. But on some level, I think I already did."

· · · · ·

In the parking lot, vendors and customers passed by on their way into the market as I rested my hands on the steering wheel, then closed my eyes and rested my head on it as well. Mudge had been poisoned. She had died of asphyxiation. The DA had called it accidental, but someone had deliberately killed her.

I was trying to think of her symptoms the day she died, of the moment she began acting the least bit strange or different. I went over everything she'd eaten or drunk, starting with that morning. I had thought she was drinking too much, that she'd had too much gin. . . .

Gin . . .

The flask.

· · · · ·

The driveway was empty, which meant Flora was running errands and Helen was out somewhere. I ran up the walk and, without thinking, turned the doorknob before reaching for my key. The door opened, which meant Flora or Helen had either forgotten to lock it behind them or they were still home. But if they were home, where were the cars?

I told myself it was nothing, just an oversight, but I pushed the door open, slowly, silently, and peered inside. Everything looked just as I'd left it that morning. I slipped off my shoes, set my purse on the hallway table, and grabbed the first hard object I could find—a sterling silver candlestick. I crept through the downstairs first, from room to room, checking drawers and valuables. The back door was locked. The downstairs and backyard appeared to be empty.

I crept up the stairs then, candlestick in hand, and explored each bedroom and bathroom until I could see that no one was there, not even hidden in a closet or under a bed. I set down my weapon and checked more thoroughly now—my room, the guestroom where Helen was staying, Mudge's room. I checked her furs and her fine jewels, the ones she kept locked up on her dresser. Everything accounted for, nothing missing.

I pulled Mudge's suitcase from the back of her closet—the suitcase she'd taken to Broad Water. I'd thrown everything in there, so it was all jumbled together: clothes and shoes and magazines. I'd gone through it all before the funeral to find her silver wings, but I'd left the flask in the bag. I would get the flask now and give it to Dr. Murdoch so he could take it to the laboratory and have it tested.

I rooted through the mountain of clothes and shoes—but the flask wasn't there.

I sank back on my heels and made myself breathe. I had put it in there myself. It must be here. It had to be here. I turned the suitcase upside down and dug through all the contents again. I was still digging when Flora walked in.

"Miss Velva Jean?"

"Flora, I'm looking for Mudge's flask. It's not here. Did you happen to see it?"

"No, ma'am."

"Maybe Helen?" Even as I said it, I knew this wasn't true.

"She'll be back soon. We can ask her." Flora started picking things up and folding them neatly, setting them on the bed.

"Did you remember to lock the front door when you left?"

"Of course, honey. I triple-checked it like I always do."

"Did Helen leave after you?"

"She was already out by the time I got to work."

"They knew."

It's gone.

"Miss Velva Jean?"

They took it. Whoever did this, whoever poisoned her. So there would be no evidence, no proof. It's gone.

· · · · ·

That afternoon, on Metro's recording stage, Rosie played back the songs so I could hear them. The truth of it was, no matter how rattled I was from the morning, I'd still been able to remember the words and hit the notes. Unless you were Judy Garland, singing for MGM meant sounding clean and sparkling and just like everyone else.

The technicians gave me a thumbs-up, which meant that was it. Cut. Print. No need to try it again.

Afterward, Rosie said, "You sounded fine, but you weren't there. I need you to show up next time."

Why, I thought, when we're all so interchangeable?

· · · · ·

Flyin' Jenny: Red, White, and Blonde premiered that night at Carthay Circle. As if we didn't have a care in the world, Hal MacGinnis and I walked the red carpet followed by Babe and Les Edgar, and other Metro stars. Babe and I posed cheek-to-cheek, sisters Jenny and Bonnie Dare in person, Mr. Mayer's newest discoveries. Hal and I smiled for the cameras, hands clasped, arms around each other. The all-American couple, except that he liked men.

Reporters wanted to know about Barbara Fanning. What really happened? Had she been drinking? How were we bearing up in the wake of her tragic death? Did we think it was strange that Nigel Gray had disappeared so quickly after Miss Fanning died? Why had MGM sent him away? Where was Nigel now? Where was Pia Palmer? Was Nigel really on a publicity tour, or was that a studio-invented excuse for keeping him out of the spotlight?

Hal deflected each question. Over and over, he brought the topic back around to *Flyin' Jenny*, to the important work Nigel was doing in England to promote *Home of the Brave*, and speaking of *Home of the Brave* . . . Bernie tried to push us toward the theater as quickly as possible, but then Zed Zabel spoke up and over everyone. "Weren't you the one who found her, Kit Rogers?"

"Yes, I was." Someone—Bernie or Hal—placed his hand on the small of my back, trying to steer me away.

Zed fixed his eyes on me. "And everything they're telling us—is that the way it happened?"

"No comment."

Everyone fell silent. Zed Zabel's eyes gleamed like an animal's. "Are we supposed to deduce, then, that all is not what it seems?"

"Why don't you ask Howard Strickling or Whitey Hendry? Or, better yet, the coroner?"

Bernie shoved me up the carpet before I could say anything else. "Do you realize what you just implied?" He gave me an earful all the way to our seats, smiles plastered on our faces so that no one would know there was a problem. Bernie pointed at me. "Stay." He marched off toward the exit.

Hal leaned in to me. "You shouldn't have done that."

"She was my friend. She was your friend too. You think I'm going to abandon her right now when she isn't here to fight for herself?" I caught his eye and gave him my worst look. "I should have told them everything."

Twenty minutes into the picture, I was too restless to sit still. Sitting still wasn't going to get me anywhere. I got up, ducking low, stepping over feet and legs, and slipped out of the theater. I asked the usher for the pay phone, and he directed me to a wooden booth in the far corner of the lobby. Inside, I dropped a nickel into the slot.

"Dunbar Hotel," someone said.

I asked for Johnny Clay Hart. He answered on the first ring, sounding out of breath. "Are you playing tonight?" I asked him.

"The Downbeat till ten or so, then we're going to join the jam session at Jack's Basket Room."

"What's the address?" Because I didn't have a pen, I repeated it twice so I would remember.

TWENTY-TWO

Jack's Basket Room sat at Thirty-third and Central Avenue and was owned by heavyweight boxing champ Jack Johnson. I parked as close to it as I could get, and walked the rest of the way through the heat of the people and the scene. I wore my premiere gown—a sleek emerald green—which made a *swish-swish* sound, like bird wings, as I went.

Men in zoot suits, bright as peacock feathers, sauntered by and shouted things at the white policemen who patrolled on foot. "Hey, baby," men called to me. "Where you goin', girl, and can I come along?" The air was smoky and smelled like curry, red pepper, garlic. I could hear music coming from an open window, wailing like a woman.

A policeman cut through the crowd, his mouth moving, already talking before I could hear him. "Turn around, Miss Hollywood. You shouldn't be here." His badge said "Phelps." He had a big red nose that looked like he blew it too much.

"I'm going to see my brother." I kept walking, which meant he had to fall in line next to me, elbowing his way through the crowd.

"These clubs are breeding places where crimes are planned and carried out. No place for a white woman, especially by herself, especially one so recognizable." He grabbed my arm, made me stop. "A little white girl about your age was found not far from here today, cut in half. Worst crime I've ever seen committed on a woman. You want that to happen to you?"

"I'm going to see my brother," I said again, snatching my arm away. I was mad—a kind of dark red mad, the color of blood. It had started with Mudge's death and the closing of the investigation and the meeting with Dr. Murdoch. *Poison.* And someone breaking into Mudge's house and stealing the flask, and now, tonight, the reporters. "My friend died and I need to see my brother. You can either walk me there or let me go."

Officer Phelps called me every name in the book, and then half-dragged me the rest of the way. "The next time I see your face, I want it to be on the movie screen."

Jack's Basket Room was a great, rickety barn of a place. All it lacked was sawdust on the floor. There wasn't a single open seat, so I stood as close as I could to the front. Police lingered in doorways and along the walls, keeping their eyes on the crowd.

I looked around at the faces, mostly colored, but also white, Mexican, Creole. You could hear the steam rising off the stage. A battle was heating up between the two tenor saxes, Wardell Gray and Dexter Gordon. I thought: The best thing about them is they don't play for anyone else but themselves. They're making music because they love to play.

When a spot opened up down front, I took it, ordering myself a Jack's basket, which was fried chicken and french fries, and a beer. Up on the stage, the musicians changed, overlapping, interrupting each other, but the music continued to build, the steam still rising. The Downbeat was one thing, with its jazz and bebop, but here, anything went.

I let myself get lost in the music, and felt myself relaxing a little, the anger fading to a simmer. I was done with my food when I thought I heard my name—not Kit Rogers, but Velva Jean—and when I turned I could see my brother and Butch and their drummer across the room. I wove through the tables and set my bottle down among the glasses of whiskey they'd collected and a stack of white napkins. Johnny Clay picked me up and hugged me hard, and Butch gave me his chair.

It was too loud to talk, so I watched the musicians and shouted along with the crowd. *Go, go, go!* The drummer, Sherman Crothers—the young colored man from Mudge's funeral—beat on the table with his sticks.

Butch leaned back in his chair, fished around in his pocket, and came up with a pencil stub. He picked up a white napkin and scrawled something down as my brother, guitar in hand, jumped onto the stage. Sherman followed, springing toward the drums like he couldn't help himself any longer. Butch stood, slid the napkin over to me, took a drink of whiskey, turned the glass upside down, and dragged his guitar out from under the table.

This is for you.

Up on stage, he said something to the horn players, the ones who'd been playing for the past half hour, and off they went, nodding and waving to the crowd. Butch and Johnny Clay plugged their guitars into an amplifier, and then Butch laid one hand on the microphone—the hand with the tattoo—and said in that whiskey-and-cigarettes voice, "Seems everywhere I turn these days, I'm hearing about folks who died too young. Someone once said, 'Sing your death song, and die like a hero going home.' Here's to the heroes." He closed his eyes and, without guitars or drums, he sang:

> They tell me of a place where my friends have gone
> They tell me of that land far away
> And they tell me that no tears ever come again
> In that lovely land of uncloudy day.

At the exact moment I almost walked out—nose and eyes stinging, feeling ambushed, feeling jumped from behind—the guitars roared in like B-29s, and Sherman began beating away at the drums. The sound was bigger than the three of them, bigger than all of us gathered there. It was angry. It was loud. It was going to raise the roof and blow it all the way to the moon. My brother's guitar throbbed out the bass line, sounding more like five guitars than one. Butch's guitar howled and moaned like an animal, like something in pain. It was everything I was feeling—a low-down, raw, bloodred angry. I sat for a long time and then I got to my feet, like everyone else, and danced where I stood.

Butch lit a cigarette one-handed, never missing a note. The broken bottle neck smoked like he did, up and down the strings. His hair fell across his face, and in that raspy barroom voice, the one he'd blown out years ago, he sang as he played.

> *Ready or not, I'm comin' around*
> *You can hide if you want, but I'll hunt you down . . .*

The music found its way under my skin and into my blood and way, way down into my bones until I was charged and electric and could do anything.

> *Not gonna stop for kingdom come,*
> *You better hide, girl, you better run . . .*

As the crowd beat on the floors and the tables, swaying and shaking body against body, white skin, black skin, the policemen who had been leaning against the wall stood straight and tense, hands on their weapons.

> *'Cause ready or not, I'm comin' for you . . .*

The crowd shouted, cheering the music onward and upward and outward so that I knew it pushed its way out onto the street, into the skin and blood and bones of the people walking by, which meant soon everyone on Central Avenue would catch fire, just like we had, and feel themselves burning where they stood.

He gets it, I thought. He always has. This music—the soft and the loud—is exactly how I feel. And that, maybe, was the worst thing about Butch Dawkins, that he got me and knew me but could only ever go so far with it before he turned tail and ran like hell. Or maybe it was that he just didn't think of me the same way I thought of him.

· · · · ·

It was four a.m. when they gave up the stage. Outside, the crowds on the street were as thick as the ones in the clubs. If anything, the avenue was busier, louder, just getting started. Police wove through the streets and sidewalks, and for all the sense of life and celebration, there was an air of tension underneath it all, as if we were inside a pressure cooker and any minute the lid might blow right off.

We left Butch and Sherman at the Dunbar Hotel, and then Johnny Clay walked me to my car, even though I wanted to keep going and find another place, other music. He blew three perfect smoke rings, which drifted over our heads like balloons. "You don't want to see it in the daytime. The whole avenue smelling like beer, cigarette butts on the ground, trash on the street. It's a place built for night, Velva Jean."

I wondered if I was a person built for night, if there was such a thing. I felt warm and dangerous from the beer and the music. I didn't want to go home and go to sleep, because that meant I would have to wake up and think about what to do and what was next and how to prove what had happened.

Too soon, we found my car. My brother chased away the teenage boys who were leaning on it, setting off firecrackers and smoking a pipe they passed around. He kicked at the wheels like he was checking the air.

I said, "Mudge was asphyxiated."

Johnny Clay whistled. "Strangled?"

"According to the chief autopsy surgeon of Los Angeles County, she was poisoned. Almost everyone who was at Broad Water that weekend has access to Benzedrine and Seconal. I should have asked Dr. Murdoch about them, but I didn't think of it. You drank from the flask the night before, in the limousine, and Sam drank the rest on the red carpet. I gave the flask back to Mudge just before the picture started. It was empty by then. She wouldn't have filled it up again till we got home, before we left for Santa Monica."

"Did she drink at the airfield?"

"She left the flask in the car. The next time I saw her with it was at the pool at Broad Water." I thought of Mudge's flask lying on her lounge chair, of all the people coming and going. She had left it out in the open, unguarded, for hours. There would have been plenty of chances for the killer to slip off the cap, drop something in, give it a shake. "It could have been anyone."

"Who's to say the guy that did this isn't after other actresses? Or maybe some of the other party guests? Or other people from the movie? Until we know why it happened, you got to be on your guard, little sister."

"I already am."

"Do you think it was Nigel?"

"I don't know. The studio seems to be doing all it can to protect him."

"My money's on the wife. You want me to come stay with you?"

"I don't need a babysitter, Johnny Clay. But thanks."

. . . . .

I was just past the oil derricks of La Cienega when a truck the size of a moving van came barreling up behind me. The street was nearly empty, but instead of passing me it moved up too fast on my tail. I slammed on the gas and shot ahead, the headlights dropping back in the rearview mirror.

I eased off the gas a bit, but only a bit, and then the truck moved into the left lane so it could pass me. I eased off the gas further so that he could go on by, but instead the truck pulled up alongside me and swerved into my lane. I slammed the brakes and went skidding off the side of the road, knocking my head against the steering wheel.

I sat, catching my breath, knuckles white. I checked my mirrors and looked around. I turned too fast, over my shoulder, and my head started to pound. The roadside was empty except for me. Wilshire was nearly empty too.

I opened the door and got out, testing my legs, making sure they still worked, and watched as, in the distance, the taillights of the truck continued west toward the ocean.

. . . . .

At home, I examined my forehead, where a bump was forming. Then I went to the kitchen and stood at the stove, waiting for the kettle to boil, ready to catch it before it whistled so the sound wouldn't wake Helen. I poured the water, dropped a tea bag in, and carried the cup into the living room.

I set the cup down and picked up an issue of *Photoplay* from the coffee table, then *Ladies' Home Journal* and *True Story*. They all featured Nigel Gray's face, brooding and handsome and dignified. "How Nigel Gray Faces Life Without Love," said one. "Nigel Gray Grieves," said another. "Nigel Gray Remembers Barbara Fanning and the Life They Could Have Had," said a third.

He was the biggest star at the biggest studio. He was worth millions to Louis B. Mayer and the rest of them.

I set down the magazines and rubbed my head. I had more questions for Dr. Murdoch, and questions for the guests of Broad Water. I had letters to write and business to take care of that had nothing to do with the death of Barbara Fanning. I thought about all there was to do, and then I picked up one of the magazines again. I stared at Nigel, as if he might tell me something. I tore the cover off. I set it aside and there, on the next page of the magazine, was Mudge in an ad for Lux soap. I tore this page out as well. Five pages later, I found Hal Mac-Ginnis. Two pages after that, Babe King. On the following page, Ophelia Lloyd.

It only took me half an hour to sort through a stack of magazines and cut out pictures of everyone who was at Broad Water the night Mudge died, except for Yilla King and Dr. Atwill. On the wall of my bedroom, I taped a picture of Mudge at her most glamorous. Photographer: Virgil Apger.

On an index card I wrote, *Found Sat., Dec 28, around 11:45 p.m. on the floor of the bathroom off the music room at Broad Water, home of Billy Taub and Ophelia Lloyd. Last word spoken: "Rebecca."*

Then, in order of suspicion, I tacked the other pictures on the wall below Mudge. I wrote down what I knew—motives; the ways everyone was related to each other; the ways they were related to Mudge; where they'd been during the game.

Half an hour later, I was in bed. I closed my eyes and told myself to let it all go for now. I could pick it up again in a few hours.

· · · · ·

By the time I was awake, minutes after nine, Helen had made coffee and breakfast. Even in the morning, she looked as smart and chic as a model for *Cosmopolitan* magazine. She said, "What on earth happened to your head, Hartsie?"

I touched the bump, where it had started to bruise. "I got up in the middle of the night to go to the bathroom and ran smack into the wall." I poured myself a cup of coffee, swallowed two aspirin, and sat down at the kitchen table.

"Now why don't I believe you?" Helen cocked her head at me.

"Any luck finding Mudge's will?"

"Okay, I'll drop it. Just know I'm interested if you ever want to tell me what really happened." She settled elegantly on the chair across from mine. "I can't figure out where she put it. She was the most disorganized person I've ever known, and she kept everything—fan letters, hate mail, movie stills, magazine clippings. Nothing's where it should be. Flora's promised to help me look. She knew her better than anyone and she might be able to make sense of her filing system, such as it was." She nodded at the morning newspaper. "Did you hear about this poor girl?"

The front page of the *Los Angeles Examiner* read: *Slain by a fiend, the body of a teenage girl was found in a vacant lot here yesterday. The nude body was severed at the waist. The girl had been killed elsewhere and her body taken to the lot and left in plain view, not three feet from the sidewalk. Death came to the girl, police scientists said, after hours of torture.*

Accompanying the article, which took up almost the entire page, was a photograph of the victim, body covered by a blanket, eyes closed, black hair a cloud around her head. She looked peaceful as she lay next to a sidewalk on the edge of an overgrown field in Leimert Park, the neighborhood where Flora lived, near downtown Los Angeles.

As I studied the picture of the girl in the field, my head throbbed.

I told myself that what had happened the night before was an accident. The man was just a bad driver. He hadn't been looking or paying attention.

But what if he had wanted to run me off the road?

• • • • •

I crept along at twenty miles an hour the entire way to the studio. I watched the mirrors, flinching at every truck that entered the street. As I turned onto Venice Boulevard, the traffic picked up. Off to my right, a train rattled past on the raised tracks of the Venice Short Line.

I made it to Metro without anyone following me, and went directly to the portrait studio, where I told the girls working there I wanted to see Virgil Apger. "You aren't scheduled for today, Miss Rogers," one of them said, finger running up and down the page of her appointment book.

The studio was filled with file cabinets and card catalogs of indexes, but I believed what I'd told Coroner Nigh. The crime scene photographs wouldn't be here with everything else. If they even still existed, pictures and negatives would most likely be under lock and key somewhere in the Thalberg Building, which might as well be Fort Knox. But I had to be sure.

"Oh, I'm not scheduled, but I wanted to ask Virgil a question. Is it okay if I leave a note for him on his desk?"

She got up and walked to his office, knocking on the door even though it stood open. "Go on in."

I thanked her and slipped inside, running my eyes over the room, the walls covered in framed photographs of his most famous subjects—Jean Harlow, Clark Gable, Jeanette MacDonald, Joan Crawford, Hedy Lamarr. There was only one file cabinet in here, behind his desk. I glanced at the open door, making sure no one was watching, and, just in case, helped myself to a pen and a piece of official portrait studio letterhead. I bent over the desk, pretending to write, and did a quick, quiet search through the drawers, looking for a key. It sat, like it was waiting, in the middle drawer, the last one I checked. Too easy, I thought.

I picked it up, and with another glance at the door, kneeled in front of the filing cabinet and opened it with a click. I waited, listened, glanced, and then slid the drawer open. Inside were envelopes of negatives, labeled on the outside—"Garland," "Johnson," "Turner," "Loy." And "Fanning." There was only one strip of pictures. I held it up to the light, heart starting to pound—but in each frame Mudge was very much alive, and naked as could be.

At the sound of footsteps, I dropped the negatives into the envelope, slid the drawer closed, turned the key, and was just bending over the desk again, the key in my hand, when Virgil Apger appeared. "Miss Rogers?"

"I was just leaving you a note." I held up the half-written piece of paper, then crumpled it and pretended to search for the trashcan behind the desk. The key in my hand felt like a hundred-pound weight.

"I'll take that," he said, and started toward me, but at that moment one of the girls called his name, and as he turned, I slid the drawer open a fraction of an inch, dropped in the key, and closed it again.

When he turned back to me, I walked over to him and said, "I wanted you to hear it from me first. About the bump on my head. I know I'm due to have photos taken in a few days, and I wanted to see if we should reschedule."

He tilted my face to the light and examined the bump. "How did you do this?"

"I ran into a wall in the middle of the night."

His eyes met mine before moving back to my forehead. "I don't think it's anything makeup and good lighting can't fix. Is that the only reason you came to see me, Miss Rogers?" I could hear the wariness in his voice, or maybe I was only imagining it.

I almost said something. Someone had told me once that he was the son of a sheriff. I knew him to be a good, decent man. But just then a figure appeared in the doorway.

"Miss Rogers," said Howard Strickling. "What a pleasure. Did you have a shoot scheduled for today?" There was a woman with him— Shelby Jordan.

What incredible timing, I thought. How surprising to see Mr. Strickling at this exact moment.

"I was just showing Virgil the bump I got from walking into a wall. I wanted to give him fair warning so he knew what he was up against."

Mr. Strickling smiled. I smiled.

"Thanks, Mr. Apger," I said. "You've made me feel much better."

Outside again, I went directly to the first-aid department, which was housed in a little building near the dressing rooms. This time, Dr. Atwill studied the bump on my forehead.

He said, "How did you get this?"

I decided to change my story to something that might sound more believable. "A dog ran out in front of my car. I hit the brakes to avoid him and bumped my head."

What was it Dr. Atwill had said about Benzedrine and Seconal? *Everyone uses them, Miss Rogers. When taken in the right combination, they're perfectly safe.*

Unless you're poisoned.

"You may get a bruise, nothing they can't cover with makeup."

"I have a nasty headache."

"To be expected." He made some notes on a chart and then reached behind him into a cabinet with glass doors that was stocked with pill bottles. As he reached for the aspirin, I practiced Babe's doe-eyed look. "It's just that I've had trouble sleeping ever since Barbara Fanning's death, and during the day I'm so tired." I was thinking of the pills, now missing, from Mudge's purse.

He handed me two bottles. "You're not the only one, Miss Rogers. A perfectly normal reaction to such a tragedy."

I held up the Benzedrine. "How many of these can I take at a time?"

"No more than two."

"And these?" I waved the bottle of Seconal.

"No more than two."

"Is it possible to overdose? I wouldn't want to take too many."

"Yes. Twenty-three hundred milligrams of Benzedrine is enough to kill a person of, let's say, one hundred twenty-five pounds." He smiled. "And you weigh a little less than that."

I smiled. "On a good day." Doe eyes, I told myself, and gave them an extra bat-bat-bat. "That sounds like an awful lot. You know, I've always been sensitive to medicine—what symptoms should I look out for, just in case they don't agree with me?"

"Oh, a pulse that skyrockets. High blood pressure. Headache, vomiting. Just the right amount helps the energy, but even a little too much can cause delusions, euphoria, and dizziness."

So it was possible to take too much, to kill yourself or someone else. I wondered who else had sought out the good doctor's services lately, because everyone at the studio was connected through Dr. Atwill. They all came to him sooner or later.

On the way back to my dressing room, I passed by the Little Red Schoolhouse, where a few of the child actors sat on the stoop under the arched front doorway. They squeezed close, too many of them to fit, and tried to knock each other off the step and onto the ground. Every time someone tumbled over, they fell on top of each other, laughing and whooping. The sound and sight of it was so happy that I stopped to watch them. I tried to remember the last time I'd felt that way, so light and worry-free.

I could go home. I could leave right now, this afternoon, and then I would be light and worry free too.

Like that, I was on my way to the parking lot. I would tell Johnny Clay and Butch, and also Helen and Flora, and then I would just go. No more studio. No more pills and accidents that might not be accidents. No more of people looking the other way and pretending nothing happened.

I climbed into the car. It would be so easy just to leave. And then I turned the key of the Oldsmobile Mudge had given me as a Christmas present, the one she'd had painted to match my truck.

"Where should we go?"

"Anywhere! And everywhere. Let's just drive."

So I headed back to Beverly Hills, because I couldn't leave. Not yet.

TWENTY-THREE

arbara Fanning had moved off the front page, replaced by the young girl found murdered in Leimert Park. The *Examiner* identified her as Elizabeth Short, twenty-two years old, of Medford, Massachusetts. She was five feet six inches tall and weighed 120 pounds. She had brown hair and green eyes and a fair complexion. Her hair had been hennaed and her brown roots had just begun to regrow. In the 1943 Santa Barbara Police Department photo that ran alongside the story, she looked eerily, spookily like Mudge.

I read the news on the front step of Mudge's house, without bothering to move inside. A man drove past, very slowly, hat drawn low over his face. I looked up to watch him, and he caught my eye. As he kept on going, I went back to the newspaper. Even after I heard my name, I continued reading.

The paper confirmed that Dr. Frederick Murdoch, the chief autopsy surgeon for the County of Los Angeles, had performed the autopsy on the person the *Examiner* was now calling the Black Dahlia because of her habit of dressing in black and wearing a flower in her hair.

"Hartsie." Helen opened the door and stuck her head out. "There you are." She pointed to the hall. "There's something I want to show you."

As I was turning to follow her inside, the same man drove by in the other direction. One door down, he pulled over and parked the car. I waited for him to get out, but he only sat there, engine idling.

"Hartsie." Helen was back again. "What are you doing?"

This time I followed her into the house. Spread out on the dining room table were a newspaper article, a photograph, and what looked like a letter.

"I found them inside a book."

The letterhead belonged to Fred Wamack, Private Investigator, Hollywood, California. It was addressed to Eloise Mudge. *Per your request, I have conducted an independent investigation into the where-abouts of one John Doe, age 11, born September 1935, birth name 'John Henry Briggs.'*

His report went on to say that the child was now living at the Dell Rapids Orphanage and Industrial School, also known as the Dell Rapids Odd Fellows Home, in Dell Rapids, South Dakota. The newspaper article was dated October 1946. It detailed a new addition to the home, originally built in 1910, and a need for funding. It featured four pictures—the home itself, a handsome English manor house of red brick, which rose out of the flat, dry landscape; children planting potatoes; children gathered around a phonograph; and four boys sitting in a freshly plowed field. The smallest boy was circled. He sat on one end, a little behind the others, his face puckered, as if he was looking into the sun. The photograph appeared to be of the same child, hands at his sides, dressed in a suit.

There wasn't much more to it

John Henry Briggs

than that. Page two of the letter was a carbon copy of a document that read *Orphan Home, Lodge #8, Dell Rapids, South Dakota, History and Record of Resident. Date of Admission: Dec. 25, 1935. When and where born: Washita Co. Oklahoma, September 13, 1935.* At the end of his letter, Investigator Fred Wamack said he was glad to look into the matter deeper, if she was interested. The date of the letter was December 2, 1946.

I picked up the photograph of the little boy. "Do you think he's hers?"

"He must be."

"But why would she have given him up? She dreamed of having kids. She said she and Nigel were going to have a houseful."

"Maybe one reason she wanted children so badly was because she'd had to give a child away."

"Do you think it's strange that a woman who kept everything doesn't have a single paper relating to her childhood or where she came from? No birth certificate. No pictures. It's almost as if she didn't exist until the summer of 1933 when she signed with MGM."

"Think of it this way—didn't we all start over, in a sense, when we went to the WASP? And then again after the war? How many people out here know about your ex-husband, Harley Bright? I think she wanted to give herself a new life, that's all."

"You said you found the orphans' home information in a book?"

"It's upstairs."

This time, I followed Helen to Mudge's room. Everything was as she'd left it—the vanity table crowded with perfumes and powders, the little desk turned toward one window, the blue embossed stationery stacked on top, the blue bedspread, the blue flowered wallpaper, a script lying atop the bedside table. *A Woman of Means* by Sam Weldon.

I flipped it open and glanced at the first few pages. "I didn't know Sam Weldon wrote another script for Metro."

Helen handed me something. "The book." *Jane Eyre.*

I opened it, searching through from front to back. On nearly every page, Mudge had underlined sentences or whole paragraphs. "Where did you find it?"

"In the drawer here." She opened it to show me.

I had not intended to love him.... He made me love him without looking at me.

"Did you find anything else?" Helen asked, peering over my shoulder at the book.

"No," I said. Maybe, I thought.

When I walked outside to my car, the man with the hat was gone. I climbed into the yellow Oldsmobile and headed to Hollywood.

• • • • •

Fred Wamack, private investigator, worked out of an office on the corner of Hollywood and Vine. The door to the building was so narrow, I almost missed it. But there was his name on a list by the entrance: F. Wamack, P.I., Suite 202. He answered the buzzer, "Wamack."

"Mr. Wamack, I'm a friend of Eloise Mudge. I understand you did some work for her."

The door buzzed and clicked. Inside, there was a door to my right and one to my left, and a rickety staircase in the middle. I walked up the stairs and saw 202 at the end of the hall. The door stood open.

It was just one room, bright with a corner view. Fred Wamack sat behind the desk, which was messy with papers, cigarette burning in the ashtray. He was thick and broad with a full head of hair and two chins. He was chewing gum, and he didn't bother standing. "You're a friend of Eloise Mudge?"

"Yes, sir." He didn't offer me a seat, but I sat anyway, dragging the chair away from the wall, closer to the desk. "I know you did some work for her."

"That's right." He eyed me like I might be a criminal. "Sorry to hear about her death."

"Thank you. I'm just going through her files, trying to put things in order, and wanted to ask if you could tell me anything more than what was in your report, about who the child was and why she needed the information."

"Sorry. I'm sure I don't need to explain client confidentiality."

"It's just that I've got a mountain of paperwork to go through, and if you could tell me anything that might help me—"

"If I were you, Miss . . . ?"

"Hart."

"If I were you, Miss Hart, I'd stop asking questions. I'm doing you a favor by telling you that. I'm saving you a lot of trouble."

I gave him a sad smile. Then I glanced down and glanced up again with a look I'd seen Mudge give Felix Roland or Tauby when she wanted to get her way. "Could you at least tell me when she hired you?"

He picked up the cigarette, pressing the gum into the ashtray with his thumb. "Last fall."

"Can you tell me why she needed to find this boy?"

"No. But it seemed awful important. Know how I know? Because she walked in here off the street. No phone call. Barbara Fanning, the movie star, just as plain as you or me, sitting right in that very same chair you're sitting in now. She said, 'I need you to find someone for me. And I need it done as fast as you can.' I told her if I'd known she was coming, I woulda dressed up."

"But she hired you as Eloise Mudge?"

"That's right." He flicked the ashes onto the gum. "Said we had to keep it confidential."

"How did she find you?"

"I've handled more than one movie star case in my career. When she asked for recommendations, my name came up."

"After you gave her the information, did she say she needed anything else?"

Before he could answer, the phone on his desk rang. He picked it up. "Wamack." He listened, dug for a file, sending other files spilling onto the floor. "Got it right here, old man." He looked at me, covering the receiver. "Nice chatting with you, Miss Hart. Or should I say 'Miss Rogers'? If you don't mind, do me a favor and close the door on your way out."

· · · · ·

Back at Mudge's house, I phoned Dr. Murdoch, and when I couldn't reach him I tried Lara Yacoubian, secretary to the coroner. She answered on the first ring, and I could hear voices in the background.

When I told her who I was, she whispered, "I can't talk right now," and then, louder, "Could I have him return your call?"

"Get back to me when you can," I said, giving her the number. "I wanted to know if Dr. Murdoch saw anything in the autopsy relating to Benzedrine or Seconal."

After hanging up, I dialed the operator and placed a long distance call. After a few rings, a voice crackled on the line. "Dell Rapids Home, how may I help you?" It was a woman's voice, pleasant and cheerful.

"Yes, I'm interested in making a donation to the children's home."

"Bless you, dear. Just one moment, please."

I heard her walk away, shoes tapping across a hard floor. My heart started to race. A minute ticked by. Through the phone, I heard the sound of shoes tapping again. A woman's voice said, "This is Ella Kingery. I understand you'd like to make a donation?"

"Yes, ma'am. I read an article about how the orphanage needs funding. I'm interested in contributing, but I'd like to know more about the home first."

"Of course. I don't know how much you know already, but we were built in 1910, and the building was dedicated in 1911. Nearly eight thousand people attended the ceremony. We have twenty-six children, ages six to seventeen, and twenty-one elderly. We have a staff of nine, including myself."

She rattled off details about the reading room, nursery, infirmary rooms, quarantine rooms, barn, machine shed, silo, and hog house, and said the home sat on 172 acres. The staff and residents ran the farm, under the supervision of a hired farmer, both to supply the home and to sell products in town. The children divided work between the home and the farm, depending on age and gender. They received lessons in etiquette and moral education, held worship and sermons in the parlor and scriptural lessons at meals. They attended church weekly, rode the horses, listened to the phonograph, played baseball and croquet, and even had visits from Santa.

I told her this all sounded fine, and I wanted to write a sizable check, perhaps five hundred dollars.

She said, "This is quite generous, Miss . . ."

"Rogers. Kit Rogers. I was orphaned myself."

I waited for the name to mean something to her, but she just said, "Thank you, Miss Rogers," and gave me the mailing address.

"Would it be possible to make the donation in the name of a particular child?"

"An unusual request, but I'm sure we'll be happy to oblige. The child's name?"

"John Henry Briggs."

"John Henry. Yes, we can do that. Are you a friend of John Henry's?"

"No, ma'am, but a good friend of mine was." I asked the next question that came to mind. "Once a child like John Henry is brought to the home, what are the odds of him leaving before he's of age?"

"By law, surviving parents can remove children at any time. In 1921, we instituted a policy that legal guardianship is signed over to the home when the children arrive, and the children are discharged when they reach an adult age, or when a single parent remarries."

As I clicked off the line, I thought, Maybe I can go there. I had visions of myself in disguise, showing up as Mudge, asking to see my son.

• • • • •

That evening, Helen and I worked in the game room, digging through boxes and books. Police had discovered another dead girl down in Bronzeville, near Central Avenue, this one strangled by a silk stocking. They'd also discovered, at the Greyhound Express station downtown, a suitcase belonging to the Black Dahlia.

Helen said, "Apparently there were these stacks of letters from servicemen, and her replies to them, sealed and unsent. The letters were wrapped in red ribbon. I don't know why I find that the saddest detail of all."

According to her mother, sister, and friends, Beth, as the Black Dahlia was often called, had been engaged to a boy named Matt Gordon. Before he could marry her, he was killed in a plane crash five days before the war's official end. The newspaper said the letters in the bus station suitcase reflected a young girl who had been deeply hurt many times by men. In the end, she appeared to be just another girl who wanted someone to love her. I thought Beth Short not only looked like Mudge; she sounded like her.

In three days' time, more than one hundred suspects had been rounded up and questioned in the Black Dahlia murder case. As nearly a thousand policemen and newspaper reporters combed the city, going door to door, exploring clues from downtown L.A.'s Biltmore Hotel to the culverts of Malibu, the late, great Barbara Fanning was forgotten.

Helen said, "It makes you think—what happened with Mudge, what happened with these girls. It makes you realize how important our time is. My parents want me to come back home and marry someone named Sterling Archer Sanford the Third." Helen never talked much about her upbringing, but I knew she came from money. "But when I marry—if I marry—it's going to be because I want to."

We worked until midnight, and before I went to sleep, I read the first few chapters of *Jane Eyre*.

When we are struck at without a reason, we should strike back again very hard. . . . I am not your dear; I cannot lie down: send me to school soon, Mrs. Reed, for I hate to live here.

Mudge hadn't underlined just the romantic passages of *Jane Eyre*. The first pages were as marked up as the later ones.

I set the book aside and picked up *A Woman of Means* by Sam Weldon. It was the story of a girl from the wrong side of the tracks who marries well and has a child, only to have that child taken away from her by the man she loves. A note on the last page read, *SW— This draft best yet. Thank you for creating something I can be proud of. xx BF.*

I laid the script and book aside thinking that when it came down to it, I hadn't really known her at all. And then I got out of bed and found my hatbox in the back of my closet. I sat down to look through it, as if I were someone discovering these things for the first time. If this hatbox was all that was found of me one day, stored in a bus station locker, what would strangers be able to tell of my life and who I was from a collection of clover jewelry, letters, carved wooden figures, a parachute rip cord, my WASP wings, an emerald from the Black Mountains, a little gold wedding band from France, and a handful of songs?

TWENTY-FOUR

It felt good to be back at work, back in a routine that would make the real world go away, at least for a while. We were filming *Flyin' Jenny Meets Buck Rogers* at the Los Angeles Airport, which substituted as Airdale, Jenny Dare's home base. The film's stunt coordinator, Bud Bowdoin, went over the plane with me—range, twelve hundred miles; service ceiling, twenty-six thousand feet; rate of climb, 1,850 feet. As the mechanic refilled the oil and swung the propellers through ten rotations to feel for resistance and any possible hydraulic lock, Bud said, "You know Mayer doesn't want you doing this."

"I know."

Mr. Mayer and I had already discussed it before the first *Flyin' Jenny* installment: *We cannot have you doing your own stunts. What if something should happen to you?* His voice had climbed an octave and his ears had turned red. I'd heard the stories about Mr. Mayer's histrionics, his ability to fall on the floor and foam at the mouth and pitch the biggest tantrum you ever saw, bigger and more spectacular than any tantrum thrown by any star.

If someone fills in for me, the audience will be able to tell, and this is Metro-Goldwyn-Mayer, sir. They're going to expect more than that. I knew it was the one thing he wouldn't be able to argue with, and he didn't.

The plane was what they called a Twin Beech, because of its two engines. It was a small, low-wing airplane that had seen war service. It could carry six passengers, and fly a maximum speed of 225 mph.

When the mechanic was finished, I told Bud I wanted to go over the plane myself. He shook his head. "He's already gone over it, and it checks out fine."

"Sorry, Mr. Bowdoin, but I'm a pilot through and through. One of the first things we learned in the WASP was that you don't take off without first going over your plane."

He looked at Leslie Edgar, who consulted his watch. "That's fine, Kit," Les said. "But move as fast as you can, before we lose the light."

As the entire crew waited for me, I went over everything—brake fluid, rudder cables, hydraulics—searching for any sign of tampering or foul play. This wasn't something to be hurried along. This was, potentially, my life.

When I was done, Hal MacGinnis and I climbed inside the cockpit, pulling on helmets. The rest of my costume was a pair of tan breeches, a red blouse, a tan scarf, black boots, and red goggles. The view out the window was wide and open. The passenger terminals were still housed in temporary, two-story wooden frame buildings that were under construction, and jackrabbits lived along the runways in the weeds that grew there. I studied the cockpit as Bud showed me the throttle levers in the center, the prop levers to the left, the mixtures to the right, all the handles and buttons and switches. We started the engines, which took a lot of priming—seven strokes with full resistance.

With props at fine pitch and throttles open, the gear warning switch clicked. I selected the RH engine and pressed the start button. It fired after five revolutions with a cloud of smoke and a roaring rumble that I felt in my bones. I pressed the start button on the LH engine and went through the same process.

Bud shouted his last instructions before he walked away: "Remember to lock the tail wheel. Line her up and push the T-bar on the lower section of the throttle quadrant. Try with one of your brakes to check if it's locked. No flaps for takeoff. Power up to thirty-six inches MAP. Get the tail wheel off the ground, and liftoff follows at sixty knots."

Hal was so broad and tall, he barely fit inside the plane. The sight of him, hunched up in the copilot's seat, knees to his chin, started me laughing, which got him laughing. Over the rattle of the engine, he hollered, "Studio wants us to go to Ciro's tonight, depending on what time we're through."

"That's fine. We don't have to stay long. By the way, do you know why Shelby Jordan is suddenly hanging around Metro?"

"Keeping an eye on her wandering husband? Or maybe doing some wandering of her own with Buck Rogers?"

"Phillip?"

"That's the rumor."

I accelerated to ninety knots on the climb, and I could see the city spread out beneath us. These first shots would be filmed from the ground, and I searched for my marks. As soon as I found them, I climbed higher and faster, higher and faster, pushing the little plane as far and fast as it would go.

I took the plane into a roll, and even though Hal had been a brave pilot in the war, he held on tight because I'd caught him off guard. I shouted, "Sorry, too fast."

"That's okay. Send her into another one."

I took the plane into another roll, and another. Over my radio, Bud said, "What the hell do you think you're doing up there?" What I was doing was thinking of Mudge and the time we borrowed the Douglas SBD Dauntless from Santa Monica Airport and went flying over the water. I was thinking of her face, of how happy she'd been, of how she'd wished she could live in the sky.

Hal flicked the radio off. "Let's give 'em a show, Kit Rogers."

I sent the plane into a dive. As the plane came out of it, we whooped and hollered, and then I sailed still higher, still faster, climbing again before I sent us into a spin. Together, we ran through every one of my songs from *Home of the Brave*, as I pushed the little plane as far and as fast as it would go.

I flew past my marks, out toward the ocean, and Hal sang louder, his face buried in his knees.

When we were on the ground again, Bud Bowdoin gave us an earful, and afterward Hal took me aside. "I know you're investigating what happened to her. Have you talked to Ophelia yet? You know she tried to get Barbara fired off the picture for sleeping with Tauby."

"But that was long ago. Or was it?"

"It may have started long ago, but it's been off and on for years, at least platonically. As you probably knew, she had a way of attaching herself to father figures, like Tauby and Les Edgar. She said her friendship with Tauby—that's what she called it—ended when she met Nigel, but I wondered. She certainly saw plenty of him when she was married to Redd."

I was getting an idea. "Do you mind if we skip dinner tonight? I can blame it on a headache, leave you out of it."

"Okay by me. Got a hot date you don't want to break?"

"Something like that. One more thing—did Mudge know anyone named Rebecca?"

"If she did, she never mentioned her to me."

$$\cdot\ \cdot\ \cdot\ \cdot\ \cdot$$

We were finished by three o'clock. I didn't bother changing out of my costume because I needed every minute. I asked to borrow one of the airport phones, and called MGM. When the operator answered, I asked for Sam Weldon in the writers building.

His voice came on the line, businesslike, as if he led another life in which he was only courteous and professional. "Sam Weldon here."

"Pipes here. I wanted to take you up on that dinner."

Silence.

"Hello?"

"I seem to remember making you another offer a while ago." His voice had warmed.

"Let's start with dinner."

$$\cdot\ \cdot\ \cdot\ \cdot\ \cdot$$

Rockhaven Sanitarium hugged the Verdugo Mountains, on the far reaches of the San Gabriel Valley, northeast of Los Angeles. The main house was made of rock, and sat behind an arched iron gate in the midst of tranquil gardens, alive with butterflies and hummingbirds. Statues lined the pathways, which led through twining California oak trees, trunks bent and twisted, and shrubs thick with flowers. The air smelled cleaner here, in the foothills—golden and honeyed—and I felt a twinge of homesickness.

The main building itself was smaller than I'd expected, large enough for only twelve or fourteen patients at a time, but Agnes Richards, the woman who ran Rockhaven, walked the property with me and said they had room for nearly one hundred residents. As if to prove it, she showed me the dozen or so outer buildings, with names like "the Willows" and "the Pines." The Rose Cottage, where the wealthiest, most famous residents stayed, was a small, red-roofed bungalow with a wide front porch.

Ophelia Lloyd was living there now, renting out the entire cottage. Miss Richards tapped on the door, and when no one answered she consulted her watch. As she looked up at me, the lenses of her glasses caught the glare of the sun. She said, "I believe this time of day you'll find her strolling the gardens."

She led me down one garden path after another, now and then passing a nurse in a crisp white uniform or women I assumed were residents, even though they were dressed as if they'd stopped in to tea. We found Miss Lloyd sitting on a bench in the shade, contemplating the azalea bushes. A book lay beside her, unopened.

"You have a visitor, Miss Lloyd." Miss Richards smiled a patient, matronly smile.

Miss Lloyd looked up, frowned when she saw me, then seemed to remember herself. The movie star manners appeared. "Kit, how lovely to see you." She held out her hand, then withdrew it before I could touch her. "Thank you, Miss Richards." It was a polite dismissal, as if she were a queen and Agnes Richards was one of the household servants.

Miss Lloyd looked accusingly at the book, as if it had sneaked up on her, before moving it aside so I could share the bench. "What brings you out to Rockhaven, Kit?"

"I came to ask how you're doing and see if there's anything you need."

"How thoughtful of you." She looked and sounded bored. I'd expected agitation, a good, old-fashioned case of nerves. Wringing hands and tearstained cheeks, a handkerchief close by. "Thoughtful girl."

"It's a pretty place. I can see why you like it here."

"Who says I like it?"

"I assumed. They said you checked yourself in."

"Did 'they'? How nice for them."

"It seems very—relaxing."

She stared right at me with large, dark eyes. "I value directness, Kit. In fact, I appreciate it. Why don't you make your point?"

"I know about Barbara's affair with your husband."

"Which one?" She smiled coldly. "A studio wife learns to look the other way. That's what they call us—'studio wives.' I get to be a movie star too, so I'm lucky. Being a studio wife is a job no woman in her right mind would ever sign up for if she knew what it really entailed. Unlike most of them, I actually love my husband. Which only makes it harder."

"He must love you."

"He does. But he's a boy, and boys will play. It never means much. I'm not stupid enough to think otherwise. But he and Barbara Fanning—or should I say Eloise Mudge? Good old Eloise." She winked. "Now that was something else. At first I thought he might leave me, but she wasn't that serious about him. I don't think she wanted him for every day, just now and then, whenever something was going wrong in her life and she needed a daddy figure. She'd snap her fingers, he'd go running, and I might not see him for a week or more. One time it was three. But he always came back." She sighed as if this wasn't necessarily a good thing. "Let's face it, girls like that only want what they can't have." As an afterthought she added, "May she rest in peace."

"Is that why you tried to have her fired?"

"Among other reasons. I mainly tried to have her fired because she tried to have Felix Roland fired. She thought she ran the show. They gave her too much power, if you ask me. When I was at Metro, we did what we were told, went where we were supposed to go, and didn't ask questions. All these actresses now with their demands." Her nostrils flared.

"She tried to have Mr. Roland fired?"

"You must have known that." She snorted. "This business with Les Edgar. Dear as he is, he was in over his head on *Home of the Brave*. That picture never would have gotten done if they hadn't let him go." Her voice had turned bitter. "No, I didn't want her working on *Home of the Brave*. I thought it was better for everyone if she didn't. So I went over Billy's head to Mayer, who told me to be a good girl, play nice, and he'd make sure to remember it during awards season. 'Best actress' sounds so much better than 'best supporting actress.'"

"Did you hate her?"

"I felt sorry for her." The bitterness was gone. She was matter-of-fact now. She pulled a pack of cigarettes out of her pocket and lit one elegantly, languidly. "I take it her death wasn't actually an accident."

"No."

"How surprising." She inhaled, exhaled, dropped the cigarette, grinding it into the soil with one delicate shoe. Then she stood and walked away, leaving the book behind on the bench. She paused, turned, arched an eyebrow at me. It was then I noticed that she was wearing less makeup than usual. In the sunlight, she looked years younger, much closer to thirty than forty. "Are you coming?"

I jumped up and followed her. We twisted down one path and another until we were at Rose Cottage. She opened the front door without a key, and inside everything was decorated like spring—flowing curtains in pastel colors, framed pictures on the wall, everything coordinated, simple yet tasteful. An enormous bouquet of lilies took up most of the living room coffee table. Miss Lloyd asked if I wanted anything to drink, and I glanced at the bar against one wall, fully stocked with liquor. I wondered if Rockhaven made a practice of supplying their famously sober movie star guests with alcohol, or if Ophelia had supplied it herself. I asked for water and sat on the sofa while she disappeared into the kitchen.

Then Miss Lloyd was back, handing me a glass, perching on the edge of the settee, one perfectly manicured hand propped in the air, cigarette dangling into space.

"The lilies are beautiful. Are they from an admirer?"

"Yes. They're from me. My favorite flower. The Chinese say, 'When you have only two pennies in the world, buy a loaf of bread with one, and a lily with the other.'" She swirled her drink. "I'm afraid I didn't kill her."

"I wasn't accusing you."

"I know. But you were snooping just the same. If I were going to kill her, I certainly wouldn't have done it in my own home. It's going to be enormously difficult to get anyone to come to the house again, and I'm fond of parties. I'm also fond of not looking like the world's worst hostess in front of the entire world. 'Don't go to Ophelia's. Unless you want to leave in a hearse.' No thank you." She swirled her glass again and took a drink.

On my way to the car, the arched gate to Rockhaven swung open and another automobile rolled up the drive, gravel snapping under the tires. Behind the wheel was Felix Roland, window down, dashingly handsome, silver hair slicked into place. I watched as he parked, swung out, and practically loped toward Rose Cottage. He wore gray slacks and a crisp white shirt, but no jacket, no tie. I turned and followed him, creeping around the trees, careful to stay a good distance behind.

She met him at the door. Immediately, their mouths were locked in one of the hungriest kisses I'd ever seen, as if they were two animals trying to swallow each other whole. He backed her inside, the door slamming closed behind them.

· · · · ·

At home, I sorted through my messages. *Butch Dawkins called*, Flora had written, along with the number for the Dunbar Hotel. I checked my watch, picked up the paper, stared at the Dunbar Hotel number until I had it memorized, and dialed the exchange.

"Dunbar Hotel."

"Butch Dawkins, please."

"One minute, and I'll connect you."

The phone clicked and then rang and rang. On the sixth ring, he answered.

"It's Velva Jean. I got your message."

"Hey, I wanted to talk to you about the record. If you're free and willing, I'd love to have you be a part of it."

"Just tell me what you need me to do."

"If you got time, I want you to give me a song. I'm picturing a record about loss and about hope and the dark places in between. I know you got things to say about that, and I want to hear them. Other folks will too."

I don't know how to write that, I thought. I'd never been one to write what I was in, especially when what I was in was a dark place. I usually had to be on the other side of things to describe them.

Butch said, "You just give me what you got. I ain't asking for more than that. And if you can't, it's okay. There'll be other times down the road."

"I'd like to. I'll try."

We talked about his ideas, about the schedule, when we would meet and go over the music, when he might need me to come to the studio. Then we said good-bye, just like a couple of old friends.

I was running late. Sam would be there soon. Still, I sat another minute or two, trying to push away the feeling that somewhere, a door had closed when I wasn't paying attention.

TWENTY-FIVE

The Villa Nova, on Sunset, was a hole-in-the-wall Italian place with a high, slanted roof and plenty of dark corners. The booths were red and curved and the air smelled warm and heavy. Sam sat looking at me, one arm hugging the back of the booth. The waiter appeared and when he asked us what we wanted to drink, I said to Sam, "You order for me."

He asked for two whiskeys, and then we ordered our food, and when the whiskey came, we clinked glasses and drank, the liquid burning all the way down. Sam nursed his along, but I threw mine back, as I'd seen my brother do, because the taste was so awful, and then I asked for another. Sam's eyebrows shot up and he said, "Easy, tiger. I'd like this evening to last longer than the next ten minutes."

We talked about my new film, about his new picture, about the Black Dahlia case, which Sam was following closely. We talked about where I came from and where he came from—pleasant, easy, interesting conversation. I thought of telling him about Rockhaven and the Dell Rapids Orphanage, and the things Dr. Murdoch had said, but instead I asked him about his parents, his brother, his childhood, and his life before MGM.

The food arrived—two bowls of spaghetti, the steam rising off them. With the first bite, I realized how hungry I was. I concentrated on eating, and then at some point I set my fork down. "There's something I need to ask you."

"Uh-oh." He pushed his plate away, tipped his glass to see how much was left. "Should I order another drink first?"

"Maybe you should get one for both of us." I decided I liked drinking. It made me feel lighter and freer, almost like being a little girl again, back before anything sad had happened.

Sam waved down the waiter, ordering another round. People crowded into the restaurant. I loved each one of them because they brought bustle and color and life, and it was good to think about life right now.

"I wish I knew something we could do to pass the time." He leaned in as if he were going to kiss me. I studied his mouth, curled up at one corner, and remembered what his lips felt like against mine. The memory was so vivid, so warm, that I could almost feel them. Suddenly, I wanted him to kiss me. Suddenly, I was thinking about a lot more than kissing.

The waiter set the drinks down between us, and just like that, Sam pulled away. He toasted me, drank, rested his chin on his hand. "All right, Pipes."

"Tell me about you and Mudge."

He lit a cigarette, and then a second, and then a third, making a show of smoking three at once. Then he stubbed one out and then another. He raised the remaining one to his lips, inhaled deeply, exhaled, and said, "She paid me to adapt a book she optioned. The idea was if Mayer didn't agree to produce it, she'd produce it outside of MGM. She said once a girl hit thirty, she had to start looking out for herself."

"*A Woman of Means.*"

"She told you?"

"I read the script."

"And?"

"It's very good."

"Ah, flattery. My favorite aphrodisiac." He winked. "She was giving me notes, not something I usually appreciate from actors, but she was smart. Not necessarily well read, as I'm sure you know, but she knew what worked on camera, and she was honest. It was important to her that the work read honestly too. She said there was enough fakery in Hollywood without printing lies on the page."

"And when you weren't working together?"

He shrugged, helpless. "She was gorgeous, and I had a reputation to uphold."

"Mmm," was all I managed to say. My insides had gone prickly, even though I knew they had no right to.

"That was when they first brought me out here, a couple of months before I met a certain girl singer." He smiled. I smiled back, waiting. "It was one night, during a lapse with Nigel."

"And that was it?"

"And that was it."

"Thanks. For telling me."

"You're welcome." He stubbed the last cigarette out. "You make a man want to say things he wouldn't normally say."

"Sam . . ."

"I'm not asking for anything in return. Not right now."

I took a breath. "I haven't been part of a couple—a real couple—in a very long time. I've never dated in the traditional way. I got married when I was sixteen, and divorced when I was nineteen, and I've lost my heart one or two times since then, but I don't know anything about going to dinners and what it's like to do normal things in a normal world where the world isn't at war."

"Los Angeles isn't exactly a normal world, and you're not exactly a normal girl."

"No, I guess not."

"Before you work up to telling me whatever you're going to tell me, I have to ask about the Indian."

"He's not 'the Indian.' He's part Indian. His name is Butch Dawkins."

"I have to ask about Mr. Dawkins, then. Where is he in all this?"

"This is about us. He's nowhere."

"I'm not sure about that."

"Butch has always been there, but not there. He's like a haint—a ghost—that just appears now and then."

"So is he in a now phase or a then phase?"

Now, then, now, then. Then, then, then.

"Then."

"Do you love him?"

"I don't know." He'd been honest with me, and I wanted to be honest with him.

"Do you love me?"

"I don't know." I took a drink and felt the recklessness of my daddy's people and their people before them surging up from somewhere. "The only thing I know is that this isn't the time for love. Not right now. Not with all that's happened." What would Mudge have done? She would have kissed him anyway and thought things through later. "Does it matter that I don't know?"

"To me, no. To you, probably."

We were interrupted by a cough, and the waiter was there to take the plates. He asked if we wanted dessert. Sam looked at me and I said, "Maybe we could take it to go."

He raised an eyebrow and turned to the waiter. "There's a five in it for you if you hurry."

Several minutes later, we were still waiting for the bill. Sam said, "I'm going to embark on a search."

"While you do that, I'll use the powder room."

I hunted through my purse for my lipstick and compact, and walked into the ladies' lounge, which was a narrow room with one toilet and a sink with a mirror above, cracked at one corner.

On my way out, a man was standing beside the door, big and amiable, arms folded across his chest. He nodded at me and started to move forward. I stepped out of the way, but instead of moving past me, he pushed me back into the bathroom and locked the door. He said, "You're the actress. Sing me a song, just like you do in the movies."

His breath was on my face, his hands on my arms, holding me in place. My eyes darted past him, to the soap and towels at the side of the sink, the little wooden stand that sat behind him, a vase with flowers, the door.

"One little sweet song." As his mouth moved toward me, and his hands slid down my arms, I could smell the alcohol on him. He could have been studio ordered or a friend of the murderer or just some drunk, obnoxious fan.

Then his hand was on mine, and I wiggled my hand so that my fingers intertwined with his. In one swift motion, I pulled hard on those fingers, bending them back to his wrist. I knew enough from self-defense, from my work in France, how to sprain a man's hand without breaking it, how to take it almost to that point. "Tell me who sent you."

"Sonofabitch. Let me go."

I pulled harder on the fingers. "Tell me who sent you."

We went back and forth like this for about thirty seconds. I pulled harder, right at the breaking point, hovering there. Then just a little harder. It would have been so easy to snap his hand in two, finger by finger.

He dropped to his knees. "No one sent me. I saw your pictures. I wanted you to sing me a song." He was starting to cry now, and I felt one last surge of anger before I went empty. I let him go and he sank back onto the floor.

He was just a fan, only a fan. I knew from Mudge that they could be as dangerous as anyone else. I took a deep breath and felt relief wash through me. My heart settled. My pulse settled. I pulled a towel from the rack and handed it to him.

"Next time, ask nicely."

I stepped over him and found Sam outside the door, a box in his hands. He stared past me at the man lying on the floor. "Great mother-of-pearl." Sam looked at me in what could only be called awe, or shock. "I don't know whether to kiss you or run like hell."

• • • • •

In his car, in front of Mudge's house, Sam said, "And there it is." We both stared up at its still and silent face, the windows dark, curtains drawn. The house looked as if it were sleeping.

I said, "Aren't you going to walk me to the door?"

I carried the box from the Villa Nova—some sort of strawberry cake. Sam and I didn't talk until we were standing on the stoop, my back to the house, his back to the street.

I said, "Aren't you going to walk me in?"

He kissed me then, as if he'd been waiting for this moment all night, his hands on either side of my face, twining into my hair, tugging at it so that my head tilted back and he could run his lips across my throat. My own hands had gone off without me, dropping the box, doing exactly what they wanted to do. I wanted him, and he knew I wanted him. I wanted his hands and his mouth, and the rest of him. I wanted to fall asleep against him, feeling the warmth, listening to his heartbeat, feeling his skin. I wanted to forget about Mudge and death and MGM and Helen down the hall and how things looked and my good Southern upbringing, as strong as any contract, and what Sweet Fern might say if she could see me. I didn't want to think at all.

Sam threw the door open, picked me up, and tossed me over his shoulder. He was up the stairs two at a time, my head bobbing upside down. He pushed open the door to one of the guest rooms, then jogged me out of there and down the hall, throwing open another door, and another. "Where the hell am I taking you?"

"Not that one," I whispered. "Helen." I pointed. "That one at the end." In my bedroom, he shut the door and said, "What's this?"

He carried me over to the evidence wall, where all the little faces were lined up, including his own. "You really have been busy."

"They're my suspects," I said, muffled, into his shirt.

"I gathered." He bent his knees, leaned in, so he could better see himself. "I can't believe it."

"I'm sorry."

"You should be. If you're going to put me up there, at least use a good picture."

Then he switched off the light, flicked on the bedside lamp, and dropped me onto the bed. Instead of joining me, he stood looking at me, as if he couldn't believe he was there, and I was there, and there we were.

I reached for his tie, just like in a movie, and pulled him toward me, so that he planted one arm on either side of me, brown hair falling over his forehead, brown eyes staring down at me, mouth set in a half smile.

"You're the damndest woman."

His forehead met mine, his lips hovering close, so close but not touching. His breath quickened. He ran his hands over my skin, my hips, waist, arms, hair. I ran my hands over his shoulders, feeling the strength of his body underneath his shirt, along his neck and down his back. He pulled the shirt off, dropping it to the floor. His skin was hot to the touch. He pulled me up so I was standing and turned me around so that I was facing away from him. My heart was racing. Then I felt his fingers below my hairline as he unbuttoned my dress—a long line of buttons down the back and a sash at the waist. I felt the air hitting my skin as the buttons came open, as my back was exposed. He pulled at the sash, tugging it out of its bow. My dress dropped next, pooling at my feet.

I leaned in then and pressed my lips to his neck, where the skin was hottest. He swept me up and onto the bed, rolling me toward him so I was on top of him, and then rolling over again so he was on top of me.

And then, for no reason, I started to cry. "Sorry," I said, and brushed the tears away. I pulled him in, kissed him again, and then felt another wave of tears, right after the first. "Dammit. Sorry." I brushed these away too. I hiccupped. "God, sorry."

He didn't say anything, just lay down beside me, my back to him, pulling me in close. I cried and hiccupped and tried to focus on his arms and his heartbeat. And then I began to cry harder.

Eventually my mind drifted off. Hours later, I opened my eyes, and Sam was gone. I sat up, looking around, and the bathroom door opened. Sam, in boxer briefs, rubbing his eyes. He said, "You didn't sleep long. How's the head?"

"Splitting."

"Do you keep aspirin in this place?"

"In the drawer there."

He opened the drawer, and the bottles of Benzedrine and Seconal went rolling into the wood. "Well now, what's this?" He held up the Benzedrine and shook it.

I sat up, gathering my hair, and then let it go. "Evidence." I heard a noise outside, or downstairs, or maybe down the street. I cocked my head, listening.

"It was outside."

"What?"

"The noise. I'm not just a pretty face, Pipes. I'm also blessed with exceptional hearing. So what's my motive?" He nodded at the evidence wall.

"That remains to be seen. Did you know Felix Roland and Ophelia are having an affair?"

"The mystery man from her bedroom?"

"I guess so." I told him about seeing them at Rockhaven.

He whistled. "We need to figure out who up there not only had a motive but the ability to poison her. They're not necessarily one and the same."

"I doubt Felix will talk to me, and I didn't get very far with Tauby."

"Maybe they'll talk to me." He smiled. "Want me to see what I can get?"

"If you don't mind. Did you—when you worked with her, did she ever mention someone named Rebecca?"

"Doesn't ring a bell, no. Why?"

"It was the last thing she said to me before she died."

He took my hand and nodded up at the wall again. "Have you thought about what will happen once you figure this out?"

"What do you mean?"

"Say you catch the killer, find the evidence, prove that he or she did it. What then? If what you say is true, the studio's never going to let you put this out there. They'll kill it as fast as someone killed Barbara Fanning."

"I'm still working on that part of it."

"Let's not worry about it tonight." He kissed me lightly on the nose. "Shall we get some more sleep? Unless, of course, you can think of something else to do."

When I made a show of yawning, he reached over me to switch off the lamp. As he looked down, his face half in light, half in shadow, there was something in his eyes that made me ask, "What is it?"

"I don't know. But I'm thinking there's more on your mind than suspects and poison and murder. Am I right, Pipes?"

I reached up and kissed him. His lips were warm. My head still pounded. It hurt too much to think clearly. "The only thing I'm thinking about right now is sleep."

· · · · ·

When I opened my eyes again, it was morning and he was gone. A note lay on the pillow next to mine along with a bottle of aspirin. *You're utter hell on a man's ego, Pipes. It's a good thing I have ego enough to spare. Gone to the studio, but will be thinking lasciviously about you the entire time. (Lascivious \la'sivēas\ adjective [of a person, manner, or gesture] feeling or revealing an overt and often offensive sexual desire.) Take two of these as soon as you wake up and call me. P.S. I don't know how I'll concentrate now that I can picture you in bed.*

I sat up, stretched, opened the curtains. I padded over to the evidence wall and studied the faces. Nigel Gray and Pia Palmer smiled out at me as if to say, *You can't get us. We're safe. There's nothing you can do.*

And there, below them, was a newer, better photo of Sam—torn from the page of a movie magazine—which he'd tacked over the old one.

TWENTY-SIX

arly Thursday, Helen found Mudge's will folded and tucked inside a book of Shakespeare's plays. In it, Mudge remembered her bunkmates at Avenger Field. She made sure that I received all her dresses since, as she noted, I could "certainly use them." She left money to the families of the thirty-eight WASP who died and to a flying school for girls, started by Shirley Bingham, a pilot two years ahead of us. She left her house, car, minks, jewelry, and several thousand dollars to Flora, and everything else—including the bulk of her money—went to John Henry Briggs of Dell Rapids Orphanage and Industrial School in Dell Rapids, South Dakota.

I took the document from Helen to read the date. "December 15, 1946. It was updated two weeks before she died."

"Do you think Redd Deeley knows he was cut out?"

"I don't know."

"So he might have expected to still get everything." When I nodded, she said, "That looks bad for him, doesn't it? I mean, in mystery books, that's usually the motive of the killer."

I thought about this as I got dressed and ready for work. Before I walked out the door, I put in a call to Redd, asking him to meet me for lunch. Outside the house, a man with a hat was sitting behind the wheel of his car, the engine running. He was the same man I'd seen parked on the street before. When he saw me coming down the walk, he touched the brim of his hat and drove away.

· · · · ·

At eleven fifteen that morning, I sat down at the piano in Rosie's studio and played what I'd written of the song for Butch's record. I only had a half dozen sheets of paper filled with lines, most of them crossed out. The only line I really liked was: "Home to me."

I'd written it because it sounded hopeful, and I remembered what Butch had said about hope. I knew people in this world who'd never been through a single sad thing, and they didn't have any more hope than a grasshopper. But somehow I'd held on to mine—through Mama's death and everything sad or terrible that had followed. But what if hope had a threshold? What if there was a limit to it? What if each of us was only given a certain amount and mine was used up?

The thing I did have was the melody, so mostly I played while Rosie listened, and afterward he sat beside me on the bench and said, "Good. This is good. What if you also add in something here?" He did a little flourish up and down the keys. "And what if you change it to a minor key?"

My first instinct was that this would make the tune too sad, that it was sad enough already, but Rosie said, "Try it. There's no harm in experimenting. Nothing's set in stone. You can go right back to the way it was if you don't like it."

So I played it again. This time through, I could feel it in a way I hadn't before. I played it once more the same way. Then Rosie and I talked about words, and about what I wanted to say. Just as I was starting to hear the lyrics forming in my mind, a messenger boy appeared and said I was wanted in Billy Taub's office.

· · · · ·

My first thought was that he looked like a madman again. He sat shuffling through papers at a wild pace, fielding phone calls, making notes, shirt untucked, glasses askew. The white streak of hair had grown to several white streaks of hair, so that you could barely see the original brown. His desk was heaped with scripts and notes and pictures—no more *Home of the Brave*. He was on to *Latimer* now. A cigar burned in the ashtray.

When I walked in, he barely looked up. He waved me to a chair, finished his telephone conversation, jotted something down, then threw the pen onto the desk and fixed his eyes on me. "I'll make this quick, Kit. I know you went to visit Ophelia. I know you were asking questions. I'm telling you this as a favor—let it be."

I wondered if he knew I hadn't been her only visitor that day. "I don't know what you mean."

"But you do. We didn't send her there so that she could be upset."

"The papers are reporting that she checked herself in."

"We don't have time to sit here and go back and forth. I know what you're trying to do, and you need to stop doing it. Let this go." There was something in his voice that chilled me. He stood. We were done. "It's best for everyone, especially you."

"You meant a lot to Barbara Fanning."

"She was a good actress. I enjoyed working with her."

"You were more than that to her. If you cared about her at all, and I'm guessing you did once upon a time, you'll help me."

"I'm sorry."

He didn't bother walking me out. At his door, I turned. He still stood behind his desk, sorting through papers. "Who is Rebecca?"

He stopped what he was doing. For a moment, he couldn't speak. "Why are you asking about Rebecca?" His voice broke.

I was filled with a sudden breathless feeling, but I told myself to stay cool. "Who is she?"

He cleared his throat. "She was my daughter. Our daughter." His voice broke again. He glanced at Ophelia's picture. "We adopted her when she was two."

"I didn't see her at Broad Water."

"Rebecca died five years ago. She was ten. It was a heart defect,

something we couldn't have known about, even though it was heredi-
tary. Maybe it could have been attended to if they'd told us. But we
didn't know. They didn't tell us."

"Did Barbara ever meet her?"

"Once. She came to . . . visit me at the house when Ophelia was
away. Rebecca was with the nanny, but Barbara ran into them on the
beach. Rebecca had seen all her films and so she recognized her. Instead of spending the day with me, Barbara spent it with my daughter.
They played in the water and built things in the sand. I knew I
shouldn't let them, that Ophelia would have my head, but it was good
to see both of them enjoying themselves like that. Barbara told me afterward it was one of the nicest days she'd ever had." His eyes had
gone misty and faraway. "Rebecca said the same thing. She didn't have
many nice days left. She died three months later."

• • • • •

When I left him, Billy Taub was sitting quietly, hands folded, staring
at his desk. I was late to meet Redd, and I hurried across Washington
Boulevard to Frances Edwards' Bar and Grill, which everyone at the
studio called "the Hangout." I was trying to process the conversation
I'd just had—was Rebecca Taub the Rebecca Mudge had meant?
And, if so, why had this been her last word?

Redd was seated in a booth and had already ordered for both of us.
As I sat, he said, "Congratulations. You've been named *Photoplay*'s
Rising Star of 1947." He talked about what a big deal this was—my
picture on the cover, a full-length article accompanied by more photographs. "Metro's bringing out the second *Flyin' Jenny* ahead of schedule in order to capitalize on the publicity."

"Do they want an interview?"

"Not necessary. They have enough information for the story without talking to you."

I was distracted, but I hoped he couldn't tell. "That's wonderful."

"What's up, Kit? Why did you want to meet me?"

"Did you know Mudge changed her will in December?"

Redd was slick, but he wasn't an actor, and his entire expression shifted. I could see genuine shock followed by wariness, which told me he hadn't known. "December?"

"That's right. Do you have any idea why she would have changed it?"

"No. Except maybe to cut me out of it. Is that what she did? I suppose she left everything to Nigel."

"She did cut you out, but she didn't leave anything to Nigel."

"When you say 'cut out,' you mean I'm nowhere in it? Not even a tie clip? Not even the goddamn car I bought her for a goddamn wedding present?"

I glanced around, catching the eyes of the people nearby, who were now looking in our direction. "Nowhere and nothing."

He threw his napkin on the table and glared at the ceiling. When he spoke again, he was quieter and calmer, as if he'd forced himself to count to ten. "I guess I shouldn't be surprised, right? I mean, she was done with me the moment she met Nigel."

"You represent Nigel." The fact had just dawned on me.

"That's right." He was staring off across the restaurant.

"How did you do that after what happened?"

"You mean after she divorced me to marry him?" He shrugged. "I'm a businessman. She used to say I was an agent before I was a man, and that was the problem with me. She always loved telling me the problem with me."

"She said you wanted Barbara Fanning, not Eloise Mudge."

"I know she thought that, but it wasn't true." He held up his hands in a gesture of surrender. "I loved her—Barbara, Eloise. I still do." He was talking to the table now, where his hands rested, empty, helpless. And then, for the first time I saw it—the wedding ring he still wore, a year and a half later.

"Redd, who is John Henry Briggs?"

He made himself look up, but I could see the effort it took. "Who?"

"She left the bulk of her estate to a boy named John Henry Briggs. A ten-year-old orphan living in Dell Rapids, South Dakota. She hired a private investigator to find him not long before she died." I opened my bag, took out the picture of the boy, and slid it across the table. "I think he's her son."

Redd stared at the photo for a minute, as if he didn't want to touch it, and then he picked it up, running his finger up and down one corner, over and over. He took a good, hard look before setting the photo down and pushing it toward me. "He's not her son."

"But she wanted to find him. And she left him all that money. It would have been before you, maybe with Cray Cordova." I was trying to remember the name of her first husband. Maybe the boy belonged to him.

Redd shook his head and smiled sadly, the corners of his mouth barely lifting. "I assumed you knew. Barbara wasn't able to have children."

"But she always talked about having them."

"Because she wanted a kid more than anything. We tried before we got married, after we got married. We were always trying. She was never able to have one with Cray, but she thought that was because he smacked her around. Her body was just anxious, in a state of stress, she said. But with me she was safe. We argued, but I'd never hit her, and she knew that. When it didn't happen—when she didn't get pregnant—she went to her doctor. Not the studio quack, but a regular doctor. He was the one who told her. She didn't believe him, and so she went to see another doctor and another, until finally I told her to stop it because eventually someone was going to spill it to the gossip columnists. All the doctors told her the same thing: She would never have a child of her own." He picked up the photo again. "Maybe this was a kid she wanted to adopt."

He handed me the picture and I looked at the boy's face. "But who was he? And why him?"

· · · · ·

When I got back to my dressing room, a note was taped to the door. *Pipes—I know I'm supposed to play hard to get, not calling you for a week or two, just to make you worry, etc., but frankly I want to see you too badly. See what you've done to me? Sam. P.S. I'm heading to Broad Water for another script-writing lock-up. Please write and provide conjugal visits. Will be interrogating the old boys' club until your arrival.*

I went into my room, came back out, and there it was—the first time I'd noticed it: "Babe King," it said on the door of Mudge's star suite. I heard a voice from inside, and then the door banged open and Yilla King barged out, pushing past her daughter, knocking Babe's shoulder too hard with her own.

Babe appeared, face a dark cloud. Just past her, I could see that Mudge's blue walls had been changed to pink.

"Is everything okay?"

She started a little. "Kit. I didn't know you were there. It's good to see a friendly face." She nodded toward the street, where Yilla stood smoking a cigarette. "I think my mother would be happy if I didn't grow up. She likes it when I depend on her, but she doesn't like it when I have a mind of my own."

"I have a sister like that. It looks as if you're all moved in."

She came out, shut the door and locked it, dropping the key into a flat red purse, which she tucked under her arm. "To be honest, that dressing room gives me the spooks. I can't help feeling that any minute she's going to reappear and tell me to get out."

· · · · ·

I told Flora the news that night—that Mudge had left the house and cars and jewelry to her, along with a great deal of money. Flora sat down with the will and started to cry. As Helen patted her back, I brought her a cold drink and a handkerchief. She said, "Miss Barbara was good people. She had a heart that not everyone could see."

I said, "We can help you move in, as soon as you're ready." As soon as we can, I thought, and out of Leimert Park, where the Black Dahlia had been found, just blocks from Flora's house.

She dabbed at her eyes. "What about the covenants?"

"We're looking into those, but you own this house, Flora. They can't take it away from you."

"I want you to stay here as long as you want." She said it to both of us. "It's your home too."

· · · · ·

On Friday and Saturday, *Flyin' Jenny* shot on location in the Valley. Les released us Saturday afternoon, and that evening Johnny Clay and Helen and I ate hot dogs from paper cartons at Pink's hot dog stand on La Brea. As we sat outside under a canvas umbrella, I told my brother about John Henry Briggs and Mudge not being able to have children and the will and Rebecca Taub and even *Jane Eyre*.

"Do you think the Taubs' Rebecca is Mudge's Rebecca?"

"I don't know. It doesn't make sense."

He asked me questions, including where was Nigel Gray and when was he expected back, and then we returned to the house, where Johnny Clay told us about the record and the band—Butch Dawkins & the Bluesmen—and all the things they were planning to do after Los Angeles. They might head to Memphis or maybe Chicago, or maybe even New York City. "Which reminds me," he said. "There's a stack of records in the car that I'm supposed to give you. Things Butch wants you to listen to."

I showed him the evidence wall and played him what I had of my song, and before he left Helen served drinks in the living room while we listened to the Grand Ole Opry. Johnny Clay said, "You still think of going on there, little sister?"

"Of course." But I said it out of habit. It used to be that singing and playing on the Grand Ole Opry was the only thing I ever thought about, but the truth was, I hadn't thought of the Opry in a very long time. I'd been too caught up in getting home from England, in coming to Hollywood, and with everything that had happened since the weekend at Broad Water.

Helen said, "Did you hear a banging?" She turned the radio down and then we all heard it—a pounding on the door.

Sam was standing on the front step, and a car idled in the street, headlights blazing. He said, "Roland and I are on our way to the beach."

"Do you want to come in?"

Johnny Clay yelled, "Who is it?"

"No. He's waiting in the car." Sam leaned in. "I just wanted to do this." He kissed me, sweet and electric. He kissed my mouth first, and then my neck, all the way to the collarbone, his hands sliding down my back, to my waist, pulling me in.

When we broke apart, he studied my eyes, my nose, my mouth, like he was learning every line. "I like your freckles. I like you best like this. No Max Factor. Just you." He kissed me again.

"Good night, Pipes."

"Good night, Sam."

Like that, he was gone, across the yard, and back inside the car, door slamming, engine revving, taillights moving away into the night.

Johnny Clay appeared behind me. "Who was it? The writer?" We both stood looking down the street. Cars went by in either direction. I shut the door and tried to think of something to say. I put a hand to my mouth, to my cheek.

He said, "Little sister. You should see your face."

· · · · ·

I was up before Helen the next morning. On the front porch, wedged beneath the newspaper and the welcome mat, was a plain brown envelope, no address, no name, nothing written on the outside.

I glanced up and down the street before carrying it into the house. I threw the newspaper aside—"Murdered Girl Discovered in Victorville"—and very carefully opened the envelope to find a thick stack of pages, and a single piece of paper, which fluttered to the ground like a leaf in fall. I plucked it from the rug.

Kit Rogers—

There's more where this came from. Let's talk.

Zed Zabel. 213-555-3499

The stack of pages was paper-clipped together, and at first I couldn't understand what I was looking at. I carried the pages to the sofa, where I propped myself against the cushions and started reading. They seemed to be phone logs—complete, detailed transcripts of every conversation I'd had over the telephone during the past few weeks, not just in my studio dressing room, but at home.

I thought: I should call my brother. I should wake up Helen. But instead I started reading again from the beginning, as if I might possibly find some clue as to who or how or why.

DEATH AT CROSSING

Movie Star Couple Hurrying to Overtake Commuter, Hit by Southbound Train

The London Times

LONDON, January 27—Believed to have been hurrying to Charing Cross to catch a train, international film star Nigel Gray, 31, was injured and his wife, actress Pia Palmer, 34, was killed instantly when their automobile collided with a southbound passenger train at Rogers Street crossing this morning.

Gray is being treated for a broken arm and broken ribs at Charing Cross Hospital.

Railroad officials said the couple apparently had waited for a northbound train to pass, and collided with the southbound local when their machine was driven onto the second track.

There was possibly only a single witness to the tragedy—T. S. Granger, fireman of the southbound train. He said the victims' auto smashed into the side of his locomotive. The Metropolitan police report indicated that the right front wheel of the machine was already on the track.

It may never be determined who was driving the car, although the police believe Ms. Palmer was at the wheel. Neighbors of the couple did not believe Ms. Palmer a good driver and said her husband had frequently protested against her operating the machine.

Gray had been in England since early last week, on a publicity tour for his most recent picture, Metro-Goldwyn-Mayer's *Home of the Brave*.

TWENTY-SEVEN

I drove Sunset Boulevard all the way to Western Avenue, which wound up to the entrance of Griffith Park. I followed the winding dirt road through the trees, which were green even in winter, up and around the mountain. At the very top I came to a parking lot, empty except for one other car, and at the end of it sat a large domed building. "The Griffith Park Observatory," a sign said.

I made my way across the lot to the sidewalk and up to the building, where Zed Zabel sat on the steps. "You're late," he said, standing.

"You said dawn. It's dawn."

The Hollywoodland sign perched on a hillside just west of us. Somewhere, birds were singing. We walked along the building to the back, overlooking the city, downtown to the left, the ocean to the right. I had the sense of endless rolling green, almost like being home again. We leaned against the guardrail that separated us from the valley below, and now I could see the sun, spreading its way across the horizon.

We stood shoulder-to-shoulder, only I was an inch taller. "What do you want, Mr. Zabel? Where did you get my phone records?"

"Ever heard of a guy named Jim Vaus?"

"No."

"He's an ex-GI with a passion for electronics."

"What does that have to do with me?"

"He's a wiretapper. And not just any wiretapper. His taps are virtually undetectable. He works for Mickey Cohen, the cops, and the studios. He plays all sides."

"And you're saying he tapped my house and dressing room?"

"That's right."

"Who hired him?"

"Whitey Hendry. Eddie Mannix. Someone at your studio."

"Why?"

"Don't ask a stupid question. You know why. Because your friend was killed and you won't let it go."

"But I don't know anything."

"Doesn't matter. You're digging. That's all they care about."

"How do you know she was killed?"

"Everyone knows she was killed. Just like Ted Healy. Only in that particular case, Wallace Beery, Albert Broccoli, and Pat DiCicco beat him to death outside a nightclub."

"Ted Healy?"

"Two-bit actor who created the Three Stooges comedy team, but he couldn't touch Beery's popularity or box office pull. After Healy was killed, Beery was sent to Europe on a four-month-long publicity tour and the press was fed some bullshit story about three college boys who attacked him."

I knew the name Wallace Beery. I'd actually seen Wallace Beery on the lot at Metro. But I still had to ask: "Who covered for him?"

"Eddie Mannix, Howard Strickling, and Louis B. Mayer. You know Shelby Jordan?" I nodded. "She was a kid publicist then, just cutting her teeth. Literally a kid, no more than eighteen or so. She was there then." My heart went thump-thump-thump. "Now, Wallace Beery's no Nigel Gray, but you have to admit that's a pretty strong coincidence. I need to know what you know."

"How did you get my phone records? Who gave them to you?"

"Everyone has a price, sweetheart. Did you talk to Dr. Murdoch?"

I didn't say anything.

"Look at this." He leaned against the rail, hanging over it. I peered over the edge and studied the sheer drop, the trees and bushes and undergrowth that straggled down the hillside. "You could murder a man and throw him down there and it might be days, maybe weeks before he was found, if the coyotes don't eat him first. Or, I figure, you could poison him." He looked at me then, a question in his beady eyes: Is this true? Is this how she died?

I decided to answer him without answering him. "And then cover up the crime scene, seal the coroner's report, send the man who did it away for a few weeks, get him out of the public eye." I studied the spiderweb of dirt roads that wove their way over and through the hills. "I have to ask you. Detective Nick Agresta?"

"Dirty."

"Coroner Nigh?"

"Clean."

"Dr. Murdoch?"

"Clean."

"The DA?"

"Dirty. Best thing you can do is play along. My sources tell me Nigel Gray will be back soon. You cozy up to him, get him to confess, I print the story, and we blow this thing wide open."

"You print the story?"

"That's right."

"What if I just start talking off-book during one of my interviews?"

"What are you going to say? That someone killed your friend, but you don't know who or how or why? Besides, you've been cut off from press conferences and one-on-ones, or haven't you noticed? None of us are allowed near you right now."

"What makes you think I can get Nigel Gray to talk to me?"

"You're a girl, aren't you? Plus he's got something not many people have in Hollywood—a conscience." He handed me a slip of paper. "You need me, call me from a pay phone, but make sure it's out of the way. The studio has spies everywhere. And count your lucky stars that Nigel's had this little accident. If the studio wasn't so distracted, you might be feeling a lot more heat right now."

· · · · ·

By the time I got to Metro, a crowd of reporters was gathered outside the Thalberg Building, stretching up to the East Gate. They roamed in front of the car, around the car, banging on the fender. When they recognized me, they began shouting and snapping photographs.

The guard waved me on through the gate, away from the mob. On the other side, I rolled down my window and leaned out. "How long have they been here?"

He took off his cap and wiped his forehead. "Since the news broke." He fitted the cap back onto his head and rested one hand on my car door, squinting toward the crowd, keeping his eye on them. "Terrible way to die, hit by a train. Mr. Gray's always been good to me. First Miss Fanning, now his wife." He shook his head. "Poor bastard."

Yes, I thought. Poor Nigel Gray. Losing both the women he loved within weeks of each other. How tragic. How strange. How coincidental.

· · · · ·

In the makeup and hair departments, the women were gossiping. *Nigel finally got rid of the old ball and chain. Pia was clearly driving. She wanted to kill him for humiliating her, and ended up killing herself. He tried to kill her for standing in his way with Barbara Fanning. He killed her because she killed Barbara Fanning. They made a pact to die together, but in the end Nigel was saved, and now he'll live with the guilt of his survival for the rest of his life.*

On the Stage 4 set of *Flyin' Jenny*, we were all so distracted that Les Edgar let us go early. "Let's pick back up tomorrow, folks. I suggest everyone go home, clear your heads, and get some rest."

Hal said, "What are you going to do with this unexpected time off?" He held the door for me, and as I walked out I heard my name.

One of the wardrobe girls came running after me. "Before you go, Miss Rogers, I need you to stop by the wardrobe department to be fitted for the new flying uniform."

Hal smiled. "I guess that answers my question. See you tomorrow."

"See you tomorrow."

. . . . .

Inside one of the wardrobe cubicles, I undressed and then dressed in the new costume, which was the same navy blue color as my WASP uniform. Through the thin wall of the dressing area, I heard Yilla King say to Babe, "First Barbara Fanning, now Pia Palmer. Lord help the next girl who gets involved with him. And Lord help those children, being dragged back here to be raised by him, as if he's fit to be a parent—"

"Mother." Her tone was sharp. "Please stop talking."

I stood very still in case they continued, but the only thing Yilla said was, "Once I marry Leland, he'll never be invited. You'll see. Nigel Gray won't ever set foot in my house." I heard the sound of the cubicle door opening and closing and two sets of footsteps tapping away.

Ten minutes later, as I stood surrounded by racks of costumes in all styles and colors, I felt an idea forming. As soon as I was done being measured, I told the girl at the desk that I was going to a costume party later that night, and needed a maid's uniform—black dress with white collar and cuffs, white apron, little black-and-white hat, plain stockings, low black heels, name tag. Exactly like the uniform worn by the servants at Broad Water.

I changed into my costume at a gas station in Venice, pinning my hair up underneath the hat and softening my makeup and lipstick. I traded my seamed stockings for the plain ones, my sandals for the sensible black shoes. Ophelia liked the maidservants at Broad Water to look clean and attractive, but not too attractive. When I was done, I studied myself in the little mirror that hung above the sink. Even in this getup, I was still recognizable.

I asked the service station attendant if he had a lost and found. He said, "I got a basket in the back where we throw things people leave. If they don't come for it in a week, we keep it."

"Do you happen to have a pair of glasses in there?"

"I can check for you."

I waited outside for him, and he was back a few minutes later carrying two pairs of glasses. The first was a man's pair, black rimmed and thick lensed. The second was round and made of wire. I picked these up and tried them on. The world slanted, but I could still see through them.

"Are those yours?" The man sounded doubtful.

"No, but I'd like to borrow them. I can have them back to you later today."

I handed him five dollars, and as he pocketed the money he said, "You can have 'em. They been in there for at least three weeks."

· · · · ·

Broad Water looked exactly the same as it had the first time I'd seen it, grand and white and columned. The sun beat down from the blue, blue sky. The waves rolled in and out, in and out, on the wide, tan beach. I parked just past the house, up the road, and walked across the sand to the oceanfront entrance, which I knew would be open.

The pool chairs were empty, tennis courts empty. I hurried up the stairs to the terrace and slipped inside. I listened for voices. During the writing of *Home of the Brave*, Sam said that he, Les, and Tauby, and later he, Felix, and Tauby had holed up on the other end of the house from the music room bathroom, where I'd found Mudge. I hoped I remembered the way.

Ophelia would still be at Rockhaven, but I needed to watch out for the servants. From the entrance hall, I headed south toward what I thought were the art gallery, the library, and the music room. I got lost, ending up in the game room, where we had all gathered after dinner that night. I turned around and went the other way. The house was a maze of rooms and hallways, somehow more confusing now than it had been in the pitch dark.

I heard voices and ducked into a sitting room, one of five or six sitting rooms I'd already seen. They were female voices—housekeepers or maids—and I crouched behind a chair as they passed. I listened before tiptoeing to the doorframe, where I looked this way, then that, to make sure all was clear.

I found the music room a few minutes later. There was the rug that Whitey Hendry had turned over. And the bathroom where I'd first seen Mudge. I wasn't sure what I hoped to find. Some obvious clue. Something to tell me what had happened that night. I flipped the rug back and studied the floor, the underside of the rug itself. I stood in the bathroom scouring every inch of tile, wall, and countertop with my eyes. The white monogrammed towels that hung from the rack were fresh and clean. I turned on the faucet, letting the water run. I turned it off. I opened the cabinet to see what was inside. Cleaning supplies, more towels. But it got me wondering— what was in Tauby's personal cabinet? The Benzedrine he was always chewing, but what else?

It took me ten minutes to slip upstairs, unnoticed, to the bedrooms. Too late, I spotted a girl coming down the hall, dressed like I was in a black uniform, white apron, and hat. I adjusted my glasses and tried not to bump into the wall. Before she could say anything, I smiled. "Golly, am I glad I ran into you. I've only been here a day and I've already lost my way. I'm looking for Mr. Taub's bedroom. I'm supposed to fetch something for Mr. Weldon."

I waited for her to call for help or chase me out, but instead she pointed to the end of the hall. "It's the grand suite, ocean side. The opposite of Miss Lloyd's." She nodded in the other direction. Then she elbowed me. "I'd like to fetch Mr. Weldon a few things myself." She walked off, laughing to herself.

I waited till the hall was empty, then took off the glasses and ducked inside Tauby's room. Once inside, I shut the door. It was a manly room—dark wood furniture, white walls, bearskin rug, framed nudes, all female, including one of a very young Barbara Fanning. She couldn't have been more than twenty at the time. In it, her expression and her body language were almost shy, but her eyes were shining as if she knew exactly what she was doing.

I made myself explore the medicine cabinet first because I didn't know how long I had until I was discovered again. The bathroom featured a black-and-white tile floor and a black claw-foot tub and shower. Inside the wooden cabinet that hung on the wall, I found bottles of pills. Benzedrine, Seconal, and others with names I didn't recognize. There were tinctures and lotions and salves and liquids. It was practically a pharmacy. I picked up one of the bottles of bennies and read the name of the prescribing physician: Dr. Atwill. I picked up another: Dr. Gabler. And another: Dr. Wakeman. Sneaky man, I thought. Billy Taub had prescriptions from every doctor in town. But then I looked at the labels more closely—"Ophelia Lloyd," they said, not "William Taub." Every single one of the prescriptions was for his wife.

I memorized the names of the doctors, and memorized the names of some of the other medicines. Then, back in his bedroom, I rummaged through the bedside tables and chest of drawers, and finally the thick-legged wooden desk that filled one wall. When the middle drawer wouldn't budge, I pulled a hairpin from my hat and jimmied the lock. Finally, I heard the click, and the drawer slid open. Inside were two bundles of pictures, tied with twine. One set was of a little girl—twenty or so photographs of Rebecca Taub from the age of two to ten. She was a delicate, sweet-faced child, small for her age. Each photo was labeled and dated, and the last featured Tauby, Ophelia, and Rebecca sitting side by side on the beach, feet stretched out toward the camera.

The other set of pictures was of Mudge. Underneath these was a stack of letters, which seemed to be from her as well, the earliest from 1933, the most recent from last month. It was dated December 10, 1946.

Dearest WT, I'm sorry about the blowup, but you've got to understand: I'm a girl in love. You said that Nigel won't marry me, and in the end I'll be the sad, old thing in the balcony. I know you mean well and you only want what's best, but can't you see this is what I've been waiting for? I loved Donald, Cray, and Redd in their own ways, but now I think they were just practice, all of it leading up to this man. If he will marry me, I'm going to grab on to it so fast, you'll have to hold on to your boots. He's my fresh start. He's my chance. I'll never forget all you've done for me. Be well, darling, and remember the girl you used to know. Maybe then you won't be so hard on the one she became. Love, B.

Suddenly, I heard footsteps in the hallway. In a panic, I slid the letter back into its envelope, shut the drawer, and ran for the closet. It was a deep, narrow walk-in, and I felt my way in the darkness to the very back. There, I rummaged around to get my bearings as voices entered the bedroom. A man and a woman. The man said, "Her name was Mary?" I couldn't tell if this was Tauby or one of the male servants.

"It was on her name tag." I touched the tag on my dress.

I could hear them making their way around the room. He said, "Check to make sure nothing's missing." This was followed by an opening and closing of drawers and the door to the terrace.

I shrank back against the wall, as far as I could, feeling for something to hide behind. And that was when I felt the latch. I lifted it and, on a hunch, pushed. Part of the wall fell away, and I tumbled backward into a hallway. As the closet door opened, I closed up the door in the wall and stood staring at it. I could still hear the man and the girl, now in the closet, where I'd been hiding only seconds before.

As their voices faded off, I turned to see where I was. A hallway, and at the end, a door. Careful not to make a sound, I opened the door and there was the love nest, just as Sam and I had left it, the covers of the daybed smoothed down, the mountains framed by the window. It wasn't Miss Lloyd's love nest at all—it was Tauby's. Had he been angry enough to kill the woman he loved once he found out she was leaving him?

I followed the hall to the secret staircase down, listened at the door to the library, and then slipped through it, out of the room, and through another and another until I was in the entrance hall, where I walked straight out the front door and back to the car.

TWENTY-EIGHT

On Monday, February 3, one week after Pia Palmer's death, Nigel returned to Metro. He looked pinched and pale, and someone said, "That's England for you," as if it was a time to make jokes.

He started rehearsals of *Latimer* that day, once again working with Billy Taub, Felix Roland, and Babe King, and now Webster Hayes, cast as King Henry VIII. Both *Latimer* and *Flyin' Jenny* were shooting on Lot 3, so as soon as I had a chance, I left the Jungle River Island and walked across the lot, past the farmhouse, to the Kismet staircase, where Nigel and Babe, still dressed in her Bonnie Dare costume, were standing.

The concrete staircase was nearly one hundred feet across and fifty feet high. It rose up out of the ground and went nowhere, the only thing left of an elaborate Baghdad set built for a picture named *Kismet*. At the top, carpenters were banging away on a plywood structure, which would become a palace or cathedral or prison.

Nigel and Babe were walking up and down, up and down, as Felix Roland gave them direction. Each time they reached the highest step, Nigel took her in his arms and kissed her. As he walked back to the bottom, I studied his face—grim and serious, no sign of the charming smile or the dancing blue eyes. He looked like a man just trying to get the job done.

· · · · ·

When I was finished shooting for the day, I went back to the Kismet staircase, which was empty except for the carpenters. Shelby Jordan chatted with the set designer, bending over a sheath of blueprints spread on a makeshift table, and when she saw me standing there she waved good-bye to him and came walking over. "Lose your way, fly girl?"

"I thought I'd watch them rehearse, but it looks like the party's over."

"For today at least. Can I give you a ride?" Her car was a shiny convertible roadster, painted racing car red. Inside, the leather smelled brand-new. As we took off, the wind whipping our hair, she said over the engine, "What can I do for you, Kit? I hear you've been asking about me."

"I've been asking about a lot of people."

"Part of your investigation?" She smiled like a cat. "Oh, don't look so surprised. Metro may be the biggest lot in town, but it's still small. Besides, it's my job to know what's going on."

"Like with Wallace Beery?"

"My, my. You have been asking around." She sped onto Lot 1, past the reporters still gathered at the gate. "I don't know who you talked to, but they probably didn't tell you I got fired over Beery. Actually, I threatened to quit. I was barely eighteen, new to the city, new to the studio. 'Beery's a bastard,' that's what they said to me. 'He's one royal pain-in-the-ass son of a bitch, but he's worth a lot of money to us. We need to make it go away.' I told them if that was the case, I would go away, and they didn't blink. They fired me that day. I didn't work again for two years."

She sped right up to the star suites, and yanked on the brake, the engine still idling. She reached past me, opening my door and pushing it so that it swung wide. "Curb service. And, Kit? If you ever have any more questions, I'd prefer you come to me directly. The good news is I'm back at Metro now, so I won't be hard to find."

· · · · ·

As I passed by wardrobe on my way to the parking lot, some of the wardrobe ladies were leaving. One of them said, "Miss Rogers, you might want to check with Trudy at the desk. I think she has something of yours."

When I walked in, the girl named Trudy said, "There you are. Sorry I didn't get this to you sooner, but when the maid's uniform went to cleaning, they found this in the pocket." She searched below the desk and then handed me a slender envelope, bent at the corners.

In the car, I opened it, and there was Mudge's handwriting, the characters looping across the page. I looked at the date: June 23, 1933. Without meaning to, I'd walked away from Broad Water with one of her letters to Tauby.

═══════

Dear Mr. Taub,

    I can't thank you enough for the interest you've shown me. It's hard to explain to someone like you, but no one in my life has ever been much interested in me. I never knew my dad, and my mother did the best she could, or so everyone tells me. As far as I'm concerned, I'm done with them and with everything that came before June 10, 1933, the day I signed my contract with Metro-Goldwyn-Mayer, greatest film studio in the world. As you said yesterday, this is my chance to be someone new. I guess I worry that 'Barbara Fanning' sounds too glamorous for me. That's the kind of name you'd give a lady, but I'll take it, especially since you chose it. I'm going to do my best to earn it. And I'm going to do my best not to let you down.

                Sincerely yours,
                Barbara Fanning

Folded in the envelope was a newspaper clipping, yellow from age. "Carmen Girl Makes Mark as Actress," read the headline, and it featured a picture of a very young, pretty, serious-looking Mudge. *Local girl Eloise Mudge, 17, a resident of the Carmen Odd Fellows Home, is succeeding in the theatrical world. After an appearance in "The Restless Sex" at the Colonial Theater, Eloise was spotted by a scout from Metro-Goldwyn-Mayer, who offered her a chance at motion pictures. Also in the cast was sister Edna Mudge, 15, whose idea it was for her big sister to audition. Says Edna, "She's more the quiet type, while I'm the actress. I thought doing the role would bring her out of her shell." Now the elder Mudge isn't just out of her shell—she's out of Oklahoma and heading to Hollywood.*

. . . . .

Helen closed the door to Mudge's office and said, "I never knew she had a sister. What do you think happened to her?" The office was tidier now and more organized.

"I don't know. But at least we know where Mudge came from."

"Carmen, Oklahoma. What's an 'Odd Fellow'?"

"I don't know that either." Suddenly, hearing her say it, I had a feeling I'd heard it before. "Where's the file on John Henry Briggs?"

She opened the file cabinet and sorted through it. "Here."

My eyes ran across the detective's report, then the newspaper article. There it was: *Dell Rapids Orphanage and Industrial School, also known as the Dell Rapids Odd Fellows Home.*

Over my shoulder, Helen said, "Do you think they're connected?"

"They have to be, don't they? It must be some sort of organization. I'm going to borrow this for a while." Then I waved at the room. "You've made good progress in here. It doesn't even look like the same place."

"It was easier once I figured out her filing system." Helen plucked a book off the shelf. "For instance, she made a donation last year to the NAACP, and they gave her a copy of the paperwork for her records. This is where I found it." She held up the book. *"Black Boy."* She pulled another book off the shelf. "In this one, I discovered thirty or so letters from soldiers, all fans of Barbara Fanning, tucked between the pages." She held up the book. *"The Good Soldier."*

"And she filed the will in Shakespeare—'will' for 'William.'" I looked back and forth between the books. "Apparently she was more organized than we thought."

"By the way, Bernie called, and also Butch Dawkins. I think he wants to hear that song you're writing for him."

Dammit, the song. The thing was only half-done because there hadn't been time. Like that, I felt my temper stir. I didn't have a moment to slow down now. I had to keep going because it was the only way to figure out who killed Mudge.

• • • • •

In my room, I sat on the floor and listened to the records Butch had given me: Ma Rainey, Billie Holiday, Ethel Waters, Sister Rosetta Tharpe, and the Empress of the Blues, Bessie Smith. He had told me that, for a long time, blues was thought of as the devil's music, but these women had sung it anyway. They taught themselves to play and sing. Most of them had come from dark, terrible childhoods and led dark, terrible lives, but nothing could keep them from singing.

At first I concentrated on the lyrics. Then I listened to the whole song, not just the words, trying to hear what it was Butch wanted me to hear. Bessie Smith was my favorite because her big, sad voice seemed to come from inside the song, as if it had grown alongside the tune and the lyrics so that it was all seamlessly entwined. And there was something else—in her voice, you could hear every emotion she'd ever had. All the pain and sorrow and struggle were there, but so were strength and hope. I listened to "St. Louis Blues" until I thought I'd wear the record out.

At seven thirty, I called Butch at the Dunbar Hotel and played him what I had so far. He picked up his own guitar and, with the receiver crooked between my ear and shoulder, we went back and forth like that for an hour, figuring out the melody, working on the words. He finally said, "If it's not too late, why don't I come over? This'll be a whole lot easier in person."

• • • • •

Helen was gone for the evening by the time he got there, telling me only that she was seeing a friend. Butch leaned against the wall of the den, stripped down to his jeans and white undershirt, Bluesman tattoo flexing with the muscles of his arms as his fingers worked the strings of my new guitar. I sat on the floor opposite him, my back pressed to the sofa, and listened. I hadn't been this alone with him in years, and in the tight, close space I breathed in his woodsiness and watched the way his hair changed color under the light.

I wanted him to play forever so I could live in the music and not think or move. But when he was finished, he handed the guitar back to me and said, "That's a good instrument, Velva Jean. You made a good choice. I know you'll treat it with respect."

Like that, the spell was broken, and I could feel my temper stir again. "Mudge was the one who chose it. It's beautiful, but I can't play it," I said as if it were his fault.

"I doubt that. You just got to break it in, figure out how it wants to be played. Every guitar's different. They're like people. Want to play me your song?"

"I'm still working on it." I waved the pages so he would know I'd been writing. "Even in the middle of everything I'm doing right now, I'm working on it. Maybe you could play me one of yours and then I could get the feel of it to know where I should go." As usual, Butch didn't have a stack of pages because he never wrote his music down.

He picked up his own guitar, pulled out the bottle neck, and slid it up and down the strings. "This record's important. Probably the most important thing I've ever done. I'm giving it everything."

"I'm doing my best. In case you haven't noticed, I've got a few other things going on."

"It ain't about you, girl. All I'm doing is letting you know I know what you're going through. I know what it's like giving everything. I want you on this record, but not if it's just one more thing for you to deal with."

"I want to do it." As cross as I was, I meant it.

"Then you should let the song tell you what it needs to be and let it take you where it wants to go."

"Like the guitar telling me how it wants to be played?" It came out testy, as if I was looking for a fight.

"Something like that. The song's in there, just waiting. It's in you, it's in that guitar. You just need to pull it out."

For some reason, that did it. "You know, I'm sick and tired of everyone telling me where to be and how to feel and what to say. Maybe I want to be the one who decides things. As far as I'm concerned, the song can be what I damn well tell it to be and the guitar can play how I damn well tell it to play." For extra emphasis, I added a few more "damns" as I went on and on about how sick and tired I was of being sick and tired, and how I was so sick and tired that I felt as if all my life I'd been trying to figure out who killed Mudge. "And don't tell me 'You'll figure out the song, you always do,' because what if I don't this time? I'm not sure I will. I'm so sick and tired of having to figure things out; maybe there's nothing left over for some stupid song."

I was still talking when he stood up, took the guitar from me like he was afraid I'd break it, set it back on its stand, and held out his hand.

I frowned up at him. "What?"

"Get up."

"I thought we needed to work on the record."

"Fuck the record."

Outside, it was deep, dark night, the stars lit overhead. He swung one leg over the motorcycle and said, "Get on." When I'd swung up behind him, he said, "Now wrap your arms around my waist and hold on." Underneath us, the machine thundered to life. I leaned forward, slid my arms around him, rested my cheek on his back, took a breath, took another, and then we were off. I lifted my face, felt the wind in my hair and against my cheeks, gentle at first. We crossed Sunset and started up the canyon, where the roads were narrower and the air was cool.

We picked up speed as we climbed. I wondered what would happen if the motorcycle couldn't make it up the hill and we fell backward. The tune Butch had been playing on my guitar started up in my head, as if it was pushing us forward and upward, helping to carry us. "Faster," I said, but I didn't know if he'd heard me.

I could feel his body tense and then, suddenly, off we went, like a rocket, as if we were heading straight for the moon. We were going so fast I had to close my eyes so the wind wouldn't blind me. I didn't open them again till we reached the top of the mountain, where we turned onto Mulholland Drive, which was a road like the Scenic, built across the Santa Monica Mountains that divided Los Angeles from the San Fernando Valley. The road was dark and winding, curving like a snake. Around this bend, suddenly a million lights reached into the horizon. Around that bend, the lights rose up on the other side.

Faster, I thought. "Faster," I said.

He pushed the motorcycle harder, hugging each curve so tightly I thought we'd go sliding across the road and over the side, or fly straight off into the sky. But I wasn't afraid. I just held on and breathed him in. With every mile I could feel myself letting go of the anger and the worry I'd been carrying for weeks. By the time he slowed the bike and skidded into a turnout overlooking the Valley, dust flying, I felt alive.

The lights spread as far as I could see. We sat on the bike, my arms around his waist, and I said, "It's beautiful." Back home, the Scenic climbed higher and stretched farther than this, but at night the mountains grew pitch-dark. From up on Mulholland Drive, it looked as if the earth was covered in stars. Stars in the sky. Stars on the ground.

"L.A.'s better from up here." His voice was low, almost as if he were offering up a prayer. "When you're down on the ground it's too easy to focus on the shit around you, like Central Avenue on a weekend morning. When you're down in it, you only see the skag and cigarette butts. Sometimes you gotta get a better view."

"In flying we call it being above the overcast."

We sat a long time, and I remembered something Daddy Hoyt once said about how a person couldn't share silence with just anyone.

Suddenly, Butch climbed off the bike, took my hand, helped me off, and led me over to the edge. The stars spread out before us like a carpet. He said, "The Hopis express sorrow by wailing on the day of death. All day. They just let it out. A year later, they do it again, in case anything built up."

"I've already cried. I don't want to cry anymore. I need to keep busy and useful because it's when I sit around that the sadness catches up, and then I feel trapped. I need to be moving. There's too much to do."

"And most of it rests on you."

"Yes."

"I'm not asking you to cry. Crying's not the same as wailing. You're carrying a lot right now, and sometimes you got to make room so you can carry more." He threw back his head and howled like a dog. His voice echoed off the canyons. "You try it. You ain't going to find a better place."

"I don't think—"

"Just try it. It'll make you feel better." He cupped his hands to his mouth and howled again.

I tipped my head back and let out a small, pitiful sound that didn't carry two feet.

"From here." He moved behind me, one arm wrapping around me as he placed a hand on my diaphragm. "Like you were singing a song." I could feel the heat of his body pressed against mine and the spread of his fingers through the thin material of my dress. His voice went soft in my ear. "Let it out. You got to let it out to let it in."

I closed my eyes and wailed, like I was taken over by the spirit. I didn't think of how ridiculous I looked or sounded, like a wild dog, howling into the night. I just let it out. Butch joined in and the two of us carried on like we were at a revival.

I wailed till my voice gave out, and it occurred to me that maybe I wasn't wailing just about Mudge but about a lot of other things I'd been carrying around inside me. When I was done, I opened my eyes and Butch said, "Better?"

"Better."

Just like that, he let me go. The air between us sparked, and as I was wondering if he felt it too, he said, "You know Bessie Smith came from nothing, and record producers said she was bad to work with. But that voice. In all that sorrow, there's something else."

"Hope," we said at the exact same instant.

His face lit into a smile and I smiled back, and I thought, This is the nicest moment I've had in a long, long time. Then, because the smile and the wailing had made me feel brave and strong, as if I could figure out who had done this and how and why and nail the son of a gun once and for all, unlike all the other sons of guns who'd walked free after sabotaging planes or capturing spies, I said, "You didn't come to Santa Monica that weekend. Were you ever going to, or did you just say it because it's what you thought I wanted to hear?"

"I was going to."

"What stopped you?"

"It ain't the time." He said it simply, as if there was no other answer but that one.

"What does that mean?"

"You're in the thick of it right now. You got things to do still; so do I. Last thing you need is some guy hanging around. Anyway, from what I hear, there's already a guy hanging around."

He climbed back onto the motorcycle and sat watching me. I got very, very quiet. He said, "Let's get you home."

I swung up behind him, holding on to the bike instead of holding on to him. He reached back and took one of my hands and then the other, hooking them around his waist. His hand resting on mine, he turned so that I could see his profile, looking back at me out of the corner of his eye. "Tell me what you need from me right now."

I need you to love me, I thought. Or I need you to let me go. Then I heard myself saying, as if it was what I needed most of all, "I need to feel part of something that isn't MGM and what happened to Mudge. I need to work on this song."

He smiled as if he'd known this all along. "Then you tell that song and that guitar what you want and let them figure it out. Everything's going to fall into place. Just you wait. You got enough on your mind right now, girl. It's time to let something else take over."

Back at Mudge's house, he walked me to the door. "Listen, it's bad on Central Avenue right now, and I don't want you coming down there. Police are rounding up anyone and everyone who might have killed those girls. I'm trying to find a studio up here. If I can't find one, I think we should wait. See what happens. Ride it out till things settle down."

"No," I said. "I don't want to wait. I'll be there."

TWENTY-NINE

The Independent Order of Odd Fellows had begun in England in 1819. Members practiced the principles of friendship, love, and truth in everyday life, and gave aid to those in need while doing what was possible to help mankind.

The man I talked to was new to the Carmen Home in Carmen, Oklahoma, and said at the start of our call that he might not be able to tell me much because a number of the records had been destroyed in a fire a few years ago. But he referred me to a woman who had worked there during the time Mudge was a resident. He said she remembered everything.

The woman's name was Dorothea Green. I telephoned her from the pay phone at Nate 'n Al Delicatessen in Beverly Hills, but there was no answer. I tried her again from a pay phone near the studio, but once again, the line just rang and rang.

· · · · ·

I concentrated on following Nigel like a ghost from the Kismet staircase to Lot 2's Wimpole Street and Copperfield Court. Whenever I was able to get close to him, something or someone got in my way. He was always surrounded.

When I was summoned to Mr. Mayer's office Thursday morning, I was sure he knew I was shadowing Nigel, or else he knew about Broad

Water. His face was sober, but he took my hand and greeted me warmly. It had been too long, he hoped I was holding up well, my goodness wasn't *Home of the Brave* exceeding all expectations?

After making the necessary chitchat, he said, "We think it's time you and Hal MacGinnis get married." The light from the window behind his desk was so bright I had to blink to see him clearly. Sitting like that, surrounded by all that white, a shroud of sun engulfing him, he could have been God.

"Sir?" I'd been expecting a reprimand, and I thought maybe I'd misheard him.

"You only have to watch yourselves on screen to see the magic there, the very magic that inspires the public. The fans love you together. We've received thousands of letters." As if to prove it, he held up a thick stack in one hand, a thick stack in the other. "There are many more where these came from." He set the letters down, neatly tapping them on all sides into a tower of paper that came up to his chin. "The two of you are *inspiring*." Above the letters, his eyes danced. "What do you say, Kit?"

"I'm not in love with Hal, and he's not in love with me."

"But you like him and he likes you. You have more of a basis for marriage than most people I know." He chuckled. "Besides, the fans want this." He tapped the stack of letters again. "This is what the studio needs right now after so much sadness. A wedding between two of our most popular stars. It'll be like a vitamin shot to the movie-buying public. They don't want to read sad stories. They want something to celebrate." Behind the fatherly smile, I could see the shrewd and driven businessman who had climbed his way to the top from nothing, willing to step over or on anyone in the process.

"But I don't want it."

His smile dropped and I could feel him measuring his thoughts. Finally, he said, "I'm going to be honest with you, Kit. I feel that I can be. I don't like the crowd of people Hal runs around with or the places he goes. He needs a stabilizing influence—a wife—to keep him grounded, to rein in the drinking, and to make sure I don't hear any more rumors, if you understand my meaning."

"It sounds like what he needs is a babysitter."

"What he needs is a wife."

"Maybe Hal doesn't want to be married."

"Hal doesn't have a choice. I've thrown Phoebe Phillips and Arlene Dahl and Babe King at him, but he will only marry you."

"But Hal doesn't love me, not like that."

"No, but he trusts you. And he likes you. And you are both *very* valuable to this studio. I'd hate to see anything change that."

"I'm sorry."

He sighed, tapped his desk, frowned. "I do understand." He seemed to think something over, his eyes going cloudy. "I'm afraid that Metro's in a difficult position. You're clearly overwrought by your friend's death. I wonder if you're really able to think clearly or capably, given all you're dealing with emotionally." He paused to let this sink in.

I could almost see the headline: "Metro Star Kit Rogers Suffers Breakdown." Which would, of course, discredit any future statement I might feel the need to make about Mudge's death.

He said, "We know about the Indian, though we haven't said a word. I'd hate to step in and make an executive decision, even if I do have the contractual right."

"According to my contract, Metro can tell me who to date but not who to marry. I'm happy to keep 'dating' Hal, going out on the town with him when our schedules allow for it, but I can't marry him, sir. I've been married before, and when that ended, I promised myself that I wouldn't marry again unless I was certain."

I knew from studio gossip that Mr. Mayer's own marriage was ending. He had moved out of his Santa Monica home and into a more modest house in Bel Air. He smiled now, sadly and faraway, as if he was thinking about it. "I understand," he said again, before pushing the button on his desk and letting me go.

· · · · ·

I met Hal for dinner at the Hollywood and Vine Brown Derby. The booths were filled with living, breathing movie stars, and the walls were filled with their caricatures. The white-jacketed, black-tied wait-ers moved up and down the aisles with trays of prime rib, curries, sweetbreads, and lobster. When a photographer asked to take our pic-ture, Hal and I smiled widely, cheek to cheek.

The moment the photographer was gone, I said, "Did you know about this?"

"I didn't know Mayer was going to talk to you." Hal sliced into his steak with the neat, clean lines of a surgeon. "So what did you tell him?"

"I told him no." I picked at my trout.

"Is the idea so horrible?"

I ate a french fry and pushed my plate away. "You don't love me, Hal. And I don't love you. This is just more studio lies. These kinds of lies are the reason Collie Fedderson switched from contract star to cos-tume designer, because he wouldn't play their game. What does he think about all this?"

"I'm not Collie. And I'm not you. You all can fight it, but I don't want to. Can you understand that?"

"No, I can't." All I knew was fighting. It was practically all I did. It was practically all I'd ever done.

"You think I wouldn't change me if I could? Do you know how much easier it would be if only I just liked women?"

"So you might as well marry one?"

"If it means keeping my career, yes. I've worked too hard to get here."

Webster Hayes, followed by his entourage of bodyguards, paused at our table. "If it isn't the two lovebirds. How's the prime rib?"

Hal smiled. "Good and bloody."

Hayes turned to one of his men. "Get me two." Then, back to us, "Where's Weldon? I've been trying to collect on a drink he owes me." He said this in my direction, without looking at me. Webster Hayes was one of those men who only liked to address a woman in conversa-tion if he was leering at her.

I said, "He's still at Broad Water working on the *Latimer* script."

"Shame about the Palmer dame. You talked to Gray?"

He was looking at Hal, but I answered "No."

His eyes jumped to me before zinging right back to Hal. "He claims he can't remember how they were hit or how they ever came to be on the train tracks in the first place. The only thing he remembers is waking up on the goddamn ground thinking, 'What am I doing outside?' If I had a nickel for every time I've wondered that myself." He threw his head back and roared.

There was the sound of a commotion. People at the neighboring tables were buzzing so loudly it sounded as if a thousand bees had been let loose in the room. They chattered behind their hands, eyes on the door. Hal, Webster Hayes, the bodyguards, and I turned to see what they were looking at.

Nigel Gray and Howard Strickling stood together, Mr. Strickling leaning on the host stand, chatting with the host as Nigel, hands in pockets, stared back at everyone who was staring at him. The host led them through the aisles, Mr. Strickling behind him, Nigel following. As he passed, people called out hello and nodded and told him he was looking well, and the moment he moved on, they went on buzzing.

· · · · ·

At home, I lay in bed and thought, as I always did, about how much I hated lying in bed in the dark in the minutes or hours before sleep. This was the only time of day when I slowed down and let down, and just as I did, there would come the sadness creeping in, trying to get inside.

Mudge was murdered and no one cares. My friend is gone, and everyone is carrying on as if nothing happened.

I sat up, turned on the light, picked up the steel guitar, and tiptoed down the stairs. I went out to the pool house, where I wouldn't wake Helen, and said out loud, "All right. Show me where to go. Show me what to do. If you're in there, come on out." Like the giant in Devil's Courthouse, I thought. Like the Wood Carver. You couldn't always see them, but you knew they were there.

"Come on, song," I said. "I don't have forever."

· · · · ·

On Saturday, *Latimer* began shooting at Castle Finckenstein on Lot 2. The medieval castle sat in Joppa Square between Verona Square and Chinese Street. Like most backlot buildings, it was only a backless shell built out of plywood, made to look as if it were constructed of stone. A crowd was gathered—crewmen and other cast members, including Webster Hayes. We watched as Nigel Gray was dragged from his castle home by a violent mob.

Babe had wrapped her scenes on *Flyin' Jenny* and was now transformed into Lady Catherine. She ran after him as he was taken through the streets, struggling at first, shouting bloody hell and damnation, before—finally—giving in, as if he deserved it. When they marched past the cameras, I got a good look at his face, chin held high, tears running down his cheeks, resigned to his fate.

"A remarkably believable performance." Sam was at my elbow, the first I'd seen of him on the *Latimer* set. He looked suntanned, but tired and unshaven. The cameramen began resetting the scene as Felix Roland spoke to Nigel. I watched as he dried his eyes and crossed his arms, listening closely to the director.

Sam kissed me on the cheek, his lips lingering. "Rumor has it you've been spending more time here than on your own picture. Anxiously awaiting my return from Broad Water? Or have you shifted your affections to Nigel Gray now that he's single?"

"You're terrible."

"I missed you too." He kissed me again, this time on the mouth. When I came up for air, I caught Babe's eye, watching us. She waved and I waved back. Behind her, I could see Shelby Jordan and Mr. Strickling strolling toward the set.

"Not here," I said.

"But you look so fetching in your flying gear."

He untied the scarf from my neck and I slapped his hand away. "Were you able to find anything out from Tauby or Felix?"

He arched an eyebrow. "You know, I'm accustomed to being used for my body, but being used for my deductive skills is a whole new experience."

"I don't have long before I'm due back on the set. Just be serious for a moment."

"All right then, to answer your question, in the midst of being locked up for ten days with two drunken, pill-swallowing egomaniacs who can't write to save their lives but *think* they can, I did a fair amount of digging, and, in summation, I'd be surprised if either had anything to do with her death."

"Weldon!" Felix was calling him, hands cupped to his mouth. Arms still crossed, Nigel looked in our direction. When I caught his eye, he glanced away.

"Duty calls. I'm not going to kiss you again because I prefer not to get my head ripped off, but are we still on for dinner tomorrow?"

I opened my mouth to say yes, but there was something in his expression—behind the smirk and the dancing eyes, I saw real emotion, real feelings. "I don't think so. I'm sorry, Sam."

"Care to give me a reason?"

"It's not you."

"It's you?"

"Yes. And the situation. And the timing. I can't do this right now—us. Not romantically. It's not fair to you. The only thing I can do is be your friend."

"It would be a first for me, Pipes."

"I'm sure it would. But I'll only keep frustrating you and I don't want to do that."

"And after all this is said and done?"

"I can't promise anything."

He sighed, and I could see the hurt he didn't attempt to hide. "I can't promise anything either, but I'll try."

· · · · ·

The Lot 1 saucer tank was filled with twenty feet of water and measured 5,250 square feet. It was an enormous aboveground watertight bowl with portholes carved into its sides, which allowed the cameras to film underwater. Here, Johnny Weissmuller had once wrestled rubber crocodiles, and Esther Williams had splashed onto the screen in her debut.

For *Flyin' Jenny*, the tank was doubling as the interior of a flooded fifty-five-foot freighter. In the scene, Jenny finds herself imprisoned in the bowels of the ship, until, in the nick of time, she finds her way out. Right now, the top of the tank was covered with a black ceiling. I would climb into it through a small trapdoor.

Les and some of the other crewmen arranged themselves along the upper rim and down below at the cameras, which were poised at all angles. I stood beside the trapdoor, dressed in my flight suit, except for my boots, which, at the last minute, they'd agreed I could leave off. I didn't want to be dragged to the bottom by the weight.

Les called, "Okay, Kit?"

"Okay."

"You won't hear me say 'rolling' because I want you to go on in."

We had practiced this again and again. I could hold my breath for nearly four minutes, thanks to years of swimming in Three Gum River. Even with that, they would have to shoot quickly.

Inside the tank, the walls were painted black to match the ceiling, and the light was dim at best, just bright enough for the cameras. It was like being in a cave. We hadn't practiced with the ceiling in place, and it took me a moment to figure out my marks.

I counted to ten, to make sure they were rolling, and then I started to swim, first here, then there because Jenny was disoriented, trying to remember the way. A body floated past, then another—both wax dummies, but the sight of them jarred me.

One minute gone.

There was a motion to the water, a churning that was meant to imitate the pitching of the ship. I could see one of the cameras through the closest porthole, but even so I felt a flutter of panic. Another body floated past. I swam to the door they had built into the side, just for the scene, just for me. I tugged on it, but of course it didn't give.

Two minutes gone.

More bodies floated past, and I dove my way through these, searching for another door. Then back again to the first one, the only one, and I tugged again. I fiddled with my belt, undoing it as I'd practiced so that I could wrap it through the door handle. I pulled with all my might, my foot braced against the wall. Then I slipped, plunging backward, only to be picked up by the water and carried forward. I hit my head on something sharp—the handle, maybe. The water changed color around me, and in the murky light all I could see was the dark inky red of blood.

Three minutes gone.

My ears rang, as if someone had boxed them, and my head throbbed as if it had been cut in two. The water rocked me, over and over. My head spinning, my ears ringing, I swam back to the other side of the tank, in the direction of the trapdoor. I wasn't supposed to do this, and I could hear voices in the distance, waterlogged and urgent, no doubt telling me to go back and for God's sake don't ruin the shot. I pushed up through the water, up toward the blackness, but when I reached for the trapdoor, it wasn't there. I was swallowing water now, and my lungs ached.

I slammed against something and my fingers scraped at the wall. I scrambled to find a handhold, the panic quickly growing. My limbs were weary and weak, weighed down as if they weren't my limbs anymore and belonged to someone else. I felt my eyes start to close even as I scraped and scratched and went tumbling away, the water lifting me and pounding me and pushing me down, down, down.

Four minutes gone.

The pants of my flying costume were wool, and I had to fight to keep from sinking. I struggled with the clasp, trying to slip them off, but then remembered they were safety-pinned to me, to keep them up after I removed the belt. I fumbled with the pin, but couldn't work it free.

With every ounce of strength I had left, I pushed my way up again and swam along the top of the tank, banging against the ceiling. Everywhere, it was smooth wood, smooth iron, smooth walls. Black, black, black. Through the porthole, I could see the men talking and laughing, tilting the cameras, as if they couldn't see that I was drowning, that I was dying. I was hitting ceiling and wall, ceiling and wall. I couldn't tell the difference anymore.

They don't know what's happening to me. They think I'm acting. I'm going to die in here before someone saves me.

Then, somehow, I found the hatch. I pushed against it, but it didn't give. I banged and pushed, banged and pushed, and my head and lungs went throb, throb, throb.

Five minutes gone.

I was sinking again, all the way down to the black, black floor. And then, from a long way off, I heard a voice say: *Let go. Stop fighting. Give in. Give up.*

I closed my eyes and drifted, and the feeling was lovely and peaceful. It was so much easier than fighting. I was warm and light, as if I didn't weigh anything at all, and I just gave in, gave up, and let myself be carried.

Suddenly, I was rising up and out and into the sky. The day was so bright, I covered my eyes with my hand. Someone had me in his arms and was moving me down the ladder and onto land and laying me down softly, gently, and then the nurse was there, the one who always stood by when the saucer tank was in use, and Hal was leaning over me, water dripping from his skin, and he was saying, "You're okay. I got you. You're okay. You're here."

Little by little, other images and sounds came filtering in, and over Hal I could hear someone shouting. Maybe Les Edgar or one of the technicians—no, it was Les, wanting to know who in the goddamn bloody hell had latched the trapdoor from the outside, and whose goddamn bloody idea was it to put a ceiling on the pool in the first place.

THIRTY

Hal drove me home in my car, Les Edgar following him in his own. Even though I could walk perfectly fine, Hal carried me into the house and set me down on the sofa as Helen and Flora fussed about. I said, "Helen, you need to go back to Connecticut and get on with your life. Why are you still hanging around here? Hal and Les, the same goes for you—go back to the studio, go back home. Flora, you're not a maid anymore. You don't need to be bringing me things and waiting on me." I was irritated with all of them.

Flora pointed her finger at me. "I'm your friend as sure as Miss Helen or Mr. Hal there. Don't you tell me what to do in my own house."

Les said, "We're nearly finished filming, but you see how you feel on Monday. If you need a day or two off, we'll make it happen."

I wanted all of them to leave me alone and go away so I could think of who might have locked that trapdoor. I tried to remember the faces of everyone on the set, of anyone who could have done this. And then, again and again, my mind kept circling back to Nigel. *Nigel and the studio. Mr. Mannix. Mr. Strickling. Whitey Hendry.*

I waited until Les and Hal had driven away and Helen and Flora had disappeared into the kitchen. Then I picked up my keys and went out to the driveway and got into the Oldsmobile.

I drove like AAA national champion Ted Horn from Beverly Hills to Brentwood, the road stretching out in front of me. That was what I liked most about driving—the forward motion of it and the sense that you were on your way to somewhere. My head ached, but I was fine. I was here. I was alive.

Nigel lived on a ranch in Mandeville Canyon, which was just west of Brentwood. The minute I turned onto Mandeville, I felt a sharp, sweet pang for home. A thick, green forest hunched across either side of the narrow road, as if it were still deciding whether or not to let the road pass. I rolled down the window and breathed in the air, which was both cool and warm, and smelled faintly of salt. I drove for miles until I thought I'd run straight into the mountains. And there, at the base of them, was Nigel's property.

A low white fence separated his land from the street, and a wide iron gate marked the entrance. I hadn't called first. He didn't know I was coming. But while the car sat idling, I tried the gate, which opened as if I'd been expected. It took me another mile or so to reach the house, a low, sprawling ranch structure that would have looked big and spacious if it weren't hugging a mountain. I could see a barn, tennis courts, guest cottages, and horse stables, and trails that spread out from those stables toward the wild, thick forest that climbed up the hillside.

I parked the Oldsmobile next to his car, which sat outside one of the garages. I rang the doorbell and waited. He might not even be home. The walls of the house were nearly all glass, so I could see through to the other side, and out into the backyard, where a couple of cows were grazing. I rang the bell again.

After waiting a minute, I walked over to his car and laid my hand on the hood. Still warm. I poked my head in each open or half-open garage door, then walked around to the other side of the house. Here, my eyes swept over the barn, the stables, and the guesthouses. I crossed the yard, passing through the back patio, and saw the cigarette, the end glowing red, resting in the ashtray. "Nigel?"

I had the sense of someone watching me, even though, except for the cows and horses, I seemed to be alone. "Hello?" My voice sounded too small to carry over all those acres. It was stopped short by the mountain and the breeze.

"Nigel?" I shooed the cows and stepped carefully to the barn, which was empty except for a nest of pigeons fluttering in the eves. I explored the stables, where the sweet, stale smell of hay and horses burned my nose. I breathed through my mouth, making my way past the stalls as the horses watched me, heads turning lazily as I passed.

Outside, I breathed the air again and this time walked to the tennis courts, circled the pool, and peered in the windows of each guesthouse. When I got back to the main house, the cigarette was gone. I knocked on the back door over and over. "I know you're here," I said. "I need to talk to you."

I shaded my eyes and pressed my face to the glass. I could make out the living room, the bar, the den, the office. I moved sideways across the house, looking in each room. When I got to what looked like the playroom, I could see a scattering of children's toys. I thought I saw a figure sitting in one of the chairs. I didn't trust my eyes and so I pressed my face closer until my nose was against the glass and my breath was making little clouds of mist. I wiped these away and gave the figure a good, hard look. It was Nigel. He was sitting in the chair, facing me, staring at the carpet, his fingers wrapped around a bottle of something. I rapped on the glass, and he raised his head.

When he didn't move any further, I rapped again. "I'm not leaving until you talk to me."

The drumming of my heart was filling my ears so that it almost sounded as if I were underwater again. If this man had murdered Mudge and his wife, I wasn't going to think about what he might try to do to me—or what he may have already tried to do.

After what seemed like hours but was probably just minutes, he stood, like someone in a trance, and walked over to me so that he was only inches away, on the other side of the window. The sun was behind me, which meant it was focused on him. I could see him clearly now. He was shirtless, dressed in shorts, and his feet were bare. He looked as if he was getting ready to take a swim.

I said, "I need to talk to you. I need to ask you about Barbara."

On the other side of the glass, his blue eyes looked clear and pale. I thought if he stood there long enough I could count every line I noticed, for the first time, at the creases of his eyes and mouth.

"Open the door, Nigel."

His eyes locked with mine. "Go away," he mouthed.

I banged on the glass. "Nigel, let me in. I almost died today on the set, and whether or not you were the one who tampered with that trapdoor, that's your fault. None of this would be happening to me if it weren't for you. So start talking. It's the least you can do. You can damn well tell me what happened."

I could see him thinking it over. Finally, he leaned one hand against the glass, palm facing me, as if the hand was the only thing holding him up. "She was upset." I could just make out his words. "She said she would never forgive me."

"Forgive you for what?"

"For falling in love with someone else."

I realized he wasn't talking about Mudge. He was talking about Pia. He began to pace, back and forth, on the other side of the window.

I banged on the glass, harder this time. "Who was driving the car, Nigel?"

He walked up and down, up and down.

"Nigel? Who was driving the car?"

He stopped and looked at me again. "She was. But it may as well have been me. I as good as killed her myself." He rapped on the window so suddenly I jumped back. "And they all think I've done it. Every last, bloody lot of them. Just like Barbara."

My chest fluttered. My hands shook. "Nigel, let me in."

He turned, as if someone was calling him, and then I could see a little boy and a little girl, no more than eight or nine, in the doorway of the room. He strolled away from the window, said something to them, and then an older woman bustled in and ushered them out. Nigel came strolling back toward me, the telephone in his hand. He picked up the receiver, dialed, and looked right at me as he said, "Yes, I'd like to report a trespasser. 3099 Mandeville Canyon Road. I have reason to believe this person is dangerous. Thank you." He hung up, wearing a sad smile. "You have approximately three and a half minutes before they get here. The driveway alone will take half that time."

"I'm going," I said. "But before I do, I need to know. Was it Pia? Was she the one who did it?"

Something in his eyes went dark, but then I realized it was the clouds, drifting across the sun. He stood temporarily in shadow just like I did. And then the clouds cleared, and I could see that he was crying.

· · · · ·

I was on Sunset when I spotted the man with the hat, two cars behind me. I moved over to the right lane and checked my mirror. In a moment, he changed to the right lane, one car between us now. I slowed down, hoping the car behind me would pass, and finally it shifted into the left lane and zoomed on by. The man with the hat was now on my tail.

He dropped back a little, as if he didn't want me to get a good look. I slowed even more, and he dropped back farther, and then I sped up, dodging into the left lane, passing the car ahead of me. I was getting ready to dart into the right lane again, when I thought, No. It's time to find out what he wants.

I slowed down until he caught up with me. I let the speedometer hover at thirty miles per hour, then let it go down to twenty-five. He eased off a little. I slowed to twenty miles per hour, and he eased off more. I crept along until other cars started blowing their horns and roaring by. He stayed two car lengths behind, and when we came to a red light, I got out of the car and stalked over to him, banging on his window.

"What do you want?" I banged on the window until he rolled it down. The stoplight turned green, but I still stood there. "Who are you? Did the studio hire you? Do you work for them? Mr. Strickling and Mr. Mannix? Mr. Hendry?" When he didn't say anything, I leaned in closer. "Please give them a message for me. You can park in front of my house or follow me all over town. You can lie down in my driveway, for all I care. But I'm not going to stop digging. If they want to scare me off, tell them they're going to have to do better than this."

I climbed back in my car and drove away, and the next time I checked the rearview mirror he was nowhere to be seen.

Back in the driveway of Mudge's house, I sat in the car trying to wrap my aching head around all the pieces of the puzzle, too many pieces in too many places, too many clues, too many dead ends, too many suspects, but nothing clear or making sense.

What kind of world was it in which men could fix events—like murder—so that they never happened, make murderers disappear as if they never existed, arrange marriages between people who didn't love each other, and use people's lives as something to be bartered and bargained with? They were, all of them, extortionists.

From inside the house, I heard the sound of the telephone. In a minute, Helen appeared on the front step, waving at me. I could have kept sitting there, but I made myself get out of the Oldsmobile and walk toward her. She said, "I thought I heard your car. Where did you go? Flora was worried sick."

"I had to run an errand."

"Sam's on the phone."

I went into the house, dropped my keys on the table by the front door, and picked up the extension. Without a hello, he launched in. "You told me she filed papers away in books."

It took me a minute to realize he was talking about Mudge. "That's right."

"What was it she said to you before she died? Was it 'Rebecca'?"

"That's right," I repeated.

"What if Rebecca isn't a person at all, but a book?"

· · · · ·

Helen and I searched every bookshelf in every room of the house until I found it in the sunroom, underneath a copy of the Bible. I opened the book—*Rebecca* by Daphne du Maurier. I flipped through it, shook it upside down, and when nothing fell out, I started at the beginning and turned every page.

I was nearly at the end of the book, and I had a sinking feeling in my heart. A little voice in the back of my mind said, *This isn't the Rebecca she was talking about.*

When I got to the last page without uncovering even a scrap of something, I shut the book and examined the cover, looking for any secret hiding place or pocket. Then I flipped through again, page after page.

Finally I snapped the book shut and sat back. "There's nothing here."

Helen took it from me. "Are you sure?" She began searching through.

"I'm sure." I reached for the Bible and turned to Genesis Chapter 24. I flipped through all the passages about Rebekah, wife of Isaac, just in case she was the one we were looking for.

When I had finished searching and Helen had finished searching, she said, "Do you ever feel like you wish you'd known her better?"

"All the time."

THIRTY-ONE

On Monday morning, from the bar and grill across from the studio, I telephoned Miss Dorothea Green, of Carmen, Oklahoma. I told her my name was Kit Rogers, I was a friend of Eloise Mudge, a.k.a. Barbara Fanning, and I was interested in knowing about her time at the Carmen home—how long she'd lived there and what, if anything, Miss Green could tell me about Edna Mudge, the younger sister.

Miss Green said, "I remember Eloise well. She was a shy thing. Polite, sweet, wounded."

"Wounded?"

"Like a bird with a broken wing. That's how I always thought of her. She carried a lot inside. I remember Edna too, of course. They were very different from each other." Her voice trailed off.

"Can you tell me how old the girls were when they came to live there? And where Edna is now?"

"I'm sorry, Miss Rogers, but I'm afraid I can't disclose that information over the telephone."

"What if I were to come see you in person?" I would have to record my song for Butch and work out my schedule with Les, but we were nearly done shooting the picture, and he'd mentioned a day off if I needed it.

On the other end of the line, Dorothea Green was silent.

"Miss Green? Would you be able to talk to me if I came to Oklahoma?"

"Yes, Miss Rogers. I would be glad to."

• • • • •

I was back on the set for my first time since Saturday, and Les Edgar wanted to know again if I was okay to continue in the wake of the accident. I wanted to say, What accident? That was no accident. Someone was trying to scare me, or worse, but guess what? It didn't work.

He said, "Do you need a day or two off to recover? Or can you finish the week? We're nearly through. We might even wrap as early as Thursday. You'd have time enough to recuperate before Monday's premier." He was referring to the second *Flyin' Jenny* installment, *Star-Spangled Blonde.*

As he talked, everyone was listening but pretending not to, anxious to get going.

"I think I can finish what you need me to finish, Les, as long as I know I have two or three days to myself as soon as we're done."

He smiled, and I could see the relief there: We would stay on schedule. We would be on time. He said, "I'll clear it with Mayer today."

• • • • •

The day we finished shooting, the night before I left for Oklahoma, I covered up the cut on my head so that no one—not even my brother—could tell I'd been in an accident. Johnny Clay picked up Helen and me and drove us downtown because he said it wasn't safe to come by ourselves. Another murdered girl had been discovered Monday morning. Across the nude body of Jeanne French, the killer had written a message to police, too vulgar to print, in dark red lipstick taken from her purse.

The Bronze Recording Company was located in a storefront on busy Vernon Avenue, an area made up of factories and stockyards, slaughterhouses and meat-packers. Leroy Hurte, the man who owned Bronze, had been making records since 1943. His was one of the first independent labels in town, holding its own against Decca, Capitol, Columbia, and Victor.

"Did Dawks tell you no one above Central wants to rent to a colored guy?" Johnny Clay had said.

"Butch isn't colored."

"Maybe not to you and me. But to them, he's just a dirty Indian."

The entire staff of Bronze Records totaled four—Hurte, his secretary, a pressman, and a printer. When we got there, the secretary greeted us and led us into the studio, a large room with a piano and a glass-windowed control room off of it. A middle-aged black man, straight-backed and dignified in a pin-striped brown suit, jacket thrown over his chair, sat in the control room talking to Butch through the speaker. Sherman stood up from behind the drums and shook Johnny Clay's hand, Helen's, and mine.

Mr. Hurte said, "Is that Kit Rogers, the movie star? Look at me, moving up in the world." He laughed.

Butch was all business. You stand here, Johnny Clay stand there, Helen sit over here out of the way. We'll get Velva Jean's song first, and then, while we have her, record another, get her to sing on that too. He moved around the room like a cat, languid, loose limbed, but with purpose. This was his show, and he knew what he wanted. When it was clear what we were doing, he said to me, "I want you to forget everything you've learned. This is Vernon Avenue. There's a slaughterhouse two blocks away. This ain't MGM, girl. This is equipment Leroy built himself. Just let everything down and play."

I thought: Don't just tell me. Tell Sherman and Johnny Clay.

To all of us Butch said, "Let's throw it down."

We ran through the song a couple of times so that we could get it stirring and get Sherman and my brother, on guitar instead of trumpet, on board. Then Leroy gave us the go-ahead, and Butch counted us off, and there we went. I tried to forget everything I'd learned and lose myself in the music, but we hadn't even reached the chorus before Butch raised his hands and then cut a finger across his throat so that Leroy would know to stop the track. We tried it again. And again. Butch stopped us over and over, and finally said to me, "MGM is all

over you, girl. That's great for the movies, but that don't work here."
He was frustrated, but trying not to be. "Don't think so much."

"I'm not thinking."

"Yes you are. I can hear you, like a dancer trying to learn the steps,
counting under your breath."

"Maybe you should sing it."

"Maybe I'll need to, but I want to see if you can do it first."

I thought, Like hell you will. I said, "All right, let's go again."

We'd barely started this time when Butch stopped, told everyone to
take five minutes, and led me outside, where the night air was heavy
with the smell of the slaughterhouse. Sirens wailed in the distance. A
man walked down the street, singing his heart out. Butch lit up a cigarette, and for a minute I thought he'd brought me out there to watch
him smoke. Finally he said, "If you ain't careful, that studio's going to
ruin you. You got a shine and a spirit I ain't ever seen before, and a
voice like I ain't ever heard. But they're going to rub the shine right out
of you."

"What are you talking about? Kit Rogers is known for her shine.
That's practically all she does."

"Kit Rogers isn't real. She's a part you're playing, I don't care about
her; I care about you. I want to see if you can remember being Velva
Jean Hart."

I thought about walking away, but Butch kept right on going.

"Let me ask you something. Do you like what you're doing over
there?" He nodded in the direction of the slaughterhouse, but I knew
he meant Metro.

"Of course." I did my best to sound sincere.

"Don't tell me what you tell everyone else. Does it feel good in
here?" With the cigarette hand, he pointed at my heart.

"It's challenging. I'm challenged. I'm learning to act. I'm learning
new styles and techniques. Things a girl like me never would have
learned if I hadn't gone there."

"'A girl like you'? Oh, man." He shook his head.

"Let me ask you something. Why do you care so much?"

"Because I know what you can do. They don't own your songs anymore. Their year is up and your songs belong to you now. But your voice has changed. It's like they still own you."

"My voice has gotten better."

"Only technically. You're a natural born singer. You got a gift. But you're in danger of losing it. If you were throwing yourself away on booze or drugs, I'd feel the same. The minute music stops being something you love, you need to walk away. There's a helluva lot of work involved, but in its best moments, it shouldn't feel like work. In its best moments it should feel like love. New love. First love. Sweet, uncomplicated, and raw. You play and sing without having to worry about what you know and what you been through. Without ever knowing or expecting the doubt and the hurt and the bullshit. It's love in its purest form before we go in and fuck things up and make it harder than it should be."

He dropped the cigarette on the ground, crushing it under his shoe. "You ready to go back in there and try again?" His voice was low and even, but his eyes were blazing. He was daring me.

My eyes blazed right back. "Yes."

· · · · ·

We threw it down, as Butch would say, and something happened—it was like a light turning on. I could feel the change. Metro would never have recorded me like this. I would have been sent back to class and told to study and find my diaphragm and think about the way I was holding my tongue. I felt like I was leaving one world and walking into another. Like I was falling in love with the right person for the first time. Everything felt brand-new, and the world seemed prettier, the air seemed prettier, as if instead of a slaughterhouse we were surrounded by greenhouses of roses. The thing I'd been missing in all the songs I'd been given to sing was soul. There wasn't room for soul at MGM.

When we'd recorded my song and one other, Johnny Clay said, "I don't know what you said to her, but it worked." He grinned at me. "There you are, little sister. Good to see you again."

Leroy Hurte came out of his booth and told Butch he'd put the first song out and then the second, and so on like that, letting each song build off the one that came before. His printing press could print a thousand records a week, and by the end of that week, the dealers would come lining up to buy them. Then he'd go back and press another thousand.

Then Leroy turned to me, shaking his head. "Honey, you should go up to Capitol Records. They won't take unknowns, but they'll take someone they figure can sell in a hurry, and you can sell. You don't need to be down here cutting race records."

"It won't be long before they know Butch Dawkins and his band," I said. "Besides, this is where I belong. Everyone above Central can just keep their studios." My face was still burning from the session. I could feel the itch in my fingers that meant I was ready to do more. As good as it felt to prove myself to Butch, it felt even better to know my voice was still my own. No one else was in charge of it but me.

I sneaked a glance at Butch and he nodded in a way that was meant just for me and no one else. His eyes said, Good job, and Yes it is, and Yes they can, and You can still shine when you need to.

• • • • •

Outside the studio, my brother danced Helen and me around the street, singing my song, while Sherman beat a rhythm on the hood of his car. Butch made a smoking gesture and my brother handed him a cigarette. Johnny Clay felt his pockets and said, "You got a light, Scatman?"

Sherman said, "Nah, man, I gave that up."

"Dawks?"

"I used my last matches. Leroy's still in there. He'll have some."

"Trying to get rid of me?"

"Only temporarily." Butch handed him the cigarette back. "Do me a favor. Smoke both of them." He grinned like someone up to no good.

Sherman said, "You want Helen and me to pretend like we smoke?"

"Yes I do."

When they were gone, Butch set his guitar case on the sidewalk and leaned against Sherman's car. We watched the people going by, the traffic rolling past. I leaned against the car, right next to him, so that my arm brushed his.

"You sure showed me, girl. That was hotter than a Louisiana summer."

"It felt good to be playing like that, all of us. To be in a studio—not a recording stage, but making a record that I want to make."

"You nailed it. Fo sho, fo sho." He shook his head. "I wanted to tell you without those buzzards hanging around. I also wanted to tell you that we'd like to record with you again and have you be part of this, if you want to be, however you want to be. I don't know where it'll lead or if it'll lead anywhere, but you're welcome anytime."

I felt like a live wire. I wondered if he would burn if I touched him. He straightened up off the car as if he could sense it. The music was still in me, making me feel bold and reckless, my face hot, my blood stirring. I said, " 'We'?"

He leaned in, one arm against the car, just past my shoulder, so close that I could smell the woods and tobacco on him. "*I* want you to be a part of it."

I don't know what made me do it, but I wound my arms around his neck and pressed my body close to his, like we were dancing. His body went stiff, and he looked down at me, eyes dark and steady. We stood like this for what seemed like hours until he said, "Girl, don't open that door if you're not ready to come on through."

"What's that supposed to mean?" I was trying not to feel foolish, standing there holding on to him like he was a tree, him not reaching back, not even touching me.

"It means that I'm not going down this road unless you know you want to go down it. But you got to be sure. I'm not going to play around with you, Velva Jean. I want more than that." The words hung in the night, settling around us. I could feel them land like wild, far-flying birds on my head, my shoulders, my heart. He unhooked my hands from around his neck. "You better get in the car. Sherman and your brother can take you home."

As if I couldn't think for myself, I got in and shut the door too hard, my stirring, reckless mind trying to make sense of it all. He walked away and then he was back again. He banged on the window. "Roll it down."

When I didn't move, he banged on the window some more. I shook my head at him. I was humiliated, my temper rising, mad at myself more than anything. It had been a good night, the best night in months, and I'd gone and ruined it.

Butch swung the car door open and leaned inside. "You stir a man up more than any woman I know. You can't just let him be; you got to get under his skin till you're part of it."

"You say that like it's a rotten thing."

"If a man don't want to be stirred up, it is."

"You say it like I do it on purpose."

"No. You're not the kind. You got a lot to get through right now. A lot going on. I told myself I'd leave it alone. This ain't the time or place. Besides, I don't like to step on anyone's territory, and up until recently you been pretty cozy with Sam Weldon."

"I'm not a car or a house. I'm not anyone's territory."

"No you're not. And the way I see it, you'll always have a lot going on. And the way I see it, maybe there's no such thing as the right moment, or the right time because life doesn't stop so you can figure things out." Behind him, I could see my brother coming, Helen and Sherman at his heels.

"All you do is talk in riddles."

"There's other ways to talk than with words, and sometimes, good as they are, words just don't cut it."

"Sometimes a girl likes words."

"Then let me give you some." He crouched down so we were at eye level. "I've known you since you were sixteen years old, a married woman up on a mountain who had a dream she would sing at the Opry. I knew you as a pilot, fighting all the bullshit the military piled on you. The war sent me my way, and you went yours, and I don't begin to know about your life, and you don't begin to know about mine. There are things about you I'll never know. You ain't the same girl I met in North Carolina. You ain't the girl I knew at Camp Davis. I ain't the same either." It was the first time I'd seen him churning and burning without a guitar in his hand. "I knew the old Velva Jean, much as I could. Now I want to know this one."

My brother leaned on the door, smoking away. "Miss me?" Sherman stood over his shoulder. Beside him, Helen gave me a look, eyebrows raised.

I said, "Go away, Johnny Clay."

"Hey now, what's got into you?"

Butch said to him, "Can't you see we're having a conversation? Go smoke another cigarette. Give us a minute here."

Johnny Clay narrowed his eyes at Butch, at me, and I guess it all must have shown on my face because he fixed Butch with one of his worst looks. "What did you say to her?" My brother looked like he was about to punch him in the jaw, and then, sure enough, he said, "I ought to punch you in the jaw." Helen laid a hand on his arm, holding him back.

"Nothing that didn't need saying. Nothing that wouldn't have been said one way or another. Besides, you're a fine one to talk. You can knock me into next week, but it ain't going to change the way I feel about your sister."

Butch smiled that crooked smile at me, but his eyes were an unsettling dark, the color gone from them. "Remember, no matter what shit comes down on you, no matter what anyone says or does, you're one down-home girl, Velva Jean Hart. Strongest spirit I know." He swept up his guitar and walked off toward his motorcycle. And then he threw back his head and howled.

THIRTY-TWO

On Friday, February 14, Helen drove me directly from the studio to Hughes Airport, where I'd arranged to borrow a plane. The man who greeted us apologized for his boss's absence, and told me Howard Hughes himself had arranged for me to land on a private farm just outside Carmen, Oklahoma. The plane he'd found for me was a P-51 Mustang, painted red. It was a single-seater, with a maximum speed of 437 mph, and its external fuel tanks had made it a good long-range wartime fighter, able to travel from England to Germany and back without stopping.

Forty-five minutes later, after I had checked out the plane myself, I took off from the world's longest private runway—unpaved and nearly two miles long. The P-51 was powerful and fast. The force of the engine shook me down to my bones. It felt good to be in the air by myself, no movie crews, no copilot. No Sam. No Butch. I could clear my head and clear my heart. I would be in Oklahoma by nightfall.

. . . . .

The farm belonged to a man named Franklin Hooper, who lived two miles outside of Carmen, on the snow-swept plains of northwest Oklahoma. He and his wife and three sons welcomed me into their house and told me I could stay as long as I needed to. The wife, Joanie, told me she had seen both my pictures more than once, but she assured me no one would know I was there. Mr. Hughes had explained to her that my visit must be kept quiet from the press. They were to tell anyone who was curious about the red P-51 parked in their field that I was a cousin from California.

The Hoopers had one telephone, which sat on a little table under the wide kitchen window. Joanie brought me a pad of paper and a pencil, in case I wanted to write anything down. I said, "This is a local call." She waved her hand at this and said it was just good to have me there, and if I needed anything they would be in the other room.

I telephoned Dorothea Green and made plans to see her the next day, keeping the conversation as brief as possible since there wasn't any privacy. Then I enjoyed a quiet evening in front of the fire with my hosts. Franklin had been born and raised in Carmen. He remembered going over to the Odd Fellows Home as a boy and spying on the orphans, trying to see if they looked different from him and the other boys he knew. This went on until the day his daddy caught him and told him if he ever went over there again, he'd find himself living there. Franklin shook his head. "I always was afraid of that place."

Joanie was from Kansas, just over the line, although she'd lived in Carmen for thirty-some years, too many to count. She brought me a cup of hot chocolate and sat down, propping her feet on an overstuffed ottoman. With her toes, she pushed one shoe off and then the other. They hit the floor with a clunk, clunk. She looked at her husband. "Are you talking about the Home?" When he nodded, she folded her hands across her lap and propped her elbows on the arms of the chair. She said to me, "The Odd Fellows have done a lot of good for the community. Can we ask what you want with them?"

"A friend of mine grew up here, at the home, actually. I'm trying to find out some information."

"Well, anything Dorothea can't tell you, let me know. Bill Dumfries had an aunt that was raised there, and the Wassons and the Tyners both have kin that could tell you stories."

· · · · ·

You could see the Carmen Odd Fellows Home for miles. It rose up out of the flat, flat land, against the open winter sky, a gloomy four-story brick Victorian with a high center tower and stair-step wings on either side. Except for an old red barn and several small structures, it was the only building—the only object—for miles. A white expanse of lawn spread to the road, and from the road it took a good five minutes in Franklin Hooper's truck to reach the front door.

I didn't see any signs of life or activity. It was too cold for the children to be outside. There was a chill in the air, and as I studied the sky I thought, A storm's on the way.

I knocked at the door, and a girl answered, plain face, plain dress. When I told her I was there for Miss Green, she showed me to a parlor with bookcases built into the walls, where I took a seat on a long sofa with spindly wooden legs and a straight back. The fire was dying in the fireplace, and the room was chilly. From upstairs or down the hall, I could hear the sounds of children's voices.

I tried to imagine Mudge here as a little girl, as a teenager. Had she sat on this sofa, in front of this fire, dreaming of leaving one day? My eyes ran across the spines of the books. When I spotted *Jane Eyre*, I walked to the shelf and plucked it off. Something fluttered out of it, a piece of paper. *J.M.—Steal two rolls and meet me in the attic after supper. L.K.*

A woman came tapping in wearing a dark gray dress, low black shoes, and glasses. She was in her sixties, as stout and sturdy as the prairie. She extended her hand to me, introducing herself as Dorothea Green, and apologized for the cold. "They hardly use this room except for guests, especially this time of year." She nodded at *Jane Eyre*, at the note. "The children leave messages for each other in the books. It's a kind of coded system." She smiled. "They don't think we know."

I felt a puzzle piece slide into place: *This is where Mudge learned her filing methods.*

"We'll be more comfortable in the office, if you want to follow me."

I trailed her through the hallway, past a dining room, music room, classrooms, passing children of all ages, from the very young to seventeen, eighteen, around the age Mudge would have been when she left.

We walked through the kitchen, large and bustling and too warm, into a small room that adjoined it, where a fat walnut desk faced two deep chairs. "There's a larger office, of course, but I always preferred this one." She took one chair and gestured toward the other. "Please." When I was settled, she smiled the patient smile of a woman used to working with children. "What can I do for you, Miss Rogers?"

"Please call me Velva Jean, my real name."

"All right. Call me Dorothea."

"My friend Barbara Fanning died December twenty-eighth in Santa Monica."

"So I've read, and so you mentioned."

I unfolded the newspaper article I'd found in Tauby's desk and handed it to her. "I always called her Mudge. We flew together in the WASP. I first met her in 1943. She never said much about her life before the WASP or before Hollywood."

Dorothea's eyes ran over the lines as she read. "I remember the play," she said at last. "She didn't much want to do it. Eloise was a shy girl, as I believe I told you on the telephone. She kept to herself, did what she was asked, not a remarkable student, but she tried hard. Still, I always had the sense that she was waiting for something."

"A career in pictures?"

"Oh no. She never talked of that. She didn't like speaking up in class or causing a spectacle, as she thought of it. No, I had the sense she was waiting till the day she turned eighteen so she could leave and get married, start a family, have a home." She opened her palms, raised her eyes heavenward. "This is a good place, but it's not a permanent one. I suppose like all orphans she dreamed of that stability and the love a family would bring."

"That sounds like Mudge. What happened to her parents?"

"The father had died or drifted by the time she was three. Edna was just a baby, perhaps six months old, when the mother dropped them off."

"No one ever tried to adopt them or take them in?"

"It gets harder as the child grows older, of course. I'm afraid very few people want to take in someone over the age of three or four.

There was one couple who considered it, but the mother swept in and took them away."

"Their mother?"

"Yes." Her smile vanished. "Every time she remarried, she would reappear to claim them, then the marriage would fail, and she would be back to drop them off. Take them away and drop them off. Over and over. Those girls were in and out of here every few months. Sometimes they were gone as long as a year, and I would think, Maybe this time the mother has gotten herself together. But there she would come, dragging those girls along, and back they would be."

"What can you tell me about Edna?"

"Edna and Eloise were very different. Edna was outgoing. Friendly. She was bright, but she talked too much in class. Eloise was prettier, but Edna was the one the boys liked." She sighed, shifting in her chair, brushing invisible lint off the skirt of her dress. "She was a lot like the mother."

"You didn't like Edna."

"I didn't trust Edna. Two different things. She was cunning."

"How did the sisters get along?"

"They had little to do with each other. I think Eloise disapproved of Edna, looked down her nose at her. She kept her distance from her. Edna made fun of Eloise behind her back. She played pranks on her, and not always in the spirit of fun. I used to wonder what that house was like whenever the mother would take them away. I imagine those two girls spent quite a lot of time on their own." She shook her head.

"What happened to Edna?"

"When Eloise was discovered and given the chance to go to Hollywood, Edna wanted to go with her. I've already told you the girls weren't close, and I think Eloise saw this as her chance to leave the old life behind and begin again. There was no living with Edna after Eloise left. She was angry with everyone. There was a married boy who worked for us—Jack Brooks, I think. He wasn't much older than twenty, twenty-one. I always thought he had his eye on Eloise, and that she would have married him if he didn't already have a wife. It was very innocent, very sweet. I think he needed a friend, and she was there for him. But then Edna and Jack became involved. We fired him, but they somehow continued seeing each other. After Eloise left, Edna became pregnant. She was only fifteen." She smiled, sadly. "That was the last I saw her."

"Did she have the child?"

"I don't know. Jack left his family for her. They moved away. He returned to Carmen not even a year later after Edna and the child were killed in a car accident. It was a terrible time. I always wondered why he came back."

"Is he still in Carmen?"

"I'm sorry. He died last summer. He was a lonely man and a sad one. He never remarried and lived alone up near Alva for all those years. I always wondered what his life might have been like if he'd never taken up with Edna Mudge."

I was out of questions, and at the end of it all, I felt as if I wasn't any closer than I had been when I arrived.

She said, "Would you like me to show you around? The children will be gathering in the dining hall for lunch, and you're welcome to join us."

As we made our way back through the kitchen and back through the hallway, I paused at a display of photographs on the wall. "Do you have any pictures of Eloise and Edna?"

"I'm afraid these were taken more recently." She reached up to tap the wall, her ring shining in the light. "We probably have some from their era in the attic. I meant to dig them out for you before you came, but there wasn't time. If I can get my hands on one, I'll send it to you."

"How beautiful. Your ring. And how unusual. Is that a dove?"

"Yes, and the crescent moon, and seven stars, and the lily flower. The D and the R are entwined, you see."

As unusual as it was, I couldn't help feeling I'd seen something like it before.

A girl of thirteen or fourteen appeared. She stared at me as she said, "Miss Foley wants to know if she'll be joining us, Miss Green."

"Thank you, Sharon. I hope our guest would like to stay."

They both looked at me, and I said, "I'd like that." When the girl disappeared, I turned back to Dorothea Green. "She was wearing the same ring."

"Yes, we all have them, at least those of us over the age of fourteen."

As she moved toward the dining room, I stood rooted. In the doorway, she turned. "Are you joining us, Velva Jean?"

"Yes, but—can you tell me what the D and the R stand for?"

She held out her hand so I could better see the ring. "The letters are for the female auxiliary of the Independent Order of Odd Fellows. The Daughters of Rebekah."

· · · · ·

The Rebekahs were named for the Rebekah of the Bible, a beautiful, godly young woman who showed kindness to an unknown stranger in need. A girl could become a Rebekah at fourteen, at which time she received her ring and learned her creed. Rebekahs were known for their humanitarianism and devotion to mankind and to God—just look at member Eleanor Roosevelt. The symbol of the lily, the dove, the moon, and the stars represented peace, love, charity, tolerance, purity. Above all else, Rebekahs believed in the Golden Rule—of doing unto others as you would have others do unto you.

As she walked me out into the cold evening, Dorothea smiled in apology. "I'm sorry I couldn't be of more help. You traveled a long way, and I get the sense you didn't find what you were looking for."

I smiled in return as I shook her hand. "Actually, I think I found exactly what I was looking for."

· · · · ·

When I woke the next morning, three feet of snow covered the walk and the driveway. Franklin Hooper went out to clear a path, and when he came back inside, shaking the snow off his hat and coat on the porch, knocking his boots against the doorjamb, he said, "I think you'd best wait till tomorrow."

"I have an appointment tomorrow night that I can't miss." I told Franklin I wanted to go out and see the plane for myself.

I borrowed a coat and scarf from Joanie. The air was so cold my teeth hurt, and my hands, deep in the pockets of Joanie's coat, were numb. In California, the sun would be shining and the air would be warm, but here, in the rest of the world, it was winter. My boots made crunching sounds in the snow.

The red of the P-51 barely showed through the white. I circled it slowly, brushing the snow off, scraping at ice.

Franklin Hooper said, "I can't let you risk it. The weather report says this is the last of it for the next couple days. You can leave early in the morning and get back in plenty of time. Better to be safe than sorry."

He turned and walked back toward the house, blowing on his hands. I ran after him, as best I could, through the thick, white mess. "Did you know a local boy named Jack Brooks?"

"Name doesn't ring a bell." We stepped onto the porch and banged our shoes against the stairs.

Joanie opened the door, her forehead creased. She stared up at the sky. "You can't leave in this. She needs to wait till tomorrow, Franklin."

"She is waiting till tomorrow."

"I'm going to make you some coffee. You can hang your things on the rack by the door."

As we let ourselves in and hung up our things, I said, "So you didn't know a Jack Brooks?"

He took his time, placing first his scarf, then his coat onto the peg. "I knew a Jack Briggs; John Briggs would have been his given name."

"John Henry Briggs?"

"That's right. He did odd jobs for me and the Tyners a couple of years ago. Died last year of pneumonia or some such, over in Alva."

"Did you know a girl named Edna Mudge? Someone he got involved with while he was married? I think they went away together."

"No, but I heard about her."

"Do you know what happened?" I hung up my coat, pulled off my boots, and followed him into the den.

"They were living somewhere up north. She was supposed to meet him, her and the baby, but she never showed. It was two weeks before a car was dug out of a lake, just a few miles from where he was living. It was her car, but she wasn't in it. Maybe the fish got 'em, folks said. Maybe they melted away, bones and all. Or maybe she had taken the baby and disappeared."

· · · · ·

The next day was colder, but clear. Franklin and his boys cleared the paths and plowed a runway with the tractor, driving it up and down to make the road as flat and smooth as possible. After I refueled, I thanked them all for the hospitality, told them I wouldn't forget them, and swung aboard.

By the time I got the plane engine humming, it was noon. There was an instant after takeoff when I thought I would overshoot the runway, that it wasn't long enough, but then I was up and climbing, the flat, white land spread out beneath me like an endless blanket.

Only then did I let myself think about what was waiting for me back home. Edna Mudge had once hurt her older sister by stealing the man she loved. It made sense that Mudge would do the same to Edna years later by stealing her husband. All I had to go on was instinct— and a cabinet full of Benzedrine, and a love of lily flowers, and a daughter named Rebecca, and a person who was younger than she claimed and who was sent away by the studio after Mudge's death, just like Nigel, just like Wallace Beery. And motive. A good deal of motive. What I needed was an early photo or the original bio and publicity questionnaire, something from before her career had started that would record the real names, the real birthdate, the truth.

And then I thought about Butch. After years of wondering how he felt and wanting him to say something—*anything*—to give me some clue to his feelings, he had laid it right down on the table, or started to.

Did I love him? Did I love Sam? The thought of Sam flooded me with warmth, as if I'd stepped into sunshine and somehow swallowed it whole. Sam was new. I was still finding my way with him.

But I couldn't think about Butch without my heart racing. *Butch, Butch, Butch,* it seemed to say as it pounded along. The thought of him warmed me in a different way that was both familiar and new, easy and electric. It was a deep, unsettling burning that reached my bones.

This was as far as I had gotten in thinking either of them through—what they meant, how I felt, where we went from here.

REBEKAH CREED

I AM A REBEKAH: I believe in the Fatherhood of God, the Brotherhood of man, and the Sisterhood of woman. I believe in the watchwords of our Order—Friendship, Love, and Truth. Friendship—is like a golden chain that ties our hearts together. Love—is one of our most precious gifts, the more you give, the more you receive. Truth—is the standard by which we value people. It is the foundation of our society. I believe that my main concern should be my God, my family, and my friends. Then I should reach out to my community and the World, for in God's eyes we are all brothers and sisters. **I AM A REBEKAH!**

THIRTY-THREE

I walked the red carpet at Grauman's Chinese Theatre as if I hadn't flown in from Oklahoma just three hours earlier. There had barely been enough time to go from airport to studio to home, to shower and dress and arrange for the studio to pick me up. I didn't want to be there. I wanted to be in my car, headed to Metro's research department, where I would find answers in the thousands of files kept on all their stars, past and present. I wanted to drive to Rockhaven Sanitarium right now. I would go tomorrow. I would take Helen with me or my brother, or maybe I would go by myself.

Reporters lined the ropes, shouting questions at each star going by. I looked, but didn't see Zed Zabel. Bernie made a beeline for me. "The next time you want to leave town, let Mayer know."

"Les gave me those days off. I didn't miss work. I'm here for the premiere."

"What were you doing in Oklahoma?"

"How did you know where I was?"

"Just do me a favor, kid—lay low and stay out of trouble."

Sam was there alone. Hal stood to my left, his arm around Babe King, fielding questions about their new romance. When did they first feel that spark? When did he know that it was Babe, not Kit, who had his interest? *And, Miss Rogers, how do you feel? You and Babe are such good friends, but is there any jealousy on your part? What happened to your romance with Sam Weldon, Kit? Is that over as well? And speaking of romance, is it true your mother recently married grocery store heir Giffard Leland, Miss King?*

While Babe and Sam talked to reporters, Shelby Jordan brushed past, holding hands with Felix Roland. They posed before cameras, the perfect Hollywood couple. The press wanted to know about *Latimer*, about Nigel, about how he was doing in the wake of the tragic death of his wife. I was inches away from Shelby. She was the right age—twenty-seven or twenty-eight. She was bright and charming and clever, and there was a steeliness about her, as if she'd been through a great deal. But she hadn't killed Mudge.

"What are you working on now, Sam Weldon? Will you ever write a book again, or is it strictly movies from here on out?"

"I'm glad you asked. I'm actually working on a new book even as we speak. It's a murder mystery set in Hollywood in which nothing's what it seems."

"Does it have a title?"

"Not yet. For now, I'm just calling it *The Great Cover-Up*."

"Will it be a movie, or is it too early to tell?"

"I'd say it's got the movies written all over it."

They were hustling us along, trying to get us into the theater. Babe and Hal walked ahead, leading the way. Sam nodded at me. "Good to see you, Pipes."

A reporter shouted something in my direction, and I turned, thinking I'd heard him wrong. He leaned forward on the rope and said, "Can you tell us why your brother was picked up by police? Can we get a statement from you, Miss Rogers?"

"My brother?" But I had just seen Johnny Clay, days before, at the recording studio.

Sam said, "When was he picked up?"

"Yesterday. They're holding him for questioning in the case of Jeanne French, the girl they found Monday. What can you tell us?"

"I'm sure it's a misunderstanding. I'm sure it's not my brother, but a man with a similar name." To Sam, I whispered, "I have to go."

He said, "I'll drive you."

. . . . .

Johnny Clay was being held downtown at the Central Jail. Sam and I were directed to the Central Division station, which sat at the corner of First and Hill Streets. It was a cold, dingy building, the walls stained with smoke. Helen and Lara Yacoubian, secretary to the coroner, sat side by side in hard wooden chairs. While Sam, cigarette burning in one hand, talked to the officer at the desk, I joined them.

"What are you doing here?" I asked both of them.

Helen said, "Johnny Clay called the house after they brought him in."

Lara jumped up. "I'm so sorry about your brother. That is so, so, so awful what they did." From her chair, Helen watched her. "I was at your brother's show. I was there when they picked him up. I came to see if I could do anything, but no one will talk to me, and I also came to see you because I figured you would be here." Lara glanced at Helen, who smiled at her. Lara took my elbow and steered me away. "Listen," she said very low, "I know you were thinking that it was Benzedrine that killed your friend, but I talked to Dr. Murdoch." Her dark eyes darted over my shoulder, back to my face. "Benzedrine wrecks the internal organs. It leaves behind damage that's easily no-ticeable—a dilated heart, congested kidneys, congested liver, internal hemorrhages. Benzedrine is easy to spot because it just messes up the body. You don't even need to test for it. But he didn't see anything like that in the autopsy."

"So it's not Benzedrine?"

"No. I don't know if that helps or hurts, but I thought you should know either way." She checked her watch. "I've got to go home and get some sleep. Is there anything I can do?"

"No, you've already helped. And, Lara? Thank you."

"You're welcome. Maybe you could tell that brother of yours to call me when he gets out."

As she rushed off, I sat down next to Helen in one of the hard brown chairs. "Women certainly do make idiots of themselves over your brother," Helen said. She was the only girl I'd ever known who seemed immune to him. "Are you okay?"

"Just worried."

"How was Oklahoma?"

Before I could answer, Sam was back and saying there wasn't any bail because Johnny Clay hadn't actually been arrested, only brought in for questioning.

"If he was only being questioned, why did he have to spend the night?"

"Isn't it obvious? To send a message." He sank into the chair next to mine and loosened his tie.

"A message for me." Well it's been received, I thought. Loud and clear. Helen got up to go in search of coffee for us, and Sam reached for my hand. "This has gone too far. They've gone too far." My eyes moved from uniform to uniform, suit to suit, at all these men who may or may not have been crooked, men you were supposed to trust but couldn't because any one of them might have been on the take.

"Velva Jean?"

Butch was standing above me, white shirt, dark pants, jacket under his arm. He nodded at Sam, his eyes glancing at our joined hands, at his cigarette. "You got a light?"

Sam let go of my hand and passed Butch the lighter.

As he lit up, I said, "Where have you been?" It sounded angry, as if all of this was his fault.

"I've been trying to get him out is where I've been." The lighter found its way back to Sam.

"Why didn't you call me?"

"I did call you, but you didn't answer and no one seemed to know where you were."

"Helen knew. She knew exactly where I was."

Butch dropped into the chair on my other side, angling himself toward us, throwing one arm across the back. He looked at me sideways. "Well next time I'll call Helen."

"Where were you when they brought him in?"

"Getting my own ass rounded up." He looked around me to Sam, as if he needed to talk to a rational person. "They've been raiding all of Central ever since the Black Dahlia killing and then all those other girls. They let me go around four a.m., told me they'd keep an eye on me." He said to me, "They let everyone go but your brother."

"They told me they brought him in to ask about Jeanne French, as if he had something to do with her death, as if he even knew that girl."

"You go ask someone else in here, and he'll tell you they brought your brother in because he killed the Black Dahlia. They've done everything but blame him for Pearl Harbor." He looked at Sam. "You think this was the studio?"

"Yep."

Butch held the cigarette like he was getting ready to write with it. He said, "This is one fucked up town."

I got up and walked away so I could stand by myself and think. It was my fault. I should have listened. I should have left it alone. And now they weren't going after me anymore; they were going after my brother.

Helen came back with a coffee for Sam and one for me. When she saw Butch, she offered to get him one, but he shook his head. She and I paced up and down, back and forth, and fifteen, maybe twenty minutes later, Johnny Clay came fuming toward us from the other end of the hall. He moved like he ached, like a man twice his age, and he had murder in his eye. He also had a beauty of a shiner and a split lip. Before he could say a word, I hugged him tight, as if he might disappear.

"Are you okay? Did they hurt you? What happened?"

"I'm okay."

He yanked his arm away and pushed past me, heading for the door. Sam called, "Uh, Junior. There'll be reporters there. We should go out the back."

Johnny Clay kept walking like he couldn't hear. He walked right out the door, and the rest of us followed. He was swallowed up by the swarm of reporters who were circling, waiting for stories. I heard him say, "They picked me up outside the Dunbar, two of them, both white, both wanting to know what I was doing in that part of town. I told them it was none of their business." He grinned meanly. "This was about three, four yesterday afternoon. The fellas that picked me up said they got an anonymous tip telling them I might have something to do with the recent string of lone woman murders. That's what they're calling it. I told them, You got the wrong guy, but they said it didn't matter, they were supposed to take me in, that I must have really pissed someone off. That's a direct quote."

Sam said to us, "And that, my friends, is the sound of Pandora's box opening. Anyone else think it's strange that Bernie Hanser, publicist of Kit Rogers, hasn't shown up yet? Or Mannix? Or Strickling?"

"No," I said. "They've left me on my own on this one. They know I went to Oklahoma, and I'm sure they figured out it had something to do with Mudge's death. It's all part of the lesson."

A reporter called out, "Did they actually question you, Mr. Hart?"

"No. Except for 'Where were you the night of February 9?' And 'Did you know Jeanne French?' I said I was playing a gig at the Downbeat February 9 and had about two hundred witnesses who could testify to that. And, what's more, I didn't know any girl named Jeanne French. That was it. One of the officers said that's all, thanks so much, now here's your cell."

"That's all they asked?"

"That's all. I been in that cell ever since."

"Did they give you that shiner?"

"And the split lip. They said be grateful it isn't worse."

Zed Zabel moved up to the front. He said, "Isn't it true you've been in trouble before? Does the name George Cuswell mean anything to you?"

"No."

"Sorry. You would have known him as 'Blackeye.'"

Johnny Clay went silent. My heart slowed in my chest. My feet, my hands, all of me went cold.

Zed rambled on. "From Texas, wasn't he? Had a brother called Slim. Worked for the CCC back in 1940, 1941, until someone nearly beat his brains in, left him to die. Would you know something about that?"

Sam stared at me. "Who's Blackeye?"

I looked at Butch and so did Sam and Helen. Butch had been there too, back on the mountain, back when Blackeye and his gang had tried to hurt Lucinda Sink, the woman Johnny Clay had loved.

"Go, all of you." Butch handed me his jacket and then pulled off his shirt. The skin across the Bluesman tattoo was a deep and angry purple-red.

I reached out to touch it. "You're hurt. Who did this?"

He smiled. "Let's give 'em a distraction."

• • • • •

We waited on the other side of the building, in the shadow of Old Central. Sam smoked cigarette after cigarette as I paced up and down. Helen leaned against the building, rubbing her arms to keep warm. I said, "I should be right there with him—with them. Standing beside them, telling those reporters what I know." Up and down, up and down. I was going to wear a hole in the pavement.

Sam said, "Which 'him' are you talking about?"

"What?"

"Nothing. You need to sit on what you know until you know more."

"But I think I know who killed her."

"So we deal with that and then you talk to them, only then. Give them something concrete. You spill things now, Pipes, and you'll be the one who ends up looking bad; I guarantee it. They'll twist the truth until they've pinned you for it. And then you won't be of any use to anyone."

I closed my eyes. I counted. When I opened them again, my brother and Butch were walking up. I caught Butch's eye as he wadded up the shirt he was holding and threw it in the trash bin. I handed Butch his jacket, and he pulled it on over his bare chest.

Johnny Clay said, "Let's get out of here. I can't stand to look at this place."

• • • • •

We found a dim, smoky bar two blocks from the jail. The five of us crowded around a table in the back, where we ordered a bottle and glasses. Johnny Clay knocked one glass back and then, eyes burning, said to me, "What happened in Oklahoma?"

I glanced around. Metro had spies everywhere. "Not here."

"Just tell me you're getting close so these sons of bitches will let it alone."

"I'm getting close. I'm almost there. I'm so sorry they brought you into this, Johnny Clay." I looked from him to Butch to Sam to Helen. "I don't want them going after any of you."

My brother poured himself another. "Too late."

"Do you think I should drop it? Just let it go? I will if you tell me to."

"What would Mudge have done, if it was you that died?"

I thought of one of the passages she'd underlined in *Jane Eyre*: *I cannot lie down.* "She would have fought for me."

"Then you keep fighting too. We both will. If they think they can mess with us, screw 'em. They haven't met Velva Jean and Johnny Clay Hart. We come from Indian warriors, little sister. Shit." His eyes were shining, mean and wicked. There was nothing my brother loved better than a fight. "They're the ones that should watch their backs." He threw down the liquor, set the glass on the table. "The way I see it, the only way to get at the honey is to chase the hornets out of there. Or bait 'em out. If it was me, I think I would stir up the hornets and see who wants that honey bad enough to sting."

Butch dropped his cigarette into his glass and said, "Just be careful you don't get stung too bad."

For the next hour, Johnny Clay sat drinking like he didn't plan to go home. When I started to yawn, Helen told me to go on, get a ride with Sam, she would make sure my brother and Butch got back to the Dunbar Hotel safely.

On the drive back to Mudge's house, I told Sam about my trip to Oklahoma, the Rebekahs, and Edna Mudge. When he walked me to my door, he said, "In the interest of being your friend, Pipes, I'm going to tell you something straight. I get the feeling there's more to your uncertainty about us than not being in a good place. Maybe you need to figure that out, and if I'm wrong, I'm wrong. For the first time in my life, I'll gladly eat crow. But if I'm right, well you need to figure that out too."

"What are you talking about?"

"Subtext. I'm flattered you trust me enough to tell me about your trip and this investigation, but does it ever occur to you that you're trying to keep Butch Dawkins separate from this for a reason? That maybe you're trying to protect him, and keep him out of it so when it's all over and done with, you don't have to look at him and be reminded of what you went through? So instead you can just focus on looking ahead?"

When I didn't answer this—because I didn't know how to answer this—he started down the walk. With every step, I thought: Stop him. Ask him to come back. But instead I stood stupidly watching as he drove away.

· · · · ·

From the shelf in Mudge's closet, I pulled down the jewelry box I'd once overturned on Christmas day when I was searching for sweaters. I dumped the contents of the box onto the bed. It was a jumble of necklaces, pins, earrings, bracelets, and rings. Some were missing a bead or a rhinestone or a clasp that worked. I pulled things out in a clump and untangled them strand by strand. I made piles—necklaces here, bracelets here, and over here, pins and medals and one black ring, all featuring a dove and lily, the moon and stars, and a D and R entwined.

I slipped the ring onto my finger. It was almost identical to the rings worn by Dorothea Green and the girls at the Odd Fellows Home. But as I looked at it in the light, I had the same nagging feeling I'd had in Oklahoma—that I'd seen a ring like it somewhere else.

THIRTY-FOUR

Ophelia Lloyd was no longer at Rockhaven Sanitarium. I arrived there at dawn to find the Rose Cottage empty and Ophelia checked out. Agnes Richards couldn't tell me where Ophelia had gone, so I had to assume it was back to Broad Water. On my way to Santa Monica, I stopped at a crowded diner just north of Culver City to place a phone call.

"Broad Water," a voice said.

"Yes, I'm calling for Miss Lloyd. This is Frances from the portrait studio. I work with Mr. Apger."

"I'm sorry, but Miss Lloyd isn't in right now. I'll let her know you called."

"When do you expect her?"

"I'm not sure, but I'll give her the message." The person clicked off.

I picked up the phone again and asked for long distance. Minutes later, the telephone rang five, six, seven times. Then a voice, thin and far away, said, "Velva Jean?"

"Talk into the receiver, Granny." I sat inside the phone booth and watched the door as people came in and out.

I could hear her saying something to someone there, then I heard the low, deep voice of Daddy Hoyt as he came on the line. "Everything okay?" It was the way he always began our conversations.

"Everything's fine." I figured he didn't need to hear about Johnny Clay. "Everything okay there?" It was what I always asked in return.

"We're all getting along as good as can be. I got your check, honey, but you don't have to keep sending them."

"I want you to have it. I wish you'd let me send more."

We talked for a minute about the news from the mountain—Linc had found a job in Asheville but hadn't decided whether to take it because taking it would mean moving himself and Ruby Poole and Russell and the new baby away from the family, Beachard had come and gone and come and gone again, Dan Presley had announced he planned to go to college, and Sweet Fern was pregnant. Granny piped in now and then, and I could picture her over my grandfather's shoulder just as clearly as if I were there.

When he was finished, I said, "I need your help." I told him what Dr. Murdoch had said and how everything was being covered up. As I talked, it all came spilling out. "All this time, I thought it was Benzedrine, but it wasn't. I was hoping I could tell you her symptoms and you might be able to figure out the thing that could have done this to her. Dr. Murdoch says this is the best way to identify the poison."

"Tell me," he said.

After I described every last detail and symptom, Daddy Hoyt was so silent that I had to ask if he was still there. "I'm here," he said. "I'm thinking." He asked me a few questions about the way she looked when I found her—were there any markings on the skin, and so on. "Are you somewhere I can call you back? I want to talk to Granny, consult my books, think about this a few minutes more without tying up your long distance."

"It's easier if I phone you back."

"Give me an hour," he said.

· · · · ·

I went to the studio to wait. I was on my way to the research department when I ran into Bernie, who told me I was needed in the Thalberg Building.

Billy Taub was the one who let me know: I was suspended for six weeks, effective that day. I didn't have to ask why. I had broken my contract to leave Los Angeles without permission. And then there were the morning papers, stacked on his desk, my brother's battered face plastered across the front pages. *Studio Fall Guy?* one headline read. *What MGM Doesn't Want You to Know,* read another.

Tauby said, "No one will know about the suspension unless you or your brother decide to announce it. You can still go to class, but you won't be working again till the suspension is over. We'll keep you in the public eye, publish some 'firsthand' articles, include some photographs from your files. If anyone asks, we've sent you on a publicity tour to promote the new picture."

"In other words, you've got it covered. Just like you always do."

He dropped his voice, as if he was afraid of being overheard. "Why won't you just let this go?"

I pulled something out of my bag and set it on his desk, on top of the papers. "Because she deserves better."

He stared at the article, at the picture of a seventeen-year-old Eloise Mudge on her way to Hollywood.

"Do you even remember that girl?" I laid her letter to him beside it. "Because she deserves better too." He picked up the letter. "As the article mentions, she had a sister. Edna Mudge. I believe Edna had something to do with her death." I waited for this to sink in. "What was Ophelia's name before the studio changed it?"

"Ophelia?" He blinked up at me, and I could see the confusion in his face.

"She's younger than she looks. How old was she when she retired? Twenty-five? Twenty-six? She would be something like twenty-eight, twenty-nine now."

"Ophelia was born January 4, 1910, in Wichita, Kansas, making her thirty-seven years old, although I'm sure she would be flattered to hear you thought she was so much younger." His eyes grew cold. "Her real name is Louise Wasselman, not Edna Mudge."

· · · · ·

I walked out of the Thalberg Building and didn't stop walking until I reached a service station two blocks away. *Just because Tauby says she was born in 1910 and that her given name was Louise, not Edna, doesn't mean he's telling the truth. He could be lying. Or she could be lying to him.*

Daddy Hoyt picked up on the first ring. "We're fairly sure it was belladonna."

"Belladonna? The plant?"

"Otherwise known as deadly nightshade or devil's cherry. 'Hot as a hare, blind as a bat, dry as a bone, red as a beet, and mad as a hatter.' One of the surest signs of belladonna poisoning is meaningless speech and uncontrollable laughter. The entire plant is poisonous. Remember Martha Simms? I treated her for days after she ate the berries. Said she thought they were blueberries, and that they tasted just as sweet. But, like a lot of deadly plants, you can use it medicinally. If you know how. You could go to a store right now and find belladonna salves and plasters, tinctures and eye drops. It's used as a pain medicine, an anesthetic, for seasickness, palsy, respiratory sickness, intestinal troubles, and menstrual cramping. There's a reason they call it a medical miracle. Some even call it the sorcerer's herb because it's such a cure-all. You just have to know how much to take."

"So it's easy to find? Easy to get your hands on?"

"It's always been available in one form or other. I've used it myself. When the war started, it was harder to come by because until then you could, for the most part, only find it overseas. But about three or four years ago, the Department of Agriculture set up belladonna farms in five or six states, including California. Now I'm not a medical doctor, honey, but I know what it can do to a body, and I would wager my life that that's what killed your friend."

"Would they have had to use the plant or the berries? Or could something like a tincture do it?"

Tauby has bottles of tinctures in his medicine cabinet, all prescribed to Ophelia, but I don't remember seeing belladonna.

"Probably the tincture. In some cases, they'd have to have a prescription for it. But a little bit here, a little there, could have built up enough in her system so that one big dose of it would be enough."

"You think it might have been going on for a while?"

"Given what you told me, I think it could have been."

"If this was caught in time—would there have been a cure? Could we have saved her?"

"You can't look backwards, Velva Jean. It does you no good."

"I realize that, but I need to know."

"The poison, strong as it is, can usually be offset by swallowing a glass of warm vinegar, mustard, even water, and following up with magnesia or strong coffee. If it makes you feel any better, I don't know that I would have been able to tell what was happening to her until it was too late."

You would have known. You can heal anyone. I've seen it. I've helped you. But where was I? And how did I not know?

He said, "The funny thing about it, if you can call it funny, is that, deadly as belladonna is to humans, certain animals are immune to it. Cattle, chickens, rabbits."

Rabbits. I stopped listening because my mind was flashing back to Carmen, Oklahoma, and the farm surrounding the orphans' home. Not just the farm, but the barn and the other structures—chicken pens, rabbit pens. I looked down at the ring on my hand—Mudge's Rebekah ring—and I suddenly remembered where I'd seen it before.

He was saying, "There's a plant researcher named Henry Walters who believed that if you crossbred poisonous plants like belladonna with carnivorous plants like the Venus flytrap or butterwort, it would be more dangerous than the cholera. He believed plants, like people, were capable of love and that they had memories. Which meant, if this were true, that they could feel pain and jealousy and even hold a grudge. According to him, belladonna is a plant filled with hatred."

Before hanging up, I said, "Daddy Hoyt? You all might read about Johnny Clay in the papers, but I want you to know there's nothing to worry about. What they're saying isn't true, and we're going to put a stop to it."

"Is everything okay out there, honey?"

"It isn't now, but it will be."

· · · · ·

I still carried the hairpins that Monsieur Brunet had crafted in his French laboratory, the ones that doubled as knives and, in a pinch, lockpicks. Babe King always locked her door. I knew this because sometimes we would come into or out of our dressing rooms at the same time. She seemed to keep the key in the flat red purse she carried everywhere.

Babe's dressing room faced north toward Washington Boulevard, which meant you couldn't see the entrance if you happened to be walking down A Street. Even with this, I needed to work quickly because I wasn't sure who was around, and I knew I could be interrupted at any moment. I had picked a lock before, but I wasn't fast at it like Johnny Clay. He could work one in under thirty seconds.

I rapped on the door first, to be sure she wasn't home. I rapped again and again. When there was no answer, I bent one hairpin like a hook and slid it inside the lock, then used another as a tension wrench. It was all by feel. You had to have just the right touch. It was like anything else—you couldn't force it. When I felt the hooked pin bending out of shape, I pressed it against the keyway to bend it back. I did this over and over, stopping now and then when a car rolled past or I heard the sound of voices.

Finally, I heard and felt the click.

Before anyone could come along, I slipped inside the suite, shutting and locking the door behind me. I hated what she'd done with the place. Mudge had made it warm and welcoming, everything in blue, her favorite color, because it reminded her of the sky and of her days as a pilot. She'd always kept fresh flowers around the room, but the only flowers here were on the curtains. The walls and carpet were a bright, blinding pink. The window treatments, the carpet, and the pillows were a sort of creamy white. Pillows and towels were stitched with "BK."

I went straight to the bathroom, where I searched the cabinets for belladonna. I found aspirin, toothpaste, Vaseline, hair spray, lipstick. I searched the vanity table, end tables, anything with a drawer, but there was nothing containing belladonna, nothing even all that personal. I stood in the middle of the room, eyes searching for anything strange or suspicious or out of place, anything that might help me.

And then I saw it.

It was sitting in plain sight, atop a little table by the door, as if she'd set it down quickly, on her way out. A simple ring—gold band, black square face, crescent moon, seven stars, a dove, a lily, and an R and D entwined.

THIRTY-FIVE

The afternoon paper carried Zed Zabel's column, where he told "the truth about Johnny Clay Hart," recounting sordid stories from my brother's past, most of them made up. The ones that weren't made up were exaggerated to make Johnny Clay seem wild and dangerous. There was no telling how many newspapers the story had reached. From a Beverly Hills pay phone, I called the Dunbar Hotel and asked for Butch. When he came on the line I said, "Has he seen the paper?"

"Not yet. What's in it?"

I read him the article.

"What do you need me to do?"

"Keep him away from them if you can. The last thing we need is for him to go after Zed Zabel and do the same to him that he did to Blackeye, even though both those men deserve whatever they get."

"Done. What are you going to do?"

"I'm going to stir up the hive."

· · · · ·

The living room of Mudge's house was stacked, floor to ceiling, with books because Helen and Flora were searching for things Mudge might have filed away. The sofa was so covered in pages you could barely see the pattern. Letters, newspaper clippings, notes, receipts, photos—years of material, years of a life.

Helen cleared the papers off one of the chairs so I could sit, and then she cleared a spot for herself and Flora on the couch. "How's your brother taking it?" She nodded at the newspaper.

"He hasn't seen it yet. I asked Butch to keep him away from it until I can figure this out."

"Wise idea. So Babe King."

"Babe King."

"Not Nigel at all."

"No. Although I'd bet the studio thinks he did it. Why else would they go to so much trouble? Babe isn't worth anything to them yet."

"I don't understand what the motive is. I have a sister I'm not especially close to, but I wouldn't wish anything bad for her."

Flora shook her head. "Poor child," she said, and I knew she was talking about Mudge.

I thought of my own sister, of how many times over the years I'd prayed for her to disappear or leave me alone or suddenly turn nice. "I wouldn't wish anything bad for Sweet Fern either. You haven't found anything in all these papers?"

"Just more things to be properly filed and put away."

I looked at the framed picture of Mudge that sat on the mantel. She smiled, her secrets safely kept.

Helen said, "Without the flask, there's no proof. There's nothing to tie her to the crime."

"Unless there's a way to stir the hive and get the bee to come after me." She and Flora looked at each other and back at me, lost. "I need you to keep going through these books. Search every book in this house, until you find something that can help me."

Flora said, "What are we looking for?"

"Anything relating to Edna Mudge or Babe King or a boy named John Henry Briggs."

$$\cdot\ \cdot\ \cdot\ \cdot\ \cdot$$

Giffard Leland lived in a pink stucco mansion high up in the Bel Air hills, a gift from his father, the grocery store king. The property was terraced and statued within an inch of its life, as if to say, *We're every bit as rich as you are and we belong here too.*

It was two o'clock on Wednesday, February 19, and I had an appointment. A maid in a black uniform met me at the door, her smile as wilted as her apron. Yilla King tripped in from the wings, as if she'd been waiting for her cue. Her bright yellow hair shimmered. The pink-orange of her lips and nails matched her blouse perfectly.

"Kit Rogers, how charming," she said, kissing me on both cheeks. She ordered drinks for us from the maid and then led me through a maze of rooms, hands flapping as she pointed out this and that. We wound up on the sunporch, where magazines were spread across the love seat. She had clearly been catching up on her reading.

She plucked a cigarette from a bowl of them arranged like flowers, but didn't offer me one. "What can I do you for?" She sat, swinging one leg over the other, shoes a glittering gold under the cuff of her trousers. I sat across from her and it hit me for the first time that this too-bright, too-loud woman was Mudge's mother. The same mother who had dropped a three-year-old girl and a baby at an orphanage, and then come to collect them and drop them off, again and again, until they were old enough to leave on their own. As far as I was concerned, Yilla was as guilty of killing Mudge as Babe was.

I said, "It's about Edna."

"I'm sorry?"

"Your daughter."

"I don't know what you're talking about."

"Yes you do. Edna Mudge. Babe King." Her leg stopped swinging. "I guess in a way it's about Eloise too." I opened my bag and pulled out a folder. On the table between us, I placed copies of the detective agency letter, the newspaper article featuring the Dell Rapids orphanage, and the picture of John Henry Briggs.

Yilla stared at them, eyes wide and unblinking.

The maid walked in then, setting drinks down in front of us, glancing as she did at the materials I'd laid out. Yilla shooed her away and picked up her drink. She took a dainty sip, and then downed half of it. She set the glass on the table with a bang, little drops of water splashing onto the papers.

I said, "I found these when I was going through Eloise's things. Take your time."

She kept her eyes on me, as if she was afraid to look down. "What do you want?"

"I want you to tell me about this boy." I leaned forward and tapped the picture. "I'll get you started. He's Edna's son. Your grandson. Eloise was interested in him enough to pay a private investigator to find him. I'm wondering why."

She swallowed the rest of her drink. This time, her hand trembled as she set the glass down. She sat staring at the floor.

I continued to help her out. "I guess it wouldn't look good for a popular young movie star to have a secret past and to have abandoned her own child, much less shaving a good ten or eleven years off her age. I don't think the studio would be very pleased about that. Especially a studio like MGM, which believes in family and happy endings."

She lit another cigarette, both hands shaking so badly that I took the lighter from her and helped her. She sat back. Finally, she let out a breath. "She didn't want anyone to know about it. She stashed the kid somewhere up north, faked her own death, ran away from the father. He was no good anyway." She sniffed, picked at her lip, inhaled deeply. She glanced at the picture, then away quickly, as if it might burn her eyes. "Eloise knew there was a child because when it happened, back when she got knocked up, Edna asked to come live with her out here. She was just a stupid, mixed-up kid, but Eloise didn't want anything to do with her. Eloise always had it in her mind that her sister stole that man from her, as if anyone would want him. Like I said, he was no good. Common, you know. But Eloise was cold that way. Same way she was with me. Coming out here, too big for her britches, making all that money. Do you know she kept me on a budget? Tried to tell me what I could spend it on and where."

"She supported you?"

"If you could call it that."

"It was her money."

"I was her mother."

A picture was beginning to form. "And when she cut you off, you pushed Edna into pictures, hoping she would take care of you instead."

She laughed, a hard, brittle sound. "No one ever pushed Edna to do anything. Anything she ever did she did on her own and for herself, and she's the first to tell you. She turned out to be as ungrateful as her sister."

"So when Edna knew she was pregnant, why didn't she turn to you instead?" As if I had to ask.

"I was married by then and living out of state. Husband number three wasn't interested in raising someone else's kids, if you know what I mean. And who could blame him? Troublemakers, both of them. Eloise phoned me up and read me the riot act, said I needed to get my act together and go get Edna and grow up once and for all." Her eyes flashed. "Me, her own mother!"

"Why did Eloise go to so much trouble to find him?"

She leaned forward, stubbing the cigarette out in the ashtray. "She tracked him down through that private eye. Told Edna to stay away from her studio, go back to Columbia, leave her alone, or she would tell Mr. Mayer and Louella Parsons and the *New York Goddamn Times*, anyone who would listen. It was blackmail. 'You stay over there, I stay over here, everyone's happy.' Only Columbia is a shithole; everybody knows that. Edna wanted more for herself. She always did. This was her dream." She waved her hands at the house, the city. "Eloise stole it right out from under her nose."

"And so you helped Edna, hoping she would help you. You pretended she was ten years younger, just a fresh up-and-comer who needed her mother as a chaperone."

She smiled. "It worked didn't it?"

It was too much, all of it. Poor Eloise. Poor Edna. This awful mother.

"Until now." I looked around at the sunporch and the statued gardens that spread beyond. "It is a beautiful house. I meant to congratulate you on your marriage. Your husband's a well-known, respected man. It must be a dream come true for you and for Edna. This house, your marriage, her contract at Metro-Goldwyn-Mayer."

"What do you want?" she said again.

"The same thing Eloise wanted: blackmail. I want you to tell Edna that I know about John Henry Briggs."

I waited just long enough to make sure this had sunk in, and then I stood and collected my purse. As she stared down at the papers spread across the table, I said, "Don't worry. You can keep those. I made them for you."

· · · · ·

And so, I waited.

I waited for Yilla to deliver my message and for Babe to get in touch with me.

I waited for Babe's next move.

On Thursday, I drove to the studio and went to my classes like a good, dutiful MGM girl, and pretended I wasn't waiting for anything. Rosie said, "You seem distracted, Velva Jean."

I said, "There's a lot on my mind. Ever since my brother was picked up by police. Did you read about it? And Zed Zabel's article too?" He nodded. "And then the suspension—1947 has been a really horrible year." It was an easy, believable excuse.

He gave me a pep talk, which made me feel worse about lying, and then, as if to make up for it, I sang him the song I'd written and told him I'd recorded it the week before. "I should get a copy soon," I said. "When I do I'll bring it in and play it for you."

· · · · ·

On Friday morning, I reported to hair and makeup and then to the Thalberg Building. I had a meeting with Bernie at nine o'clock. As I came off the elevator, I saw a man who looked like Zed Zabel but who couldn't have been Zed Zabel because this man was dressed in a suit Zed couldn't afford and walking with Howard Strickling and Eddie Mannix, the three of them looking like best friends, the conspiring kind.

In Bernie's office, I said, "Do you want to hear something funny? I thought I saw Zed Zabel just now with Mr. Strickling and Mr. Mannix, but it couldn't have been him because he's banned from the studio."

"He was banned, that's right. Until Mr. Strickling hired him." Bernie launched into what he knew: Howard Strickling had been the one to approach Zed, or that was the rumor anyway. Bernie had seen the result of it with his own eyes—Zed sitting with Eddie Mannix and Howard Strickling in Strickling's office, the three of them shooting the breeze like old friends. The next thing that happened was Zed on a guided tour of the office, shaking hands, chatting up the secretaries and female publicists, acting for all the world like a man who'd inherited a gold mine.

He showed up the next day wearing an expensive-looking suit and an expensive-looking haircut, his name on the door of one of the third-floor offices, where he moved in as if he'd always been there.

What was it Zed had told me? *Everyone has a price.*

While Bernie talked, my mind was spinning in all directions: *Now that I've lost Zed, I'll have to find someone who can get the story out there. I can go to the* Times *or, better yet, the* Examiner. *I can go on the radio, tell my story there, once I have proof.*

Sam can write something.

But I can't go to Sam because Sam isn't speaking to me.

Maybe Dr. Murdoch will come forward. He says he'll come forward if he has evidence. But I don't have any evidence to give him. Not yet.

· · · · ·

Outside, I saw her across the street, parking her brand-new car. Babe King, dressed hat to shoes in red, sashayed toward the Thalberg Building, toward me. I could tell she hadn't seen me yet, and I considered running, but I wanted to know: Had Yilla talked to her?

For the first time in my life, I wished for a cigarette so that I would have something to do with my hands. I opened my purse and rummaged around until I heard the tap of her heels on the steps. I looked up. Smiled. "Morning, Babe."

She smiled in return as she paused on the same step, so that we were eye-to-eye. "Morning, Kit." There was something in her voice that made my pulse quicken and my brain start churning in an excited, terrified way, as if it realized that finally the waiting was over.

I raised my hand to tuck the hair behind my ear, and her eyes followed it. As they settled on my ring, her expression changed. The smile disappeared. I held out my hand so she could get a better look. "Pretty, isn't it? But then, I think you have one like it." I smiled and glanced up at the building, where anyone might have looked out the window and seen two of Metro's rising stars engaged in pleasant conversation.

"Nice to see you, Edna," I said, skipping down the steps. "Have a good day."

· · · · ·

On Saturday night, I sat on a corner of the living room sofa, Butch in the opposite corner, Hal between us, Helen and Sherman and Flora taking up the chairs, Johnny Clay standing beside the record player. This was my fake birthday party for my fake birthday, and my present from Butch and my brother was a copy of the record we'd made. *Butch Dawkins & the Bluesmen, featuring Velva Jean Hart.*

The music was good. It was so good, I wanted to take the record and break it into a million little pieces so that no one but me could ever hear it, so that I could protect it and keep it for myself. There was my voice, as I'd always thought it sounded. Not my MGM voice. Not the voice of Kit Rogers. That was Velva Jean Hart, ladies and gentlemen, thank you very much, singing from deep in her soul.

I glanced past Hal at Butch. When I'd played my first record for him, years ago, up on Devil's Courthouse, we had danced. He'd held me so close that I could feel the Indian medicine beads he wore against my own chest. It was the nearest I'd ever been to him, the only time he'd had his arms around me.

Butch looked up, catching my eye before I glanced away. Somehow he had kept my brother from hearing about Zed Zabel's article, and I was grateful.

When the song was over, we all observed a moment of silence out of reverence for the fact that it was really, truly good in a way that you couldn't say about many things. Then everyone started to talk at once about how much they loved it, how great it sounded, and what came next. Johnny Clay chattered on about the record they'd made yesterday, which was going to be even better than this one, and guess how many dealers had asked for copies, Velva Jean. Go on, guess. That's right, Leroy was sold out already and having to press more.

My brother's face was lit up, and I was happy for him because he needed to be happy, even if I was too worried and anxious and on pins and needles to do anything but watch the phone and watch my back and wait for Babe to do something.

Johnny Clay, Sherman, and Butch were the last to leave. On their way out the door, my brother was off and running toward the street, as if he couldn't wait to get to the next place. I hadn't told them about Babe or Yilla, not after what had happened with the police.

While Sherman and Johnny Clay climbed into the car, talking a mile a minute, Butch stopped on the step and said, "He'll be okay. It's you I'm worried about."

"I'll be okay too."

"What are you up to, girl?"

"It's nothing, not yet. But I've laid the bait."

"We can help. You're not in this alone."

"I know." But I'd involved them enough.

"For now, maybe you should go back in there and listen to what you did, in spite of what you're going through. You need to be proud of that and know if you can do something like this now, you can do it anytime. People ask do I only write when the feeling hits, but you can't wait for the stars to align. You got to stick with it and be prepared to align your own stars. That's what you did here, Velva Jean. You aligned the stars even when you couldn't see a single one for the clouds."

· · · · ·

After they left, and after Helen and Flora had gone to sleep, I curled up on the living room sofa with the record on my lap. It was just a thin black disc labeled "Bronze Recording Company." To look at it, you'd think it was nothing much of anything—a plastic circle, no bigger than a pie plate.

Butch Dawkins & the Bluesmen. I ran my finger across his name.

I flipped the record to the other side and there was his name again. There was my name too.

The part of me that was still Velva Jean Hart, a ten-year-old girl with a mama and a daddy, who dreamed of hearing her voice on the Grand Ole Opry, thought, Once everything is over, I want this.

Velva Jean Hart

1947

THIRTY-SIX

On Saturday, March 1, a message was waiting when I got home. In Helen's neat and tidy handwriting it read, *Nigel Gray wants to meet Sunday at 7 p.m. at the Lot 2 castle. His secretary says NG knows about "Edna" and has something that might help.*

Sunday was cool and wet, the sky gray and heavy with fog. Rain fell off and on throughout the day, but by five o'clock, the clouds were starting to clear. Helen's parents were visiting from Connecticut, and the three of them were spending the weekend in Santa Monica. She called to give me the phone number for her hotel, to make sure I'd gotten the message about Nigel, and to tell me she'd left food in the icebox. "I knew you wouldn't take time to cook or even eat if Flora or I didn't see to it."

In the refrigerator, I found cold chicken salad with celery, nuts, and berries, lemon meringue pie, and iced tea. It was a summer picnic for a winter day. I picked at the food the way I picked at all my food lately, then dropped my plate into the sink, meal half-eaten, and got dressed. Because of the weather, I pulled on a trench coat and picked up an umbrella.

At twenty past six, I drove to the studio. I checked my mirrors, but no one was behind me, as far as I could tell. I arrived at the gate at ten of seven. I sat by the curb on quiet Overland Avenue, Lot 1 on the left side of the street, Lot 2 on my right. "Keep Out," the signs said, all along the chain-link fence. The gate was open, but I didn't see the guard. I waited, engine idling, for him to come out of the guardhouse, where a light was burning, but when he didn't I rolled on past, following the curve of the main road past the warehouses and boat dock, twisting through New England Street, passing the railroad tracks, the trains, and Railroad Terminal #2, and parking near the enormous and elegant Grand Central Station.

Outside the station, the gaslights gave off a hazy glow, barely burning, as if someone had turned them down but not completely. The backlot looked eerie, especially with the fog billowing in from the ocean, but I could see the moon, appearing in and out from behind the clouds. Something about it made me feel more exposed somehow, and for the first time I thought: You should have told someone where you were going, Velva Jean. Why does Nigel want to meet you here? Why not a restaurant? Why not his house or Mudge's house?

The station and terminal were dusted with fake snow so that I found myself in a winter wonderland. The ground was covered in white, icicles hanging from the train and from the eaves of the station roof. I crossed over the open ground. I could see the turrets of Castle Finckenstein outlined against the sky. The back side was nothing but plywood beams and ladders, scaffolding and propped-up wood.

I walked through the passage between Verona Square, with its fountains and statues and arched stucco walls, and Joppa Square. It was darker here, and I made my way carefully across the courtyard, blackness and shadows all around. I could only make out the shape of the castle turrets and walls, and the stairs that led to the entrance, a flight on either side of the landing.

A figure waited at the top of the stairs, framed against the entrance. I started to call out, but didn't because the sound of a voice cutting through all that night would have been jarring, even if it was my own.

I ran up the stairs, two at a time, my shoes tapping against the concrete, the only noise for miles. Nigel stood, hands in pockets, waiting.

"This is an interesting choice for a meeting place," I said, trying to sound breezy.

"My thoughts precisely." He wore a black jacket, the collar turned up.

"Before you say anything—I'm sorry I came out to your house that day."

"Why did you come out there?" I could just make out his face.

"To get information. Maybe to get you to confess or admit that Pia did it. But I know now that you didn't kill Barbara."

"So now I'm innocent? I thought it was supposed to be the other way around in this country."

"You have to admit, it looked bad. By doing everything in their power to protect you, the studio only made you seem guilty."

"It's been a bloody nightmare, start to finish." He gazed out past me at nothing, then shook his head, eyes on mine again. "I don't blame you. I guess I don't blame anyone. I would have thought I was guilty too."

"I'm sorry about Pia."

"Everyone seems to assume I'm glad she's gone, but what they don't realize is I did care about her. I wouldn't have married her all those years ago if I didn't." The moon disappeared again, and he rocked back and forth, as if he was cold. "Was that what you wanted to tell me?"

"Yes."

"You could have waited till tomorrow and found me in the daytime. You didn't have to bring me all the way out here on a Sunday night." Even in the dark, I could see his white, white smile.

"I didn't bring you out here."

"I had a message that you called, asking me to meet you."

"But you invited me."

Our eyes locked, and I could see he was as confused as I was. I looked up suddenly, toward the turrets, toward the rooftops of Chinese Street, which grew up alongside. I took his hand and pulled him into the shadows of the great doorway, where I whispered, "I didn't invite you here."

I could see his eyes now, the only spot of color in the pale light. "Then who?" His voice was barely a breath.

"Barbara's sister. The one who killed her."

"Her sister?"

"Where's your car?"

"The boat dock."

"Mine's closer."

We crept down the stairs and stayed in the shadows of the building, hugging it as close as we could. We slipped through a castle archway to the narrow and twisting Chinese Street beyond. This was acres of palaces and pagodas, ringed by the Great Wall of China. Most of it was flooded with water for *Green Dolphin Street*, a full-sized ship docked on one side of a wooden bridge, a group of small Chinese junks on the other.

We picked our way across the bridge, over sandbags that lay strewn about. We were halfway across when a shot rang out. In the night, it was hard to tell where it came from, the sound of it echoing through the buildings. Nigel grabbed my hand again and we went bumping along, tripping over the bags of rice or sand, as heavy as bodies, then off the bridge, our feet hitting dirt as we ran through the streets. The shop window signs, all in Chinese, waved in the breeze. Narrow stairways and doorways led to nothing.

At the end of the street, I could see Grand Central Station, the gaslights glowing in the fog, and, to the left of it, my car, and another car beside it.

Suddenly, a figure blocked the path.

Nigel said, "Babe?"

We froze because she had a gun, and it was pointed at both of us. Without a word, she fired, hitting Nigel in the chest or arm, I couldn't tell. The unexpected force of it sent him reeling backward.

She said, "Hello there, you two. Just the people I wanted to see. Thanks so much for coming. How are you feeling, Kit?"

"A little ambushed."

She laughed. "And you, Nigel?"

"The same. Also a little bloody."

"Just so you know, that wasn't bad aim. If I'd wanted to hit your heart or your head, I could have. After all, I grew up in Oklahoma. I was as good as married to a farm boy who taught me how to shoot."

Nigel gripped his arm, little beads of water forming across his face. In the glow of the gaslights, I could see the red of his blood.

Babe waved the gun. "Let me tell you how we're going to play this scene. I shoot you once more, Nigel, before giving the gun to Kit, after the chamber's empty, of course. Then I'm going to get in my car and drive away, and tomorrow Howard Strickling and Eddie Mannix can call in Whitey Hendry and the whole thing will just disappear. Just like Eloise. As if it never happened. As if you'd never killed each other, Kit so angry and distraught over the death of her friend, and Nigel so bent on shutting her up."

I said, "Before you do this, tell us why." I was stalling, but I had to think.

"Are you trying to stall for time, Kit? Okay. I'll play, just like in the movies. Because Eloise took everything I ever wanted and then she turned her back on me. The time I needed her most, she said no. I was just a kid, but that didn't matter."

Nigel said, "She was sorry."

"How do you know?"

"She told me. Not about you exactly, but I knew there was something in her past that she regretted. She said, 'I haven't always done the right thing. I once hurt someone very much, someone close to me, someone I should have forgiven and watched out for.'"

"Someone she should have forgiven? That sounds like Eloise."

Please keep talking.

"It's ironic, when you think about it, that she got the life I wanted and I got the life she wanted, or at least I had it for a while. She loved John Henry Briggs, but she couldn't have him because he was married, and back then she didn't go for married men." She batted her eyes at Nigel. "That changed, of course. But I guess, in the end, neither of us got the life we dreamed of."

It started to rain again, and that was when I remembered the umbrella, still gripped in my hand. Out of instinct, Babe tilted her head toward the sky, and I opened the umbrella like a shield and swung it in her direction.

A shot went off, and for a moment I thought I'd been hit because I felt the force of it go through me. Nigel slumped to the ground. I hesitated, but he said, "Go," and I ran away from the light, into the dark.

My throat had gone dry. My heart was pounding. I ran through Chinese Street, back over the bridge, the rain falling harder now, the drops sounding like a chorus as they hit the water. Babe could be anywhere and everywhere.

Three shots had been fired so far. The gun looked like a .38, the same one I'd carried in the WASP. The chamber would hold six bullets, which meant three to go before she would have to reload.

I could hear her behind me, faster than expected. I was moving too slow. Go, Velva Jean, I told myself. Go, go, go.

I was on the streets of England now, the clouds rolling out toward sea. I could see the thatched, peaked roofs of the buildings and the towers of another castle, an arched door leading to another land. I raced across cobblestones, through the door, and onto another cobbled street. My shoes were making too much noise, so I ducked into one of the open buildings, pulled them off, and in bare feet went rushing out the open, empty back side. I flashed back to wartime France, where the houses and churches were beautiful and whole, until you stepped inside and realized there was no roof, no wall, the stairs leading nowhere to floors that no longer existed.

I was on the cobbled streets again, silent this time, running. And suddenly I was in Paris. The world tilted because these were streets I recognized. I knew these courtyards and sloping walkways. There was the dome of the Sacré Coeur, the shops and alleyways of Montmartre, the chimney pots and steeples, the twisting streets of the Latin Quarter. I was Clementine Roux, Germans on my heels. I slipped through the shadows thinking: They won't take me. I will not be caught again.

The scale was wrong. The dome looked smaller the closer you got to it, when it should have looked larger. The alleyways stopped suddenly, coming up short, and the shops were empty, except for plywood and cables and dusty props. It was a world meant to be seen through the lens of the camera. Up close, in the middle of it, everything seemed upside down and backward.

I felt the sting on my shoulder before I heard the shot, and saw the blood dripping down. It might be bad, very bad, but I couldn't stop to look. I needed to reach the entrance gate on Overland because it was the only way in or out that wasn't blocked by a twenty-five-foot fence. There would be a telephone. I could call for help. Even in the rain, I was burning up. I threw off my coat, which was too heavy, and began to run faster.

I was in Hamlet's Mill, or a place just like it. In a blur, I passed city hall, a barbershop, department store, market, drugstore, all lined up on either side of a charming town square of grass and trees, the American flag waving in the breeze. I passed the little theater where I'd seen my first movie, the one Mama had brought me to when I was seven and we'd walked down from Sleepy Gap, holding hands and singing the whole way. I passed the Hamlet's Mill Hotel, but the sign said something different.

I could call Daddy Hoyt. I could call the sheriff. They would know what had happened to the hotel. The sheriff would get me home, just like he used to bring Daddy home. I would walk up the mountain and see my family, as if nothing had ever happened, as if all of it—my whole life—was just a dream, like the one Dorothy had in *The Wizard of Oz*. I would be safe and quiet and cool and still, and this pain in my shoulder would stop aching.

Babe King was on my heels, and suddenly I wasn't home at all but on the backlot of MGM. I'd completely lost my bearings. In the distance, straight ahead, I could see the water tower, which meant Lot 1 was that way.

To get there, I would have to cross open ground. I stayed low and ran in a zigzag because something in my brain remembered this from France. I wished I still had the umbrella, but I had thrown it away when I opened it, and now I had no shoes, no coat, no weapon. Nigel might be dying or dead already, and I had left him all alone.

The rain made everything blurry, just slightly out of focus. I was out of breath, my mouth so dry I couldn't swallow, my heart racing. I wanted to rest, but I had to keep going.

I reached the scene docks and heard another shot. This one brushed so close to my ear that my hair blew across my face. Without thinking, I climbed. Here were staircases that went nowhere, standing in a tangle, railings crossing railings, stairs bumping into stairs, some curved, some straight. I ran up and down, up and down, and there was Babe, two staircases over, coming up and up and across toward me. By now, we'd been trained to run up and down stairs with books on our head, not even looking where we were going, because we were MGM girls and that was what we did. She fired again, and then again. I wasn't counting anymore, but I knew she had reloaded.

I leapt to the ground, but it was too high a jump. In the dark, I misjudged the distance, and I landed hard, my ankle throbbing. I ran on, telling myself it didn't matter and I didn't care about pain. There would be worse pain if I didn't run.

Where was the water tower? I'd lost track of it, and then, somehow, I was on New York's Fifth Avenue, and it was immediately quiet. It was too quiet. She might be aiming that gun at me right now. I couldn't remember if I needed to go right or left or up or down, and then there was no time to decide because Babe was there again and she was running, looking for all the world like someone who just loved to run, who could run forever and ever.

At the end of the street, I turned a sharp right and I saw the open gate, the light still burning in the empty guard booth. The sight of it helped me go faster, and then I was inside, bending over the guard, who lay on the ground, still breathing. I shook him, but his head rested on his arm, as if he was sleeping. I picked up the phone and dialed the operator as I tried to unhook the gun from his belt. "Yes, I'm at MGM studio, Lot Two. Please send help." I hung up, wondering if I should have said more.

I didn't have time to worry or call again because something tapped against the window, and there was Edna Mudge smiling back at me. She stepped into the doorway and I picked up the first thing I saw—a half-drunk mug of coffee—and threw it in her face. She stumbled backward, and I took off, the guard's gun in my hand, crossing Overland, through the gate onto Lot 1, past the half-acre lake, until I was, once again, in France. This time, it was a French village with shingled rooftops and gabled windows and balconies that stared, dead and vacant, onto the avenue. I paused just long enough to check the pistol, which wasn't loaded.

At the foot of the water tower, another shot was fired, this one from close range. I waited to feel it go through me, but when it didn't I rested a hand on the rung of the ladder, wet with rain. I looked up at the underside of the tower, shoved the gun in my belt, and started to climb.

"How are you feeling now, Kit Rogers?"

The voice came from ten or fifteen feet beneath me, maybe more, maybe less. I glanced down and there she was, pulling herself up steadily, gun in her hand.

I didn't say anything because I was concentrating on climbing. For some reason, I knew if I reached the top everything would be all right. I would be up above the overcast. I would be beyond the keep. I couldn't go backward or stand still. I had to keep going, as high as I could, maybe up into the clouds and all the way to heaven, where Mama was waiting. My body didn't want to stop moving. I felt tired, lost, numb—but unafraid. *I should feel afraid.*

Babe might have been able to keep up for a while, on the ground, but we were in the air now, and that was my territory. I kept going.

I slipped, caught my breath, and then steadied myself and thought, How did I get here? I looked below and there was nothing but open space and air and, at the bottom of this, many miles down, pavement.

Babe said, "I hope you enjoyed the berries. I'm told they taste sweeter than blueberries, even if they do look just like them. I dropped them off yesterday, gave them to your friend. Helen, I think she's called? I said they were from Nigel, told her I was his secretary, and delivered the message that he wanted to meet you."

This stopped me for a moment. I hung on to the side of the water tower and tried to focus on what she was saying.

"You know you can buy directly from the belladonna farms, make your own medicine, or just feed your pet rabbit. They're immune to the plant. Unlike humans."

I went lightheaded, maybe from the height or the sight of the pavement. Maybe from the poison. The symptoms were there—the confusion, anger, fever, dry mouth, headache, the wild desire to laugh. Enough poison to kill me. I tried to remember how many of the berries I'd eaten. I told myself, If they can't figure out on their own what's been done to me, I can tell them the antidote. *If I can remember. If someone finds me in time.*

Down below, the street was nearly empty. No sign of the police. A taxicab stopped outside the bar and grill, and a passenger climbed in. A man walked by, his dog on a leash. A motorcycle went roaring past. No one looked up. No crowd collected. For the first time in a long time, I didn't have an audience, and this might have been the best thing—the only good thing—about being up there.

The wind tugged at my hem. Even though I was only wearing a dress and bare feet, I was burning up. *Is this how it feels before you die? Or is it one of the earlier symptoms?*

I wanted to dance, but I held myself back—gripping the rung so tightly I could literally feel the metal hitting bone. The ladder was barely wider than my waist. My fingers dug into the hard, wet surface. My mind wouldn't turn over, even though I was trying to think. I suddenly wanted to get back down, but I didn't know how to get there, and besides, someone or something had chased me up here.

I don't want to die.

A voice was saying, "I actually thought of you as my friend. Maybe that's the hardest part of all of this. I liked being your friend, Kit. I wasn't just putting that on. This isn't personal, although I know it seems that way. It's just what has to happen now."

Here is the strange thing: I feel calmer than I have in months, probably because I am doing something to fix this, once and for all. My mind feels far away, as if it has wandered off, free-falling all those miles onto the street, and from there speeding its way toward the ocean. I am waiting to see what it will do next.

From the direction of the ground, I heard my name. At first, I thought it was Babe, but then, just barely, I could make out a face. It was a good face, a friendly one. It was a face I loved.

Babe was also looking down. I hooked my arm through the rail, so that I was latched on, and then I pointed the empty gun at her head. When she turned back to me, she was staring down the barrel. I said, "Bang," and pulled the trigger. The gun made a clicking sound, and in that instant, Babe lost her grip. Too late, I reached for her hand, dropping the gun. Babe fell through the air, her eyes on mine as she went. I pulled myself in, shut my eyes tight, clinging to the ladder. I was suddenly frozen. I couldn't look. I couldn't go higher. I couldn't go down.

A voice hollered at me to come on. "Everything is okay. You're safe." But I couldn't move. I was still frozen, eyes still closed, by the time Johnny Clay reached me.

• • • • •

The next thing I knew, I was on the ground, looking up at the water tower as if it were a giant beanstalk. My brother wrapped a blanket around my shoulders, and Flora held out something foul-smelling and told me to drink every last drop of it. I didn't want to drink it, and I told her this, and she and my brother made me drink it anyway.

The guard was there, or one of them, and Butch Dawkins handed me a hot cup of coffee and told me to drink this down too. I heard the wail of a siren on the next block, and I closed my eyes just for a second, sending up a short, sweet prayer of thanks because it was important to be thankful, even at a time like this. "Nigel," I said, though I couldn't hear my voice. "He's by Grand Central Station."

The next thing I knew, I was staring at a dingy white ceiling. The part of my mind that was working and with me thought, What am I doing on the floor?

And then I saw that I was on a bed and not the floor at all, and a man in a white coat leaned over me and said very slowly, "Can you hear me, Miss Hart? Do you remember what happened?"

"Yes," I said, but my voice sounded thin and raspy, like an old man's. "There has been a murder."

"But you are alive. . . ."

"Not me. My friend. Although someone tried to kill me. The same person. They were getting away with it, you see, but not now." I started to laugh like a villain in a movie. I laughed and laughed, the sound of it echoing off the white, white walls of the room. The only decoration was a large framed painting of horses grazing in a valley, placid and dull and hanging too high on the left side. I stared at it, fascinated.

Then, as I watched, the horses galloped out of the painting, toward my bed. I covered my head, and my shoulder shot through with pain so sharp, I caught my breath.

The man in the coat told me to relax, to be calm, to concentrate on breathing. Behind him, through the window in the door, I could see a dark-haired man in a suit and another man beside him with a face like a bulldog and his hat pulled low, like a gangster. Before my eyes, they multiplied until thirty or forty of them crowded in the doorway, reaching for me.

"Don't let them in here," I said. "Call Dr. Murdoch." I clutched at the doctor's coat, my hands opening and shutting like mouths. For a moment, I thought my hands were talking, and so I waited politely, letting them go first. When they only sat dumb and silent, I repeated, "Call Dr. Murdoch." Then I pulled the doctor close and whispered, "Tell him I'm the evidence he needs. I am the evidence."

THIRTY-SEVEN

I woke up in a white room, my brother sitting beside me. I blinked at him, but he was out of focus, as if there were two of him sitting very close together. When he saw that my eyes were open, he stood up and frowned in a worried way. He looked like he hadn't slept for days.

"How long have I been here?" My voice was garbled and strange, my throat raw. That's not my voice, I thought. They've replaced my voice with someone else's.

"Since Sunday."

"What day is this?" *Where did my voice go?*

"Tuesday."

My shoulder was throbbing a little. My head ached, as if it had been split in two. I closed my eyes and opened them again. "You look blurry."

"It's the belladonna. You've still got it in your system. The doctor says it'll take about ninety-six hours before it's out of you. Your vision should clear up in a few days. You had us worried, little sister."

I tried to sit up, but it hurt too much, so I stayed still and contented myself with smoothing down the covers. "What happened?"

"Don't you remember?"

"I remember parts of things."

"It's probably better that way."

Images of scenes and places drifted in and out like clouds. I remembered the rain first. But I had a memory of snow as well. A French village. A Paris street. A waving flag. The world from much too high. And Nigel. Something about Nigel. The harder I tried to focus and think, the more my head pounded.

Finally, I said, "Nigel." Johnny Clay would know whatever there was to know and why I was asking.

"He'll be okay. He lost a lot of blood, but he used his tie as a tourniquet. Bastard saved his own life." I could hear the admiration in his voice, in spite of himself.

"He was shot." That part was coming back to me. "More than once." Something else came back—Babe's face floating toward me through the hazy, foggy mist of my brain. "Babe King. Babe King shot him?"

"And you. She was the one who gave you the belladonna. It was the blueberries, which weren't really blueberries."

"She fell." I could suddenly see her face, the wide eyes, the open mouth as she dropped away into nothing.

He shook his head, which meant Babe was dead. *Good-bye, Babe. Good-bye, Edna.*

"No one will know what she did. I mean regarding Mudge."

"They know. Your friend Sam is working on a piece about it. A nice little tribute to Edna Mudge, and the studio that created her." His eyes went bright and sneaky. He smiled, and just like that, he looked like my brother again.

"Sam was here?" I glanced around the room, as if somehow I'd overlooked him.

"That's right. We all were."

"How did you find me?"

Johnny Clay shifted in and out of focus so that there was one of him, then two, then three.

"Flora got to the house and saw the note Helen wrote you about meeting Nigel. She called Helen at her hotel because she smelled a rat, and when Helen told her about the blueberry delivery from Nigel's secretary, Flora called me. I guess Nigel Gray doesn't have a secretary,

just some business manager named Clarence So-and-so." He kicked at
the bed, studied the floor. When he looked up again, he was as serious
as could be. "But I'll always find you. You can count on that."

I reached out my hand, even though my arm felt like a dead weight.
He held my hand, gave it a squeeze, and smiled again. "Besides, I
owed you one, little sister. I figure now we're even."

• • • • •

I slept for hours.

When I woke this time, it was evening or maybe late at night, and
Butch Dawkins was propped in a corner chair, head tipped back, eyes
closed.

I couldn't remember ever feeling so tired. Everything about me
ached and hurt, as if I were coming to life after a long, long sleep. My
own eyes were heavy, and I watched Butch for a few minutes without
saying anything. When I couldn't keep them open any longer, I let
myself drift, knowing he was there.

I woke up later—minutes or hours, it was hard to tell—and this
time he was awake and sitting up, head resting on his hand. He was
staring out the window, as if he were deep in thought.

"Hey," I said.

He turned his head, dropped his hand. "Hey." He walked over to
the bed. In his eyes, I could see the worry. "How are you feeling?"

"Hungry."

He laughed, shook his head. I could see the relief wash over him,
loosening the tight, tense lines of his face. "You're one down-home,
girl, Velva Jean. That's. Fo. Sho."

I looked him right in the eye, fixing a stare on him so that he
couldn't get away. "When I had my accident at Camp Davis, when I
nearly died, I had a dream that you were at the hospital."

"Are you asking me if I was there?"

"Yes."

"What do you think?"

"I think you were. And the song you wrote, the one I carried with
me to England and France and Germany, 'The Bluesman'—was that

about me?" I could feel myself fighting to stay awake. I shifted a little, tried to sit up, but my eyes were so heavy. Why were they so heavy?

"What do you think?"

"I think it was." As if he didn't know his own song, I quoted it back to him. "'It don't matter where or when, or who or what or why—I'll love you forever and on the day when we die.'"

"Sure sounds like words to me. And not much of a riddle."

My eyes were closing again. I couldn't remember ever feeling so tired. "Will you be here when I wake up?"

"Yes."

· · · · ·

I woke sometime Thursday feeling whole, as if I'd been put back together. Butch was still sitting in the chair, as if only minutes had passed. He said, "Helen's here. She wants to see you."

While he went to find her, I tried to take stock of things. My head felt good and clear. No headache. No pain. Maybe just a little twinge in the shoulder and ankle. I felt awake. More awake than I had in months and months. I smoothed my hair and for the first time wondered what on earth I must look like.

Helen hurried in, tears in her eyes. "Hartsie." She put her arms around me and hugged me as tight as she could. Helen was not one to hug or cry, and she pulled away quickly. "This is my fault. I took the message. I put the blueberries in the salad. I believed her when she said she was Nigel's secretary. She made herself up—wore a disguise. I didn't recognize her."

I took her hand. "You didn't know."

She shook her head and gave my hand a squeeze. "That is the last time I ever cook. Mark my words." She wiped her eyes. "You had me frightened. Not just me, all of us. Your brother would have killed Babe King himself if she wasn't already dead."

"I thought you were supposed to go home with your parents."

"I couldn't leave until you were better. I've got a flight out this weekend. I need to go back and tell Sterling Archer Sanford the Third I can't marry him."

"Where's Flora?"

"She's here. She's been so worried. I'll get her for you, but first . . ." She pulled something from her handbag. "I don't want to overwhelm you or take too much out of you, but it was one of the last books I searched." She turned the spine, leather-bound and worn, so I could see it. *Ruth* by Elizabeth Gaskell. "It's a story about an orphaned seamstress who meets a man and falls in love. He takes her in, but then he leaves her, and the girl is all alone. Until she gets a chance at a new life where she can have love and respect, as long as no one finds out about her secret—the illegitimate child she's hidden away."

She handed the book to me, and then she handed me something else. "This was inside."

It was a faded photograph of two smiling girls, side by side, the older looking at the younger with love. On the back, someone had written, "Edna and Eloise, 1922."

"MURDER AND MOVIE STARS AND A TALE OF TWO SISTERS:
A Cover-up in Hollywood"
by Samuel C. Weldon
The Hollywood Reporter

The Los Angeles newspapers have been filled lately with news of what some are calling the Lone Women Murders. These women were not well-known or famous, but hundreds of people are being rounded up and interviewed as part of ongoing investigations into the deaths, and hundreds of others are coming forward each week to confess to the crimes.

A girl named Eloise Mudge died December 28, 1946, but no one is talking about her.

Why should anyone care about Eloise Mudge? Because Eloise Mudge was also known as Barbara Fanning, one of Metro-Goldwyn-Mayer's most popular stars.

There now. I've got your attention. After all, we love to read about movie stars, especially when they are very famous, and especially when there's even a hint of scandal involved.

But Barbara Fanning was just another actress. I'm more interested in the girl she was off camera.

Here's why: Eloise was the girl behind the famous face. She was an ordinary girl who grew up in Carmen, Oklahoma, in an orphans' home, left there by her mother when she was three. Her sister, Edna, was just a baby at the time, and the two girls were dragged in and out of that home until Eloise was old enough to leave for good, on her own. It was Hollywood that got her out of there: specifically, a chance to test for MGM.

The movies were never her dream. Stardom was what younger sister Edna longed for. Instead, Eloise looked ahead to marriage and children and family. She wanted a house of her own, somewhere to call home.

But Hollywood came calling before any of those things, and she discovered she was a natural on camera. After all, hadn't she been playing a role all her life? The dutiful orphan and protective older sister.

Her death is well-known, but the circumstances are not. No one cared much about Eloise Mudge, orphan girl, but everyone cared about Barbara Fanning, movie star. The men of Metro cared most of all. The death of Eloise Mudge would never have caused headlines, but the death of Barbara Fanning was worrisome business from the start. First, there was the location of the death: Broad Water, the estate of MGM producer Billy Taub and his wife, actress Ophelia Lloyd. Second, there was the potential scandal of it all. It was clear to those at the scene that night that Barbara Fanning did not die accidentally, which meant the unthinkable: Someone from the studio had murdered her.

This would never do. Particularly if that someone was another Metro star, an even bigger star—the biggest star of all. I'm talking, of course, of Nigel Gray, famous for his charm and good looks and devastating British accent, as well as, most recently, his romancing of Miss Fanning in spite of his marriage to the late Pia Palmer.

Metro, so famously run under Papa Louis B. Mayer like a very large, very affluent family, clearly believed that one of its own was guilty. And so it set out to protect him. Fortunately, there is just such a team in place for just such an occasion. I am talking about Howard Strickling, Eddie Mannix, and Whitey Hendry. These are the Fixers, folks. Every studio has them—those men who rush to the scene of a brawl or a drunken binge or any site where scandal might be brewing around their stars. But no Fixers are as powerful as Metro-Goldwyn-Mayer's.

Their main missive is to protect the image of the studio. Even if you have to call a murder an "accident," plant wiretaps and snitches and spies at every restaurant, doctor's office, or drugstore in town, use scare tactics and henchmen to keep your employees under control, round up innocent people to direct the spotlight elsewhere, deliver threats, blackmail, pass out suspensions, etc. In short, you do what it takes, and if anyone gets in the way of that, you take care of it.

Johnny Clay Hart, brother of Metro star Kit Rogers, a longtime friend of Eloise Mudge, recently witnessed this firsthand when he was brought in for questioning in the case of murder victim Jeanne French. Hart never knew French, never even met the woman, and was nowhere near the West Los Angeles murder site the night French was killed. But Kit Rogers had been poking around just a little too much about who might have killed her friend, and so her brother was implicated.

Nigel Gray did not kill Barbara Fanning. In trying to protect him, the studio pronounced him guilty.

Babe King killed Barbara Fanning. At first glance, the motive might seem clear: professional jealousy. The younger actress offs the older one for a chance at her place in the spotlight, at the same roles, the same dressing room, perhaps even the same man.

But this is a story about two sisters.

Babe King's real name was Edna Mudge. There was only one person who knew Edna's secrets—secrets she was determined to keep. That person was her sister, Eloise. Eloise, dutiful orphan and protective older sister, knew too much. And so she had to go.

Never mind the ruined lives and orphaned child Edna left behind. After all, she had found a home at MGM. When she killed once, they protected her. When she tried to kill again—her victims this time: Nigel Gray and Kit Rogers—she ended up killing herself.

But was Edna Mudge the only murderer here?

THIRTY-EIGHT

On March 13, five thousand fans waited outside the Shrine Auditorium downtown. A dozen or more searchlights panned the sky. A radio reporter was set up near the entrance, broadcasting live. He had to shout over the noise from the crowd, the sound of applause as more stars arrived, of music swelling out and around us from inside the auditorium. "I've been covering the awards since 1929, and I can honestly say this is the most glamorous ceremony of all. The war is over. The ermine and sequins are out. We've been deprived for so long that we are making up for lost time."

Inside, I took in the view—the stars laughing and talking to each other. There was Gable. There was Hepburn. There was Errol Flynn. Lana Turner. Tyrone Power. Every star in the galaxy gathered under one roof. Looking at them, in their diamonds and black ties, it was hard to believe anything terrible or tragic could ever happen. Even if the sun didn't shine here every day, it wouldn't matter. They would just paint the skies blue.

Jack Benny was our host, entertaining the crowd with his usual patter. The cast of *Home of the Brave* sat together. Johnny Clay was my date. My gown was blue, in honor of Mudge. I wore her Rebekah ring on my right hand.

Billy Taub and Ophelia Lloyd sat on the end of the row in front, Felix Roland and Shelby Jordan to their right. The rest of us fell in around them—Webster Hayes, Hal, Collie, Rosie, Redd Deeley, Phillip Drake, and Nigel, wearing a sky blue tie that matched his eyes.

"You're all here," the usher had said as he led us to the seats.

He meant, you're all sitting here, but I thought, Not all of us.

"Pipes."

"Sam."

Johnny Clay and I stood as he moved past us, followed by an ice-cream blonde in a tight white dress. He took the seat next to mine, while she arranged herself on the other side of him.

He smiled at me and I smiled back at him. "You had us worried. But you're fine." I heard the question in it.

"I'm fine. I read the article. It was terrific. It was just what needed to be said."

"I wanted to show it to you first, but I thought it was a good idea to get it out before the studio could go to work at burying everything."

"I'm surprised they even let you in here."

"That's the beauty of being a free agent. They can't do a goddamn thing except to make sure they don't hire me again. They tried to fire me from *Latimer*, but Tauby threatened to walk off."

"So he still has a spine."

"At least partially."

"Will you stay?"

"Only till I finish the job. I don't like to leave things undone once I've started them." He gave me a pointed look before glancing down at the armrest between us, at my hand dangling off. He reached for it, interlacing his fingers with mine. "You won't believe this, but I miss holding hands with you."

On the other side of him, the blonde was watching us.

I said, "She's pretty."

"Yes, and ordinary and not you."

Suddenly, everyone around me broke into applause, and Collie went walking up on stage to accept the award for costume design. Sam and I let go at the same time as we began to clap, and continued clapping as Rosie won for the score, Webster Hayes won for Best

Actor, Sam for Best Writing, and Felix Roland for Best Director. Soon, there were only two awards remaining: Best Actress and Best Picture.

Ray Milland presented the actress award. As he announced the nominees—Jennifer Jones, Rosalind Russell, Jane Wyman, Ophelia Lloyd, and Barbara Fanning—I pinched my brother's arm. "And the Oscar goes to . . ." Ray Milland paused before reading the winner. He looked down at the card and then up at the audience and said simply, "Barbara Fanning."

The applause erupted at once. I stood, Sam stood, Johnny Clay stood. In seconds, every person in the auditorium was standing and clapping and cheering until I thought I might go deaf from the sound. Then Nigel Gray walked up onto the stage, and Ray Milland handed him the award.

Nigel stood waiting for the sound to die down, blinking into the lights, into the audience, glittering and beautiful. It seemed as if the applause would go on forever, and there he would be, frozen in place, unable to walk away. He looked out at us with his blue eyes, and it hit me then that maybe the reason Mudge had loved blue wasn't because of the sky at all, but because it made her think of Nigel and of what she saw when she looked at him—the promise of a future, of love, of family, of home.

When we finally quieted, little by little, and sat, row by row, Nigel shook his head and smiled. He wiped his eyes and leaned in to the microphone. "I'm honored to accept this most deserved award for a most deserving woman." He stared down at the Oscar. "I was lucky enough to know Eloise Mudge, even if I didn't know her long enough. She would have been so bloody proud of this." His voice broke and he kissed the award before raising it into the air above him. "'All my heart is yours: it belongs to you; and with you it would remain, were fate to exile the rest of me from your presence forever.'"

Jane Eyre. Nigel had read it too. The thought of the two of them sharing something so small made me feel at once sadder and happier. I told myself to focus on the happier. It was good to know that Mudge had, for a time at least, found what she was looking for.

• • • • •

I met with Mr. Mayer at ten thirty the next morning. I thanked him for everything he'd done for me and told him he had been like a father, which was something I appreciated, more than he knew, since my own had left long ago.

"I'll never forget you or MGM for all you did for me. But I want to make my own choices. I want to sing my songs and have the public like me for me. I don't want to be Kit Rogers anymore. Of all the things I've learned here, that's the most important one—never let anyone tell you who you are."

"If this is about more money—"

"It's not."

For a long time, he held his head in his hands. I waited for one of his legendary fits to begin—for him to kick the desk and start to cry, to fall on the floor and foam at the mouth, to faint dead away. I didn't say anything. I sat with my hands folded, waiting.

Finally he looked up, and his face was hard to read. He said, "It's not the same business it was when we met, Velva Jean Hart. I won't stop you. I'll just wish you luck." I thought he seemed tired.

He stood. I stood.

He walked around his desk on the little platform, and then stepped onto the carpet so that he was beside me, standing at his actual height, which meant I had to look down. I thought, For all his power, he's just a short little man behind a desk.

• • • • •

In my dressing room, as one of the secretaries ticked off her list, I pulled the framed Opry picture off the wall and a few other things I'd left— books, one of Mudge's alarm clocks, a vase she'd given me. Everything else belonged to MGM. I said, "Come in," to the knock on the door.

Bernie walked in, something in his hand. He said, "I came to see if you needed any help." He glanced at the secretary, who went on making marks on her clipboard.

"This is it." I waved at the small pile of things. "It seems like there should be more."

"Well. That's it, then."

"That's it."

He handed me a stack of letters. "These are yours."

"What are they?"

"Something you should have had a long time ago."

· · · · ·

On my way to the car, I stopped in at the music department to say good-bye to Rosie. When I walked into his studio, a girl was singing and playing the guitar, no more than eighteen or nineteen years old, pretty, sweet face, fresh off the farm or the mountains. I stood watching her, watching me when I'd first come to Metro, maybe me when I'd first gone to Nashville. Her voice was raw and pure and big. The way she played and sang, you could see and hear how much she loved it.

When she was finished, Rosie looked up and saw me and the box I was carrying. "Going somewhere, kid?"

"Yes, and before I do, I wanted to thank you for all you've done for me."

"So you really are going somewhere, then."

"Yes. And I'll never forget you."

He began clearing his throat and cleaning his glasses with a handkerchief. I pretended not to notice how wet his eyes were or the single tear that had escaped one corner. He said, "I want you to remember, after all you've learned—just sing. At the end of the day, it's not about diaphragms and technique. It's about you and that remarkable voice."

I hugged him, and he coughed and cleared his throat and set to cleaning his glasses again.

The girl whispered something to him, too low for me to hear, and he said, "Kit, I want you to meet our newest discovery. Briana Harley, Kit Rogers."

"Actually, it's Velva Jean Hart," I said, and shook her hand.

"Miss Hart . . ."

"Velva Jean."

"Velva Jean, I'm such a fan. I can't believe I'm meeting you." She laughed. "And I can't believe I'm telling you I can't believe it. You're what inspired me to leave home and come here."

I said, "You have a gift." Not just the voice, I thought, but the spirit, bold and all her own. "You're in good hands here." I looked at Rosie. "But I'll tell you one of the best pieces of advice anyone ever gave me: Remember who you are, hold on to that, and whatever you do, don't let them change you."

· · · · ·

When I got back to Mudge's house—Flora's house now—I remembered the letters Bernie had given me. There were ten of them addressed to Miss Velva Jean Hart, a.k.a. Kit Rogers, c/o MGM Studios, Culver City, California. There was no return address.

I opened them in the order of the postmarks. One after another, months apart, spread out over the past two years, always with a different address, a different postmark. The first was dated December 7, 1945. The last one was dated February 19, 1947, from Lindytown, West Virginia.

Deer Velva Jean, I don't know that this letter will get thru, but I wanted to rite to tell you how prowd I am of you. I ain't been mutch to cownt on in the past, and I know I can't take any credut for what I see on that screen, but I shure am prowd jest the same. I can't beleeve that you have all that in you. You are the purtiest gurl in the world and I ain't just saying that cuz I'm your daddy. The only gurl I ever seen purtier was your mama. I hope they're taking good care of you in Hollywood. You got every rite to forget me, but I hope you won't. I want yoo to know that it don't matter what name you call yerself—you'll always be my dawter. Luv, Lincoln S. Hart.

All this time, he'd been writing to me, and I'd stood by and let MGM tell everyone he was dead. And the letters—I would never have known about them if Bernie hadn't given them to me. I wouldn't have known that my daddy was out there in this world thinking of me.

· · · · ·

I spent my last night in Los Angeles on Central Avenue at Jack's Basket Room, playing my National steel guitar in a jam session with Butch and Johnny Clay and Sherman. The crowd thumped and jumped, the air so smoky you couldn't see. At some point, Wardell Gray and Dexter Gordon climbed up on stage. And later, there came Clora Bryant, a beautiful colored girl who blew the trumpet so hot and heavy, you could see the steam.

We didn't know each other's songs and we didn't talk about what came next. We just got up there and played, figuring it out as we went, and the crowd shouted for more.

Afterward, Clora said to me, "The only way you're going to learn is to be a part of it. That's what you have to do. You have to go out there and be a part of that."

·····

Early the next morning, my brother and Butch came to the house to help me pack the car. The sky was a soft pink-gold, and the sun was rising fast, as if it couldn't wait to shine again. We propped the front door open and I showed them what stayed and what was going with me. Flora would move in for good soon with her daughter and son-in-law and grandbabies. The *California Eagle* reported that racial covenants around the city were lifting and blacks were starting to leave Central Avenue one by one.

I moved around Butch carefully. For years, I'd felt as comfortable with him as family, but now I found myself thinking about every word I said or look I gave him. As a result, I tried not to be alone with him, not yet, darting in and out and never landing in one place, like a butterfly or hummingbird in wild, erratic flight.

Even as he was carrying things down the walk, Johnny Clay said, "I still don't see why you need to leave, Velva Jean. Why don't you wait for Dawks and me? We're not going to stay out here forever."

"Because I've got to get going, Johnny Clay, you know that." I wanted to ask him to come with me, but I was afraid he would—not that I didn't want him to, but because I knew this was where he needed to be right now, and because this was a trip I needed to make on my own.

He said, "I love Helen."

"Helen who?"

"Helen Stillbert. I should have told you, little sister."

He walked on down to the car, leaving me standing on the lawn staring after him. When he came walking back to me, I said, "Does she—does she know?"

"She does."

"Does she love you back?"

"She will." He grinned. "Listen, I know I'm not the guy girls end up with. I'm the one they want before they settle down, you know, the one they have fun with. But I aim to be that guy for Helen." Behind the grin, I could tell he was dead serious. "I'm thinking I might even go to school. Maybe get me an education. Now that would be something to see."

Here was one more thing he hadn't let me in on, just like playing the trumpet or coming out to California. But instead of being angry with him, I told myself: This is the way life goes. He'll always be a part of me, and I'll always be a part of him, but we can't be every part to each other.

I said, "You don't need to do another thing, Johnny Clay. She'd be lucky to have you."

"You aren't mad?"

"No. I guess we're growing up."

"I guess we are."

Butch walked past, carrying my guitars. "You could always punch him in the jaw."

Johnny Clay threw back his head and laughed.

• • • • •

An hour later, it was done. Johnny Clay said, "I'm going to ride with you as far east as I can, little sister, and then you drop me off before you leave Los Angeles and I'll hitch my way back to Central."

I handed him Daddy's letters then, because whether he wanted to or not, I thought he should see them. He said, "Are these from him?"

"They are. I didn't know he'd been writing me."

"I'm not all that interested in anything he's got to say."

"You don't have to read them."

He glanced past me at Butch, and then told me he'd wait for me in the car while I said good-bye. He took the letters with him.

Butch leaned in the doorway of the house, hands in pockets, watching me. Suddenly, there was nothing left to do but say good-bye, and so I brushed past him until I was standing in the entryway. He followed me in, and then I walked into the living room. He followed me in there. When I started for the dining room, he said, "What are we doing, girl?"

"We're making sure I didn't leave anything."

"Okay." He led the way through each room, and we double-checked closets and cabinets and drawers. I suddenly wished for more rooms so we could keep checking. That way, I wouldn't have to say good-bye.

Finally, we stood in the last room, Mudge's room. I could still smell her perfume, still hear her voice.

"Time to go align those stars, Velva Jean." Butch stood smiling that crooked smile, one hand against the doorjamb.

He was right. I'd checked every corner. There wasn't any other place to look. No more delaying it. But there was something I was leaving behind that I wasn't sure I wanted to leave behind.

I made one last turn of the room, and then looked at him straight on. "Will I see you again?"

"As long as I know where you are."

"Most girls would stay."

"You ain't most girls. If you were, I wouldn't want you to stay. You got to do this, Velva Jean. What'd I tell you years ago, back when we first met? If destiny don't come to you, you got to go to it. You owe it to yourself." I didn't say anything, just nodded. "And what'd I tell you about a certain door? Anytime you want to open it and go down that road, I'm ready to go with you. You just let me know."

My heart started skipping beats. "That's true about the stars. You can't always wait on them. Sometimes you have to align them yourself."

We both seemed to freeze, as if time had stopped, and then we moved toward each other at the exact same moment. His eyes on mine, he brushed the hair out of my face, tucking it back behind my ears.

He took my face in his hands, gently, as if he was afraid it might break.

He leaned in, so close I could feel his breath.

His lips hovered, barely brushing mine.

I closed my eyes.

When nothing happened, I opened my eyes, making sure he was still there.

"Girl, I'm not going to kiss you only to send you off across the country. The first time I kiss you, it won't be to say good-bye. It'll be to say hello, I'm here, and I ain't going anywhere. I'm not going to kiss you until I can keep on kissing you."

Something inside me deflated like a balloon. We broke apart and moved away, and then I was leading him down the hall and down the stairs and onto the front stoop. I reached inside and flicked off the light switch and turned the key in the lock. Butch Dawkins and I walked side by side to the car.

"Well," I said, my hand on the door. In the passenger seat, Johnny Clay was reading the letters.

"Well."

Butch smiled. I smiled.

"I'll be seeing you, Butch Dawkins."

"I'll be seeing you, Velva Jean."

. . . . .

Johnny Clay rode with one arm out the window, checking himself out in the side mirror. He was talking a mile a minute, and I was glad because otherwise I might have turned around and gone right back to Butch and never left and seen what was ahead of me.

My brother said, "You could come down to Central Avenue, get you a room at the Dunbar, cut another record with us. We're practically famous."

He talked on and on, until finally I said, "'If now is only two days, then two days is your life.'"

He got quiet, remembering. There was nothing he could say to this because it was something he'd once said to me.

But just in case he didn't remember, I added, "If you've only got two days, you need to treat those two days like a lifetime. You've found your place, Johnny Clay. Now I need to find mine."

• • • • •

I was three miles from the Arizona state line when I caught sight of the motorcycle in my rearview mirror. It was coming up fast behind me, and without thinking twice I eased off the gas even as I told myself it might be anyone.

In the left lane, cars passed me one by one, until I was barely crawling along. Thirty miles per hour, twenty-five, twenty, fifteen . . . Soon the motorcycle was on my tail, lights flashing.

I pulled over onto the dirt shoulder, my heart thudding hard and fast, so hard and fast that it took my breath. I got out of the car, the door standing open, one hand grazing the warm chrome side of it, keeping me steady. Butch Dawkins kicked off the engine and dropped the bike on its side so that it went skidding in the dust. He came striding toward me as I stood waiting, every step bringing him closer, closing the gap between us. I wanted to go to him, meet him halfway, to help him close it faster, but I couldn't move.

And then he was there.

And the gap closed as if it had never existed at all.

I thought of a hundred things to ask him: What are you doing here? How did you find me? Why did you wait so long? But I didn't say anything because he was there. No more gap. No more space. Just him and me. Me and him. Velva Jean and Butch. Butch and Velva Jean.

Without a word, he kissed me.

I lost myself in the warmth of his mouth, that wonderful mouth. I lost myself in him. Him into me, me into him. I could feel his heart against mine, beating a fast, hard echo of my own.

This was the place we'd been moving toward since that first day on the mountain, the day he came riding up to see me in an old yellow truck. Toward his hands on my face. My hands on the firm, taut muscles of his back. Toward this kiss. This kiss that was like a song. First love, pure and sweet. New love, aching and raw. Old love, warm and familiar, bridging years and time.

I wrapped my arms around him and breathed him in.

He leaned me up against the car and stopped kissing me long enough to look at me with a crooked smile.

"You got somewhere to go and so do I," he said. "And I didn't drive all this way to slow you down. But I just wanted to say hello. I'm here. And I ain't going anywhere."

THIRTY-NINE

East of New Mexico, the landscape changed to winter. On March 25, I stopped at a service station outside of Amarillo and stretched my legs. After the attendant filled up the tank and checked the tires, he said, "I've seen your face. Aren't you that actress—the little girl who sings? Kit Rogers?"

"I used to be." I smiled at him. "Thank you for asking." I got back into the car and counted out the money for the gas. I caught sight of myself in the mirror, eyes bright, lips painted Headline Red.

"Need help with directions, or do you know where you're going?"

I nodded at the map spread out on the seat beside me. "I know where I'm going."

He counted my money, then counted out my change.

"You be safe out there, a girl like you alone on the road. Where you headed anyway?"

"Tennessee."

He whistled, and then nodded, as if he was impressed, or maybe as if to say: That's right. That's exactly where you should be going. I wouldn't have expected any other place.

He said, "You headed to Nashville?"

"Yes, sir," I said, my hands on the wheel. "I am."

"Home to Me"
(words and music by Velva Jean Hart)

I've been driving way too fast
But I don't have far to go
Over roads, across the skies
Trying to find my way back home
Home to where the stars align,
Home because it's finally time,
Home to you
Home to me

I'm hanging up the fancy gowns
Hanging up the big screen and the fame
I'm picking up my new guitar
And going back to my old name
The name my mama gave me,
The name my daddy gave me,
Velva Jean to you
Velva Jean to me

I'm heading forward on this road
Heading toward places I can't see,
I'm taking it mile by mile
Heading toward you, heading toward me
You, where all the stars align,
Me, because it's finally time,
Home to you
Home to me

You can lose the self you are
faster than a shooting star
dives to earth and disappears

in the empty, wasted years.
When where you've been is gone, gone, gone,
All you keep is the getting here

I've been flying way too fast
But I don't have far to go
Over roads, across the skies
As I find my way back home
Home where all my stars align,
Home because it's finally time,
Home to you
Home to me

ENDINGS

The year 1947 was, according to *Fortune* magazine, the greatest productive period in United States peacetime history. Before the war, the population of Los Angeles was three million. By 1946, it had grown to six and a half million.

Movie attendance in the United States was eighty million per week. By the end of 1948, that number had dropped to sixty million per week, and the studio that fared the worst was the largest and most lucrative in Hollywood, and the richest: Metro-Goldwyn-Mayer.

Men like the Fixers—MGM's head of publicity, Howard Strickling, and general manager, Eddie Mannix—suddenly, after years of ruling the town, found themselves with less and less power. As the studio system died out and the seven-year contract became a thing of the past, they no longer enjoyed complete control over their stars. But for a good many years, they ruled Los Angeles more powerfully than the mob. In the 1930s and early 1940s, the Los Angeles Police Department, the Los Angeles district attorney's office, the gossip columnists, and many of the newspapers were all famously buyable and famously corrupt, and famously in the back pocket of the movie studios and the moguls who ran them.

While the case of Barbara Fanning was invented, the actions of the Fixers in a situation like this are disturbingly true to life, right down to Howard Strickling's "talent is like a precious stone" speech. Did Metro's biggest star, Clark Gable, strike and kill a pedestrian with his car? Was Jean Harlow's husband (and MGM producer) Paul Bern murdered but made to look like the victim of suicide by the men who discovered him first—Strickling, Eddie Mannix, Whitey Hendry, and Louis B. Mayer? Did popular MGM character actor Wallace Beery beat Ted Healy to death outside the Trocadero? Did Eddie Mannix have anything to do with the mysterious gunshot death of George Reeves, the last major studio scandal of its kind handled by Howard Strickling?

Loretta Young's pure and wholesome on-screen persona was created by MGM. When she became pregnant by married costar Clark Gable, Strickling and Mannix were the ones who shielded her from the public and made certain no one found out about the pregnancy. Two years after the child's birth, they were the ones who arranged the bending of California state law so that Miss Young could "adopt" her own daughter from the orphanage where she'd hidden her.

Personal memories and first- and secondhand information confirming the preceding have become part of the public record. However, any hard evidence is long gone. Even for a dogged and determined researcher, it is a frustrating quest. Howard Strickling and Eddie Mannix seem to have done a thorough job of destroying any and all pertinent records, which included crime scene photographs taken by studio photographer Virgil Apger, incriminating evidence removed from various crime scenes, and eyewitness accounts that were later altered.

On June 22, 1951, Louis B. Mayer resigned from Metro-Goldwyn-Mayer, forced out by Nicholas Schenck, president of Loew's Inc. On Mayer's last day, Howard Strickling ordered a red carpet placed at the front door of the Thalberg Building. It was unfurled down the steps and across the walk, all the way to the street. The executives and secretaries who had worked with Louis B. Mayer for so many years gathered outside to applaud him as he made his final walk through the gate that still bore his name.

Actor Turhan Bey said, "When Louis B. Mayer left MGM, that was the end. Of contract players, of publicity departments who nursed you through the crises of studio life, of the studio life itself. In every meaningful way, it was the end of Hollywood."

MGM, once the largest and most glamorous movie studio in the world, is now owned by Sony. The famed backlots, left to decay and ruin in the 1970s, are gone. In 1986, Ted Turner purchased what remained from Kirk Kerkorian, and then sold it back to him after keeping the film library—some four thousand movies—which became the building block for Turner Classic Movies. Spencer Tracy, who read the eulogy at Louis B. Mayer's funeral in 1957, said, "All the rest is history. The shining epoch of the industry passes with him."

Louis B. Mayer, and the studio he ran, belonged to a different era, a different world. A world where men were gentlemen, where women were virtuous, where families were loyal and loving, where pictures hung straighter, grass grew greener, picket fences shone whiter, people danced down streets and sang songs, endings were happy, and everything was sprinkled with magic dust. It was an idealized America where dreams came true, especially when there were men to protect those dreams and ensure nothing spoiled them.

It was the America that should have been, and that never was—except as it existed on the soundstages of Metro-Goldwyn-Mayer.

· · · · ·

My love for Hollywood was born in 1983 at 725 North Rodeo Drive. I was an awkward preteen, braces just off, but tall for my age *with hips* and a mane of unruly hair. I was at turns bursting with confidence and painfully self-conscious. My mother was researching her first book, a biography of poet and author Carl Sandburg, and I traveled with her to Los Angeles for my first time there. Several important and pivotal things happened on that trip: I went to Disneyland. I had my first glimpse of MTV in our hotel room. I discovered a band called Duran Duran in a Westwood music store. And I found Hollywood.

As part of her research, my mom did a round of interviews with legendary writer, director, and producer Norman Corwin, *The Tonight Show* founder Steve Allen, television writer and producer William Hale, and Gene Kelly.

The vibrant and elegant Norman showed us Los Angeles. He squired my mother and me around the city, pointing out the sights, telling us the history, taking us to dinner. To me, he was Norman— kind and gentlemanly and funny. I loved my dad, but I still hoped somehow that Mom could marry Norman, because he would have been a wonderful stepfather. Only later, when I was old enough to appreciate it, would I be able to fully comprehend the scope and extent of his genius and his legacy.

Gene Kelly was the last interview of our visit. He invited us to his home in Beverly Hills, on the world-famous Rodeo Drive. He lived in a handsome farmhouse, large and white, set back from the broad, palm-tree-lined street with the same expanse of Irish-green lawn as the others that surrounded it, and a white picket fence. There was nothing remarkable about it from the outside.

An old man answered the door, rugged, broad shouldered, my dad's height or a little shorter, about five feet ten. He was balding and wore glasses with thick black rims. I looked over his shoulder for Gene Kelly, but the man shook my mother's hand, and then mine, and thanked us for coming. He led us into the house—wide and bright and spacious—and into a room that faced both the street and the backyard. It was a long room with a piano, books, artwork, an-tiques, various statues and artifacts, a Christmas tree in the front win-dow with lights twinkling, and, hung on the wood-paneled walls, hundreds of framed photographs.

Our host was a gentleman. He offered us something to drink and to eat, and then we sat, the three of us, at the end of that wood-paneled room and my mother began her interview. Oh, I thought, so this is Gene Kelly. I felt a little pang of disappointment. He seemed so *old*, and so unlike the Gene Kelly I'd seen in pictures and movies.

The primary reason for the interview was that Carl Sandburg had written a poem for Gene Kelly to dance to on one of his television specials (the poem was actually titled "Lines for Gene Kelly to Dance To"). Mom asked Mr. Kelly about Sandburg and their relationship, about how the poem came to be. They talked about the poem itself, about dancing to it. Mr. Kelly told stories relating to Sandburg, to dancing, to Hollywood, and as he did, something mysterious and extraordinary happened—the years seemed to slip away and suddenly there he was sitting next to us, the Gene Kelly of *Singin' in the Rain*.

Because I couldn't help staring at the photographs that lined the walls, he said to me, "Would you like to look more closely at them?" When I said, oh yes, I'd love to, he took Mom and me through the room, showing us each picture, each souvenir from his movies, amassed over five decades. He showed us the art he collected, the stacks of papers that comprised the autobiography he was, at last, writing, his Academy Award, and his dancing shoes. He spoke with love and affection of this person, of this film, of this experience. His warmth was genuine. He was funny and humble, for all I'd heard then or since about his ego. Perhaps *humble* isn't the right word—perhaps *grateful* is more accurate. He seemed grateful for all he had accomplished.

We spent the better part of the day with him, and then, too soon, it was time to go. There was dinner with Norman, and more Hollywood stories to come. But I didn't want to leave that room at Gene Kelly's house. Being there was like stepping back into another time, one of glamour and hard work, of camaraderie and competition, of fame and beauty and heartbreak and . . . magic.

Mr. Kelly walked us to the door and hugged first my mother, then me. The sky was still blue but the sunlight was fading. The houses and the street looked different to me. Mr. Kelly said to my mom, "She's a beautiful girl. She takes after her mother." And he flashed that unmistakable Gene Kelly smile—the one you could spot in a Times Square crowd—as he watched us down the walk and waved as we drove away. As we headed back to our hotel, I felt somehow *prettier*. Los Angeles seemed prettier too. I no longer saw the faint brown haze of smog or the endless lines of traffic or the strip malls and grocery stores and gas stations. I could suddenly see the Hollywood he'd shown us—the magical one that was still there, if you looked for it. It was a gift. In a way, he gave me his Hollywood, and I would never forget it.

On December 23, 1983, one month after our visit, Gene Kelly's home was destroyed by fire. He told reporters he had left the Christmas tree lights on because he felt a responsibility to his fans, who liked to drive by or walk by and see them. His artwork, his antiques, his papers, his photographs, his Academy Award, his dancing shoes—all of it, destroyed. Mr. Kelly and his two grown children barely escaped. His publicist said, "He has nothing this morning but a pair of pajamas."

My mother wrote him a note to tell him how deeply sorry we were, and how much we were thinking of him. A week or two later, he wrote her back to thank her. It was true, he said, that his treasures were gone. They could never be replaced. But the memory of them remained.

Six years later, my mother began working on a book with the actor James Earl Jones. The book became *Voices and Silences*, his autobiography. I once again tagged along on interviews and television and film sets, not only getting to know James Earl, but for the first time receiving an inside glimpse of the inner, everyday workings of the industry and of the world behind the curtain. At the time, I was in college in New Jersey, but often traveling with Mom, and it was after watching James Earl Jones and Robert Duvall at a grueling location shoot in a buggy, muggy Louisiana swamp that I decided: As soon as I graduated, I was going to *Hollywood*.

To this day, living here, I see the city the way I saw it after an afternoon spent at Gene Kelly's house. I see what it was, what it tries to be, where it came from, how it began. I can see the orange groves and tinsel and the klieg lights surrounding Grauman's Chinese, and all the places now gone that existed in a different era, a different world— Ciro's, the MGM backlots, Central Avenue, the Cocoanut Grove. I can hear the music. I can see the stars. I can feel the magic.

Acknowledgments

As always, I could not have done this alone. Enormous, jubilant, heartfelt thanks to my mentor (and BFF) mom, Penelope Niven, my rock of a fiancé, Louis Kapeleris, and my three steadfast (and highly entertaining) literary kitties—patient Satchmo, sweet Rumi, and live-wire Lulu, who went through her own share of eye troubles and sleeplessness in order to keep me company (often sitting by my side and gazing at the computer screen with me) day in and day out, long hour after hour.

Thanks to the outstanding Plume team—my splendid editor, Carolyn Carlson, as well as the wonderful Ramona Demme, Mary Pomponio, Elizabeth Keenan, Ashley Pattison McClay, Clare Ferraro, Kathryn Court, Phil Budnick, John Fagan, Lavina Lee, Kym Surridge, Jaya Miceli (art director extraordinaire), and Sara Wood (who created the absolute knockout of a cover)—for giving Velva Jean such a good home for the past five years, and for all they have done and continue to do for Velva Jean and me.

Thank you to the experts who generously answered question after question about all things poison-related or Hollywood-related or murder investigation–related so that I could write the most historically/technically/logistically sound book possible. First and foremost, Dr. Michael Wilks, senior forensic physician, Thames Valley Police (and his partner, my cousin Sandy McClean). But also Dr. James Klaunig, former state toxicologist of Indiana and current professor in environmental health at Indiana University; Joanne Parrent, of Parrent Smith Investigations; retired North Carolina policeman (and honorary cousin) Doy N. Newell; Glynn Martin, executive director of the Los Angeles Police Museum; author and forensic anthropologist Kathy Reichs; the Margaret Herrick Library; the Hollywood History Museum; the Hollywood Heritage Museum; the UCLA Film & Television Archive; the Louis B. Mayer Library at my film school alma mater, AFI; the USC Cinematic Arts Library; the Annenberg Community Beach House (which, back in its Marion Davies heyday, provided the inspiration for Broad Water); the Hertzberg-Davis Forensic Science Center; and the Los Angeles Public Library.

Much of my research was gleaned from my own extensive Hollywood library, but one book in particular became my bible—*M-G-M: Hollywood's Greatest Backlot* by Steven Bingen, Stephen X. Sylvester, and Michael Troyan. Thank you for writing it!

My friends and family helped keep me sane, made me laugh, forgave my long absences from the world outside my computer, and loved me anyway. Adoring thanks to the Waxhaw homefolk, especially Gay McGee Diller, Gloria McGee Hope, Patricia "Patsy" Niven Gamble McGee, Ken Collins (and the members of his amazing book club), and Dr. Haskell Eargle for their Velva Jean enthusiasm, promotion, and warm hospitality. And to the LA homefolk—Angelo Surmelis, Ed Baran, Lisa Brucker, Jack Angelo, Briana Harley (who was also one of my three trusted early readers), and the wild and wonderful Irish laddies, Joe Kraemer, Justin Speranza, and Shawn Fowler.

Thank you to my lovely and brilliant dynamo of a literary agent, Kerry Sparks (and everyone at the ultrafabulous Levine Greenberg Literary Agency, with special nods to Elizabeth Fisher and Monika Verma), for effortlessly and enthusiastically picking up the Velva Jean baton and running with it—and for surpassing every expectation.

Thanks to Lara Yacoubian, Phoebe Phillips, and Laura Burdine, Greatest Interns Ever (which is why they have cameos in this story). Thank you, Briana Harley, Shelby Padgett, and Jordan Gripenwaldt for thinking up "Kit Rogers." Thank you, Larry Edmunds Bookshop, for always magically stocking the research books I needed. And thanks to my friends at the Wilshire Boulevard Robeks (particularly the always-smiling Adriana Ramirez), who kept me nourished, and who were often the only nonfictional people I interacted with outside the world of my apartment.

Thank you from the bottom of my heart to all the remarkable readers who have faithfully followed Velva Jean from one adventure to another, and to all the Velva Jeans, Velvas, Velda Jeans, and Velmer Jeans among you.

Lastly, thank you to John A. Ware. He was my first literary agent, but this doesn't begin to encapsulate what he was to me. He was, to put it more accurately, my friend, surrogate father, champion, fellow blues lover, teller of jokes, cheerleader, editor, wizard, and a true gentleman. He was known for his honesty and integrity in a business that runs too short on both. His main concern for me—always—was that I be happy in my work, and that I honor my creative self. He saw me through seven books, and we had plans for so many more. In the midst of the hardest deadlines, he would pick up the phone and call me just to play a bit of blues on my voicemail or tell me a joke. He checked in frequently to make sure I was okay, that I wasn't discouraged, and that I had what I needed in order to do what I needed to do.

In the wake of his untimely death in April 2013, I take with me all I learned from him, editorially, creatively, professionally, and personally. I was lucky to have known him.

This one's for you, John.

"Onward," as he used to say.

Catch up with the rest of Velva Jean's adventures

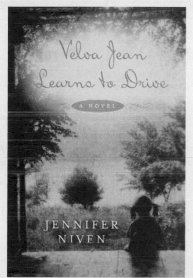

978-0-452-28945-1

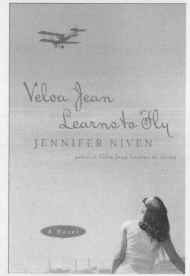

978-0-452-29740-1

978-0-452-29810-1

Available wherever books are sold